SEATTLE GREEN

SEATTLE GREEN

A Novel by

JANE ADAMS

A *Belvedere Book*

ARBOR HOUSE 🍁 NEW YORK

Copyright © 1987 by Jane Adams
All rights reserved, including the right of reproduction
in whole or in part in any form. Published in the
United States of America by Arbor House Publishing
Company and in Canada by Fitzhenry & Whiteside, Ltd.

Manufactured in the United States of America

10 9 8 7 6 5 4 3 2 1

Library of Congress Cataloging in Publication Data

Adams, Jane.
  Seattle green.

  "A Belvedere book."
  I. Title.
PS3551.D374S4 1987   813'.54   87–1818
ISBN: 0-87795-911-0

This book is dedicated to
John Dodds
with respect and affection,
and to Seattle
with love

ACKNOWLEDGMENTS

While this book is fiction, and most of the characters in it my own invention, it may interest the reader to know the historical antecedents for some of the anecdotes, events, and minor figures in the novel.

The Dennys—Arthur and David and their wives—were among Seattle's pioneer families, and were instrumental in the growth and development of the city. The facts surrounding the relationship between the brothers are somewhat clouded by time, but what is true is that by the last decade of the nineteenth century David Denny, who had speculated in electric streetcars, lost his land and his fortune and left the city he loved—forced out, some say, by his brother Arthur, who was an officer of the bank that foreclosed on him.

Asa Mercer did bring his Mercer Girls. Maddy and Sonnet are fictional additions to that company of adventuresome women. The *Continental*'s voyage under Captain Ben Holladay happened as described in these pages.

John Pennell's involvement in the brothels of Skid Road is well described by historians Bill Speidel and Murray Morgan; however, the circumstance surrounding Pennell's departure from Seattle—the embezzlement—is strictly fictional.

Joshua Green was another important figure in Seattle's history; he was a steamboater, sportsman, and banker. The "holdup" during which Catherine and Leighton first meet is based on an incident cited by Gordon Newell in *The Green Years*.

For a fuller description of Seattle's labor history, including the Everett Massacre and the general strike, Norman Clark's *Milltown*, Harvey Manning's *Revolution in Seattle*, and Anna Louise Strong's *I Change Worlds* are valuable sources.

Natalie's kidnapping is based on a similar occurrence in 1935, when George Weyerhaeuser, scion of the timber family, was abducted from his home in Tacoma, Washington. He was released unharmed by the kidnappers, who were apprehended and imprisoned.

This book, and the process of writing it, have been immeasurably enriched by the contributions of many writers and historians whose work made my own research easier and more enjoyable. I am particularly indebted to Roger Sale, Murray Morgan, Bill Speidel, Gordon Newell, Paul Dorpat and Lane Morgan, whose books provided a framework for mine and whose words brought an earlier Seattle so brilliantly and tellingly to life.

I am grateful to Carla Rickerson, curator of the Northwest Collection of the University of Washington, for her help in providing not only original source material but also a congenial environment for working. And I am especially indebted to Lane Morgan, writer, editor, historian and friend, whose encyclopedic knowledge of Seattle's past gave this book an authenticity and accuracy it might otherwise not have possessed. Any errors of fact or interpretation of events are mine, not hers.

Roger Sale's *Seattle—Past to Present* was an invaluable resource for this book, which owes a great deal to his interpretation of Seattle's political and economic development.

Finally, Caleb's Bluff bears some resemblance to that area known as Alki where the pioneers first located the city of Seattle, though I have taken liberties with the dimensions and geography of both.

Seattle, Washington
October 1986

SEATTLE GREEN

·Maddy: 1866-1889·

Chapter One

Please, please, oh, please go faster, Maddy silently implored the spavined old mare that pulled the tinker's wagon with agonizing slowness along the Post Road. They had been traveling since just after dark the previous night, and now the chilly winter sun was almost directly overhead. The *Continental* was due to sail on the evening tide from New York Harbor, and at this plodding pace, the ship would be gone long before they arrived.

If they arrived. For the tinker, Maddy realized with dismay, was steering the wagon off the road.

"I always put up for a bit here," he said, pulling the reins up short. "There's good trade to be had at the Post House. Whyn't you go refresh yourself, missy, and I'll be seeing to some oats and water for Lucy."

With that he jumped nimbly to the ground. He helped Maddy down from the wagon seat, holding her above her narrow waist a bit longer than he needed to and pulling her so close to him she could smell his musty whiskey breath.

"I might even see if they have a room for us here," he added with a gap-toothed leer.

Not likely, she thought, turning her face away so he could not see her grimace. She had run away from one evil man; his linen might have been cleaner, but he and the tinker were cut from the same bolt, and having escaped one trap, Maddy had no intention of falling into another.

In the courtyard of the inn she helped herself to water from a copper dipper hanging on a rope above the well. It was clear and cold, and she drank until her thirst was slaked. Then she took a fresh handkerchief from her satchel and wiped the grime of the road from her face and throat as best she could. She removed her bonnet and shook her hair free of its pins, tugged a tortoiseshell comb through her wiry chestnut curls, and twisted them into a knot on top of her head. In the dark water of the well, she caught sight of her own reflection, and was surprised to see it essentially unchanged. Her nose was still too long and thin, and her square jaw, dimpled though it was, still jutted forward in a most unfeminine manner. Her hair, as usual, defied her efforts to tame it—already it corkscrewed in defiant curls over her wide, smooth brow. And her eyes, which were transparent and either green or gray, according to the light, looked back at her from the shiny surface of the well as if to say, Nothing has changed—nothing at all.

But that wasn't true. It was the same Maddy Douglas mirrored in the water—the events of the last twenty-four hours had not altered her appearance. But in every other way, she thought, they had changed her life.

The tinker, to be sure, was a stroke of luck. He had shown up at the parsonage in Fall River two days before, his wagon almost empty.

"You haven't much to offer today, do you?" she'd said, eyeing the few bolts of cloth, the single barrel of flour, and the packets of needles he showed her.

"Not much," he admitted. "But now that the war between North and South is over, there'll be more goods to be had. I'll be going back to New York this evening, and the next time I come I'll bring you what you need." He sniffed the air, fragrant with the aroma of the bread Maddy had set out on the porch to cool. "Tell you what, though," he said. "I'll trade you these papers for a slice of that bread, and you can read about the feller that's taking all them women out to marry settlers in the Washington Territory." He handed her a bundle of newspapers tied round with twine. "Mr. Bennett of the New York *Herald* says they'll never get married, though," he told her. "They're going to be fancy ladies for the Indians and the sailors in the Territory. He says they're going to a fate worse than death, Mr. Bennett does." He peered at her closely. "You do know what that is, don't you?"

"Of course I do," Maddy said impatiently.

"This Mercer feller who's taking the ladies out West says Mr. Bennett's libeled his expedition," the tinker went on. "He says the country needs women to settle out there in Seattle. He says it's the richest land in America."

Maddy cut the tinker a thick slice from the coolest loaf of bread and slathered it with fruit preserves. Then she untied the bundle of papers and scanned the bold headlines of the New York *Herald*. She already knew more than the tinker did about Mr. Asa Mercer and his mission; just two months before, Mercer himself had come to pay a call on her stepfather after Sunday services. He wanted Reverend Stone to endorse his plan, and he described the new settlement of Seattle with fervor: the heavily timbered forests, the fine deep-water harbor, the lakes and rivers that fed rich farmland, and the spirited, hardy settlers who had already tamed enough land for a good-sized city.

But Maddy's stepfather was not converted by Mercer's ardor. "I'll not subscribe to sending our good Yankee women halfway around the world to be the whores of your Indians and scalawags!" he told the young man. "To cater to the evil lusts of your loggers and fishermen, your prospectors and criminals? Never!"

Asa Mercer, red-faced and embarrassed, had attempted to refute the Reverend's charges. "Not whores but wives!" he said. "Good men, strong men, and, especially, lonely men. Can you harden your heart to those who lack what every man deserves —a good woman, a clean hearth, a warm meal? To men engaged in God's work, clearing the wilderness, bringing His mercy to heathens, extending the borders of this great country? These men need wives, sir, and that is all they need and all they desire. They already have everything else that matters—in fact, they have the greatest opportunity of the century! Surely among your congregation are ladies to whom such a situation would be appealing—ladies who would otherwise be spinsters, with the flower of our nation's manhood lost in the war just concluded! I beg you, sir, do not turn a deaf ear to my pleas! These are not bounders, not wastrels, not criminals fleeing the justice of the Republic; these are good men and true, men with prospects. Look!"

Asa Mercer pulled a sheaf of papers out of his worn traveling case. "Here's a man with seven hundred and fifty acres and a sawmill. Here's another who's already built a house for a wife. Here's one with three cows, a sow, and a squaw to help the missus with the cleaning and cooking!"

Maddy's stepfather's face was even redder than Mercer's. "Enough!" he thundered. "Leave this house before I throw you out! It's the devil's plan, and my congregation will have none of it!" He strode out of his study, almost colliding with Maddy, who had been listening at the door.

Mercer was crestfallen. Maddy brought his coat and helped him retrieve his papers, which the Reverend had scattered on the floor. "I'm sorry about my stepfather," she said to the earnest young man. "Since my mother's been ill, he's . . . well, he's not himself."

"Thank you, miss," he said sadly. "But it's been like this everywhere, since Mr. Bennett started his campaign to blacken my good name. And Seattle's," he added.

"It is really the way you spoke of it, then?" she asked. "A queen among cities?"

"It will be," Mercer replied confidently. "We have everything. There's land for farming and more for timbering. Some say there's more riches underneath too—coal, surely, and copper, and maybe gold. The fish in Puget Sound, our inland sea, could feed five hundred times more than the settlers we have now. We're not just a frontier town—already we have some industries. And soon we'll have a railroad terminus as well, and then nothing can stop us! And, of course, we have the university, the only one in the Territory," he added. "I happen to be its president."

"Really?" He seemed much too young to be a university president, Maddy thought. He was thin and gangly, and his Adam's apple protruded above his high collar. A lock of hair fell boyishly over his forehead, and his ruddy face was sprinkled with freckles. "Then why aren't you back in Seattle teaching your students?"

"We hardly have enough to keep the doors open," he confessed. "But all that will change, once we find the women to marry the men to raise the families to—"

"Maddy!" Her stepfather's voice boomed out from the top of the stairs. "Upstairs. At once!"

She handed the young man his hat and walking stick. "You'll have to go now," she said. I wish I could go with you, she added silently; oh, I wish I could go with you!

He seemed to read her thoughts, and a look of hope came into his eyes. "Convince him," he told her. "Tell the other ladies of your acquaintance as well. We sail from New York after the New Year—Captain Ben Holladay has agreed to take five hundred women west on his ship. And there are at least that many good men waiting for you. Come with us—you won't be sorry!" And in less than a minute, he was gone.

Maddy went upstairs. She dreaded Sunday afternoons, those hours after services when it was the habit of the Reverend Luther Stone to inspect his stepdaughter's soul for signs of evil. Lately he was not satisfied with questioning her about her secret thoughts. The week before, he had accompanied his relentless examination of her moral character with personal attentions she found disagreeable and even frightening. He had taken her hand in his, pressed it to his chest as he beseeched the Lord to look upon her innocent virgin soul with pity, and then forced it down to the bulge in his trousers. "Make Your countenance to shine upon this innocent child," he had prayed. "Through Your guidance allow her to follow Your way, away from the paths of wickedness, the temptations of the flesh!" All the while he pushed her hand back and forth, back and forth, across his lap. His voice grew hoarser and his breath more labored, until at last the swollen thing beneath her hand seemed to burst, and she felt the wetness through the broadcloth of his trousers. He thrust her roughly away from him and stood up. From the next room, Maddy's mother called her, and the Reverend glared down at her. "The devil is in your soul, Maddy Douglas, but together we will drive him out!" he said. "Go see to your mother."

That Sunday afternoon after Asa Mercer's visit was a repeat of the previous one, although this time it was worse; he made Maddy kneel before him, held her head roughly between his hands, and forced it between his legs. Afterward, Maddy could not face her mother; she closed herself in her room, and from her bureau drawer she took the letter she had found in the minister's study when she brushed the ashes from the hearth after Asa Mercer's visit. It must have fallen out of his satchel, she thought, for she knew her stepfather would never have kept it. He had only scorn for Mercer's plan, as he made very plain to Maddy and her mother that evening. "It's no place for a Godfearing woman," he said firmly. "Better to die a spinster than submit to godless savages in the wilderness!" But Maddy remembered the high color that had flushed the friendly countenance of the awkward young university president, the enthusiasm that shone in his eyes as he told her about the brave, spirited Seattle settlers who were making a city in the far Northwest. A queen among cities, he had said. Maddy recalled his words as she read the letter again.

I am a Christian man with two mules, a horse, twenty chickens, a goat, and a house rough but strong against prevailing winds, on 320 acres thickly timbered and prime for cutting. With a wife, I can claim an additional stand of timber, and will share this and all my goods and faithful service and devotion as well. I have reached twenty-one years, and I am a clean man. If a strong, willing Christian woman of good character will have me, she will not be sorry.

The writer had added his signature in thick block letters and below his name a postscript:

If she be possessed of a musical nature and can read and write a clear hand, so much the better. [Signed] *A Hopeful Man.*

The tinker had come to the parsonage just after the New Year, two days before another dreaded Sunday afternoon. In the weeks since Asa Mercer's visit, Maddy's mother had grown weaker; nightly Maddy prayed to God to ease her misery and take her to His bosom. When He did, Maddy knew, she would leave the parsonage and the minister her mother had married after her own father died at Bull Run. "He's a good man," her mother had told the children, "and he is willing to give all of us a home." But half a year later scarlet fever carried off the twins, and within days it took Maddy's youngest brother, born the same July afternoon their father died in Virginia. And as the fever took its time, slower but just as lethal, with Maddy's mother, the Reverend Stone withdrew even deeper into his bleak silences, which Maddy feared even more than the fiery visions of Hell and the humiliating attentions he forced on her during those dreadful Sunday afternoons in his study.

Maddy didn't know where she would go when her mother's ordeal ended. She was not without abilities; she could sew, after a fashion, she could comb honey from a hive, put up fruits and vegetables, and tend babies; indeed, she had helped deliver her mother of her last infant. She could keep the household accounts and had done so since her mother's sickness.

She was a serious, plain-spoken child, always big for her age and therefore expected to be more grown up than she truly was. Her mother despaired of her bluntness. "Maddy, why did you tell Mrs. Bridges she'd gotten too stout for her dress?" she asked, when that corpulent lady departed in a huff after calling round to offer her condolences following the death of Maddy's father.

"Her button popped off and fell into the cream pitcher while she was eating the last of the scones you baked this morning," replied Maddy.

"It would have been more delicate of you to have overlooked it," her mother chided. She sighed. "You'll trip over your tart words, and not lightly either, when you're grown. No man will have you if you can't speak softly when it's solace or sweetness, not truth, he wants."

"Then I shan't be his wife, or anyone's," Maddy said with a defiant lift of her chin.

"And how will you manage, alone in the world, even a big, smart girl like yourself, who can't sew a tidy seam, or whip the cream without turning it to butter, or keep the woodstove burning long enough to boil water?"

I could do any of those things if I wanted to, Maddy thought resentfully. And more besides. I can make a butterfly light on my arm, and skip a stone nearly across the Taunton River, and go around the world to Greece or Persia or Paris, France, and meet kings and highwaymen and empresses and beggars too, and if I didn't have to serve tea to fat old Mrs. Bridges, I could be there now!

For Maddy could read, and since she was a child books had carried her beyond the narrow confines of sooty, smoky Fall River, the mill town in which she had lived all her life.

Her father had taught her her letters, and one magical day

they shaped themselves into words, and after that her doll gathered dust on the counterpane, and her toy wagon rusted in the root cellar. She had a rapacious appetite for books, even before she was old enough to hold them upright, but big enough to go with her father to his printshop and feel the heavy lead slugs and smell the ink and watch the words dry before her very eyes. Her father read aloud to her every night until he went to war, long after she was able, herself, to make sense of the pages of newsprint, the loose sheets of poems, the political tracts, pamphlets, and hymnals that were his trade. The silly games of children her own age bored her; instead, she closeted herself within the library in the cozy, slightly shabby old house on Water Street and dreamed away the long hours of her childhood. It was really her mother's sewing room, but the walls were shelved to the ceilings and from every one spilled treasure. She learned Latin from Pliny and French from Racine, poetry from Shakespeare and mathematics from Pythagoras, so that even though there was no money to school her after her father's death, she educated herself; and to escape the meager grayness of the parsonage she lost herself in the romance of novels.

That was why the cream turned to butter, and the eggs stayed in the henhouse until they were cracked and useless, and weeds ravaged the vegetable patch, and the stitches on Maddy's embroidery loosed their threads. And why she knew, despite her mother's warning, that she would get by somehow, even if she never did learn to hold her tongue.

Soon after the news came from Bull Run, Maddy's mother began selling off the contents of the house on Water Street. First the silver candlesticks went, and then the tea service that Maddy could never polish to a sheen high enough to satisfy. Then one terrible day a carter came to take away the contents of her favorite room. After the books had been removed, the empty shelves looked raw as an open wound, and when she closed the door of the room behind her, dust rose in the air like a cough from a crypt. Behind the cushions of the window seat she found a slim volume overlooked in the removal; she tucked Mrs. Browning's sonnets in the pocket of her apron and later hid them more securely underneath her feather mattress.

That was the second unhappiest day of her life; the first was when word of her father's death in battle reached them. Her big, slow-moving father, with the chestnut hair so like her own, and his special smell of tobacco and ink, and his strong arms that steadied her when she walked with him along the river at dusk and came upon a beaver building a dam or a wild swan nesting in the marshes. Her father, who whirled her lightly in his arms when he came home at night, who told her she was beautiful like her mother, when her own pier glass confronted her with the truth of her plainness. His death was a cruel and terrible blow, and Maddy thought there could be no worse.

But disaster followed upon disaster. Soon after the dismantling and removal of the books, the same carter returned to the almost empty house and took away the bed from Maddy's room —the soft pine bed, carved all around with leaves and blossoms, that garlanded her head like the crowns of Athenian heroes when she laid it in the exact center of her pillow, closed her eyes, and said her prayers before retiring. That awful night she lay motionless and uncomfortable on a narrow, iron-railed cot salvaged from a junk heap behind the printery, now closed and shuttered, and for the first time in her young life she did not ask God to bless her before she slept, for she thought that surely He had forsaken her.

The piano in the parlor was the last remnant of their old life to go and, with it, the only livelihood the family had, for Maddy's mother, Abigail, in the first months of her widowhood, had eked out a humble living for them by giving music lessons to the children of Fall River. Soon after, the Reverend Stone— a dour, unsmiling man whose very presence seemed to rob the sweetness from the lilac-scented air, and whose demeanor was so grave and glowering that even Maddy's mother made private fun of him once he had departed—stepped up his regular calls on the printer's widow.

Thus, when Abigail told her, a day after the year of mourning was concluded, that she had sold their Water Street house and accepted the Reverend's proposal of marriage, Maddy knew that the Almighty had truly deserted her. But she also knew, with a wisdom greater than her years, that any protests she might make would not be heeded; her mother, she thought pitilessly, was ill equipped to manage without a man to tend and protect her. And when, after the marriage, her mother smiled less and sang not at all and moved through the dank rooms of the parsonage like a ghost of the loving, girlish wife she had once been, Maddy privately thought it was a predicament of her own making.

Then the twins died, a fortnight apart, and next her youngest brother. At the grave, after the third and somehow saddest funeral, her mother collapsed—not with grief but with the same fever that had taken all her children save one.

Maddy did not leave the sickroom until the immediate danger was past; fear that her mother might also be taken from her caused her to renew and even redouble her prayers and to once again seek in God's love the faith that somehow, in some fashion still unknown to her, she was still within the shelter of His mercy.

Her mother recovered, but not completely; the following autumn she was confined to bed with another bout of fever. When Abigail began coughing blood, the physician who had attended her through all the births and deaths of her thirty-three years could only stroke his beard and say, "It is in God's hands."

To believe that this was so was to accept that Maddy, or her mother, had in some way angered or affronted God. While Maddy was not as pious as she wished she could be, or as respectful of her elders as she should be, she had committed no sins worthy of such punishment, and she was certain, or nearly so, that her mother had not either. True, Abigail had been terribly vain about her pretty looks and was all too used to the attentions of a man, even the dreadful Reverend Stone, and prideful in a way that had made the dwindling of her circumstances, after Maddy's father's death, as painful to watch as it had been for her to suffer. But even those lapses in character, Maddy thought, were not so terrible as to warrant the suffering visited on them so relentlessly, and for so long.

That God might not exist never occurred to Maddy; she saw Him in the birch trees and the sunsets, and she heard Him in the gurgle of an infant and the screech of a seabird. She accepted Him in the waxen stillness of a child's coffin, hard as it had been to bear. That He had somehow simply overlooked her seemed a more plausible answer, and despite the growing evidence of

His neglect she continued to pray to Him. When on that Sunday shortly after the winter equinox the Reverend first touched her in a way that made her cheeks burn with shame, she cried silently out to Him. After the second assault on her body, she looked elsewhere for her deliverance. And in the person of the tinker who chanced on her in the yard of the parsonage on the first day of 1866, she thought she had found it.

That morning her stepfather banished all books except the Scriptures from the parsonage. Fearful, he said the romantic novels that Maddy was particularly fond of were corrupting her innocence. With even this small comfort denied her, in the sadness of her soul an anger grew, mounting and dreadful, but at the same time there swelled in her breast a determination somehow to surmount the awfulness of her situation. As the church bells rang out the New Year and her mother coughed in the intervals between them, Maddy considered her possibilities which were few indeed for a girl of her limited means and education. She could be a governess like those heroines of fiction, she supposed. Surely someone would hire her; perhaps a family with a mother who sang in a high clear soprano, and a father whose pockets held chestnuts and a pitch pipe and whose muffler always smelt of ink.

Maddy's eyes filled with tears as she remembered the life that had disappeared the day General Beauregard fired on Fort Sumter. Once again she read the letter from the Seattle logger that had fallen out of Asa Mercer's case. Again she knelt by her bed and prayed to God for deliverance. And then she heard another bell, the tinker's, and as she went outside to see to it, she wondered if it was His answer.

Surely the tinker was a messenger of the Almighty, Maddy reasoned that afternoon, as she cut the fellow another slice of bread. The tinker was going to New York, and, according to the newspaper, Asa Mercer's ship was sailing from the harbor of that same city within the week. In the root cellar were jars of peach conserve and snap beans canned the previous summer, and cooling on the porch were a dozen loaves of fresh bread. In her mother's drawer were at least a dozen gold coins, salvaged from the sale of the house on Water Street. Maddy thought quickly, and in minutes she had struck a bargain with the tinker

—who believed, she knew, that there was more to be had from this determined girl than fresh provisions or even money. She could handle any affront of that sort, she supposed; when she thought of what she had endured at the hands of her stepfather, this simple lout seemed hardly any threat.

That night, while her stepfather was out making New Year calls, Maddy crept into her mother's room. The sweet odor of her sickness hung like a curtain in the air around Abigail's bed; in the moonlight, her mother's skin was the color of marble, and her breath was as tiny as a sparrow's.

"Maddy? Come here, dearest girl," her mother called faintly. Maddy came to the bed and took her mother's pale, wasted hand in her own strong freckled one. "Oh, Mamma, I love you so much," Maddy whispered. "But I have to go away now." She told her mother all of it—about Asa Mercer, and the tinker, and the *Continental*. "I have to go," she finished. "If I don't . . ." Her words trailed off.

"I know you do," said her mother. "I've seen how he looks at you. From the time you became a woman. If I were well, perhaps . . . but it's too late. He is a tempted man, and the Lord's light has dimmed in him." She stroked Maddy's curls, which the moonlight tipped with flame. "Take the money—it's all I have left from your father. It was to be your dowry. God keep you, my precious one, as I will keep you in my prayers."

Two nights later, she bundled her few clothes in a carpetbag and added her treasures—the copy of the Portuguese sonnets, her Bible, her silver brush, and her store of coins. Drawing her thick wool coat around her, she glanced at her reflection in the pier glass before leaving her bedroom for the last time.

At fifteen, Maddy was still a big girl, saved from plainness by the rich profusion of gleaming curls that refused to be tamed by braids, buns, or bonnet and the remarkable transparency of her eyes, which gave no hint of the quick intelligence and restless mind behind them. She would be a handsome woman and a hardy one, but her true strength and beauty would forever come from within. She had heart and spirit, and she was leaving the parsonage and the Reverend Stone behind her.

She met the tinker in the woods behind the parsonage, as she had agreed, and although he was a bit too familiar, he gave her

less difficulty than she had expected. They stopped at a farmhouse in Mystic the first night, and the farmer's wife gave her
a bed of clean straw in the barn, while the tinker slept in the
back of the wagon. They traveled through the next evening, and
Maddy dozed while old Lucy plodded along the dark Post Road.
They were, she estimated, less than a half day's journey from
New York. Deliverance seemed within her grasp, and what lay
beyond she did not even dare to consider. But if the tinker
insisted on stopping, and Lucy refused or simply could not
move faster, everything would be snatched away. All that stood
between her and the unknown, she thought, was a faster horse.

As if summoned by her unspoken words, not one but two
huge roans pulled into the courtyard of the Post House, snort-
ing and stomping to a halt not ten yards away. "Only a moment
now!" trilled a musical voice from inside the coach. "We mustn't
miss the *Continental!*" The livery driver handed down from the
coach the most beautiful woman Maddy had ever seen. Her hair
was arranged in an improbably glossy fall of curls even redder
than Maddy's, hardly concealed beneath a tocque of brilliant
blue and green peacock feathers. A green melton traveling cloak
was flung carelessly over a red velvet suit, and there was snowy
lace at her throat and cuffs. Her fingernails, Maddy noted with
envy and horror, were painted as scarlet as her lips and cheeks.

Reverend Stone would have called her a harlot, Maddy knew,
and her mother's nostrils might have flared at the heavy musk
of the woman's perfume as she stepped around the steaming
piles of horse manure in the Post House yard in her dainty
leather boots. Was this flamboyantly gotten-up woman, like the
tinker, another stroke of timely luck, or was she perhaps a heavenly messenger? Probably not the latter, Maddy thought, appraising her silently, but in any case she would do quite nicely.
She was going to the *Continental,* and somehow Maddy would
go with her.

It all proved surprisingly easy to arrange. Maddy offered the
stranger a dipper of water and her spare clean handkerchief,
which she accepted gratefully. She emptied the dipper in one
lusty swallow and patted her lips delicately. When she handed
back the little square of sheer muslin, Maddy noted, it bore a
faint trace of scarlet.

"Excuse me, but I heard you tell the driver you were going to the *Continental*. Would that be the sailing vessel *Continental*, leaving New York Harbor on the evening tide with the Mercer party?" Maddy asked.

"It certainly would," the woman replied cheerfully. "Why? Are you sailing with that company?"

"I hope to be," said Maddy. "Mr. Asa Mercer himself invited me."

"Oh he did, did he?" The woman fixed her with a keen, appraising look. "Where've you come from, then? I thought Mr. Mercer had been sent packing by all you New England blue-bloods."

"Oh, I'm not one of them," said Maddy eagerly. "I'm . . . an orphan." She sent a silent apology to God for her lie, but it was almost true, she was half that, and it would soon be the whole dreadful truth. She couldn't explain that she was running away from home. "From the war, you know," she added, hoping to earn the woman's sympathy.

"You poor thing," said the woman, eyeing Maddy's worn but serviceable coat, her rough woolen mittens and dusty overshoes. "Are you going out to the Territory to find yourself a husband?" She inspected her more closely. "You're just a young 'un, aren't you?" she asked. "What's your name, girl?"

"It's Maddy . . . Maddy Douglas," she replied. "I'm seventeen." She sent another brief apology to God, but what if this woman thought she was too young to accompany her?

"Not for a year or two yet, but who cares?" she said, and held out her hand, which was fashionably gloved to the middle knuckle. "I'm Sonnet McBride, lately of New Bedford, and I'd be delighted to offer you the hospitality of my coach, especially if that's your tired old gray mare at the hitching post. Why, I'd doubt she'd make Manhattan Island by sunset tomorrow."

A broad smile creased Maddy's face, and her heart jumped with happiness. "I'd be very pleased to accept," she replied. She'd never met anyone named Sonnet, and she'd never seen a feathered tocque or carnelian fingernails. But then, she reminded herself as the driver took her carpetbag from the tinker's wagon and tied it to the top of the carriage, she'd never run away from home before, either.

Chapter Two

The last thirty miles of Maddy's overland journey passed as if in a dream. The coachman had procured refreshments from the Post House kitchen—cucumber sandwiches, tiny meat pies, grapes and marzipan, and even two bottles of ale. At Sonnet McBride's urging, Maddy fell to with relish; she had long since consumed the small package of food she had taken from the parsonage, and she was a girl of good appetite. She had to restrain herself from gobbling everything in sight; it would not do to have Sonnet think her traveling companion was poorly bred, especially since she seemed to be on familiar terms with their captain, Ben Holladay, and might therefore have some influence on who would be permitted to sail with the Mercer party.

Any misgivings she might have had on that account were settled by her rescuer. "Oh, heavens, that Mercer fellow wouldn't turn away any woman under sixty, the way I hear it," said Sonnet. "He has a contract with Ben to bring five hundred passengers round the Horn, and I dare say the party will fall short of that number by far. For every lass like you"—and here she fixed Maddy with a direct and questioning gaze—"there are a hundred who'd rather let their maidenhood be claimed by worms in a land whose best young men died to save the foolish pride and ugly greed of others."

"You don't think the war was a noble cause, then?" Maddy asked tentatively. She was slightly shocked by Sonnet's lack of patriotic sentiment; after all, her own father had sacrificed his life for those ideals so movingly expressed in Mr. Lincoln's address at Gettysburg, which, while in no measure compensating for her dreadful loss, were at least a source of pride and some small solace.

"Are tariffs and territory noble, then? Cotton was king, and to keep it on the throne an entire race has been enslaved, and a generation slaughtered," said Sonnet. "And there are many who made a good thing of it, too."

"Like Captain Holladay, you mean?" Maddy had read Mr. Bennett's stinging denunciation of the *Continental*'s owner: "a ruthless speculator, that wretched breed which profits from the sacrifice of true patriots," the publisher called him, citing the exorbitant profits Holladay was rumored to have made during the war.

"It's true Ben Holladay never let the national welfare come between him and a pile of money, but he's no better or worse than the rich bankers and munitions makers who managed to turn a tidy sum these last years," said Sonnet. She popped a piece of marzipan in her mouth. "Besides,"—she smiled brightly "if it hadn't been for the war, Ben wouldn't have bought the *Continental*. And if he hadn't it wouldn't be sailing tonight for Seattle, and you'd still be safe at home, not bound for who knows what. And who's to say this all was not ever meant to be?"

Who indeed? thought Maddy. Was it Sonnet making her head spin, or was it the ale? Maddy listened to Sonnet McBride's stories with amazement. The woman was gaudy, and perhaps even coarse, but she was outspoken and refreshingly direct, though if she had truly been, seen, and done all that she claimed, Maddy calculated, she must be far older than her appearance indicated. She had danced at President Polk's inaugural ball; she had been to the Fair in Paris; she had known Old Rough-and-Ready, General Zachary Taylor, and implied that she had been an intimate of General Scott before his brilliant campaign in Mexico. Of her own birth and beginnings she said little; Maddy restrained her natural curiosity and asked few questions, hoping therefore to ensure that none would be asked of her.

She need not have worried. Sonnet McBride took for granted that Maddy would be her fellow passenger on the *Continental*, just as she was in her carriage. "We shall be companions of the open road, as Mr. Whitman said—or, rather, the open seas," Sonnet remarked, and with the familiar words of Maddy's favorite poet, she won the girl's affections.

For herself, Sonnet explained, the *Continental*'s voyage was not the beginning of a new chapter in her colorful life but a brief diversion. The general whose carriage they rode in was temporarily overburdened by certain responsibilities which had been neglected during the war—burdens she did not elucidate upon but which, it slowly dawned on Maddy, might well be a wife and even a family. "By autumn, I expect it'll all be set to rights," Sonnet said cheerfully. "And I've always wanted to see the Washington Territory, haven't you?"

"Well, yes, I suppose so," agreed Maddy. But the fact was, she hadn't thought much on where she was going, or even what it would be like when she got there, beyond the pictures her mind had created from Asa Mercer's words: an outpost of civilization in a remote and romantic wilderness, some far-flung corner of the American empire. Of the actual journey she had thought little, and, in fact, her geography was rather hazy. Until this very moment, all her considerable energies had been devoted to outrunning the bleak destiny she had left behind; only now that her escape was practically assured could she begin to consider what lay ahead. And she would, she promised herself sleepily as the carriage bounced and jostled them closer to the *Continental*. As soon as her head caught up with the rest of her, she would.

She woke for the first time when Sonnet McBride settled a coach robe around her shoulders and her own fur muff under her head. The next thing she heard was Sonnet's announcement of their arrival.

"Well. Miss Maddy, wake up and see your new home," she said, pulling aside the dusty velvet curtain of the carriage. "There's Ben Holladay's *Continental,* and may she bring you safely round the Horn to find your heart's desire!"

"And yours too, Miss McBride—I mean, Sonnet," stammered Maddy, though what that might be, she could hardly imagine.

The steamer *Continental* rode low in the water, all one hundred and twenty feet of her. Up close, she looked old and battered, a weary veteran of the wars. Her paint was peeling, and a tired-looking Stars and Stripes hung limply from a stanchion on her stern. Maddy followed Sonnet up the gangplank with some trepidation; what if Mr. Mercer had changed his mind and no longer wanted her? But the smile that creased that man's weary countenance when he beheld Maddy trailing along in Sonnet McBride's colorful wake reassured her.

"Miss Maddy!" he said with evident pleasure. "So you made it after all! Did your stepfather have a change of heart, then? And has your mother recovered her health?"

Sonnet gave Maddy a searching look, and she colored. "I'm afraid she fared poorly over the winter," Maddy said, which was certainly true enough.

"My condolences, my dear girl," Asa Mercer said, and then brightened. "Well, I know you're doing the right thing by joining our party. I hope you'll put your sadness behind you and dine with me this evening—and Captain Holladay, of course," he added. Ben Holladay, a huge, bearded bear of a man whose gold watch chain strained across his girth, took Maddy's hand in his own enormous one.

"Ben Holladay, sole owner of the steamer *Continental,* at your service, ma'am," he said gallantly, and presented her to the ship's master, a Captain Windsor, who acknowledged her presence with a brief nod. The captain's wife, a prune-faced woman with a pockmarked complexion, was too busy staring at Sonnet McBride to notice Maddy. Ben Holladay was introducing her all around: "My companion, Mrs. McBride," he boomed in a voice as big as he was, and Sonnet curtsied prettily.

"Mrs. McBride, is it?" asked Mrs. Windsor. "Will Mr. McBride be joining you, then?"

Before Sonnet could reply, Asa Mercer interrupted. "I'm afraid all the staterooms are taken," he told Maddy. "We've only eight, you see, and we have some families with small children, so we've assigned them already. If I'd known . . . I'm sure you'll find the ladies' quarters adequate, however."

"Mrs. McBride's late husband perished in the service of the Republic, ma'am," Ben Holladay told the captain's wife. And then, to Mercer, he said, "I've taken the liberty of giving Mrs. McBride your cabin, Asa. Given the circumstances, I was certain you'd be understanding."

Maddy noticed the look that passed between the two men; Asa Mercer seemed discomfited and opened his mouth to say something, then closed it again.

"What circumstances did he mean?" Maddy whispered to Sonnet as they followed Asa Mercer down a ladder to the below-decks quarters. The air was close and heavy with the odor of unwashed bodies, and Maddy felt a pang of fear. What was she doing here, on a worn-out troop ship that might well sink while still in sight of New York Harbor? What had ever possessed her?

"Mr. Mercer's party seems certain to be much smaller than expected, and he is already in substantial debt to Ben," Sonnet said softly. "And not all those who have agreed to make the voyage are marriageable young spinsters, either—less than half the company, Ben says. Asa has promised to pay Ben the rest of the money when we reach California."

"What if he can't?"

"Then we'll put you lassies ashore on the Barbary Coast!" said Ben Holladay, interrupting them—rather rudely, thought Maddy.

"But isn't that—" Maddy began and quickly bit her tongue. Even in Fall River, Massachusetts, she'd heard of that notorious tenderloin; Mrs. O'Hara, who helped Maddy's mother with the Ladies' Aid Society teas, was married to a whaler who'd lost one eye in a brawl in a brothel there and made no bones about it; when the liquor took him, Mrs. O'Hara complained, he'd declaim loudly to anyone who'd listen that he'd gladly give his other eye for another night in the arms of the beautiful, willing ladies of the Barbary Coast.

"You'd fetch a likely price there, my girl," said Holladay, pinching Maddy's cheek with a good-humored leer. "Of course, not as much as Sonnet, here," he added, and squeezed Sonnet's arm with an unbecoming familiarity.

"Stop that, Ben, you're scaring the poor child to death," Sonnet said, extricating herself easily from his grasp. "Oh, this stateroom is dreadful, Did you have the cavalry in here?"

"You'll make it just like home in no time," Holladay replied. "Be glad you're not sailing steerage with the other ladies." He gave Maddy a pitying glance.

"And neither is Maddy," said Sonnet firmly. "She'll stay in here with me. Is that all right, Maddy?"

"She'll what? Now look, Sonnet, you can't go and do that. What do you think—" Holladay began, but Sonnet shushed him with a look.

"This poor orphan child has just left everything she holds dear, set out for Land's End on a tub the Secessionists must have used for artillery practice, and she doesn't have a friend in the world except Sonnet McBride," said that lady stoutly. "Now just get me a broom and some rags and send your sailor down with our things, and we'll see you on deck as soon as we've made things right in here. Shoo!"

Much to Maddy's amazement, Holladay did just that, and she and Sonnet set to with great determination, scrubbing the salt-encrusted grime from the tiny porthole and washing the scuffed wooden decking until it shone. The sailor who brought the rags and broom came back with bedding for the bunks.

"From Mr. Holladay, ma'am," he said, and Sonnet wrinkled her nose.

"Please thank him and then hang these out in the air," she said. The sailor departed, and she turned to Maddy. "Well," she said cheerfully, "it's not much, but it's home for a time, and it will do. Now . . . shall we go on deck and meet our fellow passengers?"

"I'll join you in just a moment, ma'am—I mean, Sonnet," said Maddy. "I guess I don't quite have my sea legs yet."

"Hmm . . . you do look a bit peaked," said Sonnet, inspecting Maddy carefully. "Too much excitement, I suspect, even for a grown-up young woman of seventeen."

She grinned at Maddy's guilty look.

"Don't worry, my dear—your secret is safe with me. I don't know what you're running away from, or what lies ahead for you, but I've no doubt that whatever it is, you can handle it. You're young, but you're strong and clever, and, most important, you've got spirit." She patted her curls in the gleaming reflection of the porthole. "Mr. Mercer says that's what Seattle needs—spirit. You're going to do fine, Maddy, just fine."

After Sonnet left the cabin, Maddy unpacked her few belongings. She took out the gold coins, wrapped tightly in a cloth bag, and from a small leather drawstring pouch she removed a silver locket. Opening it, she stared at the images of her mother and father. She clasped the locket to her breast and dropped to her knees beneath the porthole. She thought of those she was leaving behind—her mother and Mrs. O'Hara—and her kitten Mistress, and even of her stepfather. She thought of the peonies that bloomed every June in the parsonage garden, and the solo she would not sing in the choir at Easter. Tears welled up in her eyes. *Dear Heavenly Father, forgive me for my sins, especially for the untruths,* she prayed. *Stop Mama's suffering, and have mercy on the Reverend too.*

As the tears rolled down her cheeks, she felt the deck of the *Continental* lurch under her and heard the heavy clank of the iron chain as it lifted the ship's anchor from the harbor bottom. *And keep this ship safe, and all who sail on her,* she added. She waited, hoping for a sign that her prayers had been heard. None was forthcoming so she rose, smoothed her skirt, and went up on deck to watch the only world she had ever known disappear in the *Continental*'s wake.

* * *

Rough seas and rain-drenched winds dogged the *Continental* the first week out of New York, and except for brief meals hastily taken at a table presided over by Ben Holladay and Captain Windsor, whose wife and daughter, a girl Maddy's own age, never smiled, Maddy and Sonnet spent most of the first week of the voyage in their stateroom. Maddy met a few of the other passengers and made special friends of a couple named Wardell, who were traveling with their mischievous three-year-old son to Portland, where Mr. Wardell's brother had already homesteaded a large parcel of land on the banks of the Columbia River. Cora Wardell was only a few years older than Maddy herself; she was a plump, red-faced woman who blushed every time her husband teased her, which he did often and with great relish. Maddy spent many afternoons playing with the Wardell child, and when the weather grew calmer she joined the family in the saloon, where a blind man, whose wife was heavy with child, played a scarred upright piano. When he ended the song-fest with "Rock of Ages," as he always did, Maddy's heart tightened, and on those nights she was glad to go back to her empty stateroom. For Sonnet spent much of her time with the owner of the vessel; through the walls that separated his stateroom from theirs, Maddy could hear, faintly, Ben Holladay's booming laughter and the low-pitched echo of her friend's.

By the end of the second week at sea, the passenger's appetites had returned but the meals served had become less appealing; dinner for most of the ship's company was fried salt beef or liver, tea steeped in salt water, and parboiled beef, and Maddy and Sonnet fared hardly better at the officers' table. On Sunday mornings, Mr. Mercer led church services on deck; the familiar words of the Methodist Episcopalian ceremony moved Maddy deeply, and she joined the impromptu choir that led the other passengers in hymns before the benediction. She passed the long afternoons with the other women, knitting or playing games— spirit rapping was much favored by the ladies. Or she read to the youngest passengers from *Alice in Wonderland,* a new book which Cora Wardell had brought on board. Being on the *Continental,* Maddy thought, had tumbled her into a world fully as strange as the one Alice found at the end of the rabbit hole. On some days when the children were otherwise occupied, Maddy curled up in one of the lifeboats and read the Carroll novel eagerly, as if searching for a clue to the adventures to come.

Nine days out of New York the *Continental* entered the Sargasso Sea. Maddy hung over the rail for hours, watching the delicate, gold-tinged seaweed drift over the water. On the last day of January the ship crossed the Equator, and the next evening they spied for the first time the Southern Cross, and Ben Holladay pointed out the Magellan clouds. They endured several days of weather stormier than any they had encountered since the first days of the voyage, and then the skies cleared and the trade winds cooled the heat of the day.

The first week in February they sighted the coast of Brazil. "That's the way Seattle looks from Elliott Bay," Asa Mercer told Maddy, as the ship neared the heavily wooded hills that circled Rio de Janeiro, their first port on the South American continent. "Of course, Seattle is a younger city than Rio, but give us a few years and we'll be just as important."

"I'm sure you will be." Maddy smiled. Poor Asa. He had spent the first few days of the voyage hiding in a coal bin from the ire of Ben Holladay, who proclaimed loudly and often that Mercer had "skinned me alive" and would "walk the plank for his treachery." Asa had promised to pay Ben the rest of the money as soon as the *Continental* arrived in California, but Holladay proclaimed that he was holding the ship's company hostage for Mercer's debt, and would let no one disembark there until the debt was repaid. "Our men will wire me the money as soon as they know we've rounded the Horn," Mercer protested, and Sonnet finally succeeded in soothing the ship's owner enough to allow Mercer free run of the ship.

"What if they've changed their minds?" Maddy wanted to know. "What will you do then?"

"Well, they won't," said Mercer firmly. "And even so, Governor Pickering told me if I needed funds the Legislature would help out. And of course, the people of Seattle will welcome you all into their homes, until you make suitable arrangements."

"What kind of arrangements?" Maddy wanted to know.

"Why—er, husbands, I suppose," said Mercer. "Which is what I wanted to talk to you about. Have you given any thought to what you will do when you arrive in Seattle, Maddy?"

"I expect I will try to find employment," she replied. "You did say there were plenty of jobs, didn't you?"

Mercer frowned. "Well, yes, but none I can think of that would be exactly right for you."

"I could teach school," Maddy offered, but Mercer shook his head.

"I'm afraid we've more qualified schoolteachers on the *Continental* than we have schools for in the whole Puget Sound."

"I can clean and cook," said Maddy.

"Oh, those who can afford the hire use squaws for that sort of thing, and the rest do it for themselves," said Mercer.

"Then I'll work in a shop," Maddy offered.

"I'm afraid we've barely enough jobs of that sort for the men who can't work in the woods," said Mercer. "Besides, why would a gently bred young lady such as yourself be a maid or a shopgirl when she could be a wife?" He smiled. "That's it— I'll find you a husband, Miss Maddy. That shouldn't be hard." He studied her closely. "Our men have been without women for a long time. . . . I'm certain I can find someone who'd be proud to have you."

Maddy was not sure whether to be worried or relieved. Now that the euphoria engendered by her desperate and successful flight from Fall River had worn off, she had begun to worry about how she would manage on the frontier. She knew that the pretty ones, like Annie Stephens, would find husbands immediately—why, Asa himself was obviously in love with her. And she knew that the plainer spinsters were equipped with useful skills or at least some small nest egg they could count on to sustain them until they too found partners. It was clear from all the conversations Maddy heard or participated in that matrimony was the object of the journey for most if not all of the women on the *Continental.*

Of course, eventually it was to be hers as well, despite the impertinences she had often expressed to her mother on the subject. Abigail had never taken them seriously, and Maddy hadn't really meant them that way. She had always expected to marry—it was what a woman did, and it seemed to be so even in the brave new settlement of Seattle, according to Asa Mercer. Still, she had hoped to postpone it for a while.

"Of course, there's your connection to Mrs. McBride to consider," Mercer went on. "That might make a suitable match difficult, unless I can arrange something for you in advance of our arrival."

"What do you mean?" asked Maddy.

"Her—mm—protection is hardly an appropriate introduction to society," said Mercer. It might even predispose our finer gentlemen against you."

Or, as Maddy's mother would have said, a lady is known by the company she keeps. Well, what of it? Maddy thought defiantly. Sonnet McBride was her friend, even if she was no lady. But before she could rise to Sonnet's defense, Mercer touched her arm sympathetically.

"I know she has taken it upon herself to look out for your welfare, Miss Maddy," he said, "and she's to be commended for that. But she's not staying in Seattle, you know. She'll be heading back with Holladay, and then who'll look out for you?"

"Perhaps I could be a governess," Maddy offered. "You've seen for yourself that I'm good with children."

Mercer smiled. "Governess? We don't have anything that fancy, Maddy. All the children in Seattle are seen to by their mothers—" He stopped in mid-sentence and contemplated the young woman before him. "Except for Abel Blanchard's little boy, that is."

He continued to regard Maddy thoughtfully, and a smile smoothed out the network of grooves worn into his forehead by the worries that had plagued him since the start of the voyage. Abel Blanchard, he thought. Of course! The girl was no great beauty, but she was exactly what Blanchard had requested: decent, moral, Christian, strong, and healthy.

Abel had not exactly commissioned Asa to find him a wife—someone to care for his child, he had said. And when Asa thought he'd have five hundred spinsters to bring to Seattle, he was sure there'd be one he could spare to be Blanchard's hired girl. But not now—not when his company of eligible females numbered less than fifty, and at least three times that number of bachelors had advanced him money to find them wives. If he brought this girl to town and told the loggers she was going to be Abel Blanchard's hired girl, they wouldn't stand for it—why, they'd run him out of the Territory! But if Maddy arrived as Blanchard's wife-to-be, no one would fault Asa; the rich got served first, that was the way things were, even in Seattle. And Blanchard, influential as he was, could pacify the settlers. Why, Blanchard might even get Ben Holladay off his back. Yes, thought Asa, this could be exactly the stroke of luck he'd been waiting for.

Asa described Abel in the most favorable terms, stressing his considerable energy, talents, and accomplishments. And when he told her about Abel's motherless son, she was especially enthusiastic.

"So there might in fact be a situation for me in Mr. Blanchard's household?" Maddy inquired. "Taking care of the child, I mean?"

Asa Mercer contrived a look of amazement. "Now why would a man want to hire a servant when he could have a wife, as well as the land he could claim in her name?" he asked.

This was the very argument he was already planning to make to Abel Blanchard, who was known to be tight with a dollar: why hire a woman for wages when he could as easily marry her and claim another section of land?

Asa's logic was not lost on Maddy. In Fall River she had only a few coins for a dowry, and few womanly ways or feminine charms to bequile a husband—even her mother had despaired of her prospects. But on the frontier that didn't matter—well, perhaps it did, but it was not all that counted. She could bring a man land, and in return he would provide her with a home and family.

"There are plenty of loggers looking for wives, and more than enough farmers, but with a man like Abel Blanchard for your husband, you'd be set up for life," said Mercer. "Most women would be thrilled at such an opportunity."

"Oh, I wouldn't want you to think I'm not grateful," said Maddy. "I certainly appreciate all you've done for me. I'd just like to consider it for a while, if I may."

"By all means." Mercer beamed. He was certain the girl would accept, especially after she had time to reflect on the good fortune he had put within her reach. "I do hope you'll give me your decision before we arrive in San Francisco, though, so I can wire Mr. Blanchard," he said. "Even in Seattle, one needs a few days' notice for a wedding."

"But what if I don't . . . what if he . . ." Maddy hesitated.

Asa Mercer patted her hand gently. "Abel Blanchard will count himself blessed to have you for his wife," he said, "and I doubt if you could do better."

He was probably right, thought Maddy. She knew she wasn't pretty, and if what her mother said about men was true, her ways weren't the right sort to attract them. From what Mercer was saying, there seemed no way to survive on the frontier without a husband. Certainly that was how the other women on the ship saw the situation—it was for a husband, any husband at all, that they uniformly seemed to have set their bonnets.

It appeared to Maddy, at that moment, that marriage was inevitable, and in truth she had never really believed it was not. She had never dreamed beyond that; she had never been interested in a profession, although she harbored a secret desire to be a writer. For that reason she had sought out the journalist who had accompanied the Mercer party on the voyage, on assignment from, of all things, Mr. Bennett's own newspaper, but what she learned from that lady about the vagaries of such a career, particularly for a woman, discouraged her.

Besides, she had no reason to think marriage was by any means a bad thing. Love she was not so certain about—in books it seemed to be both fearful and wonderful, fraught with at least as much pain as happiness, and Maddy thought it sounded rather like a fever. Apparently it could happen or not, there was no telling, but one thing was sure: you couldn't count on it. Marriage, though—for a woman, that was ambition enough.

Maddy thought about the times she had told her mother she'd never get married, especially not if it meant having to make up to a man and tell him black was white, or that he was smart and wonderful. But when it came right down to it—and the closer the *Continental* came to its destination, the more those words sounded like childish boasts—marriage was her fate.

If a man of Abel Blanchard's stature wanted a wife, there were many older, more assured, and attractive ladies aboard ship than Maddy, and if she did not agree with the match Asa Mercer proposed, surely he would choose one of the others for the man. And what if no one else wanted her? She would have to consider that, Maddy told herself.

"I'll see," she told Asa. "Before we sight California, I'll give you my answer."

*　*　*

Mercer's plan preoccupied Maddy as the *Continental* brought her closer to their destination. She thought about it in Rio, where the ship docked for a week and they went to church, to teas at the residence of the American ambassador, to a pre-Lenten feast, and to the markets. Unable to resist, she spent some of her money on feather flowers and fresh fruit and a copy of *Vanity Fair,* which she found in a shop just off the Copacabana that flew the Union Jack.

One Sunday, the Reverend Mr. Simonton, a missionary who had joined the ship in Rio and was en route to his next posting in Chile, preached a sermon that emphasized the moral danger incident upon so great a change of life as that which the members of the ship's company had proposed for themselves. Maddy felt certain his words were directed at her; thinking about marriage, even to someone she did not know, made her feel less imperiled. Perhaps she had used up all her courage in gaining her freedom; certainly the prospect of continued independence was a frightening one.

On March 1 the *Continental* entered the Strait of Magellan. All that night the ship hovered in the vicinity of the great shoal that stretched from the base of a promontory at the tip of the continent into the South Atlantic. In the morning Captain Windsor steered west, and that day they proceeded fifty miles up the Strait, with the wind rising ahead of the bowsprit. Belowdecks, the passengers secured their belongings against the wrath of the sea, but the *Continental* traversed the difficult waters of Cape Horn with little incident, and anchored safely at Prison Island. When the snowy peaks of Chile were sighted to the east, everyone aboard was relieved, and Maddy, in her nightly prayers, gave thanks for their delivery. Tamar Bay was their last landfall in the Strait. At the end of the month there was a total eclipse of the moon, and Maddy, who had begun keeping a journal, wrote that day, *It was surely a sign from the Almighty that our course is true and our mission enjoys His favor.*

In Mexico they had a brief sojourn ashore and then set sail for San Francisco. In that last month of the voyage, two babies were born on the *Continental,* one to the wife of the blind musician, and both were delivered safely by the Captain's wife, with Maddy's assistance. A shipboard romance had bloomed during those weeks between a California miner and a woman from Braintree, and the whole company celebrated their engagement in early April.

The next two weeks passed quickly as an air of anticipation swept through the ship. The complaints about food and accommodations were forgotten in the excitement surrounding their imminent arrival in San Francisco, from where, after a brief stopover, the *Continental* would proceed north to Seattle. And on April 23, when the cheering passengers sailed into San Francisco Harbor, Maddy wrote in her journal:

Delivered at last after a lengthy voyage to the golden state of California, hence to take passage for Seattle. A great Adventure it has been, and what awaits in this rugged land is in the hands of God alone, to Whom I pray once again for my dear Mother's release and my safety in the wilderness.

As she and Sonnet watched, the sailors on the wharf made the *Continental* fast and the porters unloaded their baggage. Asa Mercer was jovial. "As soon as we dock, I'll go to the Western Union office and secure Holladay's money," he said. "And of course, Maddy, I shall wire Mr. Blanchard the good news." For on the last evening before entering the Fallarones, just outside San Francisco, Maddy had consented to Asa's request that he inform Abel Blanchard that when the *Continental* arrived in Seattle, it would be carrying his bride.

She didn't see that there was much choice. Mr. Mercer had implied that any woman who did not make "suitable arrangements" would be offered transportation back East, but that was no consolation to Maddy, who no longer had a home to return to. She was not certain that she could make as good a match for herself as Mercer promised to; she had no confidence, in fact, that she could make one at all, and no idea how she would get along if she could not. Of course she did not express those doubts to anyone, least of all Sonnet, to whom she said only that Abel Blanchard seemed to be a good Christian man who had need of someone like her.

Maddy had only the faintest idea of what marriage would require of her, but, she told herself, she would face it when it came time. Meanwhile, she would accompany Sonnet to the hotel where rooms had been booked by Mercer for the party, and await word from Seattle that Abel Blanchard looked upon her arrival with favor.

Sonnet snorted at that. "If he doesn't, he's a damned fool, and you'd probably be happier for it. In any case, you can't go to him or any other man without a proper trousseau, so hurry along, or all the shops will be closed before we've even begun!"

Chapter Three

Although Ben Holladay had threatened to hold the *Continental*'s passengers hostage for the money owed him by Asa Mercer, he ordered everyone ashore immediately instead. This was as far as he was going, he declared, and furthermore, if Asa did not pay up, he was turning the ship back and heading for New York. Desperately, Mercer wired Governor Pickering: SEND TWO THOUSAND DOLLARS QUICK TO GET PARTY TO SEATTLE. Those ten words, he confided to Maddy, cost the last dollar he had. To Abel Blanchard he sent another wire, collect: HAVE SECURED SUITABLE SPINSTER SEND MONEY TO FORWARD FROM CALIFORNIA.

While they waited for replies, Sonnet and Maddy settled into comfortable bow-fronted rooms at the California Hotel on Post Street, from which they ventured forth early the next morning to explore the city. Sonnet was determined to outfit Maddy suitably for her wedding and insisted on paying for it. Dutifully Maddy admired the elegant dresses they were shown in three of San Francisco's finest stores—which Sonnet said were as fashionable as any outside Paris. But when Maddy found fault with one frock that looked especially fine on her, as she had with everything they had seen thus far, Sonnet threw up her hands.

"Marie Antoinette's coronation robes wouldn't please you today, girl. Something tells me you don't want to go through with this."

Maddy's lower lip quivered, and tears filled her eyes. "It's not the wedding," she said.

"Is it the wedding night, then?"

"No, it's not that," Maddy replied. She blushed. "Well, perhaps a bit, but I expect I'll manage."

"You might even enjoy it," Sonnet said dryly.

Maddy nodded, coloring slightly. What had happened with the Reverend had not killed the lively curiosity she felt about what transpired in the marital bed. She had some notion of it, and she had felt sexual stirrings in herself—to her everlasting shame—even with the Reverend.

"Then what is it?" the older woman demanded.

But Maddy could not tell her. Nor did she have to, for Sonnet understood her trepidations and attempted to advise her as best she could. "You're doing the smart thing, I expect," she told Maddy. "A girl like you, what choice do you have? It's hard for a woman, making her own way in the world, that's all there is to it."

"But you seem to," Maddy said.

"Ah, but I've accepted the way it is. I live at the whim of men, as no doubt you've noticed." Maddy blushed, but Sonnet paid her no mind. "No man owns me, but, to be truthful, some do rent whatever comfort I can give them. I don't think you'd care for that."

Sonnet's words, spoken frankly, confirmed what Maddy had supposed but in no way diminished her affection for her. "You're probably right," she admitted. "But what shall I do if I simply cannot abide this Abel Blanchard?"

"Why then, you'll have to learn to," said Sonnet. "That's a woman's task, unless she's independent, and that's even harder. Ah, Maddy, it won't be a bad life. He'll let you alone, mostly, and only fuss when you don't pretend he's perfect. That's the secret to getting on with a man, you know."

"I'm not very good at that," said Maddy glumly.

Sonnet smiled. "Why, you're quite good at it, dearie. Good enough to get you halfway around the world, at least, and off to a bright new start in the West. Marriage doesn't have to mean the end of your life, you know; if you're clever, it can be the beginning. Now—shall we look at the watered silk again?"

With some reluctance, Maddy allowed herself to be fitted for her wedding dress, a simple gown of heavy silk in a soft rosy color that made her look much older, and more self-possessed, than she felt. The dress was like a costume for a play—that was how she thought of her wedding. Right now, it seemed no more real to her than anything else that had happened to her since leaving home.

Until then, Maddy had always done what was expected of her. It was not hard, because only half of her was engaged in carrying out the demands of others. The other half was off somewhere, drifting in a world she'd read about or one she created —in her favorite of those, her father had never died and she still lived in the house on Water Street.

But this was no dream world, no book or play, even if it did seem to be exactly as Mrs. Austen said—marriage was the only honorable provision for her. But had she in her heedless flight run from one seduction only to have another forced upon her? She wouldn't think about that now, she decided, inspecting the sheer, delicate nightdress that Sonnet held out to her. She tried to imagine wearing it for Abel Blanchard and decided she wouldn't think about that now, either. Later, maybe—when her head caught up with the rest of her.

"That's it, then," said Maddy as they left the store, their arms full of packages. "I suppose I've no other choice now except to marry Mr. Blanchard, if he'll have me."

"He'll have you, all right," Sonnet replied. "No reason why he shouldn't—why, if it isn't John Pennell!"

"The very same, at your service as always, my dear Mrs. McBride." The portly, whiskered man standing before them on Mission Street beamed. "You are exactly where I'd hoped to find you, another favor I owe to our mutual friend Mr. Holladay," he said. Then he turned to Maddy and inspected her critically. "Is this one of your girls or Mercer's?" he asked.

Sonnet's eyes narrowed. "What do you want, John?" she asked.

"Simply to discuss a business proposition with you, Sonnet— merely a few moments of your time. There's someone I'd like you to meet. Will you join us?"

He gestured to his carriage. Through the isinglass window a shadowy figure regarded them; Maddy could not distinguish him clearly except for his eyes. Those eyes—they were disturbing, a deep, dark implausible color that reminded her of the sea just before a storm. They seemed to stare right through her, and after a few seconds Maddy turned away from their penetrating look.

Sonnet considered Pennell's words briefly and turned to Maddy. "Why don't you run along back to the hotel now that we've done our shopping?" she said. "I'll meet you back there later."

Maddy hesitated. There was something unpleasant about the man, a faint emanation of menace. Or was it only the heavy odor of his sweet cologne? But Sonnet did not seem concerned. "Mr. Pennell is an old acquaintance," she explained, "and it seems that he's come from Ben. Please do go on—I'll join you shortly."

Sonnet sounded impatient for her to be gone, so Maddy departed. She was worried about what lay in store for Sonnet— her own decision was made, her promise given, and her future temporarily, at least, secured, but Sonnet's was less certain. Along with the other passengers, Sonnet had been ordered off the *Continental* by Ben Holladay, who seemed to have broken off relations with her. At the very least, his continued sponsorship appeared uncertain; to her knowledge, Sonnet had heard nothing from him since they came ashore. Of course, Sonnet was resourceful and no doubt would find a new patron soon; perhaps it would even be this Pennell fellow. Maddy shuddered. Without a husband, a woman like Sonnet was at any man's mercy; Abel Blanchard was looking better with each passing hour.

When Sonnet rejoined Maddy at the hotel later that afternoon, she said nothing of her meeting with Pennell, or of the mystery of Ben Holladay's continued silence. Maddy did not pry—Sonnet had asked no questions of her when they first met, or even later, and Maddy took her cue from her.

In any case, she had much to think about herself, for early the next day Asa Mercer received the answers to his telegrams. From Abel Blanchard he had a reply as terse and direct as his own message had been: SEND WOMAN SOON AS POSSIBLE STOP CONFIRM ARRIVAL NEXT SEATTLE STEAMER, it said.

"Well, I expect I'm for it now," said Maddy. Blanchard's wire was her pledge accepted, her fate sealed.

"And very fortunate you are, too," said Mercer. "I wish the other ladies were so lucky." For Governor Pickering had turned down Mercer's plea for funds with the same alacrity as Abel Blanchard had accepted his proposal on Maddy's behalf.

"What will you do now?" Maddy asked. She had secured her future, for better or for worse, but her fellow passengers, who had embarked on the voyage with high hopes of their own, might be stranded in San Francisco.

"The lumber schooners will take some of them on to Seattle," Mercer said, "those ladies who still dare to go. And some have decided to stay in San Francisco—those who can afford to."

"And what of your own future?" Like all the women on the *Continental*, Maddy was quite fond of Asa. He had tried his best to help them make their own dreams come true, whatever they were, and they were exceedingly loyal to him.

"Oh, I expect the folks in Seattle will let me come home." Asa grinned. "I'm certain I can regain their goodwill, and perhaps even my expenses."

As it turned out, that was what happened. Asa Mercer left for Seattle that very evening, on the fastest steamer he could book passage on. The others came later—Maddy herself did not leave San Francisco for several more days, and the other passengers straggled up to the Northwest a few at a time. Long before they arrived, however, Asa had begun his campaign to convince Abel Blanchard that what he needed was not a servant girl but a wife —specifically, one Maddy Douglas, late of Fall River, Massachusetts.

Asa mustered every argument he had thought up since the plan to marry Maddy off to Abel had occurred to him. Abel had naturally misunderstood the ambiguously worded telegram. He thought the money he had sent was for the passage of a hired girl, not a wife. But Asa's appeal to Abel's sense of duty was persuasive. So was his dire warning that if Abel hired as a housekeeper a woman any other man would have welcomed, sight unseen, as a wife, it might cause such discontent and factionalism among the settlers as to disrupt the city's efforts to claim the great future that was in store for it. Asa proved especially canny by enlisting Mary Denny, wife of the most prominent man in the settlement, in his campaign to woo Abel from his widowerhood.

Finally, Abel agreed to the bargain Mercer had made for him, thus turning a mission in grave danger of failing miserably into what was indisputably a success—at least, for Asa. Shortly after his arrival back in Seattle, a town meeting was held at Yesler's Hall, during which Asa defended his efforts and vindicated his reputation and Abel Blanchard spoke on his behalf. Some of the first party of Mercer's Maidens were on hand to praise him, then and the next evening as well, when Yesler's hosted an evening of celebration and entertainment, including a magic show, whose miracles were not half so impressive as that by which Mercer managed to pacify the choleric bachelors who had waited almost a year for delivery of their brides.

Asa had one last task to complete, before he married his own Mercer girl, Annie Stephens, and took her off to Colorado, where he planned to be a rancher. And as soon as the steamer *Puget Sound* arrived in Seattle and deposited Maddy Douglas into the waiting arms of Abel Blanchard, it would be done.

* * *

The *Puget Sound*'s whistle tooted impatiently in San Francisco Harbor as Sonnet and Maddy took their tearful leave of one another at the wharf.

"I wish you were coming with me," said Maddy. "Especially since Ben Holladay's left. What will you do?" If she'd only known that Sonnet was staying on in San Francisco, she thought ruefully, she might not have agreed to marry Abel Blanchard. Surely, with Sonnet there, she might have found a way to manage—to find work and lodgings, and perhaps later pay her own way to Seattle, to arrive there indebted to no one.

Even now, as the steamer tooted its final call to passengers, it might not be too late, she thought, and said so to Sonnet.

But Sonnet frowned—or was she trying to keep from crying? Maddy wasn't sure. "Much as I'd like to keep you here with me, it isn't the wisest course," said Sonnet. "The general will be sending for me soon, you know. I'll just have a good look around California, and then I'll find my way back." She held Maddy away from her, as if memorizing her face. "You've been a fine traveling companion, my girl, and I'm pleased to have known you. Now give us a smile and go meet your fortune, whatever it is."

"God keep you, Sonnet," whispered Maddy, and turned and went up the gangplank.

*   *   *

When the *Puget Sound* steamed into Elliott Bay three days later, Maddy stood on deck, her head bent against the wind. She had her first sight of Seattle refracted through slanting silvery raindrops. It was a small settlement stretched out between a steeply forested bluff and a usually cerulean bay, whose chop today was frothy and gunmetal gray like the sky. As the ship moved closer, she could see on the lowlands several frame buildings of various heights, their weathered wooden boards glinting in the pale, thin light of late afternoon. On an elevated knoll that overlooked the flats stood an imposing structure, all dome and cupola, as if it had been lifted from an elm-lined green in her own New England and plopped right down here in the middle of nowhere.

They were quite close now, close enough to make out faces in the crowd of onlookers gathered to welcome the steamer. Maddy scanned them anxiously, looking for Asa.

She saw him, finally, hatless and waving. Tentatively, she waved back and retreated a few steps, adjusting her bonnet. From safely beneath it, she studied the man next to Asa.

He was very large, husky and fair of hair and complexion. His size was a matter of some relief to Maddy—at least she would not tower over him. He looked to be some years older than Asa, but Maddy expected that—she noticed that he was not as old as her stepfather, for which she said a silent prayer of thanks. He wore a black broadcloth suit and a vest and tugged nervously at his tie. When Asa pointed her out, his eyes came to rest on her briefly—then, as if embarrassed to be caught staring, he looked away. In one hand he held a hat, and in the other he clasped the hand of a small boy, whose face reflected the serious demeanor of his father. A wave of sympathy swept over Maddy as she considered, for the first time, that in the matter of his future perhaps Abel Blanchard might have no more choices than she had. Except, of course, that he was a man.

*   *   *

Elijah was jumping around like fat in a fry pan, which kept Abel from having to concentrate too hard on the girl. Which was just what she was, he saw, although at first the size of her fooled him. Why, she might not even be of age, which wasn't all that unusual on the frontier. Before the donation land law was changed, some settlers got themselves hitched to any female they could find, no matter how young, just to claim the double portion.

The girl said she was near eighteen, though just how close she didn't mention right at the start. She wasn't much to look at, which was no hardship as far as he was concerned—there was nothing about her to remind him of Sara, who had been small and dark and delicate; this girl was near as big as he was and almost as fair-skinned. She looked strong and healthy enough, and that was what mattered, She didn't need to be beautiful, or smell of lavender, or laugh like rain rippling on rooftops. What he wanted was for her to look after the boy, and keep the house, and cook his meals, and warm his bed at night, and for all that he supposed she looked fit enough.

Asa made the introductions and she spoke their names, his and Elijah's, in a deep, husky voice, like a man's but softer.

"I hope you had a pleasant journey," Abel said.

"Not especially," said Maddy. "I mean, the weather was dreadful, but my cabin was most comfortable and I was glad to keep to it." She had hardly seen or spoken to the other passengers on the *Puget Sound,* but she had not minded—in San Francisco she had purchased Mr. Melville's new novel, a romance that totally engaged her imagination as the steamer churned through the rough Pacific, so that she did not have to think very hard about the adventure she was presently having.

But since it was this man, after all, who had made her accommodations so pleasant, she thanked him for his concern.

Then Asa went to fetch Maddy's cases and an awkward silence fell between them. It was broken finally by Elijah, who slipped out of his father's grasp and ran across the pier toward a lad about his size and age who stood in the protective embrace of an Indian woman. She was a coast Salish, shorter in stature and stockier than the Indians Maddy had seen in South America. Her hair was a dark reddish brown, close in tone to the coppery cast of her skin, and her eyes were round. Her forehead was flattened, the head sloped upward to the crown, the result of the cedarbark pad that had been bound against her brow in infancy until it assumed the desired shape. Her nose was thin and her ears lay flat and close to her head. Her hair was worn in one thick plait tossed over a shoulder, and her ears were pierced and ornamented with abalone shells.

"Elijah." Abel spoke the boy's name sharply.

"It's Johnny Westwind, Papa!" his son said.

Maddy saw that the boy was a half-breed; his skin was coppery and his hair coal black, and there was a strong resemblance in other ways to his mother, but his eyes were startlingly green. By the time Abel made his way to his son through the crowd on the pier, Elijah and the other boy were chattering happily away.

"Come with me, Elijah," Abel said firmly, but the boy's face puckered and he shook his head.

"Stay here," he insisted. "Stay with Johnny."

Abel bent down and picked his son up, ignoring the Indian woman and her child. Frowning, he returned to Maddy, took her by the elbow, and turned her away from the pair. Elijah's protests were drowned by the steamer's whistle. Asa, with Maddy's cases, stood at the foot of the gangplank. "We'll collect your things and be on our way," said Abel. But before they could do that he was hailed by a man just then disembarking from the *Puget Sound*.

"Brother Abel," he said when he reached their side. "Have you come to welcome me home, or are you here on other business?" He tweaked Elijah's cheek and then seemed to take in Maddy's presence. He was a muscular, well-knit man, nearly as tall as Abel but with a more graceful carriage, and he was dressed modishly; in fact, Maddy thought he was something of a dandy, especially next to the somberly dressed, sober-looking man he addressed so familiarly. He had a sardonic, somewhat devilish appearance, which was enhanced by brows raised in a quizzical vee over eyes as green as the depths of the sea—eyes that looked disturbingly through her in a way that made her blush. His hair was a deep auburn color, and his neatly trimmed beard, like his brows, was flecked with gold. She thought she must have seen him on the ship, though she was not aware of having done so. Perhaps it was his eyes, so deep, so strangely ringed around the iris with smudgy black, like a raccoon's— where had she seen them? Why, she thought, on that little In-

dian child, who waited so impassively with his mother across
the pier. And then the newcomer saw them, and she understood
the boy was his.

"Looks like someone's glad to see you," Abel said shortly.
Maddy could hear the disapproval in his voice.

"But not you, eh?" the man said teasingly.

Abel snorted. "Didn't know you were away," he said, and
then he seemed to remember Maddy, for he turned to her and
said, "This is my brother Caleb. Caleb, this is Miss Douglas. You
know Asa Mercer."

"Indeed I do," said Caleb Blanchard pleasantly. "Did you get
your maidens all home, Asa? I heard in San Francisco you were
having a mite of trouble with that."

"I was, but it's all settled now," said Mercer. "In fact, Miss
Douglas here was with us on the *Continental.*"

"Is that so?" said Caleb. "And on the *Puget Sound* as well?"
Maddy nodded.

"I'm sorry to have missed the pleasure of your company," he
said, "but perhaps we'll meet again."

"Very likely," said Abel brusquely. He nodded in the direction of the woman and her boy. "Whyn't you keep 'em on the
Bluff, then?"

"They've got as much right here as you or I," Caleb replied.
"More, actually."

"Don't talk like a fool," Abel said.

His brother grinned lazily. "Glad to know nothing's changed
since I've been gone," he said.

"I wouldn't say that," Abel told him. "I'm getting married on
Saturday." And then he took Maddy firmly by the arm, spun her
on her heels, and marched her away.

Maddy kept up easily with Abel Blanchard's determined
progress across the boardwalk of the wharf and along the
muddy thoroughfare that paralleled the waterfront. Moving
swiftly along, they soon came to what appeared to be the main
commercial street of the town. They passed a general store, and
a dry-goods store, and a bakery from which the tempting aroma
of bread wafted out, and a blacksmith and a barbershop and a
haberdashery and a stationer's, which had books in the window
and thus caught Maddy's eye. But Abel Blanchard did not slow

down; he walked briskly and without speaking until they came
to a white house, two stories and quite substantial, tidily set back
from the street by a white picket fence. There was a garden with
lilies and daffodils blooming, and a graceful willow in the yard,
with a rope swing hanging from it, exactly like the swing that
hung from the willow tree in the yard of a certain house on
Water Street in Fall River, Massachusetts.

"Is this where you live?" Maddy asked, devoutly hoping it was
so.

"No," he said, and she felt a sharp stab of disappointment.
"This is the home of my friends the Dennys, who have kindly
offered to put you up until . . . well, for just now. My house is
presently undergoing some repair, you see, and is quite dusty
and noisy, really not suitable after all the distance you've come,
from much grander quarters, I'm sure." He opened the gate.
"Could have booked you in at the hotel, I suppose, but one
wouldn't want to give offense to Arthur and Mary, and of course
it's frightfully expensive. . . ." His words trailed off, as he carefully closed the gate behind them. "They're good friends, Mary
and Arthur, we came out together, you see, and the boy stays
here when I'm away. Although that will change now you're
here, won't it?"

Maddy was silent, looking up at the house that loomed before
her. It had bay windows, several gables, jigsaw trim, and a
pillared porch on which they stood, waiting for a response to
Abel's knock. She wondered how she was to answer that question—if it was a question—but just then the top half of the
double front door opened, and the woman whose smiling face
beamed out at them looked so much like Mrs. O'Hara, that
Maddy thought she was dreaming. Mary Denny—for that was
who it was—had thick braids streaked with gray like Mrs. O'-
Hara's, and the same ample bosom beneath her starched apron
front, and when she reached out to greet them the smell of
lemon grass that emanated from her was so like the sachets Mrs.
O'Hara favored that Maddy had to pinch herself to make sure
she was awake.

"Welcome, dear Miss Douglas—welcome to Seattle!" she said,
with such genuine friendliness and warmth that Maddy found

herself walking into that waiting embrace without a second
thought.

Mary held Maddy away from her, then, and looked at her
searchingly, as Caleb Blanchard had. Then she looked at Abel
and nodded her head; some unspoken message seemed to pass
between them.

"I expect you'll want to freshen up from your trip and rest
a bit before supper, won't you?" she said to Maddy. "Abel, why
don't you go find Arthur, I believe he's down to the bank, and
by the time you get back Miss Douglas will be all settled in."

Abel looked as though he wanted to say something, but Mary
shooed him away at the door.

"Just leave the cases here, Abel, and get along. You too, Elijah,
you go out to the barn with the other children, hear?"

She led Maddy inside. The floors were fir, the walls cedar
board and batten; rag rugs warmed the parlor, which was heated
by a fireplace of native stone that dominated the room. There
were kerosene lamps and cheerful chintz curtains, and a huge
melodeon stood in one corner against a wall covered with
cheesecloth that was papered over with a floral print design. A
decorative wreath made of moss, feathers, seeds, and sea moss
hung over the melodeon. On the other walls there were family
pictures framed in shells and pine cones.

Maddy followed Mary Denny into the kitchen, which was
dominated by a big black stove. Beyond the window she could
see a garden and orchards; chickens pecked around the back
stairs, and a cow grazed against the fence surrounding the yard.
At the older woman's invitation, Maddy sat down at a round oak
kitchen table while Mrs. Denny made her a cup of tea and
brought out scones and jam. "Soon it will be time to put up the
strawberries again," she said.

"At home I used to do that," Maddy offered. "In Fall River.
That's in Massachusetts," she added.

"Yes," her hostess said. "Asa told us that you came from
there."

Maddy expected that Mrs. Denny would ask her for more
details about herself, and she had them all ready, which was not
difficult because mostly they were true, except for things like
her actual age and why she had run away from home. But of

course Mary Denny didn't know she had run away, and in any
case she exhibited no curiosity about Maddy's past, a manner
Maddy was to learn was common on the frontier. People didn't
pry. They didn't need to know who your family was or where
you came from or why, which suited Maddy quite well.

Instead, Mary Denny turned the conversation easily to domestic matters: the rosebush she had just that morning planted
along the path to the barn, the cow that seemed to be ailing, the
difficulty of getting the children to do their chores, now that the
days were longer and there were more daylight hours for playing outside, and the amount of mud they tracked in, which even
the Indian woman who cleaned for her never seemed to eradi-
cate completely. "She only scrubs the middle of the floors, never
the corners," Mary said, "but she has the best supply of feathers
anywhere, and just when I've decided to let her go, one of the
babies is ready for a grown-up bed, and you can't find anything
better for stuffing a mattress."

Nothing she said seemed to require an answer, and Maddy
was content to listen, and be soothed by the chatter, and look
around the pleasant, simply furnished room, holding the fragrant cup of tea between her hands and looking into it as if
searching in the leaves for the answer to a riddle.

Then she allowed Mary to lead her into a bedroom, where she
hung up her clothes—including the dress she and Sonnet had
chosen in San Francisco. Mary Denny admired it greatly and
said that it was a splendid dress for a wedding, as if it were all
arranged, and Maddy supposed that meant she approved.

Somehow that was comforting—almost as if Mrs. O'Hara, or
even Abigail, knew and approved too, Maddy thought fleet-
ingly, as she climbed under the eiderdown quilt on the big
fourposter bed. Mary Denny was right—there was nothing
quite like a feather bed for comfort. And that was the last
thought she had before she tumbled into sleep, down, down,
down the rabbit hole and right into the lap of the Red Queen,
who looked remarkably like Sonnet McBride.

Chapter Four

Maddy had hoped to put off the wedding as long as possible, but Abel, satisfied that she was decent, Christian, and healthy, was anxious to get on with it. The work on their house was progressing nicely, and there was no reason to wait, he said; besides, it would be an imposition to extend her stay with the Dennys. "It's settled," Abel declared. "We'll have the wedding in the White Church on Saturday."

Abel did not so much solicit Maddy's opinion as declare his own, a tendency that squelched her inclination to speak her mind. She remembered what her mother and Sonnet had told her about pleasing men—it was surprising how similar their views were, considering the vast gulf that separated them in so many other respects.

Realizing that delaying the ceremony was hopeless, Maddy attempted in those few days before it to discern something of the character of her intended. It was difficult: Abel was not comfortable talking about himself, and much of what she learned came from Mary Denny, who had known Abel since the Blanchards and the Dennys came out from Illinois together fifteen years earlier. "He is not a man of fancy words or romantic notions," Mary said, "but I believe Abel hungers for a Destiny."

Abel put it more prosaically: "Whatever was out here at the end of the continent, I was going to see it," he said, "and danged if I'd let anything, including redskins, stand in my way."

In fact, the Indians that plagued some of the Conestogas of the pioneers had not bothered their party. Though once, in the

Platte River country, in the half-light between dark and dawn, Abel was wakened by the nervous shuffling of the oxen. He looked around him and stiffened—a band of mounted Shoshones ringed the rise behind their camp. Everyone else was asleep. His breath caught in his throat so that he could not speak and his limbs froze. And in that timeless moment as he watched, the Indians disappeared back into the shadows of the dwindling night, so swift and silent he thought thereafter that he might have dreamed them.

He described the incident to Maddy: "With no closer touch than that, thank the Lord, we arrived at the eastern border of the Territory." Abel was not sure how he might have acquitted himself had an Indian attack materialized, but once in safer country he was eager to push vigorously on to the last and hardest stage of their journey. Then a painted brave leading a string of ponies had galloped into their camp on the Umatilla.

"Did you kill him?" Maddy asked.

Abel shook his head. "No need to—it wasn't our scalps he wanted."

At first Abel hadn't been sure, but Caleb said he had seen the man before, at Soda Springs. Caleb wasn't worried—he believed that Indians, like any other creatures of the wild, were not dangerous unless provoked. Whether the great westward migration of settlers counted as such provocation, Abel wasn't certain.

"Caleb and David Denny—that's Arthur's younger brother—had been making a study of the Chinook trading jargon, and they parleyed with the feller," said Abel. "Seems he was after Sara—said he was willing to trade her for that string of ponies."

"Your wife?" Maddy asked, horrified.

Abel smiled. "She was comely," he said, and Maddy felt a stab of anxiety. No one but her father had ever called her comely—and probably this man never would. Abel's first wife, Mary Denny told her, had been more than comely—she'd been beautiful, a small, delicate woman Abel had married three months before leaving for the West.

Mary had been Sara's closest friend, and Maddy pressed her for details—she wanted to know what she had to live up to. The more she heard, the more she worried—surely she could not hope to equal Sara Blanchard's accomplishments. "There was always a smile on her sweet face, and a song on her lips," Mary told her. "Oh, she could sing like an angel, and when she did, we felt the Almighty's protection settle on us like a sweater on a chilly night. She made Abel bring her spinet piano with us on the crossing, and even though his pa grumbled, we were all glad he insisted. When we listened to her playing the familiar hymns out there on the prairie, we all felt less like strangers in that strange and hazardous place."

All across the plains and into the West, Mary said, Sara's soft words smoothed out quarrels and comforted children, and her pleasant ways made the rigors of the trail easier for everyone to endure. Early on in the journey, it became apparent that she was with child herself, yet she asked no special treatment because of her condition. And when the Indian brave demanded her and offered his ponies in payment, Abel scowled, but Sara teased him until his bad mood went away.

"I was blessed to have her," Abel told Maddy simply, and it was true. Why Sara had accepted him was one of the great mysteries of his life; in the long silent stretches of the crossing he wondered at it and concluded finally that she was a gift of the Almighty, Whose ways man cannot know. She weathered his somber moods, put up with his silences that sometimes glowered like the sky before a storm, and accepted his piety, which was sterner and harsher than her own.

Some nights she retired early to her wagon while Abel and Arthur Denny quoted Scripture aloud to the party, attempting to impress upon them the almost holy nature of their journey. She told Abel she felt closer to God when she spoke to Him alone, and he did not press her to wait up for him. She rarely did, although often when he came back to their wagon, after making a last check to ensure that the camp was secure for the night, her woman scent hung so heavy in the air that he could not help himself, but wakened her and pressed her close to him, burrowing into her sweet warmth until his fears and dreams and prayers were silenced by the thunder of his blood.

It was in Burnt River, on the Umatilla, that Abel first heard talk of the opportunities said to abound in the Puget Sound country, about as far away from the spot where their wagons stood as Oregon City itself was, but in a more northerly direction. The trail was open only to Oregon City, but it was Abel's contention, then and later, that if the land proved to be as fertile and the climate as clement up in Puget Sound as it was in Oregon City they might be wise to push up north, where the best land wasn't already claimed and even planted. "You got a good site, the people will find a way to it," he said, when they arrived in the Willamette Valley and, true to his prediction, found the best opportunities already undertaken. So they made the difficult overland journey two hundred miles to Olympia, a small settlement at the southern reach of that selfsame sound, which led at its northerly border to straits that pushed into the Pacific.

It is hard to say what aspect of a given piece of land calls out to a man, what arrangement of rock and soil and water, of plains and meadows, rivers and mountains, touches a hungry place in him and makes him say: *here—this is for me.* But in the region of the Nisqually, where the soil was rich, the weather mild and the roses bloomed year round, Abel's pa made his desires known, and their party was divided further. John Blanchard staked his claim in the fertile river valley, while Caleb, with his friends David Denny, John Low and Lee Terry, went north by the overland route, there to explore the upper reaches of the sound and determine if settlement was feasible. And Abel and Sara took temporary lodgings in Olympia, where they would wait out the weeks remaining before her confinement.

Thus it was a month after their child was born that Abel first encountered the Duwamish Indian known as Kinnikinnick Jim, who approached him outside Mike Simmons's general store on the main street of Olympia. Simmons owned a steamer that supplied his store with goods from San Francisco, and Abel had it in mind to do some business with him if he got the word he was expecting from his brother. Never a man to let dust settle under his feet, Abel had made good use of his time in Olympia, searching out information and connections that would help him secure his future.

"Abel Blanchard?" The Indian was close enough for Abel to smell the rancid odor of the dogfish oil that plastered the black hair to his head. Equally pungent was the aroma of kinnikinnick which rose from the cedar-bark pouch that hung, suspended on a hide thong, from the Indian's thickly corded neck. Except for the pouch, he was dressed much like Abel himself, in heavy black trousers, a broadcloth shirt, and a vest made of tanned leather. It was to the pouch the Indian pointed as he repeated what Abel finally understood to be his name—kinnikinnick was the Chinook word for the smoking mixture favored by the redskins.

Abel spoke no Chinook, he told Maddy, but from the Indian's few English words and gestures he determined that he had been sent by Caleb to guide him to the place the natives called Alki Noo Yawk. From the pouch, the Indian produced a letter whose creases were stained the color of ancient madder from the bark of the pouch. Abel read the letter twice; satisfied, he proffered a coin to the Indian and instructed him to be ready to leave for the north the next day.

But that very night Abel fell ill with ague, and it was nearly a month before he could leave Olympia for the settlement where not only Caleb but by now the Dennys, too, waited. Sara and their newborn son, whom they named Jacob, would follow by steamer in a few weeks. Abel was a man in a hurry, so eager to set eyes on the land his brother described that he overcame his distaste for Indians and accompanied the one sent by Caleb to the beach in town. There he felt again that nameless tug that had brought him this far, and without looking back, he stepped into Kinnikinnick Jim's canoe.

The Indian and Abel became well known to each other after that time, for Kinnikinnick Jim continued to serve Abel's brother Caleb in all manner of ways. His loyalty to the younger Blanchard was unquestioned, even through the Indian War that nearly destroyed the outpost a few years after the first white settlers arrived. After that conflagration, the Indians in the region were forced onto reservations across the sound. But Jim remained with Caleb on the bluff, where he had homesteaded and continued to live even after Abel, the Dennys, and most of the other settlers had moved across the bay to the city they called Seattle after the old Indian chief Sealth.

Abel thought that was going too far to pacify the redskins, whose claims to the land the whites homesteaded were, he felt, entirely without merit. After all, Indians didn't do anything for

the land they lived on. They didn't cultivate it, except for a few
mealy potatoes, or clear it, or build permanent structures on it,
or trade or swap it for advantage. Therefore they had no need
of it, but if it would cement good relations between the races,
as Arthur claimed, he would not oppose it. So it was done. And
when Caleb later told him the old Indian chief didn't want the
city named after him—believed, in fact, that having his name
spoken after his death would disturb his departed spirit—Abel
was secretly gratified. In his opinion, Indians were not to be
flattered, cajoled, or trusted, which was proven later when they
attacked this town named after one of their own. That the hos-
tilities were initiated not by Sealth's band, but by the hostile
Klickitat and Nisquallis whose treaties had been broken, made
hardly any difference to Abel—redskins were all alike, and he
for one, wasn't sorry when they were all deported from the
town. Even so, many came to the settlement, a few to work and
others to loiter, drink or gamble, and in a way he couldn't
understand, their very presence was to Abel a reproach. He
approved the efforts of the churches to Christianize them, and
supported that holy work with his own charity. And those Indians who worked for him, in his enterprises or his personal
household, he treated fairly as he would a white man.

Abel described how it had been when he and the Dennys
arrived, and Maddy could see, as they walked through the
streets, that he was proud of his part in carving a settlement out
of the wilderness. From his earliest months in Seattle, Abel dealt
in land—his own and everyone else's. He and Arthur talked
Carson Boren and William Bell into giving some of their land
to Henry Yesler for his sawmill, and to Doc Maynard for his
salmon salting business. He was partners with Arthur Denny
in a dozen enterprises—as soon as they were going concerns, he
sold them and started more. He eschewed profitable opportunities that offended his religious beliefs. Whiskey was never sold
on any premises he owned, and though some of his friends grew
rich on profits from saloons and even worse establishments
located down on the Skid Road, Abel never saw the inside of any
of them.

He started a general store and a bank—a few empty coffee
bags in the back of the store at first, and then a safe that stood

next to the flour barrels, under the farm implements. He constantly exhorted his fellow settlers to more and more diverse activity, though he himself was no speculator; he could see what he owned, knew the exact relationship between a dollar invested and the dollars it would return. But the town's business was his own, and they did well by one another.

Abel took personal pride in every example of Seattle's progress. He was a serious man, seemingly older than his years, except with his son Jacob, Mary Denny told Maddy. "When he held that small dear face close to his, the love that shone from his eyes came near bringing tears to Sara's," she said, "and when Jacob died of the whooping cough, that tender place in his heart was buried even as Pompeii. Sara tried her best to unseal it, and when Elijah was born, Abel was so proud and happy, we thought she had succeeded. But the effort, I fear, may have been too much for her, because after the birth, she became distant and distracted, not like herself at all. Abel said he used to find her rocking in the chair by the fire, tears streaming down her cheeks, unable to say what plagued her. And sometimes she was very giddy, and her face burned like she had the fever. We all feared for her mental stability and did what we could, but she grew melancholy. Some women get that way after their babies come, you know, and Doc Maynard prescribed a tonic, but it didn't help." Mary's face was sad, remembering. "Nothing did," she said, "nothing on earth."

Maddy listened, fascinated—it was like a novel. Abel hardly mentioned Sara so the details of his widowerhood came to Maddy from Sara's dear friend, a woman who obviously still mourned her passing.

Abel had been off scouting timber for the Stimsons for a week when Sara Blanchard's body, swept along by a strong southwesterly current, washed up at the foot of Caleb's Bluff. It was taken by the Indian who found it to the shack owned by Kinnikinnick Jim at the western edge of the property. He wrapped Sara's body in a Hudson's Bay blanket and placed it in the same canoe that had brought Abel to Seattle ten years before, and paddled the heavy burden back across the Bay.

Sara's absence had just been noted and an alarm raised when Abel returned home on the afternoon packet from Port Gamble.

According to the Boren girl, whom he had engaged to help his
wife around the house, Sara had left the house some hours
before, never saying where she was going, only that she would
come back by sunset. When she failed to return, the girl was not
overly concerned; the weather had turned freakish that afternoon, and Sara might have taken refuge at a neighbor's. So she
fed and calmed the baby, and put him to sleep in the warm
room, and the next thing she knew it was morning, and Sara had
not come home yet. Then she gathered Elijah up and went in
search of her own mother, who immediately raised a search
party.

Later it was reported that Sara had been seen the previous
day, getting into the canoe that, despite Abel's objections, was
her common and preferred mode of travel from the day she
arrived in Seattle. As far as could be determined, no one ever
saw her alive after that.

It was a mystery that was never solved. All that is certain is
that when Kinnikinnick Jim arrived at Yesler's Landing in his
canoe, and old Henry Yesler himself stepped forward and saw
the face of the dead woman laid inside, he took off his hat in a
gesture of respect and went in search of his good friend Abel
Blanchard. And when he found him, searching with the others
in the wood behind the town, he led him back to his landing and
to the Indian's canoe. And Abel keened, a high thin cry that was
totally unlike him, and threw himself on Jim in a rage so blind
and total that he had to be pulled off him else he might have
ripped his limbs from his body.

"It was as if a light had gone out," said Mary of Sara's death,
"as if the vision we all shared of the bright future dawning
around us was somehow dimmed. Jacob's death had been a tragedy, but this was even more terrible, and harder to accept."

With Sara gone, so too went Abel's dreams for his own happiness. For Seattle and its future, however, he continued to hope.
And in his second son Elijah those hopes abided.

Mary Denny never told Maddy about the rumors and specula-
tions that Abel's wife's death occasioned, or of how, when they
reached her ears, she confronted the gossip, and those who perpetrated it, directly. Sara was dead and nothing could change
that, said Mary; talk of where she was going, or why, and of

what might have drawn her away from her hearth and small infant on that afternoon could serve no purpose.

Still, there was talk. The Boren girl, privy to the goings-on of the Blanchard household, spoke freely about how often, in the weeks after Elijah's birth, Caleb Blanchard had called at the small house on Second Avenue, especially while Abel was away surveying. Nonsense, said Mary Denny, no one was more gentle or tender with Abel after Sara died than Caleb. Of course Sara's brother-in-law had loved her—there was hardly a soul in the town who did not. Caleb Blanchard's unconventional behavior had caused talk before this, and no doubt would again, said Mary; that was the nature of the man. His arrangement with Celia Westwind, daughter of Kinnikinnick Jim, for instance— well, that was appalling but understandable. To imply, however, that he and Sara . . . Mary would not countenance such conjecture, she declared, and no one who did would be welcome in her house.

Society in Seattle was small and close then; to be shunned by any prominent member of it, especially by Mary Denny, was to court unbearable isolation. The gossip dissipated in the gray-green winter mist; eventually the talk died down, and the towns-people no longer lowered their voices when Abel came near. They grew used to the sight of the tall, slightly stooped man carrying the small boy on his shoulders, stepping carefully around the mudholes or tramping noisily on the board side-walks of the rough, ugly settlement carved out of the forest's edge.

Those were hard times for Abel, and for Seattle too, as the Civil War absorbed the attention of the nation, and the stream of settlers coming west slowed to a trickle. Abel was as surprised as anyone when Asa Mercer brought the first shipment of women around the Horn from Boston. He missed most of the commotion surrounding the arrival of the Mercer girls—he was away at the time, surveying in the Snoqualmie Valley, where coal deposits of exceptional quality had been discovered. Abel did not like to be away from Elijah, but his business and the Territory's often called him to places where the boy's safety and well-being could not be assured. On those occasions Mary Denny was Abel's savior—she took Elijah into her own home and her ample heart. But when Sara had been dead two years, she spoke clearly what was on her mind.

"I don't mind keeping him, Abel, but it's time you found a strong young woman," she told him as he warmed himself by her hearth.

"Indeed, but where am I to get such a treasure?" he replied, as close to teasing as he ever came. He counted Mary as one of Arthur's greatest assets, but he was fond of her for her own sake and her own qualities, not the least of which was the way she listened to him go on about what Seattle needed, as attentive to his dreams as Sara ever had been.

"The Mercer boy is bringing another shipful of women here, if he can," Mary said. "Since Mr. Lincoln died, the lad is having trouble raising the funds for the voyage. If you were to help him, I should think he might return the favor by finding someone suitable for you."

"A woman to help with the boy, you mean?" he asked, for the Boren girl had recently given notice that she was getting married herself and so would be unavailable to care for Elijah any longer.

"No, I don't mean that, and you know it," Mary replied. "You can't keep someone whose only debt to you is wages. Back home in Knox County, you could easily find someone to take care of the boy, and your house, and be happy to have the position. But not out here, where a woman can have her pick of men, and her own land as well." Mary's voice softened. "Not that that's the only reason a woman would favor you, Abel," she said. "Not just for land."

Abel's face reddened. "Thank you, Mary," he said. "I know you mean well. But no one could be to me what Sara was."

"Of course not," Mary agreed. "But a wife could give you children, Abel. You're always going on about how we women have a duty to give Seattle sons and daughters. What about you? Isn't it your duty too?"

Abel said nothing. Such highly personal talk unnerved him. His silence did not deter Mary, however.

"Abel, the nine girls Asa brought here last year have all found husbands, those who wanted them, and the others have accepted positions with better futures than being a cook and nursemaid in that cabin of yours—which, by the way, you must do something about," she added bossily.

Abel looked genuinely confused. "Why? Why must I do something about it?"

"Because it's entirely too small, and too rough, to expect a woman to live in it," Mary replied. "For heaven's sake, Abel, it's only a log cabin!"

"It was good enough for Sara," he said testily.

"Sara was after you for years to build a proper frame house and you know it," Mary said. "You were so busy starting up other things you never got to it."

Abel's face darkened, and Mary thought she might have gone too far—Abel Blanchard was a prickly man, and she feared she had offended him. Still, convinced of the soundness of her argument, she persisted.

"Abel, talk to Asa. Help him out with his enterprise. And tell him to look for a wife for you. It's your duty."

Abel picked up his son, who was sleeping on a bed of quilts next to Mary Denny's youngest child, a girl of the same age. "I'll take it under advisement, Mary," he said, and went out of her warm, cozy frame house into the moist and salty night.

Mary told Maddy much of that tale; Abel himself told her the rest before their wedding. He was modest about his own accomplishments but fulsome in his praise of the other pioneers, and optimistic about their goal of attracting the transcontinental railroad. Then, said Abel, Seattle would truly be the queen city of the Pacific Northwest. He waved his arm with a flourish, as if to take in all they could see. They were on the Knoll, where the university was located—and where, the day after Maddy arrived, he had taken her, as much for his great pride in its very existence as for its commanding view of the surrounding environs. From where they stood, they could see the steamer that had brought her to Seattle disappearing around a point north of the bay on its way to Victoria. The waters of the sound were exceptionally blue, and so was the sky, across which stretched a swath of billowy clouds. In the west rose a line of sharp-edged mountains, their snowy peaks like frosting on a cake.

It was huge and magnificent, in contrast to the mostly barren, stump-strewn landscape beneath them. An ungraceful collection of nondescript buildings lined streets laid out north and south, paralleling the waterfront. Above the sawmill down near the flats the sky was brown and smoky. "Henry Yesler's running the mill around the clock, now that things are picking up," Abel said approvingly.

Some hills rose steeply away from the bay to the east, and roads had been cut into them, of which the sharpest grade was the one above the mill—the Skid Road, Abel explained, down which the logs were "skidded" right to the mill. The same mill that birthed the town and kept it alive during the hard years that followed, would supply the materials for its second chance at greatness now that the war was over.

But today Seattle didn't look like much of a city. The biggest buildings, of which there were only a few, had but two stories; the Masonic Hall and the Occidental Hotel, which Abel identified for her, were hardly as large as the smallest public edifice in Fall River. Most of the activity that could be observed from their vantage point was centered on the waterfront; two lumber schooners, a stern-wheeler, and a brigantine were tied up at the wharves, and a smaller steamboat was rounding the outer limit of the harbor, bound for Olympia.

There were hardly any trees in the settled part of the city, and here and there a horse or pig roamed the packed dirt streets between the fenced-in gardens surrounding some of the houses. A thin stand of firs on the eastern horizon stood like an advance guard for the dense forest behind it. And beyond that, a gigantic snowy mountain rose up like a cry in the throat, filling a huge space in the vast sky. Other peaks surrounded it, but seemed as nothing in comparison.

There was a great contrast in Seattle between what God had made and man had wrought, but in Abel Blanchard's eyes the town was Jerusalem. Maddy tried to imagine the thriving metropolis Abel envisioned—it was hard for her to picture, though the effort helped hold at bay the apprehension that threatened to overwhelm her. This man beside her was a stranger, and in two days he would be her husband. His hands would undress her and his eyes would look upon her naked body, and even though he had not yet addressed her with any words that were not formal and impersonal, she knew by the intentness of his gaze that some of the same thoughts must be troubling him.

There was no indication of that, however, in his dry census of the population of Seattle; there were 430 men, over half of them unmarried, 143 women, including 9 spinsters, and 38 children. He pronounced those numbers as though they were sacred, and later, when she watched the pleasure it gave him to enter the name of each newcomer to the city in his ledger, she saw that she had not been far from wrong—the growth of Seattle's population was a holy thing to Abel, and each new citizen was a convert to the true faith.

Was she, she wondered, part of God's plan for Seattle too? Was this marriage a divine scheme or a human folly? Could it possibly come to anything, this setting out together on such an uncertain journey, strangers to one another, without reflection, really, or even some understanding of who each was, or thought, or wished for?

Abel dismissed the spinsters as if they didn't count, like the Indians, whose numbers he did not enumerate either. Maddy wanted to know more about those females—was their independence their affliction, as Abel seemed to think? Maddy wasn't certain; perhaps they were to be praised, not pitied. Perhaps they were prudent, not rash like her, setting out on a course even more perilous than theirs. For what was marriage but a gamble, full of trials and tribulations, embarked upon with expectations that were sure to be crushed when the true natures of both parties emerged—as they surely would once the strangeness of the situation wore off? Even in the romantic novels to which she was addicted, marriage required something more than practicality to survive that disappointment—if not passion, then at least a pleasure in the other's company, a common bond of affection and affinity or, most hoped-for of all, love.

Indeed, when Abel mentioned the spinsters Maddy almost backed out of the bargain then and there. Not only had it come to seem unholy, a commercial transaction not unlike the ones women like Sonnet made with men—even though sanctified by the church—it might even be unnecessary. Or so she thought as she and Abel toured the city. There might be possibilities of employment—if not in the schools then in one of the commercial establishments they passed, like the dry-goods store, where she could be a clerk, or the hotel, where there might be need of a chambermaid. They went into the newspaper office and Abel introduced her to Mr. Briggs, the editor. On learning that she had been aboard the *Continental,* he said he would be interested in her description of the voyage, as would the paper's readers, and a ray of hope leaped in her. Perhaps, if she wrote an article, he might pay her for it, and that might lead to other work.

But then she realized what a groundless fantasy that was. No one would pay her to write—she was only a girl, not even graduated from secondary school, for when her mother fell on hard times Maddy's education was sacrificed—only temporarily, she said, but the Reverend Stone saw no reason for Maddy to continue it. And she was no journalist, either, a vocation that required more than a love of books. The journalist on the *Continental* had been bold and gregarious, always asking questions, taking everything in without missing a nuance or a detail. All Maddy could write were the kind of thoughts she scribbled in her journal—the feelings and ideas that filled her head, the fantasies and daydreams that kept loneliness at bay. And who would pay for that?

No, there would be no salvation there or anywhere else. For as they made their way through the town, it was clear that events would proceed as planned. People seemed to know of the forthcoming wedding; many of those to whom Abel introduced her said they would see her at the church! Sara Yesler said, "You must come to our next dance, they are jolly events," and Louisa Boren Denny, a sweet-faced woman who was Mary's sister in fact as well as her sister-in-law, said she hoped they would come to supper soon. Catherine Maynard invited them to a social the following week, and Carson Boren declared they were expected at his picnic on Independence Day, and through it all Abel beamed and accepted every invitation.

No, thought Maddy, she could not shame this proud, decent man before his friends and fellow pioneers. Clearly he was a personage of note in the town—that was evident from the respect with which he was greeted and which, as his betrothed, she also enjoyed. Even down around the shabbiest part of the

waterfront, the Skid Road—home of the notorious Lava Beds—
men tipped their hats to Abel Blanchard.

Abel hurried her through that raffish quarter of the town. It
was clear he did not approve of much that went on there, nor
of the slovenly, unshaven white men who loitered purposelessly
in the streets in the middle of the day. He remarked darkly on
the street's numerous drinking establishments, and disparag-
ingly on some heavily painted, immodestly dressed women who
staggered out of one saloon as they passed. "Sawdust girls," he
muttered, and when Maddy asked him to explain, he told her
that they lived in the cheap hovels thrown up on the landfill
created south of the Skid Road by sawdust from the mill.

A man came out of an oblong board house, long and rectangu-
lar like the school Maddy had attended in Fall River. He smelled
of whiskey, and his shirt was unbuttoned, and as they passed he
scratched himself and hailed Abel. "Hey, Blanchard," he said
rudely, "glad to see one of you boys has got hisself a white
woman at least. Ain't nothing but the Illahee for the rest of us!"
He laughed coarsely as Abel colored in embarrassment and hurried Maddy along the street.

"Who was that?" Maddy wanted to know.

"A fellow I had to fire from a job once," Abel replied. "He was
a shirker and a complainer. And a drinker, too," he added, as
they turned the corner onto Commercial Street and left the
tawdry area around the Skid Road behind.

"And what was that place? Was that where he lived?"

"No," said Abel. "That was the Illahee." His face darkened,
and he looked so stern and forbidding that Maddy did not question him further.

There seemed to be a great deal Abel Blanchard did not approve of, and she wondered how he would feel if he knew the
truth about her—about how clumsy and lazy she was, the way
her mother said, and absentminded, which all her teachers
called her, and stubborn too, according to Mrs. O'Hara. And
what if he knew about the Reverend's darker habits—what
would Abel Blanchard think then?

Of her own history she told him most of the truth, omitting
the difficulty of their circumstances after her father's death and
of course of the abuse she had suffered at her stepfather's hands.

She said that her mother had recently died, and that she had sought to put her unhappiness behind her and make a new life in a place that held no painful memories of happier times. Then she told him her true age, as if hoping that he might have cause to reconsider on those grounds either her character or her suitability, but it did not appear to concern him. In response to her confession he told her an anecdote about how Reverend Bagley had performed a marriage for a couple once when the girl was clearly underage. Doc Maynard had given her a slip of paper with the number 18 written on it and told her to put it in her shoe before the wedding. Thus he could truthfully assure the sceptical reverend that the bride was over eighteen.

"I figured you weren't that yet," he said, and Maddy wondered what else he had figured. Did he think she was what she seemed; submissive, tractable, respectful, and respectable? And was that what she wanted him to think? For now that she was here—and doubtless would stay, there being no realistic alternative she could think of—she knew that sooner or later Abel Blanchard would discover the truth about her. Which was that she was none of those things, not really. If she were, she thought wistfully, she would still be in Fall River.

There was another Maddy underneath the one he saw, one it took, as it always had, every speck of her will to extinguish. That was the girl who rebelled against authority, protested the invasion of her person with silent screams of outrage, questioned every truth that others told her. That was the Maddy who thought independently and was given to speaking her mind, usually without regard for what people wanted to hear. That was the Maddy who had impelled her on this madness, probably, and it was one she knew he would not admire. So she sought, in her fumbling way, to tell him—even warn him.

But he had made up his mind and hardly heard her words. By the time they turned in at the gate of the Denny home—which turned out to be their last opportunity before the wedding to be together without the company of others—Maddy knew it was too late. Abel Blanchard was determined to claim his bride. After all, he had claimed a wilderness already—who was she, only a girl, to stand in his way?

Chapter Five

Caleb couldn't get over it—his self-righteous, priggish brother was marrying a female Caleb had last seen in the protective companionship of one of the most notorious women of the day! Sonnet McBride had been the kept companion of heroes and generals, scoundrels and speculators, Ben Holladay being the most recent example. Holladay had told Caleb that Sonnet had brought along a girl on the *Continental* and implied that she, too, had shared his bed. And that girl, it appeared, was to be his brother's bride!

She certainly didn't look like any of the girls Caleb had seen on the Barbary Coast during his trip there with John Pennell. He was relieved that she had not recognized him—of course, there had only been that one glimpse through the window of the carriage. It would not do for his future sister-in-law to know of his association with Seattle's whoremaster, for that was what Pennell was. If this Maddy Douglas were to tell Abel she had seen them together, it would be as awkward as—well, as Caleb telling him that his bride-to-be was a whore's companion.

Perhaps Holladay had simply been boasting and the girl had turned to Sonnet McBride for simple companionship, Caleb reflected, as he played poker in Mother Damnable's saloon the night before the wedding.

"That's it—a full house," said Caleb, laying down his cards. "Bring us some more whiskey, Rosie; and Doc, you deal the next round." He patted the girl's behind and leaned back in his chair.

"Keep your hands off the girl, Blanchard, you got some of that to home, don't you?" grumbled David Maynard.

"You can afford to be all high-and-mighty, Doc, you being a married man and all," said Caleb easily. Maynard had gotten the Territorial Legislature to pass a special act allowing him to divorce his wife back in Ohio and marry the widow Broshears, but most of the men in Seattle were bachelors and many kept Indian women to see to their personal needs.

Despite Doc Maynard's remarks, Caleb's domestic arrangements with Celia Westwind did not trouble any of his friends greatly. Although Seattle had its share of moralists who thought miscegenation was a sin, the men at Mother Damnable's were not among them. Many of Seattle's bluenoses, in fact, treated the Indians most shamefully, making slaves and concubines of them. Maynard, who was a frequent guest at Caleb's home on the Bluff, was fond of Celia and thought Caleb ought to have married her, especially after he had delivered her of Caleb's child. "Half-breeds have a tough enough time of it," Doc said once when drink had loosened his tongue. "Give him a name, and you'll give him a chance." Caleb ignored him. When Doc was drunk, everyone did, though often his truest words were said when he was in his cups and feared no man's anger—or any woman's, either.

Seattle was still a village, and many people knew about the boy. But not all, for Celia and the child rarely left the bluff across the bay. It had been the site of the first settlement, but it had no deep harbor and was inadequately protected from the fierce southwesterly storms that raged across its exposed western flank. The townspeople deserted Alki, as they had named it, when they moved the city across Elliott Bay, but Caleb remained. He had come into his majority, then, and formally filed a claim, which led to his first argument with his brother Abel.

The earliest settlers had logged enough of the bluff to fill the order placed by the captain of the lumber brig *Leonesa,* which had come to Puget Sound for timber to replace the burnt-out piers of San Francisco, and Abel saw no reason why moving the town across the bay should interrupt the work they had begun.

"We can log the rest of this bluff before the *Leonesa* returns," he told Caleb.

"Not my bluff, you can't," said Caleb shortly, and despite Abel's pleadings, he refused to budge. "There's a whole forest over there," he said, pointing in the direction of the tall stands of fir, pine, and hemlock behind the new settlement across the bay. "You can log over there. The Bluff is sacred to the Indians. Their ancestors are buried here."

"Sacred, hogwash!" sputtered Abel. "How can something be sacred to them? They're not even Christian. Besides, it doesn't belong to them, it belongs to us. We cleared it. And you surveyed it and you put your stakes in it."

"Legally, it's mine," Caleb said. "But none of it really is. None of it is mine, or yours, or anyone's. It belongs to them, and I won't log it—not any more than I need to finish my house."

Furious, Abel strode out of the rude log building which was the settlement's communal dining room those first hard months in the wilderness. Caleb, he thought, was an innocent who knew nothing about how to build a city. He was a dreamer, a man whose ambitions could be thwarted by a pack of redskins. And when the other settlers left, Caleb stayed behind with the Indians, which never ceased to amaze his brother.

Alki was a narrow plain between water and forest, about a mile long, a hundred and fifty yards wide, rising above a thirty-foot clay bank. The soil was sandy, studded with small trees, and there was an encampment of Duwamish Indians at the mouth of the river that bisected it and flowed into the sound. It was thick with vegetation; salmonberries and blackberries, thimbleberries and huckleberries grew in profusion, and the land was blanketed with bracken fern, Oregon grape, honeysuckle, and sword fern. In the spring miner's lettuce grew thick between the vine maples, and in the autumn after the first rains boletus and chanterelles appeared as if by magic.

Caleb added dandelions, Scotch broom, and foxgloves and, like the Indians, killed wolves and elk for meat, hides, and skin. Deer fed from Caleb's hands, and in the summer bears lumbered into his gardens, despite his fences; cougars fed on his chickens and occasionally on his calves. Abel predicted that a man would go broke farming such inhospitable soil, but Caleb managed to make a good thing of it, taking over many of the enterprises the first settlers had begun and adding to them. Near Duwamish Head, where the land was richest, he planted gardens and cultivated orchards, and his crops, together with the clams and oysters of his beach and the fish netted by the Indians who worked his land, supplied him with a good income, so he did not need to log any more of his holdings than sufficed to allow for further planting. The land supported him comfortably and the rift between him and his brother was healed. But from that day, the two distinct visions that had brought them to the Northwest set them on different paths and were reflected ever after in the city they helped build.

Nor was that the only difference between them. In temperament one was phlegmatic, the other mercurial. Caleb loved a good joke; these days Abel rarely smiled—not that he was much given to laughter even when Sara was alive. Caleb often wondered what that gentle, laughing, spirited woman had seen in his dour brother, and Sara had never been able to explain it to him, not even in their closest moments.

Caleb had envied Abel Sara, but even though there were no marriageable women in the settlement, he did not contain his own sexual desires, despite Abel's urging that he do so. Before his marriage to Sara and after the tragedy that befell her, Abel was chaste; when the blood rose up in him, he picked up an ax and cleared more land or took down the Bible from the shelf above his bed and read until the soothing rhythms of its familiar phrases calmed him. Caleb, who believed that all that was "natural" was holy, indulged his appetites with a ferocity that made Abel fear for his brother's everlasting soul. "God put woman here for man to use, as he did the soil and the trees and everything else," Caleb said, "and only a fool goes thirsty when there's sweet water all around him." He knew that his liaison with Celia mortified Abel, who had even offered, the previous year, to pay Asa Mercer three hundred dollars to bring a suitable wife to Seattle for his brother. But Caleb refused. "You can buy a pig in a poke if you like," he told Abel, "some thin-blooded spinster from New England who'd never last one rainy season out here, but I'll wait, thank you."

Well, now Abel had done it, Caleb thought, and although this Douglas girl his brother was marrying looked hardier than most of Mercer's girls, she was no beauty. He hoped Abel would be satisfied with his bargain.

Caleb lived for the present, not the future. He took pleasure in what he could see and touch and smell and use. What he loved about Seattle was not what Abel thought it could be someday but what it was now—its presence, its essential landscape, palpable and to him beautiful. He took strength from the fecund, forgiving soil, awe and inspiration from the mountains that stood between him and God, and pleasure from the natural riches spread out around him like jewels dropped carelessly from celestial fingers. He believed the land had life and that progress killed it; some part of him mourned its transformation even as he conceded its necessity. What he saw as devastation, others saw as development. Still, he took his portion from the land, the donation due him, and used it to further his own ambitions; Caleb was a man who revered nature, and he had a mystical side, but he was no saint.

He was quick to gamble on anything that might be profitable, as long as it didn't threaten his precious Bluff, and the business he'd been conducting in San Francisco when he first laid eyes on Maddy Douglas was just such a gamble. Things were picking up in Seattle—The anticipation of the Northern Pacific railroad was enough to stimulate renewed interest in the town where the main source of capital in the decade since the Indian War had been lumber and, especially, Yesler's mill. To this now was added the wealth generated by a round of selling, buying, and swapping of real estate, fueled by speculation about the proposed route of the Northern Pacific and, especially, its terminus. Opportunities were finally multiplying for people like the Blanchards, and for the others who had come there first.

This very evening, Caleb was thinking about those opportunities. Maynard's words had provoked the usual round of complaints from the mostly unmarried cardplayers about the shortage of women in the settlement.

"Hear your brother's got hisself one of Mercer's women," said Charlie Terry. "How come you didn't just tuck a couple of them girls in your satchel and bring them back with you?"

Caleb grinned. "Charlie, you don't even own a clean white shirt. If you got one of Asa's girls, I doubt she'd have a thing to do with you." He picked up his cards. "You'll just have to make do with one of John's sawdust girls."

Terry grimaced. "By God, Pennell here may have cleaned up

his women and doused 'em with perfume, but they still smell like squaws, and that stinks to me."

John Pennell responded with a loud belch. He was the owner of the Illahee, a bawdy house that employed Indian women. The Illahee had thrived even during the depression that followed the Indian War; loggers came to it from every camp on Puget Sound. But Siwash squaws, Pennell knew, were not to the taste of every white man. In San Francisco, which was suffering a recession of its own, he could find white women willing to come north—if he could finance the lavish new building that he envisioned where they could ply their trade. It would have handsome appointments, luxurious furnishings, and beautiful women, all white, the equal of any house on the Barbary Coast. And it would be a moneymaker—every potential investor understood that, but none of them wanted to be associated with it. Certainly not Abel Blanchard, whom Pennell had first thought of approaching. He didn't know the man well, but he did know his brother, who shook his head when Pennell outlined his plan.

"Not Abel," Caleb had said. "Why, he won't even sell whiskey in his stores." Pennell himself was tolerated in Seattle, if not welcomed into what passed on that frontier for society. He was a necessary evil, and every man there knew it, even though the matrons of the town, like Mary Denny, lobbied their husbands for his removal—or, at the very least, the permanent closure of his oblong building at the foot of the Skid Road.

Pennell, of course, knew that. And he knew he was safe from people like Mary Denny because Seattle needed him. What he provided was more than simply a service, it was a civic obligation. And since he was never a man to pass up an opportunity to promote his devotion to the cause of Seattle's growth, Pennell proceeded to regale every man at the table with a vivid description of the benefits Seattle would reap from the new establishment he was planning to open within a few weeks' time.

In Caleb, John Pennell had found a willing partner for the expansion of his business. For that purpose, in fact, they had gone together to San Francisco, though no one knew or even guessed at the connection between them, a condition Caleb insisted on. His liaison with Celia Westwind was one thing, but if word got out about his connection with Pennell's enterprise, his reputation would be as badly compromised as Pennell's. The doors of Seattle society, such as they were, would be closed against him. Caleb was too gregarious to risk that. More important, he would be excluded from the profitable opportunities that lay behind those doors. Whether it was coal deposits over in the valley or shares in the bank his brother and Arthur had started, he would no longer be among the first to get in on a good thing.

No, it would not do for people to know he was backing Pennell's new whorehouse. No man in the saloon, however, had any notion of it, and as Caleb watched his partner rake in the coins of every player at the table, himself included, on what he was almost certain was no better a hand than his own, he felt confident that no one ever would.

As for Maddy Douglas, Caleb wasn't sure what the truth was. But he felt that some gesture of support or fraternity should be forthcoming on his part, so he offered to help in the nuptial celebration.

"Well, brother, we'll give your marriage the proper Seattle flavor," he told Abel. "I will host it; we'll have a potlatch."

Abel favored potlatches no more than any other relic or ritual of the natives he so disliked. However, he kept his feelings about the Indians close, bigotry being un-Christian—and besides, Caleb Blanchard's potlatches on the Bluff were Siwash only in the quantity of food and entertainment served up. He held them on all manner of occasions, great and small, not only holidays but special events, such as the arrival in the settlement of a distinguished visitor or the birth of his friend David Denny's twin sons. Caleb was proud of his prowess as a cook, and he was a genial and expansive host. People in Seattle liked to go to a potlatch at Caleb Blanchard's, and on an occasion such as his wedding, Abel thought, it might be suitable.

"Thank you," he said stiffly, and later he informed Maddy of the plans for the wedding reception. She nodded without comment. Events had so far overtaken her—her own choice in them seemed so limited—that she dared not say anything at all. They would be married as Abel planned, and they would be feted as his brother proposed, and they would live comfortably and happily together, as Mary Denny assured her. Ever after, she added.

But much as Maddy would have liked to focus on that distant future, she could not. First there was right now to be got through.

Her dress was tight and uncomfortable, and the church was hot and very crowded—everyone in the settlement, it seemed, had been invited to celebrate the wedding of Abel Blanchard, a true Seattle pioneer, to Maddy Douglas, late of Fall River, Massachusetts. The minister pronounced the covenant and Maddy was both glad and frightened when he said that Abel would henceforth be her best earthly friend. For her part, she promised to cultivate for her husband's sake all womanly endeavors and assist him in his life's work and in all things esteem his happiness as her own, but to her own ears the words sounded false.

Abel's voice rang clear and confident through the church. And later they made their way through the crowd of admiring well-wishers and down to the dock at the foot of Front Street, where Abel helped her into a gaily decorated cedar dugout sent by Caleb to transport the bridal couple to the Bluff. The canoe was manned by two half-naked Salish braves who ferried them with breathtaking speed across the water despite the strong and capricious currents of the bay. Behind them, a line of additional canoes followed with the wedding guests. The sun sparkled in the sky, where clouds billowed like a chenille spread on a blanket of blue. It was, as the Seattle newspaper reported, "the most glorious spring day there ever was."

Maddy sat in the canoe, relieved that the singing of the Indians made it impossible to carry on any sort of conversation with Abel, who was separated from her in the boat by boughs of cherry blossoms, their petals blowing in the breeze and leaving a pink trail across the bay. Occasionally she stole looks at Abel, wondering what he was thinking. His face revealed nothing. When the wind blew a fine spray of salt water across his brow he flinched slightly, but his expression did not change.

They arrived at the Bluff, and Caleb, who had remained there preparing the feast and had not come to the wedding in town, helped Maddy out of the canoe. He held her arm a second longer, a little closer, than convention or balance required, there on the rocky beach. He looked deeply into her eyes, so intimately and knowingly that she felt herself blush. And his own eyes held a hint of mockery she recognized but did not understand. He looked at her as if he knew a secret about her that nobody else did, and that made Maddy burn with shame, for the only truly personal secret she carried within her was of her stepfather's fumblings and the dark thrills they had begun in her. Thrills not unlike, she supposed, the ones that this Caleb Blanchard—yes, her own brother-in-law—might inspire in her if he were to touch her. If he were to put those long slender hands on her body. If he were to caress her skin with those soft, full, sensuous lips. If . . .

Enough! She must be dizzy from the sun, the sea, the strange events of the day. Surely she was fevered to be thinking like this, she decided, and from somewhere inside her she summoned the will to banish those forbidden images from her mind. And she did, all through the long hours of the potlatch —the feasting, the singing, the gifts, and the dancing. Caleb's culinary skills were as fine as promised, and he had done himself and his brother proud this day. There was salmon, baked on coals on the beach at the foot of the Bluff; long trestle tables were spread with clams, mussels, roast duck, and a sugar-cured ham. There were tiny new potatoes and peas that still tasted of the sun, and a dried fruit compote of apples and peaches, as well as rhubarb pie—the first of the season, Caleb told her. And crowning the groaning board was a fancy cake iced with cupids and clasped hands.

After the last torches were damped and the last straggling reveler had gone from the Bluff, Caleb led Maddy and Abel to the bedroom of his house overlooking the western promontory. "There's a fire laid, and Celia will see to your needs," he said pleasantly. "Maddy, welcome—to Seattle, and to the family."

Before she could thank him he was gone, and she was alone for the first time with her husband. She saw that her things were neatly laid out on the bed, whose counterpane had been turned down. Pitchers of sweetbriar scented the room—and Maddy thought of Rochester, proposing to Jane Eyre in the midsummer twilight of his garden, and that same bloom "yielding its evening sacrifice of incense."

"I'll wait outside for a bit," Abel said, closing the door behind him. Maddy undressed slowly. Her head still throbbed from the beat of the wedding drums, which had tattooed their rhythm into her skull during the potlatch. The events of the day passed in review through her mind as she slipped into the nightgown Sonnet had bought her in San Francisco. She heard herself repeating the words of the marriage service, and the minister pronouncing her and Abel man and wife. It chilled her skin, as she dropped to her knees next to the bed to pray. But while she reached for that elusive communion, a man's face stubbornly intruded. A face whose eyes seemed to ask, Who are you, really?

It was not the face of the man who waited outside that door, and Maddy felt her whole body give way as the image in her mind came clear. It was like the sudden onset of a fever, but it was not that. Maddy rocked on her heels, hugging herself tightly. In her imagining it was not the big-limbed, slow-moving, taciturn man she had married that brought on this loosening in the thighs, this burning in her breasts, this wild excitement she had never felt before. She got to her feet, her prayers unsaid. How could she now petition God to sanctify this union? How could she even ask His blessing? For she knew at that moment—knew as completely and lucidly as she had ever in her young life known anything, knew with every particle of her soul and body and her keen mind—that she had married the wrong Blanchard.

Chapter Six

That first summer after Maddy's marriage, Mary Denny was a godsend. She showed Maddy where to shop, how to bargain with the Indians for fish and feathers, when to gather herbs for poultices, and whom to see about delivering the baby due the following spring.

She cared for Elijah when Maddy grew too heavy and awkward to chase after him, and when rainy weather confined Maddy to the house, Mary brought her the books and newspapers she craved. She was a chatterbox, as talkative as Abel was silent, and Maddy listened intently to her chatter for some clue to the nature of the morose and phlegmatic man who was her husband. Occasionally Maddy glimpsed another side of him—a shy, sweet boyishness that was at odds with his usual solemnity. He was not ungenerous; when Maddy told him about the pine bed in the house on Water Street, he had found a carpenter to replicate it, down to the last detail, the garland of leaves and flowers carved into the headboard. On her birthday he had presented it to her, covered with a new feather quilt hand sewn by Mary Denny and festooned with wildflowers by Elijah, who had taken to Maddy immediately, as she had to him. And there was a practical joker in Abel too, who loved to grease one of Mary Denny's pigs so that when it got loose from her yard she had the devil of a time catching it.

The very day after their wedding Abel had returned to his usual routine, which involved a good bit of traveling around the sound, so it was Mary who provided the companionship that

Maddy lacked, and the practical help as well. When the baby came earlier than Maddy or the doctor had expected, and Abel was away, it was Mary who bathed Maddy's face and heard her screams and Lucas's first cry.

"We are lucky to have such good friends as the Dennys," said Abel at Lucas's christening, and though Maddy agreed, privately she thought that Mary's sheer goodness might, in time, drive her to drink. Abel had nothing but praise for Mary, and Maddy wrote in her journal:

> *I sometimes think they would have made a better pair than Abel and I. Of course, there is Arthur to consider, but he and Abel are cut from cloth so similar that Mary might not notice the difference if Abel took Arthur's place in her bed.*

That was unthinkable, of course—Abel would not covet his friend's wife, even if he was sometimes exasperated with his own. And besides, where would that leave her? Here she allowed her thoughts to wander a bit, and they fastened, as they often did lately, on Caleb. Her infatuation for him she had got over—indeed, when she thought of the strange passion that had gripped her on her wedding night, she tried not to associate it with her brother-in-law but with the very real fever and delirium that had struck her with its full force a day afterward and was due, no doubt, to the duress of her long journey and the oddly changeable weather typical of the region—when she awakened sick and headachey the morning following the wedding, the mercury had fallen twenty degrees and a wintry front had moved in that lasted for almost the rest of June.

When she recovered from the grippe, her feeling for Caleb was gone, replaced by wonder at the new circumstances in which she found herself. And soon thereafter she was pregnant, and then once Lucas was born she hardly had time to think of anything except caring for her family. Less than two years after Lucas's birth she was pregnant again, much to her dismay—she was still only a girl herself, one child was enough for now, but when she voiced those feelings to Mary and saw the disapproval on her usually pleasant face, and heard for the umpteenth time how Abel and Sara Blanchard had wanted a big family, she wished for a friend closer to her in spirit if not in years.

One morning in the last month of her second pregnancy, Maddy saw Elijah off to school in a driving rainstorm and then cleaned and tidied up the house, resisting the impulse to climb back into bed once she had settled Lucas into his cradle for his morning nap. It was not yet eleven, but the darkness of the sky made it seem more like evening, and when she had finished all the necessary chores and decided to put off the more onerous ones until later, she settled herself heavily into the overstuffed wing chair before the fireplace and read all the newspapers and magazines Mary had brought from Mr. Kellogg's store. Then Lucas woke up, hungry and wet, and by the time she had fed him lunch, bathed and changed him, and set him to playing in a corner of the room with the rag dolls she had stuffed for him and the wooden blocks Abel and Elijah had carved and painted for him, she was too tired to attack the pile of mending she kept meaning to get to, or even boil the diapers that stank in a tin pail outside the kitchen door. Instead, she drew the curtains closed in the front room, made a fire to ward off the chill, and lit the gas lamps; on days like these, when it seemed that the wet, gray afternoon would never end, she pretended it was already evening, even though the clock said otherwise, and by the time she finished reading *Lorna Doone*, which Caleb had brought her from San Francisco, it was in fact close to nightfall and time to prepare supper.

She rose heavily from her chair when she heard a familiar knock at the front door—pregnancy had swollen and distorted her body, and it was difficult to pretend she was that spirited young girl of Mr. Blackmore's novel whose adventures she followed so avidly.

Perhaps if I don't answer she'll go away, she thought crossly, but then, knowing how it would displease Abel if she was rude to his best friend's wife, she thought better of it and with as much grace as she could muster admitted Mary Denny into her home.

When Maddy had announced she was pregnant, Abel built them a new house in town, close to the Dennys, which at first pleased Maddy but now irritated her.

She resented Mary's constant presence—the houses were so close that she dropped in to visit almost every day. Often Mary

would find Maddy buried in a book, and by her immediate and
sweetly phrased offer to wash up the dishes or sweep out the
front room she managed to point out the deficiencies in Maddy's
housekeeping. She commented on the gusto with which Abel
always enjoyed her fruit cobblers, with a meaningful glance on
the apples going to rot under the tree outside the kitchen door;
she monitored Maddy's activities during her pregnancy with
such fidelity that, as Maddy complained to Abel, "She felt the
baby kick before I did."

Still, when Maddy learned she was pregnant again, it was
Mary who convinced Abel to get a squaw to help out around the
house. In fact, she told Maddy, that was the purpose of her call.
"I have found exactly the right person—Betty Westwind. You
know her—she's the sister of Caleb's—uh, housekeeper," she
announced. "Oh, I know Abel disapproves, but she's exactly
what you need, especially since Abel's off surveying in the
mountains so much now."

Mary seemed to know as much about Abel's movements as
Maddy herself did—more, even, for he and Arthur were engaged in a number of joint ventures, about which Mary seemed
to know a great deal but which Abel rarely talked about to
Maddy. It wasn't that he didn't want to, but Maddy wasn't
terribly interested—Abel went on and on about his precious
city till it bored her to tears. Some nights she could hardly stay
awake to listen. After a while Abel gave up, and after the children were asleep and Maddy had withdrawn into a book, he
would walk the few yards to the Denny house, where he found
an attentive ear, as well as hot coffee and the fruit cobbler he
favored.

Today, Maddy tried to feign interest in Abel and Arthur's
plans for constructing a pass through the Snoqualmie, which
Mary said was under serious consideration as a way to link up
with the transcontinental railroad at Walla Walla. But Mary was
not insensitive. She knew the subject was not one to engage
Maddy's attention, and she soon began to talk instead of Betty
Westwind.

"Of course, she'll have to bring her child with her when she
comes, but he'll be good company for Elijah," she said.

Maddy frowned. Abel did not like Elijah to play with Indian
children.

As if reading her mind, Mary said, "I know how Abel feels about that, but it's the way things are, and Betty will be such a help to you he'll just have to put up with it."

That was where Mary was wrong, thought Maddy. Abel Blanchard put up with very little that he didn't want to, and because she knew it, she tried to hide from him those things about herself he did not value. She was fond of him, and grateful to him, for her life since she married him had been a mostly pleasant one. That rebellious Maddy who simmered under her skin like a bone at the bottom of a soup pot she kept hold of, though not without some difficulty, and she curbed her habit of speaking her mind when she saw how cross and even sulky Abel became when she disagreed with him.

She kept to the bargain she had made with Abel in the White Church before Reverend Bagley and the people of the town, and it was not, most times, a hard one. Neither was it often sweet to her soul, though it comforted her in other ways, not the least of which was the security of knowing she would continue to be well taken care of, and enjoy considerable status as Abel's wife.

The more Maddy read of romantic love, the more she was certain it was folly, for didn't it always end badly for the woman? Madness was not only a novel's metaphor for what happened to women when they loved unwisely or too much, it was, from all Maddy had seen, a reality. She respected Abel, and he put up with her poor housekeeping, distracted airs, and occasional irritableness. He was at all times considerate in their marital relations, and if he awakened in her not passion but only tenderness, and if he minded, he never reproached her. As far as Maddy herself was concerned, if passion was that awful thrill she'd felt once or twice when she was young and then only on occasions she'd just as soon not remember—well, she'd rather not be troubled by it.

Seeing Maddy distracted, Mary Denny searched again for a subject closer to the younger woman's heart. "I hear that you're having some trouble raising subscriptions to your reading room," she said.

Maddy nodded. "Mrs. Maynard's offered us rooms in her house, and the doctor has made a substantial contribution, but they've had difficulties of their own lately, and I believe their new boarder has need of that space herself," she replied. For the wife Doc Maynard had left behind in the Midwest had lately come to town to claim the parcel of the land Maynard had registered before he persuaded the legislature to abrogate that marriage. The sight of the much-beloved pioneer walking up Commercial Street with a wife on either arm had amused his fellow citizens. Catherine Maynard had taken her predecessor into the home she shared with Doc until affairs could be straightened out, however, which brought Maddy's plans for the library she envisioned as her contribution to the town to a standstill.

"However," Mary went on, "I also hear that a substantial amount has been pledged by a newcomer to Seattle, a woman of some means but rather dubious reputation."

"Oh?" said Maddy. As she drew nearer to term, she cared less about the library—she had plenty of books of her own to read for now, and while she assumed that once the new baby came she would renew her efforts, she was content to wait.

"Yes. From what I understand, this woman—a Mrs. McBride, I believe—is the proprietor of John Pennell's bawdy house." This last she pronounced with distaste, but Maddy's heart leaped, and her face was more animated than Mary Denny, for one, had seen it for some months.

"Would that be Sonnet McBride?" she asked. It was a slim chance, for hadn't Sonnet returned to the East with her general? Perhaps—perhaps she had remained on the West Coast, and if that was true, it was not implausible that she might, in fact, be engaged in some enterprise with John Pennell, the very fellow Maddy had encountered with Sonnet that day in San Francisco.

"Why, yes, I do believe it is," replied Mary, at which Maddy's frown disappeared and in its place a radiant smile appeared. "You don't know her, do you?"

"Of course, I—" Maddy began, and then she stopped; for once, thankfully, her head caught up with the rest of her, or at least with her tongue, and she remembered what Asa Mercer had told her aboard the *Continental*—that claiming friendship or even acquaintance with a woman as notorious as Sonnet McBride might prejudice Seattle's leading citizens against her. Not that she cared particularly for their custom—but after all, she had Abel's reputation to consider.

"Well, I'm not certain," she amended, to Mary's questioning glance. "I once met a lady by that name"—for she was certain now, and while Sonnet might be no lady in Mary Denny's terms, to Maddy she remained one, and a great one at that—"during my voyage to the West, actually, but of course it could be someone else entirely." She got up from the kitchen table and cleared the tea things away, even though Mary had not finished the banana bread that she herself had brought. "I really should be getting supper now—Abel will be home soon," Maddy said pointedly.

Mary, who knew perfectly well that Abel would be away until quite late that evening, as he was off in the Snoqualmie with her own husband, nevertheless took the hint and prepared to leave.

"If there's anything I can do," she began, preparing as usual to be put off. But to her surprise, Maddy replied.

"As a matter of fact, I'd be most grateful if you could watch Lucas tomorrow—I've some errands to do in town, and he's grown so that it's quite a strain to carry him."

"Of course, dear—but wouldn't you prefer that I do them? It would be no trouble . . . and besides, you're in no condition to be gallivanting around. Why, you could go into labor at any time."

"No, really, I'm quite well, it'll be a few weeks yet," said Maddy. "Oh, Mary, you're a dear, I don't know what I'd do without you. . . . I'll bring Lucas by as soon as I've got his midday meal, then."

"Well, if you're certain—" began Mary, and, quite to her surprise, Maddy hugged her warmly.

"I'm certain," trilled Maddy, propelling Mary to the door and embracing her again.

"It's so important for a woman to have friends, isn't it?" said Mary, believing herself once more to be the one Maddy counted on, and cared about, and cherished, much as she and her own dear sister Louisa loved one another. Of course, Louisa and David had moved out to the swale beyond Lake Union, and she and Louisa didn't see each other as much as they once had . . . but she had Maddy now.

"Oh, yes!" said Maddy, and as she closed the door behind

Mary she felt a lightness in her heart that even the glum, gray, rainy skies outside could not dampen. If it was truly Sonnet McBride that Mary spoke of—Mrs. McBride of the dubious reputation, even Sonnet McBride the madam of John Pennell's establishment—then somewhere the sun must truly be shining.

* * *

Caleb Blanchard's initial business venture with John Pennell was so successful that he didn't hesitate when Pennell came to him with a plan for expanding the enterprise. The even more extravagant establishment he proposed would be a showplace, offering everything a man might want for pleasure and relaxation. Called the White House, it was designed to attract the carriage trade, not only from Seattle but from around the entire Puget Sound. Caleb's investment in the luxurious, many-gabled mansion Pennell erected on Third and Washington streets proved to be as profitable as his first one had been. Everything a man required for delectation of body and spirit was available to him there: the prettiest women, the liveliest entertainment, the gayest music, the finest wines and spirits. High rollers en route to Alaska or San Francisco often stopped for a night or for a week, and many of Seattle's rich men made it their home away from home as well.

Much of this was due to the canny management of Sonnet McBride, who had turned John Pennell down flat the first time he proposed a partnership. But when he ran into her in San Francisco two years after Ben Holladay stranded her there, she was ready for a change. The years in California were not easy ones. Time had had its way with her looks, but it had not dimmed her shrewd intelligence, and she came to an arrangement with John which vastly improved her financial condition, though not quite in the way she expected. She arrived in Seattle, installed herself in the White House, and personally recruited every one of the girls who labored there. She was the only person in Seattle who knew who John Pennell's silent partner was—and why he was silent. She had glimpsed Maddy Blanchard a few times since her arrival in Seattle. At a Library Association lecture on "Republican Liberty and Government" she sat quite close to her, and at various entertainments and civic functions they had passed within inches of one another, but Maddy did not expect to find her old friend from shipboard days there, and so she did not notice her, though she might not have recognized her—Sonnet had grown rather stout and had toned down her dress and makeup so that she looked like any other well-turned-out elder matron of the town, not like her old flamboyant self at all. Sonnet would dearly have loved to fold the girl in her capacious embrace again, but she refrained from renewing their friendship. The girl had married Caleb Blanchard's brother, and she understood from her own shrewd observations that the last thing Maddy needed was for Sonnet McBride to turn up and claim friendship with her.

But when the little Indian lad turned up at the back door of the White House with a note inviting her to tea that very afternoon, she put her own fond memories of Maddy above her concern for the girl's reputation, penned an equally formal note of acceptance with alacrity, and made herself look as decorous and ladylike as she could manage before setting out some hours later for the house on James Street.

Maddy, knowing that truth was stranger than fiction, was so certain the Mrs. McBride Mary Denny spoke of was her old friend Sonnet that she had not hesitated to contact her, though for a while the exact means of doing so stymied her. It would not do for her to approach Sonnet on her own territory; though she personally would not judge her old friend for her occupation, others would, and if Abel knew his wife had gone to the White House—which he would soon discover from some loosetongued old fogy—he would disapprove and might even forbid her to see Sonnet. Not that he ever forbade her anything outright, of course—that was not Abel's way.

Still, there was no sense making him angry, and going to a bawdy house would certainly do that. So when Tommy Westwind turned up that afternoon after school with Elijah, she gave him a coin and directions to take her letter to the big white house on the Skid Road. Nothing would keep her from seeing her old friend again, and surely even Abel could not complain if she had to tea the woman who had donated such a plentiful sum of money to the new library. At least, not until he knew exactly who that generous benefactress was.

Chapter Seven

From the kitchen, where she was washing up the supper things and listening to Elijah drill Lucas on his multiplication tables, Maddy could hear Abel and Caleb arguing in the parlor.

It was the Bluff they were fighting about, of course—it was always the Bluff. "If you want the damned railroad so much, you give Cooke your property, but you're not getting one acre of mine!" she heard Caleb say, and moments later the front door slammed so hard the glass rattled in its leaded panes.

Abel, fuming and red-faced, stomped into the kitchen. "He won't listen to reason," her husband told her, "not where his precious land is concerned." He accepted the mug of steaming tea Maddy handed him and barely noticed his sons disappear from the room—they knew that when Uncle Caleb got their father's dander up they'd best get out of sight until he cooled down.

"A few acres of undeveloped land, that's all the railroad wants," complained Abel, "and Caleb refuses."

"Caleb says that's only the beginning . . ." began Maddy, but her husband's face darkened, and she let her words trail off.

"Caleb can't see beyond his own selfish desires, but I'd think my wife, at least, would try to understand how important the railroad is to Seattle's future," Abel replied.

Maddy continued washing up while Abel ranted on. It wasn't just a few acres; the price Jay Cooke was exacting in return for locating the Northern Pacific terminus in Seattle was closer to three thousand acres, plus 7,500 town lots, half the waterfront, and a quarter of a million dollars in cash and bonds. Many people thought that was too much, among them Caleb Blanchard, who would not, for any amount of money, consider allowing the road to encroach on his sacred Bluff or the land nearby. He had bought up the land, bit by bit, until he owned not only the Bluff, and its western flank, but that part of its eastern border that curved around the bay like a sheltering arm and almost touched the town's southern limits.

Maddy couldn't understand Caleb's intransigence. After all, it was just land, and there was plenty of that to go around, more than enough for the two thousand or so inhabitants of Seattle and those who were still coming—not fast enough to suit Abel, perhaps, but steadily, and in sufficient numbers to attract industry and even some semblance of culture.

What such growth meant to Maddy was that she no longer had to wait months for the newest books and magazines to arrive from San Francisco; now she could get them almost immediately from the stationer's in town. The previous day, she had purchased *Captain Gray's Company*, the novel by Abigail Scott Duniway, the leading female literary figure in the Northwest, who was speaking that very night right here in Seattle, at the Methodist Brown Church, and Maddy was looking forward to the entertainment.

She was also looking forward to seeing Sonnet, and while there would be no opportunity for a private conversation, they could look at each other across the aisle and exchange their own raised eyebrows or amused smiles, which would have to do until Abel went out of town again and they could manage a meeting.

Maddy was not a deceiving woman, but there was simply no other way to continue her friendship with Sonnet McBride, who was a pariah in the town. Why, Abel had even made her return Sonnet's contribution to the library fund, which had occasioned a huge row between them that was not healed until Sonnet herself urged Maddy to give it up. "You can't blame a man for acting on his beliefs, even if they're wrong," said Sonnet, "and you can't go against them, not if he's Abel Blanchard and you're his wife. At least, not in Seattle."

So she returned Sonnet's money and agreed that she would not embarrass Abel by visiting with the town's notorious madam. And no one ever saw the two women together or even knew that they were friends—at least, no one except Caleb and Celia Westwind and the other inhabitants on Caleb's Bluff, which was where Maddy and Sonnet met, on those occasions when Abel was away and Maddy did not have to account for her movements.

Maddy didn't like Caleb's knowing she was deceiving Abel, and it pained her to be beholden to him for helping her do so, as if at some time he would exact a price she could not afford to pay. Yet Caleb made Maddy smile more often than Abel did, and he made her feel witty and pretty, and, most disturbing of all, he seemed to see right into her own true, rebellious nature —perhaps because he was something of a rebel himself. That he knew the part of her she struggled to deny made her cool to him, but he charmed her anyway, despite her best intentions; he had beautiful manners, a natural elegance, and handsome features and was in many ways compelling. As she wrote in her journal:

> If one were to take pen to paper and dare to compose a novel, and if it required a dashing and romantic hero, as a novel always does, one could with only some slight alteration do worse than to model such a protagonist after C.

In her private writing Maddy admitted feelings and ideas she would not in any other way accept or countenance—as if by limning them she understood and satisfied them. Once she put them down on paper, she felt them slip away from her, leaving no other evidence that they had existed, even in her mind.

It was Sonnet who suggested the Bluff as a place where she and Maddy might meet in private. According to Sonnet, she and Caleb had met through John Pennell, who owned the White House. Caleb, Maddy supposed, was a regular customer there, though why a man like her brother-in-law would descend to such a level escaped her comprehension. After all, he had Celia. But it was not up to her to judge him—especially not when she was indebted to him for making his home available to her and Sonnet so they could see each other away from the disapproval of her husband or the prying glances of people like Mary Denny. It troubled her to conspire against Abel with his brother, but so strong was her affection for Sonnet and her need for her friend's good humor, common sense, and refreshing frankness that Maddy put the wariness she felt in Caleb's presence down to his ready willingness to help her put one over on Abel.

* * *

Abel looked up now as she took off her apron, smoothed her hair, and took down her hat and coat from the peg on the wall.

"You're not going out alone, are you?" he asked.

"Don't be worried, dear, Mary is accompanying me. I may be late, so don't bother waiting up," she told him.

"It's all foolishness, you know, this suffrage business," he grumbled.

"Yes, perhaps it is, but to meet a great writer one must be prepared to put up with some distractions, even Mrs. Anthony, who is accompanying her on this engagement. Though I do hope she doesn't run on too long about women's rights, or Mrs. Duniway may not have time for a literary discussion."

That was what she told Mary Denny, too, and suffered in exchange a long tirade on the plight of women that bored her near to tears. Mary could be so tiresome sometimes, Maddy complained to Sonnet at their next meeting, but for once Sonnet disagreed with her. "It's easy for you to say the vote isn't worth anything," she told Maddy. "You're quite comfortable with a husband who doesn't make you grovel for your keep or force you to endure the humiliations many women must. But there are those less fortunate. I don't see how you can admire Mrs. Duniway's writing so and ignore what she is saying."

"Oh, Sonnet, I don't exactly ignore it, I just skip over the boring parts," Maddy said.

Sonnet shook her head. "An idea like suffrage is not boring," she replied.

"Or romantic either," said Maddy, and there ensued a lively discussion that occupied them until it was near dark, and long past time for them to separate. They parted reluctantly, with hugs and kisses and promises to meet again as soon as they could manage.

* * *

As things turned out, the Northern Pacific eschewed Seattle's compliance with its demands and located the railroad terminus in Tacoma. Seattle responded by setting out to build its own road east over Snoqualmie Pass to Walla Walla to link there with the NP. But a year later the speculation in railroads collapsed, and Jay Cooke went broke. The track laid by the citizens of Seattle did not go unused; it was extended to Renton, Newcastle, and the Cedar River valley and used to transport coal from the mines, which further cut down Seattle's dependence on San Francisco and contributed to its growth. And women did get the vote in the Territory, at least long enough to elect a slate of reformers who closed down the town's saloons and in other ways made things uncomfortable for entrepreneurs like John Pennell. Almost as soon as suffrage was given to women it was taken away again, which Maddy did not think was such a great loss. She and Sonnet continued to argue about it, though, as they did about so many things. With Sonnet, Maddy could speak her mind without fear of reprisal, and it was for that, as much as for her warmth and succor, that Maddy loved her.

It was Sonnet who first discovered that John Pennell had not only disappeared but had also embezzled the entire contents of the safe in which the clients of the White House were accustomed to leaving their valuables. And it was Sonnet who brought the bad news to Caleb Blanchard.

It was when a miner asked for his gold that Sonnet went to the safe in the back room and discovered the theft. Quickly she dispatched a servant to find Caleb. When he realized the dimensions of the crime, he knew he had no choice but to pay back every "depositor" whose belongings had been appropriated by John Pennell—it was either that or risk the disgrace of public disclosure of his ownership in the brothel. He was not John Pennell's brother or his keeper, but he was his partner, and it was on his shoulders that the burden of making good Pennell's treachery descended.

This burden severely taxed Caleb's resources. As quickly as Caleb made money, he lost it, and every time he lost it he sold more land. When times were good he speculated, and consequently he accumulated holdings in various parts of the area. He had some land in Renton, where valuable coal deposits were discovered, but he lost that in '73, when the collapse of the railroad boom started a depression that spread to the farthest reaches of the nation.

By the time of Pennell's embezzlement, all Caleb had left was the Bluff and the land surrounding it. The Alki Land and Development Company, of which Abel was president, had made him several attractive propositions for his holdings. By 1880 the ferry had brought regular service to Alki, the company had already developed some of the property nearby. Despite his attempts to fend off what Abel called progress and Caleb said was devastation, the firm had put up a yacht club and a boathouse and plotted view lots along the choicest acreage of the Bluff, although they had yet to wrest them from Caleb's control. Abel had shown the plans to Maddy; there would be vacation cottages where Caleb's orchards grew, and in place of the dense stands of fir and alder there would be streets and businesses and shops and even a school—if Caleb agreed to sell.

"I suppose you'd turn it over to that half-breed son of yours instead of your own family?" asked Abel.

"I'm not turning it over to anyone," Caleb said, and that was the end of it, until John Pennell disappeared, and Abel discovered Caleb's part in the brothel. Abel was chagrined, but he had to admit that his brother had done the honest thing in paying the claims of the men who'd been robbed by Pennell. If they'd put their valuables in his bank, no such thing would have happened, and he told Caleb as much, but his brother just laughed. "They never would've gone into your marble temple to begin with, Abel," he said.

He wasn't certain which bothered Abel more—the fact that a Blanchard was a partner in a place that trafficked in what Abel thought was sin (and Caleb believed was only human nature) or that by doing a favor for his "customers" Caleb had robbed Abel of banking business that was rightfully his. And when Caleb refused to allow Abel to proceed with the company's plans for developing the whole of West Seattle—thus diminishing not only his personal profit but his dream for the ever-increasing expansion of Seattle—relations between the brothers cooled considerably. When Abel took the first chunk of Caleb's Alki holdings from him to settle his losses from the White House, people said he ruined him. But what really ruined Caleb was whores, Indians, and a Chinaman named Ah Chin Chee.

Feelings had been running high against Orientals ever since the depression that followed the end of the railroad construction boom. There were lynchings and other acts of vigilantism, and a coalition of Populists and organized labor urged immediate deportation of the Chinese—not just the coolie labor gangs but the domestic workers as well. Everyone agreed the Chinese had to go, but disagreements were heated about the way to get them to leave. Abel was all for doing it peaceably and legally—it would not do, he said, for Seattle to get a reputation for being unable to maintain law and order, not if it wanted to continue to attract capital and "the right kind of people."

Caleb, while tolerant about Indians, held no such brief for the Chinese—he could not sell the produce from his farm because John, as every Chinaman was called, sold his for less. It was the People's Party versus the Business Man's Party, and while Caleb had nothing good to say about the strong reform element of the People's Party, which would have closed down the White House, he championed their militance on the Chinese question.

Caleb had another reason for wanting to get the Chinese out of town—the huge sum of money he owed to Ah Chin Chee, who ran the gambling in the Lava Beds. Caleb's Indian friends had introduced him to gambling years before, and he was a regular at Chee's establishment. Seattle had always been a gambler's town and Chee a gambler's friend, until the day a handful of white men invaded Chinatown and forced the residents who had not left when the Restriction Act was passed to pack their things and board the steamer *Queen of the Pacific*, which was waiting to deport them.

Ah Chin Chee, with the others, boarded the steamer. But when it sailed with the Chinese who had had enough of Seattle, he was not among them. Under the protection of Sheriff McGraw, the Home Guard, and deputized volunteers from the Law and Order Party, Abel Blanchard among them, he was marched back to Chinatown to await the arrival of the *Elder*, which would deport the remaining Chinese a few days later.

Ah Chin Chee was not planning to be on the *Elder* either. Just because the residents of the city had finished with John didn't mean he was finished with them. He returned to his establishments in the city and set about calling on his debtors. Among the largest of these was Caleb Blanchard.

* * *

Maddy answered the front door to Caleb's knock. He looked worried and angry, and when she led him into the parlor where Abel sat reading his Bible, he did not even have his usual joke and smile for her. She retired to her bedroom to lose herself in small household tasks and, when they were done, her journal. Finally, though, she could no longer ignore the raised voices of her husband and his brother.

"You won't help me, then?" That was Caleb—he was shouting, so Maddy could hear his words clearly.

Abel must have answered negatively, for the next thing she heard was the angry slam of the parlor door.

She went downstairs, mindful of her duties as hostess, and fetched Caleb's hat and coat. The anger that coarsened his features was frightening to see, and he must have realized it, for when he caught sight of the expression on Maddy's face he relaxed his own somewhat and attempted a smile.

"I'm afraid I've disturbed you, Maddy," he said. "Forgive me."

She saw the effort it cost him to rein in his emotions, and gently she touched his arm.

"It can't be that terrible," she said, "to turn you and Abel against each other for long." For always before the brothers had made up their quarrels; they might have strong differences, but they stood together against outsiders, and each felt an equal concern for the Blanchard name and reputation. It was this concern that caused Abel to overlook the moral outrage he felt upon discovering his brother was in partnership with the notorious John Pennell. And it was this concern that brought Caleb to his brother's house to borrow money to pay his gambling debts.

"You've already mortgaged your other holdings," said Abel. "I can't advance you any more on them—the bank wouldn't permit it."

"So the Chinaman gets a Deficiency Judgment and takes the

whole thing, right?" Under the laws of the day, creditors could force the sale of all a debtor's property, even if it was worth much more than the debt, and keep the surplus.

"There's your land," said Abel. "What's left of it."

What was left was the entirety of Caleb's original claim, minus some land he had swapped Doc Maynard for the property on which the White House was now located. Business had fallen off there drastically since the suffragettes had succeeded in their campaign to clean up the Lava Beds, and Ah Chin Chee was not interested in taking the property off Caleb's hands to satisfy his gambling debt. Nor was Abel much interested in it—he had no truck with the sinful goings-on in that area, even if he had not joined the reformers in their campaign to clean up the dens of iniquity. Once, some years before, the city had closed the only brothel in town, and business had fallen off so drastically in the rest of the town that the city fathers had not only allowed the brothel to reopen but even, for a time, encouraged it.

The only thing of value that Caleb owned was his land, and Abel, on behalf of the Alki Land and Development Company, was prepared to pay him well for it.

Caleb had no choice. Either he sold another part of it to his brother or lost it all to a Deficiency Judgment. And that night, as he left his brother's house, he was resigned to the fact that a full third of his precious Bluff would soon fall under the ax of the developers. Not the part where the Indian burial grounds were, and not the view sites along the Bluff, and not his orchards or horse trails. He would still retain the heart of the site. But for what he was being forced to give up—and by now he seemed to be giving it up not to the Chinaman but to his brother—he vowed to extract revenge.

The breach between Abel and Caleb healed on the surface. Neither would admit publicly that their relationship was strained. But people knew how Caleb felt about the Bluff, and when Abel's company made its first incursions onto the property, they knew that Abel Blanchard had had to catch his brother between a rock and a hard place to get it. When the brothers chanced to be together at the same event, they were polite, and Abel never understood how deeply he had wounded Caleb. As he told Maddy, "Caleb did the only thing he could, selling the land to me. He was lucky we wanted it." That Abel paid Caleb exactly what the land was worth despite his poor bargaining position was a generosity that Caleb did not see fit to acknowledge. Abel spared hardly a thought for the grievous loss Caleb felt he had suffered. "He's just like those damned Indians of his," he fumed to Maddy. "He believes it's a crime against nature to cut down a tree, just because God grew it. Or maybe he prays to the Great Spirit these days—we certainly haven't seen him in church."

Nor was Caleb able to see his brother's point of view. From his perspective, what Abel did in the name of growth, especially on his land, was worse than a crime against nature—it was a dagger aimed directly at his own heart.

And when he saw what Abel's efforts did—when he felt in his own blood the agony of the land, saw the gaping raw holes in the earth, the angry slash of road through the swale where the wild strawberries had bloomed—he felt as if the dagger had just plunged into him and he was bleeding to death. In his own fevered imagination, it was his brother who held the knife. And as he left Abel's house, he contemplated, not for the first time, what means of reprisal, in a civilized society where fratricide was outlawed, might still be available to him.

Chapter Eight

The *City of Seattle* ferry knifed through the bay this hot, still June morning like a shingle weaver slicing cedar, the rhythmic slap of hull against curl lulling Maddy nearly to sleep until the whistle signaled the ferry's imminent arrival at the dock in West Seattle.

She considered hiring one of the horse-drawn cabs that waited at the pier, but dismissed the idea in favor of the fresh air and began the long walk to the Bluff. Once out of sight of the landing she took off the wide-brimmed hat that had concealed her face from the other passengers on the ferry and removed the net that confined her hair in its usual severe bun. This far from the mainland there was little chance that anyone would recognize her. And as the day grew warmer, she doffed her shawl, rolled up the sleeves of her starched pink shirtwaist, and hiked up her petticoat so that her lisle stockings peeked out above her French calf boots. Not a passerby who had glimpsed Mrs. Abel Blanchard at one of the innumerable civic functions she and her husband attended—or even been a guest at one of her own annual Library Association luncheons—would have known the slightly disheveled, surprisingly youthful-looking woman with the chestnut curls cascading over her shoulders to be that same prim and proper matron.

Maddy's friendship with Sonnet McBride was one of the few secrets she kept from Abel. These days the reformers were up in arms once again about the sinful conditions in the Lava Beds, and the name of the doughty madam of the White House was

known even to those who had never seen at first hand the brothels, opium dens, and box houses that made Skid Road a mecca
for those Mary Denny was fond of describing as the "elements."
No, Abel would not understand, Maddy thought, as she ambled
lazily through the town of Milton, which by now all but encir-
cled Caleb's land. She and Sonnet managed an occasional meeting in the city, a seemingly chance encounter at the milliner
they both frequented or a clandestine picnic in one of the public
parks that people like the Dennys and the Borens generally
avoided now that the streetcars made them accessible to all
manner of people. These too infrequent and necessarily brief
visits were supplemented by their private correspondence.
Maddy sometimes copied out pages from her journal, especially
regarding books she had enjoyed or interesting visitors she and
Abel had entertained. She gave them first to Tommy Westwind
and later to his son, Ethan, who took them to the back door of
the White House and received in exchange a generous tip and
Sonnet's own letters to Maddy, thick missives written on thin
onionskin sheets. These were lucid, clever, and amusing—like
the one that described Sonnet's abbreviated tenure on the jury
for the case of a man who had shot an intruder found in his home
one evening. When the intruder was revealed to be the longtime
paramour of the householder's wife, Sonnet wrote, *The Territorial Legislature passed a law that released the female members of the
species from the corrupting possibilities of jury duty, while at the same
time apologizing to us for the salacious details we had been forced to
appraise.*

Sonnet tended to go on and on about women's rights, which
Maddy found tedious, but it was a delight to receive her letters.
But it was still at the Bluff that Maddy and Sonnet spent their
happiest hours, away from the prying eyes of outsiders and the
need to conceal the pleasure and comfort they continued to
draw from each other.

When Maddy topped the last rise, she was stunned by the
panorama spread out before her. Another huge chunk of Caleb's
land had been clear-cut—ax and crosscut saw had toppled the
fir, cedar, and hemlock, and the deep ruts in the earth where
horse teams dragged the logs out along a skid road were dry,
dessicated gullies. The waste was tremendous—treetops, bases,

shattered trunks and branches were scattered over the once densely forested acreage. Stumps nine feet in diameter dominated the landscape of brush and debris. Not a bird nested in the dead snags that reached heavenward, as if in supplication, twisted and uprooted, stripped of their limbs. Hummocks and hollows had replaced green tree-studded meadows. And in their place stood a cluster of squat, ugly houses, each with its own tiny patch of earth and one lone, scraggly tree dividing it from its neighbor.

Maddy did not have Caleb's feeling for the land, but even she saw the desecration that had been wrought, and her heart ached for her brother-in-law, whose original holdings had contracted as his financial situation continued to worsen. It was still Blanchard land, but the greater part of it was now his brother's, whose Alki Land and Development Company signs were posted in front of the houses.

Relations between the brothers had now grown so cold that everyone knew there was bad blood between them. Caleb was barely polite on those occasions, familial and civic, when he was forced to be in Abel's presence. At John Blanchard's funeral some months earlier they had nearly come to blows in a dispute over land again—this time over the rich farmland in the rolling Nisqually River country. Caleb had been in monetary straits as usual, and Abel had offered to buy his share of their father's estate from him; Caleb had refused, but the bank of which Abel was president had called in his loans, and that land, too, had gone to his brother. Only weeks later, another of Caleb's schemes had collapsed, and still more of his acreage—this time on his beloved Bluff—had been forfeited to Abel. Caleb had moved into rooms in town to escape the dreadful sounds of the developers and spent less and less time on Alki. But he would probably be there today; he enjoyed Sonnet McBride's company as much as Maddy did, and while he did not intrude on the women, he often prepared a light repast for their trysts and sometimes shared it with them before excusing himself so they could talk privately.

Maddy enjoyed his lively conversation; he was a superb raconteur and a delightful gossip, with a way of puncturing the pretensions of the establishment—Maddy's usual social matrix—

that never failed to amuse her. She could say whatever she pleased to Caleb, and she did; and occasionally she caught him staring at her in a deliberate, cool, knowing fashion that made her skin tingle beneath her garments.

Probably he would not be very lighthearted company today, she mused, picking her way through the loggers' debris. But once she crossed onto what was left of Caleb's land—posted against trespassers, she noted, for all the good that had done thus far—and made her way through the apple orchards, and traversed the freshly mown grass sweetening the salt-tinged air, it was easy to forget the ugly wasteland beyond the fences. Here the Bluff was as it had always been, and there, just ahead, was Caleb's farmhouse. Obeying an impulse blown in on the summery breeze, she stripped off her boots and stockings and ran, barefoot and careless, to her rendezvous with Sonnet McBride.

* * *

The house was strangely empty—deserted, bearing an air of desuetude that defied explanation, as if its inhabitants had been called away suddenly and left without securing it against intruders. She was not one, of course—she had been invited to treat Caleb's house as if it were her own and did so habitually. She walked through the empty rooms, wondering where Celia was, or any others of Kinnikinnick Jim's descendants, who still lived on the Bluff and worked for Caleb at a variety of jobs.

There were dirty dishes in the kitchen sink—unusual, as Celia was a careful housekeeper—and the odor of whiskey permeated the parlor where no table had been laid, as was Caleb's custom, for his expected guests. Sonnet was nowhere in sight, either, which Maddy found even more surprising—usually she preceded Maddy to the Bluff.

She found Caleb, finally, in the horse barn—around him was the same reek of liquor, and he was haggard and unshaven. His linen was soiled, and his eyes bloodshot, and though he raised his head in acknowledgment of her greeting, he did not speak to her, just went on wiping down his big mare, Jenny, whose huge chest heaved with exertion and whose flanks were soaked with sweat, as if she had recently been ridden to near exhaustion.

"Where is everyone?" Maddy asked, mystified. "Where's Celia and Jim?"

"Gone," he said. "All gone, to the happy hunting grounds."

"What are you talking about?" He was drunk, she knew—he lurched alarmingly so that she had to grab him to keep him from falling. She was uncomfortably aware of his closeness. This was not the Caleb she knew—she had seen him tipsy before, but never like this.

"Jim took the fever two weeks ago, and Celia cared for him," Caleb told her, slurring his words so she could barely understand him. "He died three days ago."

"Oh, Caleb, I'm so sorry," she said sincerely, for she knew the story of how the old Indian had saved Caleb's life so many years before when, cold and alone, separated from the companions who had come north with him, he had caught the fever himself and would have died but for Jim's help.

"Buried him yesterday, up on the mound," Caleb continued. His face darkened. "They won't disturb his spirit—not my brother, not any of them. I promised him: his bones won't ever be touched."

"And Celia?" Maddy asked softly. "Where is she?"

"Burnt up," Caleb said shortly. "Some of them pals of Abel's, those esteemed land sharks, set fire to Jim's cabin while we were burying him. I expect they thought it was empty, and firing it seemed easier than tearing it down. Celia was in there. She'd taken sick herself, from nursing Jim, and was too weak to go with us to the mound."

His words were matter-of-fact, but Maddy could feel the pain as well as the anger in him.

"Son of a bitch," he said distinctly, and Maddy knew he meant Abel, but she did not rise to defend him. Caleb had a right to his hate, she thought. She hardly heard the rest of what he said, a long drunken tirade against Abel and the Alki Land and Development Company. On his handsome face there was such a mixture of sadness and anger that she could almost feel the pain that consumed him—as much for his land as for the Indian woman who had lived with him, cared for him, and loved him for so many years—and had borne his only son. Maddy remembered the first time she'd seen them, Celia and Johnny, standing apart on the wharf the day she herself had arrived in Seattle. And she thought of the many kindnesses Caleb had shown her over the years, though always with that slightly mocking smile that said, I know you—you can't fool me.

Celia's death was doubtless a great blow. Caleb and Celia had been together almost since Caleb's arrival in Seattle. There had been other women in Caleb's life, dozens of liaisons. And there had been some more serious affairs as well—a woman from the Okanogan, a small slender blonde Caleb had squired about all one autumn, whom Maddy thought surely he would marry. But he had not; in the end, there had been only Celia. Caleb was not an old man—he was ten years Abel's junior and barely past his fiftieth birthday. It was not inconceivable that he might marry yet, and in a clumsy attempt to console him, she said as much aloud.

"As if she never existed, eh?" Caleb said sardonically, and she colored. "After all, she was just a redskin, a savage, not a real person at all, hm? That's certainly what Abel thinks . . . thought."

At his own use of the past tense in speaking of Celia, his voice broke, and Maddy's heart went out to him. So did her arms, as he stumbled again. She meant to comfort him, and as for what he meant, she never knew, then or ever, but as they tumbled together into the hay he had spread for the mare that panted above them, her last thought was not of him, or even of Abel, but of the handsome stranger who had stared at her through the window of John Pennell's coach on a street in San Francisco over twenty years before.

*　*　*

Sonnet never arrived that day, and much later, as Caleb's carriage conveyed her back to the dock, freshly combed and as presentable as she had been when she disembarked from the ferry that morning, she understood why. For across the bay, the entire city seemed wreathed in a thick haze of smoke, as if one of the volcanic mountains, Rainier perhaps, had awakened from its long sleep and thundered destruction over the settlements built in its western shadow.

The fire that leveled sixty acres and thirty city blocks of Seattle's downtown had begun early that afternoon, and at nightfall it was still burning. When Abel returned late that night, their house was still standing; Matthew and Lucas, along with other volunteers, had doused the roof with buckets of water in case an errant spark should ignite the frame structure. The house stood a goodly distance from the spot on First Avenue near Madison where the conflagration had begun, but it was by no means out of the danger zone.

"We'll rebuild," Abel said. "We'll build a better city on the ashes of this one, and while we're at it, we'll build our own new house, too." They were brave words, but that night, for the first time in many months, he came to her for the solace and comfort she had, earlier that day and for very different reasons, given Caleb—his brother and his enemy.

·Catherine: 1906-1936·

Chapter Nine

"Aren't you coming, Catherine?" Molly regarded her with a fishy stare. "Catherine Abigail Blanchard, if you miss one more Latin class, Miss Larsen will have your hide!"

Catherine shifted the weight of her book bag on her shoulders, surprisingly broad for her slenderness, and tugged her middy down over her skirt. "But Molly . . . look, the sun's out. We haven't seen the sun for weeks!" All that winter of 1906 it had been dark, the mountains ringing the city west and east hidden beneath a misty shroud, except for one dazzlingly clear fortnight during the February thaw, a false spring, when Mount Rainier had suddenly appeared, sharp-peaked and snowy against teal-blue skies, and roses bloomed, lulled to life after endless months of soft green rain. But now it was April, and Catherine yearned to gallop her big chestnut, Mr. Rochester, along the beach at the foot of the bluff at Alki.

"If everyone in Seattle took the day off when the sun shone, the whole city would close down," her schoolmate protested.

Catherine thought that might not be a bad idea. The city seemed to be growing too fast. Daily it seemed to gulp down more of what she loved. What was one day a dense meadow, thick with the rustle of small game and the yellow profusion of Scotch broom, seemed to metamorphose overnight into a gaping hole in the earth, from which rose almost instantly another steel-sheathed building. Streams where she had watched salmon fingerlings cluster and disperse and mature fish return, to hatch and die in the waters that spawned them—they too were thick with the detritus of growth and overuse. Like her Uncle Caleb, she mourned the pace of progress, the loss of nature's comforts: the maple trees on First Avenue, ripped up when the street was widened to accommodate automobile traffic; the lake, where swans once nested but no longer did; the flower-scented gardens of Madison Park, trampled by too many feet since the advent of the trolley lines.

"We're a couple of old mossbacks, you and me," Uncle Caleb teased her often. "Guess it's a good thing all the Blanchards aren't like us, or we'd still be fetching water from a well and lighting candles in the darkness."

Catherine wrinkled her nose. "Ugh, those electric wires on our street are awful," she said. "And they cut down at least a dozen cedar trees to make those poles they've strung them from."

"That's progress, darling girl," her uncle said. "If some people in this town heard you say that, they'd try you for heresy."

"Like my father, you mean," she said, and Caleb Blanchard nodded.

Abel thought his brother mad—and that was as charitable as he ever got. "He'd keep Seattle in the horse-and-buggy age if it was up to him," he fumed, until Catherine's mother said gently, "Don't get started on Caleb, Abel, you'll set your stomach to souring again."

Maddy Blanchard had to listen to her husband complain about Caleb's stubbornness, but Catherine refused to. She wouldn't hear a word against her favorite relative. Her father said, "You're more like him than your own father is, Catherine," and looked so hurt she wanted to hug him. He wasn't a very approachable man, even then; it was like Aunt Sonnet said, "He'll break, but he won't bend."

Aunt Sonnet! Catherine remembered guiltily. She'd meant to stop in and visit with her; the old lady was ailing again, and even Maddy feared she might not last much longer. "She was at least forty when I met her, which would make her eighty now," Catherine's mother said. "Of course, she's as tough as an old hen, and the Lord knows she's lived enough for a dozen lives, but still"—and here her face had softened—"I'll miss her when she's gone."

So would Catherine. She had known her Aunt Sonnet since she was born, a day Sonnet never tired of recounting to her in detail. "I was watching them rebuilding the downtown—after the fire, you know, it was all cinders and ashes." She chortled, reliving the memory. "Some fire that was! We thought the town was done for, but they were so busy starting over they never even got around to punishing the real culprits."

"You mean whoever let that glue pot in the paint store boil over?" Catherine asked, but Aunt Sonnet snorted in derision.

"Hell, no!" she said. "Everybody but the damned mayor knew the Spring Street Water Company hadn't checked those flues or hoses since they lined their pockets building the damned thing and then got out of town." She sighed and fanned herself. "Of course, as soon as I heard the bells go off, I knew what it was, and I knew they wouldn't be able to stop it once it really took hold."

Fearing she would be lost in reminiscing about a history that, as far as Catherine was concerned, didn't really start until the day nine months after the fire when she was ushered into the world, she nudged Aunt Sonnet toward that most important event.

"And then Ethan Westwind came to tell you Mama'd gone into labor, and Papa wasn't anywhere to be found, so the two of you got on up to our house and carried Mama to the hotel," she prompted. She knew the story, word for word, and never tired of hearing it.

" 'Course, the Continental wasn't much of a hotel then—not like it is now," Sonnet said, "but yes, that's about the way it transpired."

Even before the Great Fire, the establishment that Sonnet managed for her silent partner, Caleb Blanchard, had fallen on hard times. First suffrage had brought the reformers to the Skid Road, and Sonnet had had no heart for the trouble that heralded their arrival. "My girls are having difficulties with the law," she had told Caleb, "and it's going to get worse. Business is way off, ever since the terminus went to Tacoma; that's where our customers are going too. Last week the fire inspector was here twice, and yesterday that Denny woman and her friends from the temperance group were picketing the saloon across the street. They'll be doing the same to us, one of these days soon. I think it's time to get out of the business."

But Caleb had demurred—the White House was his only source of income by then, and while it wasn't much, the earnings he pocketed from it enabled him to hold on to what was left of his property in Alki; shrunken though his holdings were, they still occupied over a hundred acres, from the Bluff to the tide flats. The tide flats had been filled in with the wash from the hills in the southwest part of the city, which were being leveled and sluiced into the bay. Speculators got rich selling the filled lands, but Caleb held on to his, even when the shipbuilders Skinner and Eady approached him with a proposition to locate their new yard on the flats. As they later reported to Abel Blanchard, "Your brother cares more about beaver dams and water hens than he does about the future of the city," and Abel, who had long since given up trying to understand his brother, just shook his head, as if to say, What can you do?

Then the Great Fire erupted, and in the aftermath, with hundreds of people burned out of their homes and every one of the few remaining hotels and boardinghouses crammed to the rafters with refugees, Sonnet brought up the subject of the future of the White House again.

"There are people sleeping in the streets when there's a perfectly good building here, but they won't come in as long as it's a whorehouse," she told Caleb bluntly.

"Just what do you have in mind?"

"I think we should close down for a week or two and then reopen—after all, we're one of the only structures left in this part of town."

"And what would happen during that interval?" Caleb inquired lazily, his words slurred. He was drinking a lot in those days—he seemed to have given up on life. A fuse was burning in him, not just anger at Abel about the incursions his Alki Land and Development Company had made on his precious Bluff but something else. These days he hardly went out to the Bluff, just drank himself into such a stupor in the White House that Sonnet would have her houseman carry him upstairs and put him to bed in one of the rooms on the second floor.

"Why, we'd redecorate a bit—nothing fancy, just get rid of

some of this stuff," she said, gesturing at the garish red-and-gold
color scheme of the room in which they sat. "And hang up a new
sign and start taking paying guests. Men *and* women," she added
pointedly. "A hotel is what I had in mind—after all, who knows
more about hospitality than Sonnet McBride?"

"Who indeed?" inquired Caleb, and grinned at her in the old
way. "You got a hankering for respectability, Sonnet?"

She colored but ignored him. She had some money put by,
and with it she embarked on the refurbishment of the old bawdy
house. And her generosity in setting aside for the benefit of the
victims of the fire fully a third of the rooms in the Hotel Continental—which was what, with a sense of irony not lost on Caleb,
she renamed the White House—came near to purchasing the
respectability that, as Caleb had guessed, she yearned in her old
age to acquire. In time, people tended to forget who she had
been—even Abel Blanchard, on whom her role in helping his
beloved city rise again from the ashes was not lost. While he
never warmed to her as his wife did, he was polite and well-
mannered in her presence and gave no sign that he remembered
her past. The story was put about that Caleb Blanchard had
purchased the brothel from the estate of John Pennell, on behalf
of some California investors who had engaged the former
madam to manage their new hotel. And while Abel thought
Sonnet was—well, a bit garish, he did nothing to discourage the
friendship his wife had struck up with the woman who ran his
brother's sole remaining enterprise. Certainly, Mrs. McBride's
companionship seemed to make Maddy happier than she had
been in some time, although it might have been Catherine's
birth that did it, too.

Abel was delighted with his daughter; the child of his old age,
she could tease a smile from him when no one else could. As for
his wife—well, like Maddy, he was mostly satisfied with the
bargain he had struck with Asa Mercer so many years before.
She had been a good wife to him, given occasionally to long
periods of silent withdrawal into her beloved books, and to a
dreaminess that sometimes exasperated him, but on the other
hand unlike Sara she stirred in him neither the disturbing passion nor the alarms caused, before her untimely death, by her
deteriorating mental state. And she had given him two fine sons,

Lucas and Matthew, who were dearly loved by their half brother Elijah. Elijah had followed his father, as would Lucas and Matthew, into the business of developing land to accommodate the newcomers who had streamed into the city after the Gold Rush and now, in the first decade of the twentieth century, continued to arrive.

Abel's family was a strong unit, a bulwark against the forces that were changing his city in a way that sometimes troubled him. A new breed of people was coming—restless, speculative, looser in their habits and moral standards than he would have preferred, some of them recently emigrated from Europe and possessed of traditions of a different sort, a foreignness that made him uneasy. He knew they were necessary to Seattle's continued growth, and he could not control the floodgates he had been so anxious to see opened, so he came to depend even more on the stability and predictability of his own home and family. He would not have jeopardized that stability by protesting his wife's right to select her own friends. Still, he did not go out of his way to encourage her relationship with Sonnet McBride. He much preferred Mary Denny.

Maddy, delighted that circumstances permitted her to publicly claim Sonnet's friendship, did not insist on entertaining her in their home. Instead she went to the Continental, and if encountering Caleb was part of the price she must pay for being with Sonnet, well then, she would do it, though he made her uneasy, and she took care to avoid him if she could. It was not difficult—he made no overtures to her, although, later, he took a special pleasure in Catherine, and for private reasons not divulged to anyone, Maddy permitted the relationship between the tall bearded man and the small, red-haired child to flower. Caleb came rarely to her house; the split between the brothers was all but in the open, though Abel, for one, would not have admitted it to anyone. That people guessed—or knew, as they by this time surely did—that a deep, true enmity existed between the brothers was of little concern to him. Family, as he said often to Maddy, was family. Blood was thicker than water, Abel pointed out, as proved by Caleb's alacrity in getting his brother's wife to the infirmary before she delivered his only daughter in what, no matter how fashionable it soon became, was still, to him, a whorehouse.

"Oh, it was quite a day when you were born," Sonnet told Catherine whenever she pestered her to recount the story of her birth, as she often did. "The sun had broken through after nothing but rain for months on end—it started pouring the day after the fire, and for a while there folks thought it was the Flood, it just kept coming. But that day was different. Your Uncle Caleb and me, we took your Mama to the infirmary and she was so out of her mind with pain she hardly knew where she was—she'd gone into a faint, and it was something to worry about, since she was near forty then, pretty old to be having a young 'un. And then she woke up, and she says, like she hadn't seen me in years, 'Why, Sonnet McBride, has the ship sailed without us?' and then she just fainted dead away!"

"Because your hotel—the Continental—has the same name as the boat that brought Mama to Seattle, isn't that right?" Catherine asked.

Neither Maddy nor Sonnet had found it necessary to explain to Abel or anyone else that their friendship predated Sonnet's new respectability. They kept their secret. Nor did Sonnet ever tell Catherine any different.

"The Continental—yes, that's right," she said. "In '66 it was, if I remember right. 'Course, that was long before my time here. I was an old lady by then, and I'm an older one now."

She winked at Catherine, and they both laughed. There was nothing old about Aunt Sonnet except her body; Catherine thought she was the youngest person she had ever known. Her mind was sharp and clear; she was a lady of strong opinions, and she voiced them frankly to anyone who'd listen, with a tongue Catherine's father declared was as salty as the ships of the Mosquito Fleet.

Catherine could hear the story of the day she was born over and over again; there was nothing she liked better than a good chat and a gossip with her Aunt Sonnet. And on this extraordinary day, as the morning sun moved tantalizingly higher in the sky and Molly impatiently waited for her to get over her spring fever and come inside, she considered that her opportunities to enjoy just such an interlude might be numbered. As her mother said, Sonnet wasn't getting any younger.

The Latin mistress of the Forest Ridge Seminary for Young Ladies was going to have a tizzy, but Catherine would not be there to witness it, she decided. First a visit with Aunt Sonnet, then a ferry ride to Alki and a good gallop on Mr. Rochester and a chat with Uncle Caleb. After all, this was Seattle—who knew when the sun would shine again?

*   *   *

Catherine was not fond of school—at least, not the one she attended. She wanted to go to South High School, but her father refused. He didn't care for the students who attended these public high schools—the Filipinos and Japanese from Washington Street, the Chinese from Jackson Street, the Negroes from Beacon Hill, the Jews from First Avenue. All of them, and more —the Irish, the Swedes, and the remaining Indians—went to South. And so did many of the sons and daughters of the city's reigning society, which, while not an aristocracy entirely of birth, required more than simply making a great deal of money for admission to its inner sanctums or participation in its rituals. There were Stimsons and Schwabachers and Bagleys and Dennys at South High, and even Blanchards—Catherine's brothers —because Abel thought it would be beneficial for his sons to mix with the immigrants who were coming to Seattle in such multitudes. Some day they would be working for Blanchards, after all. But Catherine was a girl and needed sheltering from the rough ways of the lower classes.

Catherine was confused by her father's decision. The schoolmates Abel wanted to protect her from were mostly youngsters she'd known all her life. In her childhood, the family had lived within five blocks of the center of the city. From the time she could walk she'd roamed its streets and lanes, playing in the sawdust of the cabinet shop, having cakes and tea with the clairvoyant who lived across the street. She spent hours watching the blacksmith and begged feathers from the dressmaker to pin in her curls. She talked to anyone, and everyone talked to her, for she was a sunny, curious child who expected the world to love her and was rarely disappointed. From the first, she was spoiled shamelessly by her mother and her Aunt Sonnet, and what her own father did not provide in the way of affection—hugs, kisses, teasing, and tussling—her Uncle Caleb did.

In 1898, less than a year after the steamer *Portland* docked in Seattle carrying a ton of gold from Alaska's Klondike, Abel moved his family out of downtown and into a big house on Minor Avenue. On First Hill the streets were wider, the homes more graceful, the rhododendrons and maple trees more luxuriant. Not everyone who lived there was as rich as the Blanchards —a carpenter could live next to a banker, a laundress across the street from a lumber baron. The best thing about Minor Avenue, Catherine thought, was that it was near the trolley line, and by the time she was out of braids she had explored every part of the city accessible by streetcar. She had been to places she was certain her brothers had never seen, like the seal pen at Leschi, and the old shack on Shilshole Bay where Indian Charlie lived.

Which was probably why her father had enrolled her at the seminary, she reflected as she trudged down Madison Street. That, and what he called the "elements." She didn't understand why she couldn't be best friends with Lin Yen any more, just because she was the daughter of her mother's laundress and went to South High. Or why she couldn't ask Sam Bergman to the dance at the Seattle Golf Club, since she had to go anyway.

"Because your father has become a snob, that's why," Aunt Sonnet told her when she posed the question to her later that day. Sonnet was delighted to see her; she was sitting up in bed, a frilled nightcap on top of her head and a feathered jacket draped around her shoulders, and she poured Catherine thick, dark chicory coffee from a heavy silver pot. "Oh, he was different in the old days," she said. "He didn't care who you were as long as you wanted to help him make Seattle the biggest city west of the Mississippi."

"What happened to him?" Catherine wanted to know.

"It's hard to tell," Sonnet said. "He made as much money as anyone off the boom times in Alaska, but when everyone who didn't get his strike came back here, he fussed at that, said they ought to go back where they come from, unless they had something to offer Seattle other than another hungry mouth to feed."

"But there's plenty of room for everyone," Catherine protested. "Why, they're even sluicing off the top of Denny Hill to build up there."

"Maybe on Mr. Denny's hill, but not on your father's," Sonnet said. "And that's where he wants his daughter, not down to the Pavilion at Leschi Park spooning with that young Bergman fellow you're so keen on."

Catherine colored, and Sonnet cackled.

"Caught you, didn't I, girl?" she said gleefully. "Oh, I may be an old lady, but I've got friends, you know." Then she was serious. "And so does your father, I'd wager. You'd best be a sight more cautious unless you want your daddy all stirred up, at least until you go off to college in New York."

"Oh, Aunt Sonnet, you know I don't want to go East to college. I don't see why I can't go to the university like everyone else."

"That's exactly the reason, sweet girl," Sonnet replied. "Everyone else. Besides, your mama wants you to have the kind of education she never had. She's had her heart set on you going East practically since you were born."

"But I don't want to," wailed Catherine. "I couldn't stand to be away from Seattle for four whole years. New York is cold, and it's ugly, and I'm sure the girls are all terrible snobs. I'll hate it!" She slammed her fist on the bedcovers and flashed a coquettish smile at the old woman. "Aunt Sonnet, couldn't you talk to them? Please?"

"You can't change your daddy's mind once he makes it up," Sonnet replied. "Or your mama's either. Why, the first time I met her, when she was no bigger 'n you, she had herself fixed on a dream and she didn't let anything stop her." She smiled to herself, remembering the spunky young girl she'd met on the Post Road.

"Well, I've got myself fixed on going to the university, right here in Seattle, and I'm not going to let anything stop me either," said Catherine stubbornly. She looked at Sonnet closely. Her eyes were closed, and she seemed to be in pain. "Oh, Auntie, am I tiring you out?"

"No, of course you're not, child. I drift off sometimes, that's all," Sonnet replied, but Catherine gathered her things and bent down to kiss her good-bye.

"I'll stop in tomorrow," she promised.

"I expect you'll find me right here," said Sonnet.

"I expect I will," Catherine replied.

She skipped down the hill from Sonnet's house to the water-front and dug a nickel out of her pocket before boarding the ferry. She made her way to the pilot house and perched on a stool as Captain Olafson steered his craft across Elliott Bay.

"Haven't seen you much lately, missy," said the skipper, who'd ferried her across to Uncle Caleb's ever since she could remember. "Thought you'd be in school today."

"Not on a day like today," she said, and the captain grinned at her. The sun made everyone conspirators in Seattle; on a beautiful morning, strangers tipped their hats to each other and everyone seemed to be in good humor.

She disembarked at the dock in West Seattle and took the short cut along the beach to the barn that marked the outer limit of Caleb's property. She took an apple from her pocket and rubbed it on her sleeve before offering it to her horse, who was stabled with Caleb's other animals. Then she saddled him, changed into the riding breeches she kept in her uncle's tack room, and set off across the meadow to the apple orchard.

She found Caleb there, inspecting the graft on a new variety of fruit tree. He was dedicated to improving the yield of his trees, and though his richest farmland, near the mouth of the Duwamish, had long since fallen to the developers—rapists, he called them—he was inordinately proud of his apples, which everyone said were the juiciest this side of the Cascades. "Missing school again, eh, Cat?" he said with a raised eyebrow. "What will your mother have to say about that?"

"Maybe she won't know. She's stuck up there in that library Daddy built her, most likely. Sometimes she doesn't even come down for dinner."

Her uncle frowned. "Really?" he asked. "I guess it's been a while since I've been to Broadview."

That was an understatement—Catherine couldn't remember seeing him there for ages, not since she was four and almost died from the scarlet fever. She never knew how he'd found out, since he hardly talked to her father. Aunt Sonnet must have told him, for she remembered how he had pushed his way into the sickroom, past Maddy and Abel and the doctor, refusing to leave her side until the fever broke days later.

"Well, to be fair, Papa is away a lot in Washington," she said.

Abel had been elected to Congress two years before, but despite his urging Maddy had declined his invitation to accompany him to the nation's capital. "It's no place for a young girl," she'd said, and Abel had not pressed her. It was quiet in the big house since her brothers had married and moved into their own homes; Broadview never felt quite lived in, which Catherine didn't mind all that much. It was easy to get around Mrs. Erickson, the housekeeper, who looked after her when her mother was otherwise occupied in her book-lined room. But sometimes Catherine was lonely, and when she was, she headed for the Bluff like a pigeon coming home to roost.

Uncle Caleb wasn't like her father at all. To begin with, he didn't care what a person did or how rich he was; he was genuinely interested in everyone he met and as open and friendly as Abel was closed and aloof. When Catherine was six, he had taken her to the funeral of Princess Angeline, the old Indian woman who was the last of Chief Seattle's children. Her face was painted with strange markings and her body clothed in a heavy brown shroud, and she lay in a coffin shaped like a canoe, with a paddle resting on the stern. Much to her parents' dismay when they learned about it later, Catherine and Caleb followed the hearse, drawn by a span of black horses, to the Lakeview Cemetery. It was quite the most exciting thing Catherine had ever seen, even though she had nightmares about dead Indians for weeks.

Every home in Seattle, it seemed to Catherine, was open to her Uncle Caleb. He had friends among the earliest settlers and the city's most recent arrivals. Those who didn't know her father thought she was Caleb's daughter, and sometimes, in her most secret thoughts, she wished it were true.

She was a very sociable girl, and she loved to go visiting with Uncle Caleb. But the best times were just with him, hiking along the bluff, losing themselves in the cool green woods, finding the first jack-in-the-pulpits in the spring and the last wild oyster mushrooms in the autumn. He knew every bush, every tree, every flower, and every animal that frequented his land. In his boat shed on the beach were canoes, a kayak, and a variety of other water craft, and, having satisfied himself that she could swim, Caleb encouraged her to use them. On rainy afternoons when she came to the Bluff, they worked on his "collections," specimens of leaves and flowers and insects and even animal spoors, which she traced on thin sheets of paper and he labeled in a neat, precise hand with a quill pen that rested in a crystal inkwell. Other times she read aloud to him; she did not care that much for books—not like her mother—but Caleb encouraged her to read, dismissing with a chuckle Abel's complaint that too much learning would make her too smart for any man to marry.

Today he gave her Mr. Darwin's diaries, which she promised to read as soon as she had time. And then he saddled Jenny, his mare, and they rode slowly in companionable silence, side by side where the trees had been carefully logged and reseeded, and single file through the denser stands of mature evergreens. The sun glinted down through the trees in drops and sparkles, and birds whistled their arrival to the small game that scampered along the needle-carpeted forest floor. They passed the afternoon united in their pleasure at the fine day, and by the time they arrived back at the ferry dock, the setting sun had stained the bay scarlet.

"I don't want to go home," Catherine complained. "I don't see why I have to. Nobody will miss me, anyway. Can't I stay here?"

Her uncle shook his head. "If it were up to me, of course you could, Cat, but you can't keep missing school. They won't have you at that fancy college if this continues."

"That would be perfectly sublime. Uncle Caleb, can't you talk to my mother and father for me? About going to the university, I mean?"

"No, I don't think so," he said. "Besides, one would think you'd be delighted to shake the dust of Seattle off your heels. Most girls your age would love to. Don't you want to see something of the world?"

"Everything I want to see is right here," Catherine said stubbornly. "I don't see why everyone makes such a fuss over going East."

"Perhaps they think it will polish your manners," her uncle replied with a gentle smile.

"Well, they're wrong," she said with a shake of her curls. "G'bye, Uncle Caleb. Will you give Mr. Rochester an extra ration of oats tonight?" She got down from her horse, tucked the bundle carrying her skirt and a dozen apples from Caleb's orchard under her arm, and slung her book bag over her shoulder. There was a smudge of dirt on her nose, and her hair was full of pine needles.

Her uncle nodded. "Keep safe," he said and, turning the horses, cantered away toward the Bluff.

It was dark by the time the ferry docked at the foot of Front Street, crowded with people returning to their homes for the evening meal. Some of them worked for the Blanchards; the household maids, and the man who kept her father's automobile polished and sometimes drove her places in it; the loggers, land salesmen, and bank clerks who hailed her by name or tipped their hats to her as she passed. Doubtless there were many more who wondered who she was, this disheveled, untidy young woman who made her way with casual familiarity along the waterfront, stopping only for a moment to stare in the window of Ye Olde Curiosity Shop, whose wares always made her gasp in disbelief—the enormous snail, said to weigh 67 pounds, the 800-year-old Chinese dog, the yellow sea crab that was easily thirteen feet from claw to claw, the enormous jawbone of a whale.

A few blocks from the wharf, she caught a trolley up the hill to Minor Avenue and walked the short distance home. "I'm home," she called in the direction of the kitchen, where, she knew, her dinner was being prepared by Mrs. Erickson. Before the housekeeper could intercept her and lecture her about the state of her clothes or demand an explanation for her tardiness, she ran upstairs, taking the steps two at a time. When she came back down a short while later, she was wearing a clean shirt-waist, her face was washed, and the pine needles were brushed out of her hair. The faint spray of freckles on her pink-tinged cheeks was the only indication that she had not spent the day at school. This telltale sign escaped the notice of Mrs. Erickson, however, who was almost as old as Aunt Sonnet and practically blind, thought Catherine, as she sat down at the long mahogany table in the dining room in solitary splendor. Her mother would have noticed and remarked upon it. But her mother was upstairs in the library, and by the time Maddy looked up from her journals and saw that it was dark and another day was over, Catherine was upstairs, fast asleep.

Chapter Ten

The first time Catherine saw Leighton Blake, he was wearing a mask and pointing a pistol at her. He was clearly the leader of the half dozen masked riders, all identically garbed in full-length ulsters and sinister black hats, who surrounded the gleaming four-horse tallyho.

"Afternoon, ladies," he said politely, tipping his hat to the five women in the carriage. "I'd be mighty grateful if you'd put your jewels and valuables in here." He presented a feed bag and handed it to Catherine; when their eyes met, over his mask, she saw amusement and something else, too—a cool, appraising stare so frank in its intent that she felt it like a blow.

Behind her she heard a sharp intake of breath from her sister-in-law, Emily, and a high, keening cry from Emily's mother. With effort, she turned away from the masked bandit and caught that amok matron as she collapsed in a swoon. Catherine's mother began to comply with the bandit's request, removing her amethyst brooch from her dress and stripping the rings from her fingers. "Do hush and do what the gentleman says, Emily," Maddy reproached her daughter-in-law, who looked as if she might scream. And just as calmly, she unclasped the gold watch from the wrist of the unconscious woman beside her.

Catherine could only watch, stupefied. This was not the Wild West of the James Gang, this was Seattle, in the year of our Lord nineteen hundred and nine, and the coach the masked men were so ignominiously—and successfully—robbing had not been out of the Treats' stable for years except on ceremonial occasions.

This was such an occasion—a charity luncheon at the Seattle Golf Club to celebrate the opening of the Alaska-Yukon-Pacific Exposition. On this day Missy Green had leased it to transport her guests to the luncheon. Almost no one traveled by coach any more, and while there were still horse-drawn vehicles in the streets of the city, a holdup was a rare occurrence—as far as Catherine knew, there hadn't been one for years.

This cannot be happening, Catherine thought. True, she had only recently returned to Seattle after finishing her second year at Vassar and taking a grand tour of the Continent. As she expected, she had found the city vastly changed in her absence. It was noisier and more crowded; she noted the passing of landmarks of her childhood and evidence of bulldozing, building, and paving that had replaced them. But there were still places unmarked by the frantic boom of the Gold Rush, whose anniversary the Exposition celebrated. Beside these pleasant trails that wound along the shore of the lake and meandered leisurely among the gnarled madrona trees, there were few signs of the thriving metropolis of 300,000 inhabitants only a few miles away. When the masked robbers surrounded the carriage, she thought for an instant that she had been yanked back in time to an era that lived only in the memories of people like her parents and her Aunt Sonnet.

"Go ahead, Catherine, give him your necklace," her mother said. Catherine looked first at Maddy and then at the man whose masked face was just inches from her own.

"Certainly not!" she retorted. And with that she hoisted her skirts, climbed swiftly over the tonneau that separated the passengers from the driver, and took the whip from his shaking hands. "Giddyap!" she shouted, and cracked the whip; the team of horses bucked sharply and, with another touch of the whip on their flanks, sped away.

She heard the pistol shots behind her, and the screams of her passengers, but she did not slow the horses until an approaching car forced her to pull off the road. Then she got down from the box seat, smoothed her skirts, and climbed back into the coach. By this time Emily's mother had recovered consciousness, and the air was rent with her frightened shrieks. Her sister-in-law and Missy Green, Catherine noted, were sobbing heavily into their handkerchiefs, and her own mother was regarding her with a look of stupefaction.

"They might have killed us," Maddy said crossly, "or worse."

"They wouldn't have dared," Catherine said, although she was not as certain as she sounded. The look the bandit leader had given her had shaken her deeply: it had seemed to say, You are mine, whenever and however I like.

Several cars had stopped by now, attracted by the screams from the tallyho; Catherine explained what had happened, declined any further assistance, and instructed the driver to take them home. Almost on their heels, Colonel Blethen, publisher of the *Seattle Times,* careened into the driveway of the big house on Minor Avenue; he demanded first-hand details of the great coach robbery, which the ladies gave him willingly.

"Oh, Em, there were only six of them, not two dozen," Catherine told her sister-in-law, "and they didn't hurt us, anyway." Leaving the others to answer the publisher's questions, she went up to her room to dress for dinner. As she bathed and dressed and pinned her reddish curls into a knot at the top of her head and touched her cheeks with rouge, she thought about the dark-eyed bandit and smiled in spite of herself. She didn't for a second think they had been in real danger, and she wondered how long it would be before she saw him again.

* * *

The drawing room was crowded with the cream of Seattle society, assembled to dine with her father's guest of honor, President William Taft, and his party, present to mark the opening of the Alaska-Yukon-Pacific Exposition. It was not until the President moved his enormous bulk away from the huge Gothic fireplace that Catherine saw, resting on the mantel, the feed bag into which only a few hours before she had been requested to deposit her jewelry. Standing next to it was a tall, lean man, impeccably dressed in formal evening clothes, who grinned down at her with the same sardonic, amused eyes she had last seen above a mask.

"You!" she gasped. "What are you doing here?"

"Returning your valuables," he replied.

"I knew it!" she said delightedly. "This was one of my father's silly pranks, wasn't it? The robbery—that was all an act, wasn't it?"

The stranger laughed and made a sweeping bow before her. "Leighton Blake, at your service, ma'am," he said.

"And quite the scalawag too," said her father, who had joined them. "Leighton, may I present my daughter, Catherine."

"Father, you nearly frightened Mother and Emily and Mrs. Burke and Missy Green to death!" she scolded.

Her father looked almost sheepish. "Well, Harry Treat's wife has been after him for years to sell that team and carriage, but you know how he is—sentimental, like you. Doesn't realize the horse-and-buggy days are over. So I mentioned it to Joshua and Leighton and they came up with this scheme, staging the robbery and all."

"And here I thought we'd all been such heroines, especially you, Catherine," said her mother, coming up to steer them toward the dining room. "I don't know what got into your father," she whispered, "unless it was his cronies at that club of his, and all the excitement of the Exposition."

But of course she did, and so did Catherine. Abel Blanchard, habitually the most serious and stolid of men, possessed as well a boyish streak that was expressed only on occasions of civic celebration and then only for his friends, old pioneers like himself. The staged holdup, he explained to Catherine, was an appropriate reminder of how far Seattle had come since those days, just as the Exposition was.

"Well? Am I forgiven?" Leighton Blake whispered in Catherine's ear as they entered the dining room.

Catherine didn't reply, but she allowed Blake to seat her at the dining table. His hand brushed her arm, and a delicious shiver went through her.

"You have spirit, I'll say that much for you," he said.

"Just like Seattle has," her father said happily. After all, they'd had a good chuckle, and no harm had come to anyone, as he told the President.

Leighton Blake, Catherine discovered, was her dinner partner. Someone has gone to a great deal of trouble to see that we meet, she thought, and she knew just who that person was. Deliberately, she turned to the guest on her left, a deaf old lady with an ear trumpet who had been in Seattle, Catherine soon learned, since the schooner *Exact* landed there sixty years earlier.

She should have known; after all, she had set the place cards around the table, according to the list her father had drawn up. She had recognized most of the names on the cards, paying little attention to the few unfamiliar ones. She had been away from home for nearly three years, but her father's dinners were all the same—dull, stodgy affairs at which the men talked business and the wives murmured quietly among themselves about their homes, clubs, and children. She had not expected this evening to be any different, and in many respects it was not. The guests might have been more fashionably attired than usual, and wine was being poured, which was not typical, but that was due, no doubt, to two things: the presence of the recently inaugurated President—whose 300-pound frame rested in a chair built specially for the occasion—and the strong spirit of civic pride glowing on the faces of the assembled company.

Catherine did not need to be told that Leighton Blake had been selected by her father to be her husband. That he had someone in mind she had had no doubt since her return from Europe; that it was Blake was clear from the elaborate way in which he had arranged for them to meet and the almost childish delight he showed in introducing them before dinner.

She did not wonder why he had been chosen; probably, she thought, there was a useful commercial alliance to be gained. Like most of the early settlers, her father had made the most of his pioneer claim, much of which now comprised a large portion of downtown. He had extended his hegemony to the surrounding timberlands with the help of one Jim Hill. Hill had sold him a substantial portion of the 900,000 acres of railroad right-of-way he had extorted from Congress for six dollars an acre, far below its market value. In return, Abel had cooperated in bringing the Great Northern to Seattle, thus making up for the Northern Pacific's error in placing the western terminus of its railroad in Tacoma.

By the time the party had assembled in the music room, Catherine had placed Leighton Blake. His steamship company had started the rate wars that fueled the great Alaska gold rush. In recent months he and Joshua Green, another steamboater, had challenged the Canadian Pacific Railway's attempt to monopolize the Seattle–Victoria steamship service by continuing to cut rates, despite the recession of the previous year. The Great Rate War had received attention in the national press, and the acrimony it generated was reflected in waterfront brawling between crews of the competing lines. The president of the Northern Pacific, who felt that the rate war was benefiting the rival Canadian Pacific more than it was helping his own line, was a guest this evening too; she noticed him disappear into the library after dinner, along with her father, President Taft, Joshua Green, and Leighton Blake, and wondered, for a moment, if she had misjudged Abel's motives.

Of course, her father rarely made any overtures from which he could not wring at least one advantage, and two were even better. In any case, he had accomplished his primary goal: Catherine, who would never have believed that she could experience this weakening of the knees, this flutter of the heart, this rush of heat through her entire body—Catherine was completely and blindly in love.

Chapter Eleven

L eighton Blake took his own time courting Catherine. She did not see him again for nearly a month, when a gala ball was held in honor of James Scott and H. B. Smith, winners of the Transcontinental Automobile Race, who had left New York in their stripped-down Ford motorcar the day the AYP Exposition opened and arrived in Seattle there twenty-two days later.

The ball was held in the Stimson mansion a few blocks from the Blanchard home on First Hill. Henry Ford himself was in attendance, presenting the victors with a check for two thousand dollars and a trophy that had been put up by Mr. Guggenheim, the New York philanthropist. Catherine and her escort, a naval officer related by marriage to the Simpsons and assigned temporarily to one of the American warships moored in Elliott Bay for the Exposition, stood in line for champagne that was being poured, amidst great hilarity, from the prized trophy.

"Why, it's the courageous Miss Blanchard," said a voice from behind Catherine. "Have you foiled any holdups recently?"

She knew who it was before she turned around, though nothing in her equally casual response provided any indication of the excitement she felt at his presence. She was glad she had worn her new Paquin gown, a fire-red silk muslin draped in bengaline with gold and filigree, which had arrived from Paris only a few days earlier. Although she would not admit, if asked, that the East Coast or even Europe was superior to Seattle in any way, she had to admit that the Northwest, in matters of fashion, still had some catching up to do. Her father had been more than generous with money during Catherine's years in New York and her travels in Europe, and she had indulged her weakness for beautiful clothes. Her mother, who was tight with a dollar and cared little for clothes, had been horrified when the first boxes began arriving from the Continent, but tonight Catherine was pleased she had spared no effort to look her best. Her red-blond hair was piled high on her head in a fashionable tumble of curls; her green eyes danced as she beheld the splendor of Leighton Blake.

"It's my understanding that the ladies of Seattle are once again safe from bandits," she replied. "According to Missy Green, anyway."

"I believe we can agree that Missy, at least, has nothing to fear," he said lightly, but his deep-set eyes, compelling even without a mask to attract her gaze, pinned her again with the same knowing, insolent look.

For Catherine, time seemed to stop at that instant. Everything around her faded away—the babble of voices, the tinkling of glasses, the music from the ballroom. A wave of heat swept over her; she heard only the pounding of her own heart and thought Leighton Blake must surely hear it, too.

But he smiled easily and introduced his companion, a Miss Deirdre Flood, who was visiting from San Francisco. Next to this striking brunette beauty, Catherine felt pale and washed out—she would have traded her Dresden-like prettiness for the young woman's exotic charms in a minute. She introduced her own escort, and then Leighton Blake related the story of the faked robbery. By then they had reached the front of the queue and were separated by the crush of celebrants gathered at the table.

She saw Blake several times during the dancing, noting jealously the way he held the Flood woman against him while they waltzed. Catherine made a point of being amusing and flirtatious, bolder and livelier than she usually was, in case Leighton was watching; she knew the power of downcast eyes and girlish blushes, but tonight she eschewed them. As soon as she saw Leighton leave the ball with Deirdre Flood, Catherine reverted to her usual self—with men she was never very bold; she was content to wait until they came to her, as, in most cases, they did.

And shortly after Leighton Blake left the party, she pleaded a headache and asked to be escorted home.

All that long week before she received Leighton's note inviting her to a theater party, she thought of him. Even out at the Bluff, cantering Mr. Rochester along the beach, his face intruded on her thoughts, his knowing eyes eclipsing all else. At home she was distant, moody, and irritable; Maddy threw up her hands in disgust, and even Sonnet, who was having one of her good spells, was cross.

"You're brooding over that fellow Blake, aren't you?" she said one afternoon. Catherine had told her about the "bandit" who'd held up Missy Green's party at gunpoint and come to dinner at Broadview that evening. In the following days, she'd mentioned his name at every possible opportunity, and her eyes softened dreamily when she did so.

Leighton Blake was not unknown in her social circle, as Catherine learned by the simple expedient of keeping her ears open. He was said to be somewhat of a gambler who had amassed considerable wealth with his shipping company and was thought to be clever and enterprising; a bachelor, he had squired many of the young ladies of Seattle around town, particularly the pretty, wealthy ones. He hunted at Joshua Green's duck club and sailed with Bill Boeing, and while he had come out to the Northwest less than a decade earlier—from the South, they said —it was generally agreed that his prospects were promising, if the right woman could be found who would settle him down properly and secure him firmly in the harness of respectability.

Catherine, hardly knowing the man, wished desperately to be that woman. But although Leighton called on her all that year, took her to parties at the tennis club that summer, shielded her from the rains that dampened every Husky football game that autumn, and escorted her to the Christmas cotillion at the Rainier Club, he treated her with a teasing politeness that first charmed and then exhausted her.

She went to New York for a month, visiting her friend Ruth Straus from Vassar, and he seemed not even to have noticed her absence. She was purposefully distant and elusive on occasion, which caused him to smile in that same knowing way, and when she was coy and coquettish he was appropriately courtly. But he did not respond the way the other men Catherine allowed to call upon her did; his affection for her, when he showed it, was measured and deliberate, and his manner unfailingly and aggravatingly proper.

Yet she knew he was a passionate man; she had seen desire light his eyes; or perhaps it was only her own, reflected in his cool stare, which brought the flush of color to her cheeks. One evening, returning her home after a quiet sail on the lake, he kissed her, and she nearly swooned with pleasure. It was all she could do not to clutch him tightly to her, keep him from leaving in any way that she could, drag him into her home and upstairs to her bedroom. But of course she did not, though later, in the darkened privacy of that room, she touched herself with eager hands, imagining that they were his.

But despite her yearning, Leighton Blake did not fall easily into her arms, or she into his. The courtship, if such it could be called, continued; the kisses grew more passionate. He could have had her any time, if not by his own desire then by her own failed will.

And then, suddenly, tragedy struck twice in the Blanchard family. Within a month, both Sonnet McBride and Caleb died.

Sonnet was hardly gone a fortnight, still grievously missed by both Maddy and Catherine, when one of Kinnikinnick Jim's grandsons brought word of Caleb's death from pneumonia. The news greatly distressed Catherine, who felt guilty for her recent neglect of both Sonnet and Caleb—caused largely by her obsession with Leighton Blake. But Maddy was devastated. She walked through the rooms of Broadview like a ghost stalking some ancestral mansion; she closed herself in her room, emerging infrequently—and when she did, she was uncharacteristically disheveled and her eyes were swollen with tears. Catherine did not understand it—Maddy had never seemed all that fond of her brother-in-law—and even Abel was surprised by the duration and magnitude of his wife's grief.

When he heard of Caleb's death, Leighton Blake sent a note to the Blanchards, as was proper; two weeks later, on a Sunday evening, he came to call. When the conversation turned to the disposition of Caleb's Bluff, he listened with interest. For the

Bluff, where Caleb Blanchard had made his first and final home in Seattle, had been willed to Catherine.

Caleb's last testament had been much under discussion that weekend. Abel pronounced himself satisfied, if perplexed: "At least he didn't leave the Bluff to the redskins," he said.

"But Father," Catherine protested, "the Indians were living on the land when Uncle Caleb claimed it."

"Of course, there's all that nonsense he added to his will about not disturbing their bones, but we can get around that," her father continued, as if he had not heard her.

"What do you mean?" asked Catherine, astonished.

"Now that Caleb is gone, there's no reason to let the Bluff be," Abel replied. "I understand there's some Canadians who want to develop it. Of course, we'll have to clear it first, and timber prices are down some. But even so, it will turn a tidy profit."

"Father," said Catherine, "that's not what Uncle Caleb had in mind at all!" The Bluff was in her care; she was its steward, not its ruiner. "You may tell those gentlemen in Canada that there will be no development of the Bluff," she said firmly.

"Now, Catherine—" Abel began, but she interrupted him.

"Uncle Caleb would positively spin in his grave, that's what he would do, and I refuse to hear another word about it!" she said, and Abel, who couldn't understand why both his wife and his daughter were behaving so oddly, retreated. In time, he thought, Catherine would listen to reason. After all, development of the Bluff was to the city's advantage as well as her own, and she was a Blanchard, wasn't she?

*　　*　　*

Catherine had not returned to Vassar after Caleb's death, or ever. She had had enough education, she declared; her real interest had always been music, not arts or letters, and she wheedled a new Steinway out of Abel, to replace the old spinet that had come across the plains with her father's first wife. Abel was delighted to have her at home again. Two years was enough education, he declared, at least for a woman. Her brothers had graduated from college—Elijah from the university, and Matthew and Lucas from Stanford, which was where the sons of wealthy Northwesterners who wanted polish as well as learning went—but too much learning, Abel said, made a woman hard to get along with. Miss Nellie Cornish had started an arts school on Capitol Hill, and Abel was pleased to encourage Catherine's musical studies there. "It is as good instruction as I could get anywhere else, Papa," she told him. "And you know how much I've missed Seattle." That was true—however, Leighton Blake was at least as important a cause of Catherine's decision not to finish her degree in the East. She might have fooled Abel, but if so he was a willing dupe; he had had Blake in mind for his daughter from the beginning, and by remaining in Seattle she might yet achieve what he wanted for her. If not Blake, Abel reasoned, it would be someone else; he would find her a suitable match so that he need not worry about her bringing home some Easterner he knew nothing about or, worse yet, one of those socialists or anarchists who were stirring up so much trouble in town lately. As he told Maddy when Catherine declared her intention to cut short her studies at Vassar, she'd be married and gone from Broadview soon enough, and he saw no reason to sacrifice any of the time he had left to enjoy her.

On a spring afternoon almost a year after Catherine met Leighton, she took him to the Bluff. He rode Caleb's mare and she rode Mr. Rochester. She showed him the orchards, the trees bursting with new blossoms, the swale where the trillium bloomed sweetly, and the caves under the cliff where the Indians had stored their potatoes as well as the sacred mound where their ancestors' bones were interred. Finally they stopped the horses at the highest point on the Bluff, above the silvery curl of a steamer's wake that lapped gently against the deserted beach.

"I could dock my entire fleet down there and never even notice it from here," said Leighton, who had been thinking for some time of acquiring a drydocking facility to refurbish his wooden steamers, or perhaps a shipyard where he could build boats that, like Josh Green's *Flyer*, could cut an hour off the twenty-eight-mile trip between Seattle and Tacoma and more on the runs to and from the mill towns on the sound.

Catherine hardly heard him. She was trapped once again in the time-stopped lethargy that habitually gripped her in his presence. She got down from her horse and walked slowly to the edge of the cliff. For a moment she considered throwing herself off it, giving herself up to sky and wind and disappearing beneath the green waters that glistened dangerously below. To end this torture—for so she thought of her passion for Leighton —to have done, finally, with this fever that possessed her, turned her into a weak, mewling thing who wanted only to hear the silken murmur of his voice, feel his hands on her, his touch, his body against hers—that, she thought, would be a relief.

"Come, now, it can't be as bad as all that," he said, and for a startled second she thought he had seen into her thoughts.

She turned to him. "Can't it?" she said boldly, and at that he took her into his arms and kissed her for a long time. Her mouth opened of its own volition; her tongue sought his and he consumed it, licking, nipping, sucking at it with a hunger that thrilled her deeply.

When she finally pulled her mouth from his, her knees buckled; had he not held her so tightly, she would have plunged from the cliff as surely as if, a moment earlier, she had willed it to happen. Instead she fastened her arms even tighter around his neck, and tumbled with him down the few yards of the slope. When their bodies came to rest, he lay atop her, and she breathed in the smell of him—tobacco and leather and the salty air, mixed with a spicy orange scent and something even stronger and sharper, the odor of a man's desire. He tried to rise, but she would not let him.

"Please . . . now," she whispered, and he hesitated. "Yes," she added. "Now."

"You don't know what you're saying," he said hoarsely. "Catherine, you're so young . . . we mustn't . . . I shouldn't. . . ."

She drew him to her with her arms and moved her body beneath his. He fell on her with a soft moan, and only the terns, wheeling and screeching overhead, heard the sounds they made as, trembling with pleasure and delight so overwhelming that she never felt the instant of pain when he entered her, she possessed him, and he her.

Shortly after sunset they left the Bluff. He would be departing for Alaska the next day, he told her; he had business there and would be gone for some time. On the drive back to the city, he was very quiet, and Catherine was filled with apprehension. Surely he would bring up the subject of their future, she thought. Unless . . . because . . . because she had . . . and then she banished that idea as quickly as it had surfaced in her jumbled thoughts. True, he had not said he loved her. But certainly he must be feeling as she was, that what had occurred between them was but a promise of the happiness to come.

Or was it? She knew that Leighton Blake was no innocent—rumor had it that he spent a considerable amount of time at Lou Graham's palatial three-story brick house on Washington Street, along with other prominent men of the town. Her mother's friends, especially Mary Denny, had been trying to close down Mrs. Graham's establishment for years; it was notorious from the Barbary Coast to the Canadian border. But the more perspicacious and profit-minded men of the city refused, and the mayor, knowing whose goodwill mattered more, allowed the madam to conduct her business without interruption.

Leighton would have no further need of the services of Lou Graham's young ladies, Catherine decided. From this day forward, she would love no other man, and she would keep him in such thrall that he would desire no other woman. After a suitable interval—as brief as propriety demanded, given her recent bereavement—they would be married, and that would settle everything.

*　　*　　*

The weeks following Leighton's departure seemed to Catherine like the strange contraption she had ridden the year before at the Exposition, which whirled her up in the air one moment and dashed her earthward the next. She spent long hours in the music room, playing sentimental Chopin preludes over and over again on the Steinway. She wrote long letters to her friend Ruth, describing in loving detail the man who had captured her heart. She went to the Bluff once, but without Leighton it was a lonely, empty place, even as its hillsides turned yellow with Scotch broom and the rhododendron trees that stood as high as the roof on Caleb's house blossomed into luxuriant pink and white abundance.

Her mother seemed somehow to know that something had

occurred and was uncharacteristically sympathetic; she treated Catherine with the exaggerated gentleness of one tending an invalid, and although she said nothing directly—for they were not in the habit of intimate conversation—Catherine could feel her understanding and was comforted by it. She did not tell Maddy what had happened on the Bluff, and soon she did not have to.

Leighton was back in the city for several days before he called on Catherine; she had known almost the moment he set foot in Seattle, for her circle comprised that select company of people who knew everything of importance that occurred in the city, since their husbands and fathers and brothers made much of it happen. A few surmised that Catherine had a particular interest in Leighton, especially Dorothy Stimson, cousin to the Miss Flood who had accompanied him to the gala ball nearly a year before. Dorothy, thought Catherine, took an unhealthy pleasure in revealing that Leighton Blake had visited not only Alaska but also San Francisco, where he had called on her cousin—not once but several times.

Catherine was completely undone, as much by the news of where Leighton had been, and with whom, as by the information that he was back and had not yet called on her. Until then she had not doubted for a moment that her affections were returned.

She was sure her father shared her views. Without knowing of Catherine's condition, he would have welcomed Leighton Blake as his son-in-law. On several occasions he had voiced his opinion that the man had "the right spirit"—which to Abel meant that he was a hard worker who believed in progress, and in Seattle's destiny. Though still hale in body and constitution, Abel was nearly eighty, and he wanted his daughter's future settled before he died. He was leaving her well-off—she would be a wealthy woman, even without Caleb's Bluff, which young Blake, if he married Catherine, would convince her to relinquish for the greater good of everyone concerned.

Maddy was not as pleased as her husband with the prospect of Leighton Blake as a son-in-law. She had never voiced her misgivings to Abel, but she thought Blake was a bounder, an opinion she kept to herself even on the morning she found

Catherine retching helplessly into the china basin in her bedroom, a few weeks after the young man's departure from Seattle.

She took away the basin and helped Catherine into bed. Bathing her face with a clean cloth, she said, "You mustn't marry him if you don't love him, Catherine. That would be an even greater sin."

"But I do love him, Mama," she replied. "I'm not certain, though, that he loves me."

"Why, of course he does!" Maddy said briskly, as if that settled everything. "But just you remember . . . if you're going to change your mind, do it before you marry him. We'll take care of things." She hesitated, as if to say more, but then she stopped. "Your father will want to speak with him as soon as he returns."

"Oh, no!" cried Catherine. "First let me tell him . . . please, Mama!"

"All right," said Maddy. "But I wouldn't wait too long. People will talk as it is." She frowned. "Still, there's worse things."

"Like what?" In spite of herself, Catherine was interested—she didn't know of anything worse than what had befallen her, at least as far as Maddy was concerned, and she was surprised that her mother was taking it so calmly.

"Like doing the right thing for the wrong reason," Maddy replied, and then she leaned down and kissed Catherine. "Rest now," she said, and left the room.

When Catherine finally saw Leighton again, she was shy with him. They went to the Bluff as before. and she waited for him to take her in his arms once more. When he did—after they made love, she decided—she would tell him.

But he did not touch her, not that afternoon. Instead, he chatted lightly about the places he had been, the things he had done; while mentioning that he had been in California, he said nothing about Dorothy Stimson's cousin.

Finally, awkwardly, she reminded him of what had occurred on their last visit to this very spot. He agreed that it had been wonderful and referred to the abandon with which she had met his own passion with such frankness that her cheeks burned, though his voice was gentle and unteasing and his manner loving. But he made no effort to repeat what had happened, and she was flooded with embarrassment and horror when she concluded that he no longer desired her. How could she tell him now? she wondered—and worse, how could she not?

She stumbled over the words, got them out somehow—the words she had rehearsed so carefully, spoken aloud to her pier glass, imagining how love would soften the hard planes of his face, and happiness glow in his eyes. The words stuck in her throat with such agony that finally, as understanding dawned in those same inky depths, he stopped her.

"Well," he said. And then, "Well, well, well."

Confused, she waited for him to continue. This was nothing like the scene she had imagined.

"I suppose you'll want us to marry," he said finally, and Catherine flushed an even deeper red.

"Not if you don't want us to," she said. "Not if you don't . . . love me."

He smiled. "Why, of course I love you," he said, and then his eyes grew thoughtful. "It's just that this is not a very good time. I've had some business reverses, you see—revenue is down, it's this damn rate war we don't seem to be able to stop, and—oh, but things aren't that bad, don't look so worried, you don't want to hear this, do you?" Finally, he took her in his arms and kissed her gently. "That's it, then," he said. "I'll speak to your father this evening."

For the first time in five weeks, Catherine was happy. Leighton Blake loved her, and they were going to be married. If his initial reaction had been less than she had hoped for, it was doubtless due to his worries about business. Her father could help him with that, she thought confidently. He was a very important man, and he would want to do everything possible for his son-in-law. Of course, Leighton Blake was not without resources of his own. But anything he lacked, the Blanchards could provide.

Chapter Twelve

Catherine was an exquisite bride—everyone said so —and hers was a wedding Seattle society talked of for months afterward. Maddy, rousing herself from the queer funk into which she had slipped after the deaths of Sonnet and Caleb, was uncharacteristically free with Abel's money and executed the lavish celebration as if she had had a year rather than only a few weeks to plan it.

Remembering how she and Sonnet had shopped for her own wedding dress, she took Catherine to San Francisco to purchase a trousseau. In an elegant shop on Maiden Lane she found a discreet dressmaker, who was understanding about allowing for a slight increase in fullness, particularly in bust and waist. The resulting creation was a masterpiece of camouflage, a gown of shirred white georgette crepe frosted with princesse lace that trimmed a lappeted bertha, which draped softly over the pouched waist and full trained skirt shirred in lace-trimmed folds. The day of the wedding Catherine's gold-red hair was teased into a pompadour of the sort worn by Gibson girls—that style was long since passé in New York but just coming into vogue in Seattle.

The full veil that hid Catherine's eyes and shaded her creamy skin from the sun that summer day in Maddy's rose garden at Broadview was crowned by a rounded puff of pearl-encrusted tulle. In silk-gloved hands the bride carried a bouquet of peonies, orchids, and asparagus ferns, which she tossed directly to Ruth Straus after the reception at the Sunset Club. Then she and Leighton drove away from the assembled company of three hundred guests in Harry Treat's tallyho, that same vehicle in which she had been a passenger the first time she laid eyes on the handsome stranger who was now her husband.

For stranger he was, she realized, despite the intimacy of the act that had led directly to the celebration just ended, an act that had not been repeated since that day on the Bluff. That was the one cloud on Catherine's horizon: that she had not rushed so precipitously into marriage only because she could not bear to be separated from Leighton for an hour, or even a day, but because in six months she would have his child. She expressed that doubt to Ruth Straus, who had come to Seattle to be her maid of honor and guessed Catherine's condition as soon as she laid eyes on her.

Catherine had written Ruth immediately, despite Abel's disapproval—he could not understand why one of Mary Denny's daughters, or Dorothy Stimson, or even one of his daughters-in-law was not a proper attendant for the occasion. But Ruth was Catherine's dearest friend, and she wanted—no, she needed—her by her side on such a momentous, life-changing day. For she was not so far advanced from that feisty young girl she had been, who knew that love, for all its sweetness, could dissipate a woman's courage to be true to herself; she and Ruth, in their dormitory room at Vassar, had spent endless hours analyzing it. Free love was very much the fashion in those days, and Ruth, for one, proclaimed herself a champion of it.

Of course, Ruth was more of a rebel than Catherine had ever been—she had shocked her own parents by defying convention in ways Catherine never dreamed of. Why, she had even lived openly, for a time, with a young muckraking journalist who was not only poor but Christian—which of these traits disturbed the elder Strauses more was not certain, but what was clear was that Ruth and her young man had had a serious falling-out, which made Catherine's invitation to come to Seattle for her wedding particularly well-timed.

Vassar, and especially Ruth Straus, had exposed Catherine for the first time to ideas that most of her Seattle friends, and certainly her family, would have found heresy. Marriage was not a covenant of true minds, nor maternity the highest and best use of a woman's talents, but a male conspiracy, Ruth told her, which turns a woman into someone who is not a person at all but a unit, social and economic, in which the good of the individual is sacrificed to that of the state. Catherine feared Ruth might be right, for though she was still consumed by love and desire for her husband, she felt invaded by the child she carried in her womb, changed in both shape and essence. The last weeks had not been easy. Maddy had cautioned her to avoid her usual activities, especially riding, and she missed Mr. Rochester almost as much as she missed that innocent, girlish self she had abandoned when she fell willingly into Leighton's arms—shamelessly and hopelessly, like a girl with no education or common sense.

Free love indeed, she mused—for her, at least, it had extracted an expensive price. Not that she didn't want to marry Leighton —she had always expected, someday, to marry, and she truly adored him. But there were other things she wanted to do too, dreams she supposed she would now have to abandon. She knew she possessed musical talent, which Frank Damrosch, the director of the Institute of Musical Art in New York, had urged her to pursue it. And she had. Nellie Cornish's little arts school was growing, and she had engaged Dent Mowrey, the pianist and composer, to teach the most advanced pupils. She would study with him—although how she would play when her stomach intruded between her hands and her instrument was a matter of some concern.

"You mustn't give up your music," Ruth had told her, "no matter what." That conversation, the night before the wedding, with the two of them tucked into bed and chattering away as they always had, each secretly worried that time and distance had dimmed the specialness of their friendship, was the first time Catherine had admitted her doubts to anyone. Maddy's words rang in her head. Was she, as her mother had warned, doing the right thing for the wrong reason? Ruth said no. "After all, if you love him, that is the right reason," she told Catherine.

Well, of course she did, Catherine thought, and in her secret heart the real source of her doubt resounded. Did he, in fact, love her?

Catherine's shyness with Leighton had dissipated, and her

independent and questioning nature had reasserted itself, but she was still plagued by uncertainty about his true feelings for her. There had been those agonizingly long weeks when he had not called her. There was Miss Flood in San Francisco. And there had been other young ladies, too numerous to mention, with whom he was known to have dallied. Lou Graham's girls she did not worry about, but there was the fact that he had not made love to her since that one occasion on the Bluff—had, in fact, approached her since then with a chaste respect that tormented her, for the memory of his body on hers, in hers, remained with her as strong as ever. And under the net-swathed russet tocque that complemented her traveling ensemble, she felt herself blush.

As if he had read her mind, Leighton turned to her, and his warm, admiring, and, yes, loving glance stilled her doubts. If he felt forced into this marriage, nothing in his manner betrayed it. Of course, no pressure, overt or otherwise, had been brought to bear on him by her family. Maddy had kept her knowledge of Catherine's condition from Abel, who in any case had no objections to hurrying the wedding along if Maddy and Catherine wanted to. Weddings, after all, were women's business, and he'd just as soon see his only daughter settled and taken care of as quickly as possible. The death of his younger brother made him feel the hot breath of mortality on the back of his own neck, and although he did not mention it to Maddy, his chest had been paining him for some months now.

Maddy went about planning the wedding, and Catherine on that day squeezed herself into her stays and hoped her condition was not obvious. And now, as the tallyho arrived at the pier and her handsome husband lifted her down from it, she determined that she would not permit her probably foolish concerns to spoil one second of the honeymoon.

"It's not as grand as our house will be," said Leighton, leading her along the dock to his sloop. "But for now I think it'll do just fine." And she nodded in agreement. She was silly to doubt his love, this dashing, generous man who wanted so much to give her the kind of life her father had raised her to expect. As he had told Abel only the night before, while she was up in her room gabbing with Ruth Straus, within a year Catherine would be the mistress of the finest home in the Northwest.

Leighton's elaborate plans for the estate he was having built out at the Highlands met with Abel's approval. Of course, he would have preferred that the couple be closer—say, on the fine lot a few blocks away from Broadview which he had at first planned to give them as a wedding gift. But, he had to admit, young Blake was smart to have snapped up a spectacular five-acre site north of the city in the exclusive compound laid out by the Olmsteads, who had designed Seattle's extensive, graceful parks and boulevards.

Abel himself had thought the Highlands a good investment and had been tempted to buy some property there, but Maddy pooh-poohed the idea. "It's at land's end," she said, "and you'd be beside yourself, that far away from your old friends." The cronies she referred to were dying off with alarming frequency. Abel was one of the last of the original pioneers extant, and he spent a good number of hours each day visiting those who were still among the living, most of whom had homes within walking distance of Broadview and were happy to sit with him and relive the good old days. Maddy herself wasn't the most garrulous of companions—she always had her nose stuck in a book, and since Caleb's death she'd been especially withdrawn, which sometimes caused Abel to remember how Sara had gone daft on him just before she died.

No, the Highlands wasn't for him, although he could understand the opportunity it presented for a young couple. He listened as Leighton outlined his plans—why, he'd even engaged an architect who was coming all the way from Alabama to design the house. The Highlands had been an immediate success with wealthy Seattleites who felt crowded by the increasingly fractious and demanding hordes stirring up trouble in town. Loggers and laborers, socialists and anarchists had drifted into the city after the recent recession and, finding that no more jobs were available there than anywhere else in the country, were demanding that people like Abel and Arthur and the Skinners and Eadys and Boeings and Weyerhaeusers share the riches they had wrested from the sweat of the working class. And that wasn't all they wanted—they wanted the resources they found in the city, and the means to control them. They were agitating for public ownership of power, streetcars, water, and other utilities, and not a man jack of them, Abel declared, knew more than a gnat about what to do with them if they got them, which in his lifetime, he fervently hoped, they never would.

Leighton Blake agreed. The lower classes were causing him some trouble too, demanding higher wages than he could afford to pay. It might not be the best time for it, but he persisted in his plans to build Catherine a mansion in the Highlands. Abel admired his spirit—it was people like Leighton Blake, who refused to give up on Seattle in the tough times but instead redoubled their efforts, who made the city as great as he had always envisioned.

Abel wished he knew more about Blake's background, although, he told his wife, "Who he'll be is more important than who he was." And who Leighton Blake was, as far as he could determine, was a transplanted Southerner who still, ten years after he'd emigrated to the Northwest, carried a trace of his Alabama drawl. His grandfather was a wealthy cotton grower before the Civil War, and his father had been successful enough to educate Leighton and provide him with sufficient capital to buy his first paddle-wheel steamer. And now he was building his own maritime empire. It wasn't near as big as Josh Green's yet, but someday it would be, said Leighton, and Abel believed him.

"I know you're keen to build, son, but you've said yourself, times are hard, and there's a certain amount of risk involved. And even if you do go ahead—mind, I'm not telling you not to, just suggesting you hold your horses a bit before you start—it will be months before your house is ready for occupancy," said Abel. "We've a whole lot of house here that will be mighty empty when Catherine leaves." He rubbed his eyes. "Lord, it seems only yesterday she was a baby, just when Maddy and I thought our family was complete. Elijah was already in college and Matthew and Lucas in high school when she came along." His face softened, and Leighton could have sworn he saw tears glisten in the corners of the old man's eyes. " 'Course you never knew Elijah," he went on. "A fine lad . . . a fine lad." Leighton listened in respectful silence as Abel reminisced about the son he'd lost in the Spanish-American War. He knew Abel's other sons, both of whom seemed to have inherited their father's rather plodding personality along with his devotion to conserving the Blanchard fortune.

That was the trouble with the pioneers, thought Leighton, not for the first time. They had made their pile and they were content to sit on it, avoiding anything that smacked of risk, even if it promised an even greater fortune. Abel Blanchard himself could not be moved to gamble with any of what he'd wrested from Seattle—today, as ever, he refused to speculate on anything he could not see or touch and had bowed out of some business deals that weren't grounded, literally, in land. He'd put all his eggs in a very few baskets, notably the Alki Land and Development Company, and he'd made a pretty good thing of it, too. Not all Abel's land was over in West Seattle; his holdings extended far beyond the city's borders, in coal and gold mines, in real estate throughout the state, in wheat ranches east of the Cascades and timberlands west of it. Blanchard's considerable wealth was certainly not on display in this big house, which, while comfortable enough, was nowhere near as lavish and elegantly appointed as the great mansions of Leighton's native South. Not like Belle Rive, his grandfather's magnificent plantation, for instance, and not like the fine old homes in the Garden District of New Orleans, where his sister lived. He returned there often to visit, not as much out of fraternal devotion—even if she was his only surviving relative—as to avail himself of the beautiful mulatto women of the French quarter.

It was not typical of even the richest families in Seattle to display their wealth ostentatiously or to live in great luxury. They tended to retire behind the ivied walls of huge old houses like this one and live modestly, with none of the showy splendor Leighton loved. In that respect he was different from most, even his friend Joshua, whose wife, Missy, still saved string and served the most niggardly meals, with the smallest portions, as if at any moment her larder might be empty. Leighton Blake swore he would never live like that.

His home in the Highlands would be as splendid as Sam Hill's castle up on Queen Anne Hill, furnished with the finest that money could buy. His ships would fly his flag from Puget Sound to Skagway. He'd make a fortune bigger than Abel Blanchard's.

After all, he considered as he smiled down at his bride, he had a pretty good start on it already.

* * *

No one could say that Ruth Straus had not been treated courteously during her visit. As Catherine's friend, she was accorded respect, and the Blanchards had not indicated in any way that she was not welcome at Broadview. But as she packed her clothes the day after the wedding, she reflected that no one had been especially warm or even more than polite. So why, she wondered, was she seriously considering remaining in Seattle?

She pulled aside the heavy curtains and opened the leaded glass windows. The air was sweet and salty, heavy with the fragrance of roses wafting up from Maddy's meticulously tended garden and tinged as well with a damp, briny bite. The sun had been playing hide-and-seek with the clouds all day—the sky was the color of pewter, and a blanket of soft gray mist enveloped the city.

There were no sharp edges here, no extremes, she thought, not in the climate or the people. No one appeared to be very rich —not even Broadview or any of the other fine houses of the city held a patch on some of the great homes of Manhattan, like her own family's opulent Fifth Avenue mansion. Nor did there seem to be, on first view, many truly poor people—"I expect you'll be disappointed by our slums, there really aren't any here," one friend of Catherine's had remarked, on hearing that Ruth had been working in a settlement house on the Lower East Side of New York. And Catherine's father, shaking his head in agreement, had proclaimed in a voice that brooked no opposition, "Anyone who's not afraid of hard work can find a job here, and good riddance to the rest of them."

In the days before the wedding, while Catherine was occupied with a thousand details Ruth couldn't help with, she was left to her own devices; an inquisitive and independent young woman, she had set out to learn what she could about the city. As far as she could determine, Seattle seemed to be much as the Blanchards and their friends portrayed it—a place where the evils of filth, disease, poverty, vice, and corruption did not appear to exist. Yet there were indications that all was not as rosy as it appeared to be. Loggers, migrant workers, and seamen were flocking to Seattle, voicing their dissatisfaction with the "interests" on every soapbox in the downtown area—anarchists, socialists, Wobblies, Reds, yellows, reformers, populists, and progressives of every stripe. At an impromptu rally one afternoon, she listened to a bunch of rough-looking sourdoughs who had tried and failed to make their fortunes in the Alaska goldfields cheering an I.W.W. organizer. The I.W.W. representative played skillfully on their discontent, bringing the crowd's resentment to fever pitch. In their thunderous roars of approval at the Wobbly's words, she felt their anger at the callous disregard of the powerful and wealthy for the fate of the lower classes. At the Red News Wagon on Fourth Avenue and Pike street, she picked up a copy of the labor newspaper, the *Union Record*: "Who brought this anarchist trash into my house?" Abel thundered when he found it in the parlor where she had inadvertently left it. Making a sound in his throat like a dog deciding whether to attack an intruder, he deposited the offending tabloid in the fire; Ruth, in an act of moral cowardice she later justified as a guest's obligation—"when in Rome," and all that—made no move to claim it as her own, but she assumed from the icy stare Abel leveled at her that he knew she was the culprit.

The daughter of a cultivated family of German Jews who had come to America the same year Abel Blanchard arrived in Seattle, Ruth's politics were as much a burden to her own parents as they might have been to the Blanchards had it been Catherine who espoused them. After finishing college and returning to New York, Ruth had fallen in with a group of bohemians, artists and musicians, and through them met a young journalist named Lincoln Steffens. Lincoln had awakened in her a social consciousness and a judgment of her own privileged life. The trouble was that she didn't want to live among the less fortunate, and when she returned to Fifth Avenue from her work at the settlement house, she wanted to wash the grime away from her soul the way she cleansed it from her hands and face. But in New York there was no way to escape the wretchedness of life—it was everywhere, even outside the gilded porticos of her own home. Yet she did sincerely want to help the helpless, the women and children whose labor was being so ruthlessly exploited by men no different, really, from her father—or Catherine's. If there was a way to do that and still enjoy the feel of a silk dress on her creamed skin, or allow the beauty of a sonata to transport her beyond the world's ills, she thought she could make a contribution.

Catherine's invitation had come at an opportune time for Ruth. Her romance with a colleague of Lincoln's, which had so scandalized her family, had ended badly—despite her attempts to shake off her bourgeois upbringing, she discovered, something in her yearned for a more conventional relationship than the one she had enjoyed with him. Without him, their flat in a tenement on Delancey Street soon lost its charm, yet in the genteel and rarefied atmosphere of her parents' home she felt stifled. And even the work she had so assiduously undertaken, helping the poor Eastern European Jews who had fled the pogroms of Russia and Poland for the safety of America, seemed unimportant—especially when her father, simply by reaching into his capacious pockets, could do so much more for them than all her efforts to find them jobs, teach them the language of their new country, and guide them through their first months as greenhorns.

Not that Eli Straus's philanthropy extended to his less fortunate brethren—not often, anyway, and not until Ruth told him that she would cease her settlement house work only if he made a generous contribution to the cause she had adopted as her own. Like most wealthy German Jews, he considered himself unrelated to the unfortunates who followed his own migration to the United States. Coreligionists they might be, but that was all Eli Straus had in common with his wretched *landsmen*, and it was only his desire to get his favorite daughter away from them that stimulated his charity.

Ruth moved back into her childhood room and, within months, back into the life she had been so eager to throw off. Only it was worse this time around—after her lover's passion, the timid kisses of the escorts her parents considered suitable made little or no impression. After the exciting companionship of the best minds of her time—loud, noisy, beery evenings arguing politics with Steffens or Charles Edward Russell or Ida

Tarbell—she could not bring herself to feign even the remotest interest in the financial coups of a Schiff or a Warburg. Only music interested her; it was what had drawn her and Catherine together and made possible, in the beginning, the friendship between two girls of such vastly different backgrounds and—on the surface, at least—such dissimilar temperaments. Ruth played the violin, and Catherine the piano. Ruth, the older by two years, was a more technically accomplished player, but Catherine, she knew, was eminently more talented. "We could make some beautiful music together," she had laughingly ventured the first time she heard Catherine play. And the delicately lovely girl with the arresting green eyes and porcelain skin had smiled tentatively back at the plump black-haired girl in the practice room and replied, "Do you know the second movement from the Jupiter?"

It had begun then, and when Catherine wrote her of her decision to remain in Seattle instead of returning to college, Ruth was crestfallen. For they had shared everything—clothes, scores, confidences. Catherine's brief visit to New York the previous autumn had made Ruth realize how much she missed that closeness, even though all Catherine talked about during the entire time was Leighton Blake. Ruth was predisposed to dislike the man, and when she met him, she did. It might have been the sneering way he dismissed her as not worthy of his attention that hardened her conviction that he was simply not the right man for Catherine. That Leighton had no more use for Ruth Straus than she had for him did not bother her, unless he interfered with her friendship with the woman who was now his wife. And that really didn't matter either, she thought, if she returned to New York as she planned, the next day, to do.

"Oh, do stay!" Catherine had urged her. "We'll have such a wonderful time—we can play together again! Did I tell you, Leighton is building me a music room?" She couldn't believe her good fortune—with both the man she loved and her best friend in Seattle, her life would truly be complete. Of course, she thought but did not say, Ruth might have difficulty making friends here. People in Seattle were funny about Easterners, Jews in particular. But that was because they didn't know many. With her sponsorship, no door in Seattle would be closed to Ruth. And that was exactly what she told her.

Ruth, who was not unaware of the close scrutiny that followed her in Seattle, told Catherine she would think about it. Only Harry Ault, a printer who had started *The Young Socialist* at the Equality colony, a utopian community that had sprung up near Puget Sound, had given her a truly warm welcome. She had appeared, two days before the wedding, at his office in the ramshackle headquarters of the *Union Record* and reminded him of their meeting in New York, with Lincoln, and he had taken her to Blanc's, a workingman's café, to reminisce happily about days in New York. "Why, of course you should stay," he told her enthusiastically. "Seattle needs people like you."

"Well, perhaps not exactly like me," she said meaningfully, and Ault nodded his head.

"You mustn't think everyone here is like the Blanchards," he said. "Those old mossbacks—their days are numbered, though they don't know it. Why, I wouldn't be surprised if we elect a Socialist mayor in the next election, and then we'll take back the means of production and—"

He was off on a spirited tirade, and she listened with more politeness than interest. She wasn't concerned about finding others sympathetic to her political views in Seattle—she had seen for herself that there was a well-organized minority who believed that revolution was, if not imminent, at least possible. But the undercurrent of xenophobia and, yes, anti-Semitism that she sensed in the city bothered her. Her family's unassailable social prominence had shielded her from the worst effects of such bigotry in New York, and she had assumed that out here, at the far edge of America, her religion would be no barrier to acceptance. For wasn't this the frontier, where what one did counted more than what, or who, one was? But that, like the tales she had heard of Paul Bunyan and his great blue ox, seemed to be a myth; more than one of Catherine's acquaintances had remarked that Ruth was the first Hebrew they had ever met. One young woman, at the final fitting of the attendants' gowns, had studied her undressed form so closely that Ruth could not resist asking her what she was staring at. "I've never seen a naked Jew," she had remarked blithely. "I heard you had tails at the base of your spines."

"And cloven hooves, too," Ruth had snapped.

If she stayed in Seattle, Ruth wondered, would she always be regarded as such an oddity? Would she never be accepted for who she was, as she was? For it no more occurred to her to deny her faith than to pretend that black was white, or that the ten-hour work day was just, or that bread was something to be traded for political advantage, not a commodity to feed hungry people.

Still, she considered, if she returned to New York she would hardly be able to escape that same privileged society which, if she remained in Seattle, would never accept her. And there was as much useful work for her here as there. Perhaps there were no slums, at least not as she knew them, but there were under-privileged people who would allow her to help them, social conditions still needful of remedy. And, of course, there was Catherine.

She was still thinking about it when Maddy's soft knock sounded on the door of the guest room. "May I come in?" she asked, and Ruth nodded.

"I'm just finishing my packing," she said. Of all the people she had met in Seattle, she liked Maddy Blanchard best, which had surprised Catherine.

"Mother's usually so withdrawn, buried in her books and her library work," she told Ruth. "I never believed you two would get on so well."

Maddy liked this spunky girl—had hoped, in fact, that she would succeed in dissuading Catherine from marrying Leighton Blake. In many ways, Ruth reminded her of Sonnet McBride: the same outspokenness, the same liberal political views, and a similar disregard for social convention. While she was glad she wasn't Ruth's mother—my, wouldn't that be a handful!—she had enjoyed her visit immensely. She knew how much Ruth and Catherine loved each other, and from her own experience, she knew how important it was for her daughter to have a woman friend she could really trust.

"I'd hoped you'd stay," she told her now, but Ruth shook her head.

"It's very tempting," she replied, "and you've been very kind to me. But I think I'd always feel like a stranger here—a fish out of water."

Maddy nodded her head. "I suppose so," she said. "Folks in

Seattle don't take kindly to outsiders, especially Easterners. But I hope you'll come back to visit us."

"Oh, I will," Ruth said. "I told Catherine I'd come out and help when the baby comes. And I've promised Harry Ault I'll come back and campaign for the Socialists in the next election."

Maddy smiled. "Won't that get Leighton's dander up?"

"I hope so," said Ruth frankly, and Maddy laughed.

"Well, if it does, there'll always be a room for you here," she said.

"Even if I get Mr. Blanchard's dander up too?" Ruth asked.

"Even if," said Maddy. "A little fresh air blowing through a room never did any harm by raising some dust."

Chapter Thirteen

The golden days of September ripened into a coppery autumn, and the brant geese honked noisily as they headed south from Canada, flying overhead in thick, raggedy vees that blacked out whole slices of the sky. Catherine had never been so happy. She had everything: her husband, with whom she was completely and passionately in love; their child, growing within her, visible testament to Leighton's love; and, to make it all perfect, Uncle Caleb's Bluff.

It was not hard for her to convince Leighton that Caleb's cottage was the logical place to live until the house in the Highlands was finished. "It makes no sense not to," she told him. "After all, we can't live on the *Hera,* much as I'd like to." Her eyes roamed the small but comfortable cabin of the handsome sloop that had been their honeymoon home. Leighton had outfitted it as much for living as for sailing; though he kept rooms at the City Club, he spent many nights on his boat, especially those bachelor evenings when he entertained female companions. Catherine was not unaware of that—she had found traces of them here and there, like the hairpin wedged between the pillows in the salon and the lavender-smelling handkerchief that had somehow found its way into the sail bag. She did not mention it to Leighton—now that he was married, of course, that would stop. What she did say was that it was foolish to pay rent when there was no reason to. Despite her father's oft-repeated contention that she had no head for business, as evidenced by her refusal to sell a valuable piece of property like Caleb's Bluff, she was not impractical.

At first Leighton would not hear of it. "I'm well able to provide for my wife," he told her stiffly. "I've already taken a suite of rooms for us at the Occidental Hotel—temporarily, of course, but it will do until the baby comes, and by then the house should be completed."

"Leighton, that's ridiculous!" said Catherine. "Daddy says rent is money you never see again!" Fearing that she'd wounded his pride—money was a man's business, after all—she put her arms around his neck and stroked his forehead, running her hands through his soft, thickly curling hair. "Besides, it's wonderful out at the Bluff now; this is when it's at its most beautiful. And there's a lot to be done—the orchards need seeing to, and the vegetable gardens, as well as the horses—it's my responsibility now. I have to look after it."

"You've got that Indian tribe out there to take care of it, don't you?"

"It's not a tribe, silly, it's just the Westwinds, Johnny and his family," Catherine replied. "They live in a couple of cottages out behind the cow barn. Uncle Caleb used to have a dairy, you know. Oh, lord, the butter he made—you can't get butter like that any more. And the cheese . . . oh, the cheese was marvelous!"

When she was a girl, Caleb had sold Abel his best pastureland—the dairy had never been especially profitable, since he was so often away from the Bluff, and cows need more attention than fruit trees, so it was the pasture that went to his brother's company. As Abel said, there's people willing to plunk down a lot more money for land than for milk and butter, and Caleb had no answer for that. Caleb lived simply toward the end of his life, but he was land-poor, and it was either the pasture or the orchards. To Abel's credit, he didn't take undue advantage of his brother; he gave him better than fair value for the acres of sweet grass and clover. Catherine was glad Caleb hadn't let them strip the Bluff of the plum and apple and cherry trees that stood bravely against the howling winds of winter, bare and stark against the slate gray sky, and grew plump and full in spring with pale airborne blossoms. From summer to early autumn they dropped their fruit like tribute on the rich, rolling hills, and Catherine always loved the first press, an event accom-

panied by feasting and merriment. She intended, this first year
of her ownership of the Bluff, to continue that tradition.

Though most of her uncle's business ventures had gone bad,
the house he had built some fifty years before was still sound.
Its roof was staunch against even the strongest westerly winds,
and warmth from the huge hearth in the front room that faced
the sound, or from the wood stove in the big country kitchen,
kept the house cozy as the crisp fall days followed, one beautiful
golden afternoon after another. It was clear and dry, all scarlet,
green, and yellow; Catherine thought there had never been such
a glorious autumn. She glowed with life and health, felt a kin-
ship with the land and gratitude for its abundance, as she stirred
the last of the Gravensteins into applesauce, or put up the final
batch of cucumber pickles. She had Johnny's daughter in to
help, and her youngest girl too, and, as Caleb had, she gave away
more of the Bluff's bounty than she kept. She enjoyed the tasks
of making and doing for her husband and her home. At Broadview, Maddy had retired to her library and left the care and
feeding of the house and its inhabitants to Mrs. Erickson, who
had not wanted anyone underfoot in her kitchen, but Caleb had
been an enthusiastic and exceptional cook, and Catherine had
spent many halcyon hours watching him prepare the recipes she
attempted to replicate for her new husband.

She was a good shot—although her mother disapproved and
her father thought it unsuitable for a woman, she could handle
a gun as well as Leighton could, and they roamed the Bluff
together, flushing small game from the fields and marshes. She
stuffed pheasant with walnuts from her own trees, and grouse
with oysters from her beach; she basted succulent quail and
plump rabbits with cider pressed from her trees, which were
harvested with long-handled pickers or shaken from the leafy
branches by Johnny Westwind's grandchildren. The muscles in
her arms and shoulders ached from turning the cast-iron crank,
but she loved to watch the chipper rotate and crunch the apples
into pieces small enough to place under the press plate. When
the lid was tightened, the cider flowed in a steady stream, and
the sweet aroma filled the air around her. Most of the liquid she
boiled, to kill the wild yeast and keep it sweet; some she let turn

to vinegar, which seasoned the salads she made with wild greens and Dutch cabbage. Apples became cakes, cobblers, chutney, and fritters—some she fried with the chanterelle mushrooms that grew beneath the licorice fern and salal, and she served them for breakfast with venison sausage. She could not bring herself to shoot the brant, but there was plenty of other game; the wetlands were full of mallard, teal, widgeon, and sprig, and they were tasty, especially when flavored with sage and juniper berries. She brought down grouse and doves, fried them in a pan with sweet butter, and simmered them in sauce from the ripe Nubiana plums that were sweetest in October, so that the tiny house brimmed over with a fruity fragrance when Leighton came home. And that was later and later these days, it seemed to her, although she accepted his explanations of the many demands on his time, the press of his business as well as the tasks required by the building of their "real" home.

She harvested the garden's bounty herself: plump golden onions that she stuffed and boiled, green tomatoes she put up until she ran out of room to store them, pumpkin that soon became pie and soup and sweet breads. In winter there was steelhead trout; at Christmas, along with the goose and turkey, she baked an enormous trout—filleted into two huge slabs, placed skin side down in her uncle's special extra-long pan, and sprinkled with pungent garlic buds and thyme, pepper, and celery-flavored salt. She basted it with butter, oil, and lemon juice, and when it was done baking she covered it with fresh cream she had soured the week before, then sprinkled it with scallions, and when the cream bubbled she covered the trout with parsley.

"I haven't had a feast like this in years!" her father said enthusiastically. "Not since our wedding dinner, Maddy—do you remember that?"

A shadow seemed to cross her mother's face, or perhaps it was Catherine's imagination; by the time she brought out the flaming plum pudding that capped the fine meal, Maddy looked herself again. But Abel, in spite of his good cheer, seemed suddenly old—there was an unhealthy pallor to his skin, and his arms, when they hugged her good-bye, were weak and thin. She said as much to Leighton after her parents left.

"He's a tough old bird," her husband said. "I wouldn't worry

—your father has a lot of good years left. Besides, he's got something to look forward to," he added, patting her belly, which seemed to be growing bigger by the hour. "I'd say you're carrying twins in there," Maddy had said to her that very day, eyeing Catherine's enormous stomach. In most other respects, her figure was unchanged by her pregnancy—her legs were still slim, and her arms round and firm, and her face was not noticeably fuller. From behind, she thought, catching a glimpse of herself from that vantage point in the cheval mirror as she slipped a nightdress over her head, I hardly look any different. But then she turned around and frowned at the grotesque image that looked back at her.

"Mama thinks I'm going to have two babies, not one," she said to Leighton, who grunted something unintelligible and turned over. She came to bed, feeling a little sad now that the holiday was over, and more than a little uncomfortable. She lowered her bulk onto the bed, grimacing as she heard the protesting creak of the springs, and put her arms around Leighton. But he did not respond, and she lay awake in the dark, her hands on the mound of her stomach, wishing he would turn to her and love her. Lately he had not seemed very interested in her that way, and who could blame him, she wondered, ugly and fat as she was. She began to cry then, small pitiful tears, and suddenly she was exhausted, tired from the long day on her feet, which she could hardly see beneath her bulging belly but knew were puffy and swollen. Then she thought of the time, soon to come, when she would be slender and pretty again—"my China doll," as Leighton called her—and hold her baby in her arms, or maybe babies, she considered. And she slept, knowing nothing until the next morning, when Leighton woke her and told her as gently as he could that Abel had died in his sleep the night before.

*   *   *

Catherine sat down heavily in the big wing chair by the fireplace. The last of the hundreds of people who had come to Broadview to pay their respects was gone, and her mother was upstairs—probably writing in her precious journal, Catherine thought irritably, for in truth Maddy had seemed removed from the entire day's melancholy proceedings. She had not shed a tear, not during the long drive out to Lakeview Cemetery, or during the interment, or even when the pastor spoke of her late husband's abiding love for the woman who had shared his life for forty-five years. She had greeted those who came to call with a brave smile and an appropriate measure of decorum, but it was as if they didn't really exist for her.

Perhaps she still doesn't realize he's gone, Catherine thought sadly. For her, too, it was hard to believe that her father's bulky frame would never fill the doorway again, that they would not hear his cheerful exhortations to get up, go, move, work, do, improve—"be of use," as he was often heard to say, or "show some spirit." He had been a good husband and father, she thought; she wondered whether her mother appreciated him. Though he was a man of few words, and solemn except on those occasions that drew forth his considerable sentimentality, she had never doubted his love for her. And if she had, the generous gift that was settled on her by the terms of his will was proof enough.

"I don't understand why he gave you a quarter interest in the company," Lucas had said to her an hour earlier, when Mr. Brewster, who had been her father's lawyer since his old friend Arthur Denny died, told them how Abel had disposed of his estate. "After all, your husband is pretty well fixed, isn't he?"

Catherine thought it was unseemly to be talking about money at a time like this, but her brothers showed no such scruples, and she thought their attitude—at first disbelief, and then something close to anger—was worse yet. "Of course he is," she replied. "But I am Abel Blanchard's child too." Matthew's face darkened, as if he was about to say something, but his brother put a hand on his arm to restrain him and moved to smooth things over.

"Of course, Cat," he said, "but that's not the point. The company is not like the Bluff, you know—it doesn't run itself. And you know nothing of what's involved in managing a business of so large a scope." He turned to Leighton. "I take it you'll have no objection to our continuing to manage Catherine's share."

Catherine's temper flared. It had been a long and tiring day, and her father was barely an hour in his grave—what right did these two lumbering brothers of hers have to be picking his bones, and what right did they have to assume that Leighton controlled her affairs?

She said as much to Lucas, but before he could reply Matthew said, "Well of course, since your husband put up your precious Bluff to secure that fancy new steamer he's building, we thought he'd be handling Father's legacy to you as well." He twirled his silky mustache between his thumb and forefinger, a habit that had never failed to irritate his sister.

She turned to her husband. "You put up the Bluff?" she cried. "Why? How could you? What right did you have to—" and then she stopped, seeing the anger that dimmed the light in his eyes, turning them into two lifeless chunks of coal.

"We'll talk about it later, Catherine," he said. "At home," he added meaningfully, and she suddenly became aware of the people surrounding them—not just her brothers but their wives: fat dumb Dora, who was married to Matthew, and Emily, who on the best of occasions was a bore and a gossip and at a time like this simply a snoopy presence, butting into affairs that did not concern her. "Lucas, Matthew," began Leighton, "Catherine is distressed and exhausted. In her condition, I hardly think this is the time to go into matters of this sort. I understand your concerns about Catherine's plans for her inheritance, and when she and I have discussed it, I'll certainly share her ideas for its disposition with you. Right now, I think she should lie down." And with that he took Catherine firmly by the arm and led her upstairs.

"Your mother would probably be grateful for your company now," he said, as if nothing at all had transpired in the last few moments.

"She doesn't need me," Catherine said angrily. "Leighton, how could you? The Bluff is mine. Uncle Caleb would never forgive me if—if—"

"Hush," he said, "nothing will happen to your precious Bluff. It's just security against the loan for the new boat, that's all."

"But how could you do it?" Women might not have had the vote for very long, but even in Territorial days they had been able to own property. And the Bluff was hers—she had the deed to prove it. Come to think of it, she had not seen the deed since Leighton took it from her, when he put their valuables—her good jewels, as well as bank notes and stock certificates given to her over the years by her father—into the special vault he'd had built into the grand new estate in the Highlands. "Safer there," he'd told her, and she'd agreed—the house on the Bluff, after all, was entirely made of wood, and this was right after lightning had struck a small outbuilding on the property, sending it up in flames in no time.

"Catherine, let's discuss this later," he began, but she stopped him.

"I asked you a question, Leighton," she said. "How could you do it? The Bluff is mine!"

"I thought you said it was ours," he replied coolly. "At least, that's what you said when you insisted that we move out there to that damn land's end!"

"I thought you loved it as I did." She began to weep—for her father, for the Bluff, for herself. "I thought you were happy there."

His eyes darkened with concern, and he put his arms around her, although with the bulk of her stomach between them, it was almost impossible. "I do love it, darling," he soothed her, "and of course I'm happy there. It's been a wonderful place to live, a long and beautiful honeymoon. But our own home will be finished soon, and we won't need Caleb's again."

I will always need it, she thought silently, no matter how many other homes I have. But she was silent as Leighton explained that the power of attorney she had signed, enabling him to sell those old Spanish-American war bonds that could be much better invested elsewhere, had also enabled him to use the property left her by Caleb Blanchard as collateral for his bank loan. "But I promise you, the Bluff is safe," he said. "As soon as the *Whitecloud* goes into service, I'll pay the bank back. There's never been any danger of losing the Bluff—don't you believe me?"

She stared into his eyes—this was her husband, after all, the man she had entrusted with her life, and her child's. Of course she believed him, and of course the Bluff was safe. Nothing would happen to it. But as soon as she could manage it, she was going to find, and destroy, the piece of paper that had given someone else—even the man she loved, even her husband—the right to put her land in jeopardy.

Chapter Fourteen

Catherine heard the three short staccato toots of the airhorn of her husband's automobile and wondered what had brought him home this early. Lately she rarely saw him before the evening was well advanced, and when she complained that he was a stranger to his family, he snapped at her peevishly.

"Why do you think I'm doing this anyway?" he demanded. "Do you think it's for me?" Before she could answer, he launched into a dramatic recitation of his unceasing efforts to secure the comforts—and, yes, the luxuries—that she seemed to take for granted. "I don't see how you can accuse me of neglecting you, when it's because of you, you and the children, that I'm driving myself this hard!" he said.

"I wasn't accusing you," she said soothingly, not wanting to irritate him further. Certainly he had been preoccupied with business lately—she knew from the little he told her that his steamship lines were losing money. The Seattle–Tacoma run was no longer the Blake Line's biggest profit maker; his friend Joshua Green's fast new express steamer, the *Tacoma*, had cut the time on the run to 77 minutes, and the new electric trolley that ran between the two cities—the Interurban—was attracting a growing number of passengers. The rate wars had weakened Leighton Blake's position considerably. He did not think he could hold out much longer.

For the pioneers of Abel Blanchard's generation who amassed substantial wealth, the twentieth century was a time to consolidate what they had won and conserve it; for the men like Leighton Blake who came after them, the past was only prologue. There were still fortunes to be made in the Northwest, and the war clouds that hovered over Europe looked to Leighton like opportunities. By the time of his marriage to Catherine, he had already made a great deal of money, and he was cavalier, despite her warnings, about spending much of it on the house of his dreams.

"I want a home as perfect as you are," he had told her before they were married, "a magnificent setting for a rare and precious jewel." And she was too deeply in love to disagree, even though she would have preferred a smaller, cozier house, closer to town and nearer the Bluff than this secluded enclave. Leighton was often away, and she had only the children and the servants for company. And the house, though ideally suited for lavish entertaining, was cold, drafty, and less than welcoming most of the time.

Catherine had bent every effort to make the estate a warm and welcoming haven for her husband. She had spent months looking for the right fabric, the proper wallpaper, the perfect piece of furniture. She had sent to Marshall Field in Chicago and Gump's in San Francisco for the things she could not find in Seattle, yet the house resisted her attempts to make it a home, just as Leighton ignored her efforts to bind him closer to her.

After the twins were born, she rededicated her efforts to make herself appealing to him. She had her hair cut in the new, fashionable sleek cap she saw pictured in the women's magazines, even though its natural tendency to curl, especially in damp weather, was not well served by the style. And though she enjoyed nursing the twins, she weaned them abruptly and dieted with grim determination, despite the babies' fussiness and her own discomfort; they would adjust to a bottle in time, and as soon as her milk dried up she would be fine too. It was worth it, if only to have Leighton look at her again, reach for her in the same way he once had. There was nothing she would not do to recapture his interest, even if all the talk these days was of women claiming their independence, speaking their minds, being "modern"—whatever that was. To Catherine it looked like a prescription for unhappiness. What kind of woman would want to be modern if it meant being lonely and alone? she asked

Ruth Straus the summer after the babies arrived. "Your so-called modern woman is just unhappy and unfulfilled," she told Ruth.

"Do you think I am?" Ruth asked.

"As a matter of fact, I do," said Catherine, "but which causes which, I'm not exactly sure."

"Well, I'm not either. But I would dearly love a fat, jolly baby like one of these," Ruth said, as they played with the twins on the floor of the nursery.

"And a husband like Leighton too?" In those first few months after Kurt and Nicholas were born, Leighton was a model husband, tender and considerate, perfect in almost every way. Catherine thought her life complete; she could not imagine any greater happiness than this, and only wished her friend could find it too.

"And a husband too, I suppose—after all, one can't have one without the other, can one?" Ruth said, not unkindly.

But that had been before Leighton's coolness toward her, his seeming disregard for the love she lavished on him. Though tonight he was home early; perhaps all her hard work on herself and on the house had been worth it. But after dinner, when Leighton brought up the subject of the Bluff, she knew that it, and not she, was the real reason behind his unaccustomed attentiveness.

She realized as he began to outline his plan that Leighton was not thinking about her, he was concentrating on how he could maximize the opportunities the war in Europe might put within his grasp. Every shipyard in Seattle was operating at maximum capacity, he told her, including the one that had built the *Nootka*, the first ship to carry his flag, and the *Seacloud*, the latest.

The *Nootka* had foundered some years before in heavy seas off Bellingham Bay; its cargo of lime had caught fire and burned the stern-wheeler to the water line, though not before Leighton had personally seen to the off-loading of every passenger and crew member onto one of Josh Green's steamboats.

The loss of the *Nootka* was sad, but not tragic; no lives were lost, and the ship and cargo were fully insured. The Blake Line, in the heyday of inland freight and passenger traffic, was financially sound, with a fleet of other boats to handle the demand.

Leighton and Joshua Green competed fiercely for the water trade, a rivalry that never grew bitter because the two remained close friends. They fished and hunted together in every slough and mud flat on the sound and, later on, in more exotic terrain, like Kodiak Island and even Africa. Their individual holdings increased until, between them, they virtually controlled the Mosquito Fleet.

"What do you say we get into the shipbuilding business?" Leighton asked Joshua over a bridge game at the Rainier Club a few weeks after an assassin's bullet at Sarajevo plunged Europe into war.

Joshua had misgivings; he had seen enough booms followed by busts, and what was different about this one, he said, was the growing dissatisfaction of organized labor, especially the unions in the shipyards.

"We can control them," Leighton replied. "Skinner and Eddy and the rest won't let the Reds run them out of business."

" 'Course not," said Joshua cynically. "They'll just keep giving in to their demands, the way they have already. And every time those fellows give their workers higher wages, we'll have to follow suit or they'll shut us down. You mark my words: the Reds have taken over the Metal Trades Council, and people like Ault down at that Red-backed newspaper of his are hoping the Wobblies will make good their threat and organize all the workers in Seattle into one big union, under that scalawag Colin McKay." He snorted. "Besides, where are you planning to put this shipyard of yours? I don't suppose Bob Moran's going to sell you his for a song, or even a fair price, with this boom going on."

"I was thinking about the Bluff," Leighton said, and his friend's eyes brightened.

"Well, now, if you can swing that, I might be a mite more interested," said Joshua. "I've been wanting to get my hands on that sweet little piece of land—leastaways, the tide flats—almost since your wife's uncle died. Weren't no hope of getting it away from old Caleb Blanchard before then, and I ain't sure there's hope now, either." He looked at Blake closely. "You told Catherine about it yet?"

"I don't have to," Leighton said confidently. "Catherine will do what I tell her."

Which is why he had come home early that day, it slowly dawned on Catherine. Why, after putting the twins to sleep, he had caressed her until she thought her legs would give way, and the pounding in her blood drown out even the children's cries, if they should voice them. But before she could lead Leighton to the bedroom, he told her what he had in mind for Caleb's Bluff. And then, abruptly, the pounding ceased; she heard him clearly and felt the cold invade where heat had only seconds before coursed through her.

Catherine was not a stupid woman. Leighton Blake had married her because he had got her with child and because she was Abel Blanchard's daughter. She had not known that immediately, not in those first months at the Bluff or even later, when after Abel's death they moved into Broadview to be closer to Maddy in case she needed them. But Leighton chafed under his mother-in-law's close scrutiny, and in those last two months before the twins came, although he was almost always home for dinner, he often went out again, working until nearly midnight in the Blake Line's ramshackle offices down on the waterfront.

Although no one doubted that Leighton Blake was a comer, and working harder than most men at his business, the lights burning in his offices late at night were not always illuminating his balance sheet. Sometimes they cast a flickering glow on the naked skin of one of the clerks or secretaries or schoolteachers who made up his procession of concubines.

Leighton's infidelities were not as secret as he believed. People talked. On more than one occasion, women had been seen slipping out of his office late at night, and in a city that thrived on gossip—what else was there to while away the gray mist-shrouded winters, the long rainy autumns?—his affairs were much discussed. Still, no one would have dared reveal to Abel Blanchard or to Maddy, later on, that their son-in-law was a chronic womanizer and that he was deeply in debt. Ironically, it was Abel Blanchard's death that saved Blake from financial catastrophe; though the legacy Abel left Catherine was small compared to the holdings in the Alki Land and Development Company willed to her brothers, it was still substantial enough to serve as collateral for the loan Leighton negotiated to stave off bankruptcy.

When the new house was finally finished, Catherine was torn; it was so enormous, she told Maddy, and so far away. "I'll never be able to get to the Bluff," she said, and Maddy shook her head. "You spend entirely too much time out there anyway," she said, "especially for a woman with tiny babies. Your place is at home, with them, and with your husband." So Catherine left, and it was as if that combination of events—her father's death, and her removal to the isolation of the big house in the Highlands—loosened the tongues that until then had kept her husband's illicit activities a secret. After enough veiled references, Catherine began to understand—but when she brought her suspicions to Leighton, he put them down as jealous gossip.

"You're a Blanchard, and so you are a target—we all are—for the jealousies of the rabble," he said. "The have-nots envy us; the anarchists encourage them. And those pussy-footed progressives, traitors to their class who should know better, understand that the way to attack the interests"—and here he sneered, curling his lip in such a way that he actually resembled the caricature of the war profiteers Harry Ault had run in the previous week's *Union Record*—"is to spread gossip about us." He had taken her in his arms then, and the next evening he brought her a magnificent pair of emerald earrings, which he said matched her eyes, and made love to her with such passion that she concluded that Edith Blaine couldn't possibly have meant what Catherine thought she had when she remarked that Leighton was apparently a very generous employer—his secretary, with whom he had been seen lunching at the Olympic Hotel, had taken to driving to work in her very own automobile, which was remarkably similar to the one Leighton had given Catherine when they moved out of Broadview. And that elegant gold watch, which had been Leighton's second anniversary gift to her: hadn't Miss Weems—for that, according to Mrs. Blaine, was the secretary's name—hadn't Miss Weems been wearing a remarkably similar, and similarly expensive, gold watch as well?

The rumors did much to explain Leighton's increasingly peevish behavior. Often he came home late, smelling of whiskey and cigars and something more—a woman. Or rather, women, for by now Catherine could not ignore the gossip that seemed to hang in the air whenever she joined her friends for whist at the Sunset Club or met them for lunch at the Tennis Club.

But that evening he had seemed almost like his old self—tender, romantic, loving—and so when he brought the conversation around to the subject of the Bluff, she was caught off guard.

She had thought by now Leighton understood why she could not bring herself to part with her legacy from Caleb, but it was clear as she listened to him outline his plans for the property that he did not. Since the time she learned that he had put up the Bluff as security for his new boat, they had not discussed the subject. And her brothers continued to pressure her to sell the Bluff to their company.

"I don't see why you're so stubborn about that damned Bluff," Lucas had said. "After all, Leighton's built you a huge place out in the Highlands, and a stable too."

"It's not just the horses," Catherine replied.

"Then what is it?" Matthew asked impatiently, but she had been hard-pressed to answer in a way that either of her prosaic, practical, exasperatingly logical brothers could understand.

Catherine had a difficult time putting into words the way she felt about the land. The way her heart really did leap up when she beheld it, rising almost from the water's edge to towering heights as the ferry rounded the last curve before the Bluff came into view. The way the world fell away as she hiked or rode through the fir and pine trees, their needles so thick on the forest floor that even the horse's hooves made only a muffled thud, like the Indian drums she knew had once beat their solemn tattoos in this very same place. She could not explain how or why she felt so peaceful after an hour stretched out under the flowering fruit trees in Caleb's orchards, where a gentle breeze in early April blew their blossoms over her and bathed her in their sweet, fragrant softness. She had no words to describe the comfort the landscape gave her; the peace she knew when she considered that this world had been here long before her and would remain after she was gone; the strong bond she felt, not just with her Uncle Caleb, who had loved this land and taught her to treasure its natural beauty, but with the Indians who had cherished it, even worshiped it, before the white man came.

No, Matthew and Lucas would not understand, and so she did

not try to explain. They would not understand any more than Abel, who had attempted, at first patiently and later with marked annoyance, to convince her to put her inheritance from his brother to better use.

"But what does that mean, better use?" Catherine had asked him. "What could be better than to leave the Bluff as it is—as Uncle Caleb wanted it? You've already got the biggest part of it anyway."

Abel Blanchard's face reddened, but Catherine ignored it. That Caleb Blanchard had been forced by circumstances—or, as her father put it, "his own stubborn willfulness"—to sell off part of his beloved homestead claim to his brother was family history. While Catherine loved her father, she was also loyal to her uncle, who had been a closer, realer presence in her childhood. And Caleb had never made any secret of the fact that he held Abel responsible for the ugly use to which the land had been put. The tawdry, cheaply built houses that had gone up on the land held by Alki Land and Development Company were old before they were completed. The roads had been cut through the property with only one aim: to maximize the number of lots that could be platted. Trees were cut down to clear more land, so that the hills eroded and the soil loosened, and in the torrential rains of the previous winter, several houses had tumbled into those built below them.

Catherine knew that if her brothers developed the remaining hundred acres of the Bluff, the result would not resemble their elegant drawings of gracious homes separated by tall stands of trees, belts of green between almost invisible roads, miles of horse trails and untouched orchards. No, what they would do would be quite different—would, in fact, be another version of the crimes her own father had already perpetrated against nature. And to what end? she wondered. More money? No, her brothers had plenty of money. Growth? More likely, for Matthew and Lucas, like their father, believed in the unlimited potential of growth to create wealth—more people, more business, more of everything—even though they, just like Abel, professed distaste for what growth necessarily brought about. Neither her father, before his death, nor her brothers, after inheriting his real estate empire, wanted anything to do with the people their boosterism had lured west. Behind their tidy privet hedges they maintained a wall of indifference to the newcomers. And when Catherine made friends with some of them, she was not encouraged to bring them to Broadview, or later, to the home she shared with Leighton. "They're not our kind," her father said, and Leighton echoed his words.

She had not disagreed then, respectful of her father and enamored of her husband. But now she was prepared to contradict Leighton, at least in the matter of the Bluff. She was determined to keep it safe from further despoilment, and while Leighton had encouraged her to accept her brothers' offer for the property three years before, he had not demurred when she declined.

The dispute with Matthew and Lucas severely damaged her relations with her brothers, who went so far as to engage an attorney to determine whether they, as Caleb's nephews, could reasonably lay claim to a share of the estate he had left his niece. This enraged Catherine, who was further angered when they tried to lobby Johnny Westwind to join his claim to theirs—Johnny, who everyone knew was her Uncle Caleb's natural son.

"They're not going to leave it this way, Johnny," she told him as they hiked the Bluff together one afternoon shortly after Matthew and Lucas had first approached him. "If they win, they'll destroy it. They'll dig up your father's bones, and your grandfather's, and your great-grandfather's, and their spirits will be disturbed for all eternity."

"And you?" he asked dispassionately. "What will you do with it then?"

"Not that," she said passionately. "Never that. Caleb left it to me, not them. I won't let them destroy it. If you want to fight me for it, go ahead. I think what Uncle Caleb did to you and your mother was shameful, but I can't make up for that. He wanted to keep the Bluff safe, and I intend to do that. If it's money you want, I'll give it to you. My father left me some, you know—oh, nothing like he gave Matthew and Lucas, but enough."

"Enough for what?" he teased, and she relaxed. Johnny had not been entirely ignored by his father; Caleb had provided for his education, and he had, as a result, done much better than most Indians. Of course he was only half Indian, and the other half of him was Blanchard—and though her father would have been horrified to hear her say it, he was more like Abel than Caleb. Industrious, thrifty, and hard-working, he too dealt in land, which was why Catherine feared he would ally himself with her rapacious brothers. But he showed no inclination to do so. He had no interest in "raking up the past," as he put it, especially since he had more than enough money for his own needs. "I'd rather have the Bluff in your hands than theirs," he told her. "Frankly, I doubt that I could win, on my own, and I have no desire to do so if it means being in partnership with them."

It was not her brothers Johnny Westwind hated, any more than he hated any white man. It was what they stood for, old injustices that still ate at him, despite the education and the patina of manners and civility he had acquired over the years. It was that they were Blanchards, like the man who had spawned him and refused him his name. Of course, Catherine was a Blanchard too, but that was different; she was a woman, and she loved the Bluff as he did. It was safe in her hands for now, he decided, and he refused her brothers' entreaties to join their cause, which in any case collapsed with their first efforts to legally invalidate Caleb's will. It held as written, and the Bluff remained in Catherine's control. And there it stayed until that evening several years later when Leighton Blake tried, and failed, to take it away from her.

Chapter Fifteen

Leighton dropped sail and in a few deft motions brought the *Hera* around the breakwater, unaware as he guided the sloop smoothly alongside the dock that Catherine was watching him, through binoculars, from the upstairs window.

It was on the *Hera* that they had honeymooned, what seemed like a lifetime ago. In balmy, sunny, golden days they had sailed her in and out of every tiny cove and hidden harbor in the islands that studded the Strait of Juan de Fuca like emeralds on velvet. Each night they had dropped anchor in some secluded moorage, and after hours of passionate lovemaking they would fall asleep to the gentle rhythm of the waves lapping against the boat, their naked bodies twined together on the narrow bunk, cool breezes blowing across their skin. She had discovered in herself in those weeks a deep, abiding sensuality that had thrilled her and surprised him. It was a happy surprise, she had thought then; now it seemed like a curse, for she knew that only he could ever draw it from her, like the music only a great artist can coax from an instrument; music that, once heard, renders everything else lifeless and uninspired.

She shivered, as a cold gust of wind blew in through the open French doors, and moved to close them against the storm that would arrive with the low line of clouds on the distant horizon —not long now, judging from the speed at which they were scudding south by southeast.

She was right. By the time Leighton had secured the *Hera* and traversed the hundred yards between dock and house, rain was falling in thick, glassy sheets.

She was waiting for him when he came in, with sandwiches and brandy-laced tea, but he pushed past her, stripping off his wet clothes as he went.

"You'll catch your death," she said, following him up the curved staircase to the second-floor landing and into his dressing room, where she had laid out fresh clothes.

"I have no time for that," he said brusquely. "I'm due in town in less than an hour for a meeting with the bankers." He looked at her darkly. "I'm certain my financial troubles are of no concern to you, so I shan't bother you with them. But I must bathe now, so if you'll excuse me—" And with that he strode into the bathroom, where she had drawn his tub, leaving her to ponder whether she should follow him and settle this business about the Bluff once and for all.

If he had made one gesture of conciliation then, she thought the next morning, she might have considered his arguments. She had stayed up past midnight, waiting for him to return. But he had not, and when she came awake at the sound of a wail from the nursery, she saw that it was dawn. While she'd dozed in the overstuffed chair by the window, the sky had lightened almost imperceptibly, the night's darkness evaporated into a transparent grayness that tinted the treetops' black shadows green and absorbed the gold of the lamplight at the gateposts that guarded the entrance to the Firs.

Even by the standards of the Highlands, the estate Leighton Blake had built was extraordinary, a southern plantation house faithfully recreated on a high point of land above Puget Sound. Catherine had had little say in the plans—the Firs was all Leighton's idea, based on his grandfather's great estate in Alabama that had been burned by Yankees during the Civil War. That morning the house seemed as cold and lifeless as the fire that had gone out on the hearth during the night; in spite of the fur rug wrapped around her legs, Catherine was chilly. She rose from her chair in the early morning stillness to go to her children.

In the cheerful nursery, with circus animals painted on the walls and a careless jumble of toys and books spilling from the shelves, the boys were just stirring. Kurt and Nicholas had always been light sleepers—when one cried, he woke his brother—and when the boys were only a year old, Leighton had moved out of the master bedroom and down the hall into a suite of rooms at the east end of the house.

"We'll all be more comfortable," he explained. "Of course you should be close to the children, but I can't abide their fussing and crying in the night, and I must be able to sleep—after all, I have to be in top form to provide for you all, and I can't do that if I'm tired."

She knew that for an untruth; Leighton was quick on his feet, and the number of hours he slept had little to do with it. But she did not say that, and she did not complain when he said his involvement in labor negotiations meant that for the next few weeks, or even months, he would often be coming home late. "That damn McKay and his goons are quick to take advantage, you know, and the bargaining sessions run so late I'd wake you when I came in. You need your sleep too," he said, putting his arms around her and kissing her tenderly.

Catherine didn't protest. But after that round of labor talks was done, and Leighton departed with Josh Green for a pheasant shoot in South Dakota, she called in the architects and carpenters and had a new nursery installed on the mansion's third floor. She engaged a cheerful young Swedish woman to care for the children, purchased a set of expensive, alluring French lingerie, and moved Leighton's clothes and personal effects back into their bedroom.

"You won't be disturbed by the twins any more," she told him happily when he returned. "I've moved them upstairs. Now we can be together again." And she led him up to the nursery, where the boys were happily playing a game with Inga.

Leighton said nothing, but she could tell from his tight-lipped expression that she had miscalculated. That night he made love to her for the first time in months—if you could call it that, she thought, recalling the rough way he had handled her. The intimacies he had forced on her that night had never before been part of their lovemaking, and after he had gone to sleep, she lay awake, her body smarting, her cheeks burning with remembered embarrassment. It was not love he had made to her, but something else. Always before he had treated her tenderly, though she had felt that he was holding something back. Perhaps he had been afraid to reveal himself fully to her; perhaps this was what, until then, he had never dared show her. If this was the dark side of his nature, this animal sexuality, this too was part of him, she reflected, as she shifted her sore body, seeking a more comfortable position. And if he knew that she could accept it, perhaps some good could come of it.

The next morning she had gone to the Bluff to ride, as was her custom. The Highlands had perfectly adequate trails, and Leighton had built an excellent stable as well as purchased an expensive Arabian mare. But it was not just to ride that she went to the Bluff—it was to think. And in the cold gray light of day, she knew she had been deceiving herself. But there was no one around to see her tears, and by the time she unsaddled her horse, freshened her face, and drove away from the Bluff, she could forget that she had shed them.

Arabella had been conceived that night. and Catherine thought her birth might improve things between them—Leighton had always wanted a daughter, he said. But he had remained cool toward her, and when she refused him the tidelands on the Bluff for the shipyard he wanted to build with Joshua Green, he dropped any pretense of tenderness. Instead, he purchased an existing yard, but it was not a good investment. When the war ended, business had fallen off drastically, and increasing labor troubles now cut even deeper into his slim margin of profit. Colin McKay led the shipyard workers in a walkout, and Leighton could not complete the few orders he had. The effects of the postwar recession on Leighton's business were severe, and he was convinced that the Bolsheviks were behind it. "McKay is marching to Moscow's tune," he said, "but I'll not be put out of business by those damn Reds!"

The Bluff was the solution—even at depressed prices, the property was worth a great deal. But Catherine was adamant. "I'll give you my shares in ALKCO," she offered, but he refused. "Then we can sell this house and move somewhere smaller," she countered.

He glared at her. "Out to your precious Bluff, I suppose?" he said. "Thank you, but I'm not interested." And there it remained, like a black shadow between them, robbing their marriage of the last thin rays of light it had possessed.

* * *

"Why don't you divorce him?" Ruth Straus said bluntly. They were having a late luncheon at Blanc's—it was August, the time Catherine loved most, with her dear friend here for a long visit.

Maddy had asked her the same thing—she no longer attempted to hide her distaste for her son-in-law from Catherine, although she was tolerably polite when Leighton was in her company. Since Abel's death, Maddy was much more outspoken, more outgoing, as if she'd come out from his shadow and into her own light.

Catherine shook her head in response to Ruth's question, as she had when her mother posed it.

"I don't understand," said Ruth. "You say yourself there's no love between you any more. Certainly you don't need his money. So why do you stay with him?"

Why indeed? Catherine wondered. Was it simply for appearance' sake? Or was it because, deep in her heart, she hoped somehow to regain his affection? There had been no man in her life except Leighton, and she could never imagine that there ever would be. Divorce, in her circle, had been unthinkable though her mother said that was nonsense—"Convention is simply an excuse for not doing what you don't care to do in the first place," she said. Since Maddy had come out of her library and joined the world, she said a number of things like that, surprising even her children. Not only that, she had embarked upon what Ruth called her "second career."

Catherine agreed with Ruth's assessment that being a publisher was quite a suitable occupation for her mother. But the day Maddy told her assembled family of her plans, no one could believe anything other than that the old woman had lost her head.

"I've purchased a newspaper," she had announced. The silence that greeted this statement was at first complete; then they all spoke at once, so that she had to rap her spoon sharply against her glass to gain their attention.

"I don't suppose it will give Colonel Blethen anything to worry about, but it will keep me busy, and I'll be useful. You know how your father put such store in that." Her voice faltered as she looked about her at the members of her family, children and grandchildren, seated at her dining room table. At church that morning she had dedicated a window in honor of Abel; and three generations of Blanchards gathered as they always did for Sunday dinner at Broadview, a tradition begun by Abel and continued by Maddy after his death.

Before anyone could voice an opinion, she proceeded to describe the *Journal*, which had become available for purchase after the death of its owner. Its political views were progressive and reformist, against sin and saloons and in favor of moral living and honest, open government.

"But Mother, what do you know about running a newspaper?" asked Lucas.

"How much did Phil Gorton's heirs take you for?" Matthew questioned.

Maddy fixed both her sons with a steely glare. "I assure you, I have not been taken," she said. "I have had the figures gone over by your father's lawyers and bankers. I believe the *Journal* can be profitable and, more important, provide an outlet for excellent writing. I shall see that you all receive complimentary copies of our first issue. Now . . . would anyone care for more roast, or shall we have our coffee in the parlor?"

Leighton derided Maddy's venture when he and Catherine returned home after dinner. "I think she's gone mad," he said. "I only hope your brothers are able to stop her before she loses her money as well as her marbles."

Catherine said nothing, though Maddy's announcement had come as a shock. For as long as she could remember, Maddy had been a quiet, withdrawn, and self-effacing presence who, when she wasn't attending to her family's needs, lived in her library and in her own head. Perhaps after all these years of filling it with other people's ideas, Catherine reflected, her mother wanted to express her own.

As it turned out, she did not—at least, not in her own words. Every Monday she had Henry Erickson drive her to the small brick building on Western Avenue where the *Journal*'s offices and printery were located. There she would pick up Jonathan Cape, the Yale-educated New Englander she had engaged to manage the newspaper. They would proceed to the Olympic

Hotel, where over luncheon Maddy outlined what she wished him to write in the publisher's column. "I'll leave it to you to work out the language," she said, and he did, even when he thought her opinions were outlandish. "You pay the piper, you call the tune," he said, which was an accurate description of Maddy's role in the *Journal*'s editorial content. The *Journal* rarely turned a profit, though Cape's careful management kept it from costing Maddy more money than she could afford to lose. She subsidized it from her own income, and when her sons protested, or suggested as they did annually that she sell it—"Or give it away, if you can find someone foolish enough to take it," Lucas said—she refused.

They had no recourse. Maddy was in full control of her faculties. In fact, as people often observed, she almost seemed to be growing younger. She began to go about the city more—to the symphony, to the theater, to receptions held for important visitors to Seattle, to political dinners and civic celebrations. Jonathan Cape was her escort, a small, effeminate man with prematurely white hair and bright, beady eyes behind round wire-rimmed spectacles. His voice was high-pitched and reedy, and sounded to Catherine like a badly tuned violin. When he spoke, an echoing whistle caused by the prominent gap between his two front teeth punctuated his words. He was clever and ironic, a tasteful man who seemed content with his position at the *Journal*. He lived in Washington Park in a small house near the lake, with two Siamese cats and a conservatory in which he grew begonias. He was very fond of his employer, and the feeling appeared mutual; though her sons thought her a foolish old woman—"her head filled with a lot of crazy Bolshevik ideas by that Boston nancy," as Matthew put it—she paid them no mind.

Catherine did not recognize this Maddy as the one who had raised her, but except for enjoying the discomfort her mother's actions caused her brothers, she paid little attention. She had three children to care for, a huge home to maintain, a chamber music group to which she was devoted—and her problems with Leighton occupied her thoughts as well.

"Perhaps we're each given a ration of happiness of that sort, and I've had mine," she told Ruth that day at Blanc's. "It isn't a terrible life, you know. I've the children, and my music, and the Bluff—and you, dear heart, at least for August."

"You've your mother as well, but that still isn't enough," Ruth said firmly. "You're a young woman, Catherine; you ought to..." her voice trailed away. "Why, hello, Colin, I didn't expect to see you here. What a pleasant surprise. Catherine, I don't believe you've met Colin McKay, have you?"

Catherine shook her head. Of course she'd never met Colin McKay. She'd never met the devil either. But that didn't mean she didn't know both of them existed—might even be the same, if Leighton was to be believed. Still, this sandy-haired, slightly shaggy, comfortable-looking man who held his hand out to her as Ruth made the introductions didn't look like evil incarnate. And as he accepted Ruth's invitation to join the women and sat his bulky frame down in the booth next to her, gazing into her green eyes with his friendly blue ones, Catherine thought that in this as in so many things her husband had told her in the ten years of their marriage, Leighton Blake might very possibly be wrong.

"It's good to see you again, Ruth," McKay said. "Are you staying this time?"

"Not long," Ruth replied. "I come every summer, you know, to see Catherine."

"And her other friends too," Catherine added, for in the several years since Ruth had first come to Seattle, she had widened the scope of her connections in the city and now counted among her acquaintances many of those who shared her politics. She had introduced some of them to Maddy, who aired the views of the least radical among them in the *Journal,* and to Catherine, who found them livelier and more interesting than most of the people she and Leighton socialized with.

The fondness her mother and her best friend had for each other pleased Catherine. Ruth divided her time during her visits between Broadview and the Highlands, which was actually a blessing, Catherine thought, since Leighton made no secret of his dislike for Ruth. Not that that would be a problem this month, for Leighton had been off sailing for two weeks now.

"Oh, look, Catherine, there's Anna Louise Strong," said Ruth, waving at a woman who had just entered the café. "You must meet her—she came to tea at your mother's yesterday."

"She did?" Abel would turn over in his grave, Catherine thought, if he knew that his widow had entertained the woman who'd been recalled from the schoolboard for her wartime pacifism and labeled a traitor and seditionist for her inflammatory editorial about the general strike that had crippled Seattle for three days after the war.

"Yes, Maddy wanted to meet her—you know, we've worked together in New York, known each other for years." Anna Strong, like Ruth a social worker and sometime journalist, joined them at their table, and while she and Ruth discussed her proposed trip to the Soviet Union to witness the Bolshevik miracle, Catherine studied Colin McKay.

To her surprise, he was a cultivated man. He told her that he had not missed any of the recitals presented by her chamber music group and even expressed interest in joining it should an opening occur.

"My husband would never believe it," she replied. "No one would—a man like you playing Mozart when your workers are trying to close down the shipyards."

"Not all of them," he told her, and then changed the subject, as if suddenly remembering exactly who her husband was. "I was one of Nellie Cornish's first students," he said. "That was a long time ago—my mother scrubbed floors to pay for my flute lessons."

"I didn't know you'd been in Seattle that long," she said. According to Leighton, McKay was an outsider, an agitator sent by the Communists in New York to disrupt the peaceful relations between labor and business in the Northwest.

"I grew up on Minor Avenue, three doors away from Broadview," he replied. "I used to cut your mother's lawn and prune her rosebushes—my mother was a maid for the Stimsons for a while, and we lived in their carriage house. I went to Broadway High, but when she died, I dropped out of school. I kept up with my music, though—she made me promise to."

Before the war, he told her, he had worked in the shipyards and had his first taste of labor relations when he helped organize the workers who were agitating for higher pay and an eight-hour day. He had shipped out as a seaman, and after the war he attempted to unionize the dockworkers. Like Dave Beck, who was welding the drivers and teamsters into an effective labor force, he thought the general strike was pointless. "It won nothing," he said, "and set labor back a dozen years."

Anna Louise Strong and Ruth disagreed with him violently on this point, and Catherine said, "My husband would be surprised to hear you say that. He thinks you're a Bolshevik."

"Not me," said McKay. "I don't believe that labor can make a decent wage unless business makes a profit. Leighton Blake and I probably have more in common than you think." He looked at her appraisingly, and she colored.

"I must go," she said, "It's Inga's day off, and Leighton is due home this evening. Ruth, are you coming?"

"I don't believe so," her friend said. "I told your mother I'd join her for dinner tonight. But tomorrow—shall we work on the Bach together?"

"Oh, yes!" said Catherine. "Henry will drive you out to the Firs, and we'll have the whole day together." She kissed Ruth's cheek and allowed Colin McKay to escort her to her automobile, a gleaming Pierce Arrow.

"I know these things are here to stay," he said, opening the car door for her. "Mr. Ford's put the auto in reach of even the poorest workingman. But to tell you the truth, I miss the horses."

"Do you ride?" she asked.

"Only a milk-wagon horse," he replied, without a trace of self-consciousness. "I used to drive one, you see. But sometimes at the end of the run I'd unhitch old Ned and climb up and ride him around a bit. Of course, he was practically ready for the glue factory. I used to wonder what it would be like to ride a real horse."

"Perhaps sometime you'll come and ride with me," she said, surprised at her boldness.

"I doubt that Leighton Blake would welcome me to the Highlands," he answered, and while one part of her wondered how he knew so much about her, the other thought that it would serve her husband right if she did just that—invited his nemesis to join her in a leisurely canter through the compound. He would have apoplexy, she thought gleefully. But then her good sense reasserted itself. Leighton, she thought, would simply make this nice man uncomfortable.

"I wasn't talking about the Highlands," she replied. "I usually ride out on Alki; I own some property there." Hesitantly she added, "It's quite lovely. And private, too."

"I'd be very pleased to ride with you," he said, "if you'll promise not to laugh at my clumsiness."

"I promise," she said, and climbed into her automobile. All the way home she thought about Colin McKay, and when she arrived back at the Firs, her heart was lighter than it had been in some time. Leighton, who as it turned out had come home earlier than expected, had spent the hours drinking himself into a nasty temper.

"Where have you been?" he demanded.

"Out," she said calmly.

"With those Bolshy friends of yours, I suppose," he sneered. "Your friend Ruth Straus—you know, I think she's queer," he declared.

"And what makes you say that?"

"It's unnatural—a woman like her not being married. They say Jewesses are hot-blooded, but perhaps her blood has turned, like curdled milk. I hear she's very thick with the Strong female, and you know what they say about her."

"No," said Catherine coolly, "I don't. And frankly, Leighton, I don't especially want to." She turned to go, but he blocked her way and put his arms around her. She was sickened by the smell of whiskey that emanated from him.

"Not so fast," he said, embracing her. His hands slid up under her skirt, and she tried to free herself from his grasp, but he was insistent.

"Please, Leighton," she began, "it's been a long day, and I'm tired."

"Not too tired to go gallivanting around with your queer friends," he said, and when he tried to kiss her, she turned her head away. His fingers pushed aside her lace underclothes, demanding entrance, and as she stiffened her body against the unwanted intrusion he cursed.

"You're a cold, dry bitch," he said contemptuously, and

released her so abruptly that she fell to the floor. He looked down at her, anger suffusing his still handsome features. It had been several months since he had approached her that way—had he not been drunk and abusive, she might have acquiesced, even welcomed his advances. But as she glared back up at him, she felt the last spark of her desire for him snuffed out, like a fire extinguished by a shovel of dirt. "I didn't want you anyway— I never wanted you," he said.

"Then why did you marry me?" she demanded. And then, more bravely than she felt, she added, "And why don't you leave me?"

His laugh had no humor in it. "One doesn't seduce Abel Blanchard's daughter and then abandon her. Not in Seattle, anyway."

"My father has been dead for years."

"That's true, but the old bastard has just as much power in the grave as he had when he was alive. And there are certain advantages to being the husband of his daughter, and of Caleb Blanchard's niece."

"If you're referring to the Bluff, forget it," she told him, picking herself up off the floor and rearranging her clothes. "You'll never touch it—not as long as I draw breath!" She swept by him, a cold fury propelling her up the staircase and through her bedroom door, which she closed behind her with an emphatic bang.

Infuriated, Leighton burst into the room. He threw her roughly on the bed and his hands ripped at her garments.

"Stop it!" she cried. "Stop it!"

Ignoring her protests, he pinned her to the bed and tore at her clothes.

"Now," he muttered roughly, "now we'll see who's the boss around here!" He forced her legs apart and pushed himself into her, squeezing her breasts painfully until she cried out in what, in his drunkenness, he thought was passion. With a satisfied grunt he emptied himself in her and then rolled over, a triumphant smile on his face. "Are you finished?" she demanded, and his smile widened into a leer.

"Not yet, my dear," he replied. "Not yet."

Chapter Sixteen

"Is my wife here?"

Leighton had been home only to change his clothes during that October week in 1929. All hell had broken loose on Wall Street. He had not needed the call from his broker to tell him that his financial position, already precarious, was rapidly approaching disaster. Almost everything he owned was heavily mortgaged, even the Firs, and the failure of the stock market made whatever he had not borrowed against practically worthless. It had been a fortnight since the event the newspapers were calling "the great crash," and in that time he had done everything he could think of to stave off ruination. He had only one chance to save himself—to save his name, his company, and especially to save the Firs.

"I believe she's at the Bluff, sir," said Mason, the butler. Leighton scowled. "Shall I bring you tea?"

"Tea, hell, bring me a drink," he replied angrily, and strode into his study. Rummaging through the rolltop oak desk, he tossed files and papers onto the rug, a snowy hide from a polar bear he had shot on a hunting trip to the Arctic with Josh Green. Other trophies lined the walls of the comfortable room, which Catherine had furnished with overstuffed leather chairs and couches. Carved oak bookcases with glass doors displayed his collection of antique duck decoys; on a leather-topped secretary, crystal decanters rested on a Georgian silver tray, their contents sparkling gold and amber in the light reflected from the cheery blaze in the hearth.

Finally Leighton found what he sought. Triumphant, he downed the drink the butler poured and motioned wordlessly to him to refill his glass. Prohibition was observed in some places in Seattle, but not in Leighton Blake's house. At Sunday dinner at Maddy's the previous week, he had shocked his mother-in-law by producing a flask and filling his water glass from it.

"We do not serve spirits in this house," she had said warningly, but Leighton had ignored her, despite Catherine's restraining hand on his arm. Sunday dinner at Broadview was a custom Leighton would not ignore, but that didn't mean he wouldn't have a drink if he wanted to. Still, at Maddy's words he replaced the flask in his hip pocket and did not remove it again until he and Catherine and the children were in the car on the way back to the Highlands.

As he drank his third glass of bootleg Canadian whiskey, he reread the document he had not studied for years. As he had thought, Abel Blanchard's will named Catherine's husband as the conservator of her stock in the Alki Land and Development Company. Leighton's other investments might be worthless, or nearly so, but ALKCO was as solid as a rock—Matthew and Lucas had managed it prudently, investing, as Abel had, only in what they could see, if not touch. Some of the company's assets were in gas, oil, and mining stocks, which might be devalued right now but would certainly be worth money once this damn emergency was over. Meanwhile, by the terms of Abel's will—bless the old fossil, Leighton thought—he had the right to "buy, sell, convey, or trade said shares with the consent of said beneficiary, Catherine Blanchard Blake."

Using ALKCO stock as collateral, Leighton had managed to keep his troubled shipping empire afloat during the lean years that followed the war. But the days of the Mosquito Fleet were numbered; his friend Joshua had seen it coming and diversified his own company some years before. Now even the steel steamers that sped between Seattle and Tacoma could not lure passengers away from the independence afforded by their automobiles. And while his Alaska steamers still did a good business, the increasing demands of the crews that manned them, stirred up by that bastard Colin McKay, had cut into Leighton's profits so severely that he had been forced to sell his shipyard to subsidize the Blake Lines.

Idly, he spun the elaborate world globe that railroad magnate Sam Hill had presented to him years ago. Dietrich Reimer had hand crafted it in Berlin. On it, Seattle was prominently labeled, in larger letters than any other West Coast city except San Francisco, whose port was slightly bigger. The high and low harbor soundings of Seattle were included in a side map, as were isothermal lines and population figures. Hill's globes were greatly prized by his friends and business acquaintances, and except for Joshua's, Leighton's was the only one that included the maritime data.

Even Josh could not help him now, Leighton reflected; his friend's bank, like every other one in Seattle—hell, in the country—was reeling under the succession of blows that had followed the market's collapse. There was nothing to do but borrow against Catherine's ALKCO shares. If her brothers would not lend him money on them, he had Josh's word that he would. "If ALKCO goes belly up, the whole city will," Josh told him. "Bring me her approval, and we'll give you the money to meet your margin calls."

Leighton glanced impatiently at the clock on the mantel. Damn it, where was she? He climbed the stairs to the second floor, thinking that perhaps she had told Inga when she would return.

"I'm sorry, Mr. Blake, but she didn't mention it to me," the Swedish governess said. The twins had departed for prep school in the East, but Arabella was only thirteen, and Natalie seven. Natalie had been conceived the last time Leighton had had marital relations with Catherine—an occasion that still caused him shame when he recalled it.

He had raped her—there was no other word for it. Drink had loosed the cruelty he knew he was capable of but tried, usually successfully, to suppress; drink, and something else, some perverse desire to see his wife helpless beneath him like the whores he occasionally frequented. He had felt his hold on her slipping —his own fault, perhaps, for he had not been a very good husband. He had loved her once. Or had he only wanted to possess the daughter of Abel Blanchard, the man whose favor and goodwill could open so many doors? He remembered how she had been when they were first married—innocent, but with an abandon, in their private moments, that was thrillingly unlike her publicly demure and compliant manner. Then she had looked at him with such love and trust that he was glad he had not given in to his impulse, when she told him she was pregnant, to cut and run from the respectable, comfortable, certain future that awaited him as a member of the Blanchard family.

He had hoped that marriage would change him, curb his desire to possess every attractive female he met, his penchant for drink, and his delight in risk of any sort—stalking dangerous game of the four-legged as well as two-legged variety, gambling on his wits, never walking away from a challenge. She had been a challenge—beautiful Catherine Blanchard, who had wanted him enough to take him without benefit of clergy.

And paid for it, he thought sadly, the liquor and sentiment merging in him so that when he left the house and climbed into his Cord roadster, he felt contrite and loving toward her. Perhaps it's not too late, he thought as he drove toward Alki, toward the Bluff, scene of some of their happiest times. Perhaps we can make a new start. And he pressed the accelerator into the floor, as if by going faster he could outdistance the past.

* * *

Catherine reined in her horse and waited for Colin to catch up with her.

"You jump that horse like you were glued to the seat," he told her, pulling his mount alongside hers. "You're so reckless sometimes, Catherine, it frightens me."

"Does it?" she asked. "That's sweet, Colin—no one has worried about me for quite a while."

He frowned. If Leighton Blake only knew what a treasure he had in this woman, he thought, he'd take better care of her. But maybe if he knew, she wouldn't be here this autumn afternoon with him, galloping along the driftwood-piled beach and through the dense stand of trees that was the last remnant of a once-mighty forest.

He had never expected to meet a woman like Catherine Blake. Nothing in his life had prepared him for the way he had felt when he had first met her, eight years before: that this was why God put him on earth, to cherish and care for Catherine all the days of his life. It was not that she was beautiful, or that she smelled of gardenias, or that the light in her green eyes, like the gold that tipped her halo of curls, gleamed like the setting sun when it set the sky on fire.

It was not that she was graceful, either, that she moved like the wind through the trees; that in the woods, while he crashed and thrashed clumsily and she held up a warning finger, she could approach a doe so silently that, if the breeze was blowing in the right direction, she could get almost near enough to touch her before she bolted.

And it was not that she was gifted, although the sound as well as the sight of her bent over the old upright piano in her uncle's cottage moved him almost to tears, especially when she played the Chopin he loved so.

Colin McKay knew other gifted, beautiful women—many who were Catherine's match in those respects, and with whom he had a greater affinity, political and intellectual. Catherine's intelligence was of a different sort; it was an aesthetic sensibility, expressed in her love of art and nature, in her appreciation of beauty and of those who possessed or created it.

There was in this woman, beneath her soft exterior, a strength, a grit, that was not unlike his mother's, although no two women could have been more different. One was an aristocrat, born to wealth and position; the other was a working-class woman who had known only poverty before her marriage to Teddy McKay and hardly better after it; as she often said, "Your father couldn't keep two pennies long enough to rub them together." Ted and Loretta McKay had emigrated from Wales with a dream, but by the end of the century, those who had come for land had to settle for wage labor instead. The land was squeezed out between the lumber cartels and railroad syndicates, and what they did not own, the federal government reserved for itself. Absentee owners controlled the raw commodities and also the local wage scale. Colin grew up in poverty, and when his father died in a logging accident and his mother moved herself and her children to the city, the economic circumstances of his life changed hardly at all. Loretta went to work as a maid for one of Seattle's richest families. She worked herself to exhaustion to provide clean clothes, nourishing meals, and a roof over their heads. Colin helped out as best he could, working at odd jobs throughout his childhood to supplement her meager earnings. He had shined shoes at the Rainier Club and shot rats for bounty under the university bridge. He worked in the shipyards and on the boats, and along the way he had educated himself so that, except when he was with Catherine, he never felt the lack of a more formal education.

The men who replaced his father in Loretta's life were working men who carried the red card of the Industrial Workers of the World. When deputies fired on union men in Everett, killing seven of them and wounding fifty others, Colin got his own red card. When the government raided union halls across the state and charged the Wobblies with sabotaging the war effort, he went to sea; after he was demobbed, when vigilantes and Centralia policemen castrated a union man and hanged him from a railroad bridge, he used his badge of solidarity to get into the labor movement.

Then, he had thought militancy was the only way to bring the leaders of the establishment to their knees, to make them recognize that without the working class they would have nothing. But in the divisive years after the war, he saw that no good could be accomplished by making unreasonable demands or staging wildcat strikes. The Palmer raids, trials, and deportations brought the power of the Justice Department down on what was left of the I.W.W. Colin understood that accommodation was necessary if the people he represented were to get anything at all. The establishment was terrified by the specter of Bolshevism, frightened that what had happened in Russia could happen in America. And Colin realized that the most radical elements had to be purged from the union so that the majority of workers might get at least part of what they sought. He threw away his red card and redoubled his efforts to find a new way for labor to work with management, and in the process he made enemies of some of his former supporters, who called him a traitor to his class.

The radicalism that flourished in the lumber camps and granges and among the longshoremen in California and Hawaii had no place in Seattle, Colin declared. And that earned him, finally, the grudging respect of business leaders. All except Leighton Blake, who held him personally responsible for the failure of his shipyard and viewed the reasonable requests of the longshoremen who worked his Blake Lines boats and the leader who represented them as part of a Communist conspiracy to ruin him.

For Colin did not entirely disavow the traditional weapons of organized labor. He chose his targets carefully, avoiding the strong rich ones like Skinner and Eddy, who could hold out against his demands, and concentrating instead on those he knew could not afford a long and expensive strike—like Blake. He had actually done him a favor by striking his yard—forced to close it, Leighton concentrated instead on his shipping line and the more lucrative Alaska trade.

Colin did not pay court to Catherine to revenge himself on Leighton; that was not his nature. In fact, after the afternoon he met Catherine at Blanc's, he had tried to put her out of his mind. What good could come of it, he wondered—Abel Blanchard's daughter and Loretta McKay's son? Worse, she was a married woman and a mother—and that was more trouble than he needed or wanted.

Catherine did not immediately repeat her invitation to him— in fact, it was two years before he met her again, though he sometimes saw her at concerts at Cornish or recitals of her chamber music group. She was usually with her husband. When he encountered her a few months after their first meeting and saw that she was pregnant, he put her out of his mind. And then she bought a radio station, a purchase reported in all the newspapers, and when, each evening at seven o'clock, he tuned into KBBB and heard her husky, beautifully modulated voice recite the musical program that was to follow, he dreamed of the woman behind the voice.

That might have been the end of it, had he not run into her unexpectedly on the street one afternoon and been surprised by the warmth of her greeting and the repeated invitation to ride with her at Alki.

"I haven't been riding for some time," she explained. "The baby, of course—and then, afterward, I was ill, and the doctors forbade it. But I'm fine now . . . and I really would be delighted if you'd come."

He had accepted that invitation—and true to her word, she hadn't laughed at his clumsy efforts to sit the gelding she saddled for him. Since then, he had become quite good at riding, and even more than the freedom of the Bluff, which was by now the closest thing to a wilderness within the city limits, he loved the pleasure of being with her, hearing her lilting laugh and breathing in her sweet scent.

They were quite proper with each other; not once did he indicate in any way that he thought of her as anything other than a married woman, and not once did she tell him by any word or deed that she was not content with her marriage. But he knew that her relationship with her husband was not a happy one—Leighton Blake's womanizing was well known. How any man could stray when he had Catherine for his wife was a mystery to Colin. If she were his, he thought jealously, he would devote his entire life to teasing a smile from those sweet lips or lighting the amber glints in her green eyes. And often, when he sat across the bargaining table from Leighton Blake, he thought how satisfying it would be to say as much to the bastard.

But what would he tell him, if his temper ever got the best of him and he blurted out the truth of his relationship with Catherine? That they managed an occasional afternoon together here at the Bluff, or a coffee at Blanc's after a rehearsal of her chamber music group? That he wanted her, desired her, as he had never wanted a woman before? That he was a better man than Blake, and that she deserved much more than the disregard with which her husband treated her? No doubt Blake would throw him out of his offices—or, worse, laugh at his effrontery for daring to worship her. So, with difficulty, he curbed his tongue, if not his desire, and tried to be satisfied with the little he had of her.

"You're so pensive this afternoon," she said as they rode toward the stables. "Is something wrong?"

"No, nothing," he replied. "I've brought us some lunch, and the score of that Mozart piece you mentioned. Shall we try it?"

"Oh, yes!" she said eagerly, and they stabled the horses and went to the farmhouse, where he took his old, tarnished flute from its velvet-lined case and she seated herself at the piano.

They played together, so engrossed in the music that they did not hear Leighton's car as it ground to a halt in the driveway of the farmhouse. Leighton's shock at discovering that his wife was not alone was no greater than Colin's when he beheld the obviously inebriated man advancing toward him, his fists waving menacingly.

"You son of a bitch!" Leighton thundered. "You low-down, rotten, no-good Commie scum, what are you doing here?" He was red-faced with anger, fury coarsening his features as he realized that the man who was there with Catherine—his wife —was Colin McKay, his enemy.

Leighton's wrath turned to Catherine, and he stumbled to her, dragging her away from the piano. His strong fingers gripped her slender arm painfully, and she fell, her head glancing off the edge of the bench. Blood poured from the wound into her eyes.

Colin roared in pain at the sight of Catherine's injury and attacked Blake, delivering the punch that had knocked out scores of rowdy sailors and that now turned Leighton's nose into a bleeding, puffy mess.

"Stop it!" cried Catherine. "Stop it . . . Leighton, Colin . . . you'll kill each other!" She forced herself between them, but Leighton raised his fists again, and Colin grasped his wrist and twisted it until he heard it snap.

Leighton retreated, nursing his injured arm, but not before loosing a stream of curses at his wife. "You treacherous bitch," he sputtered, "you deceiving whore!"

"Watch your language, Blake, or I'll break your other arm," Colin rumbled, but before he could make good his threat, Catherine interrupted him.

"Please, Colin," she began her hand on his arm, but the look on Leighton's face, a look she had never seen before—not even the night he forced himself on her—stopped her.

"It's not what you think," she told her husband.

"No?" he demanded. "I suppose it's just a musical interlude, is that it?"

"As a matter of fact—" But before she could explain, Colin interrupted her.

"It's none of your damn business, you wife-beater!" he

shouted. Colin was not often violent, but the damage done to the woman he loved made him murderous. He had two inches and twenty pounds on Blake, and a lifetime of breaking up brawls in waterfront saloons, all of which he dearly wanted to employ now in Catherine's defense. But at her urging, he let his hands drop to his sides and controlled his voice.

"If you lay a hand on her, I'll kill you," he said quietly, and there was no mistaking the truth of his words.

"You come near her again—ever again—and you won't be able to," Leighton said with equal fervor, "because I'll beat you to a bloody pulp and throw your body off this goddamned Bluff!" Then he turned to his wife, who stood speechless between them. "And I'll make sure the Blanchard name is dragged through every stinking mudhole in this town!"

"And make yourself the laughingstock of your friends?" she said defiantly. "I doubt it. I don't believe you can afford to do that."

She knew how financially strapped he was; she had already arranged to sell some of her ALKCO holdings to bail him out. Although she no longer loved him, he was still her husband, and she owed him that.

"I can change my mind about those ALKCO shares," she told him. "And if you threaten Colin again—or me—I will. Now get out of my house and off my property!"

He had no choice; she had him completely in her power. The hope that he could salvage anything except money from the ruins of their marriage dissipated along with the remnants of the whiskey that coursed through his blood. He realized finally that anything he might do against her would only, as she well knew, destroy him as well. She was a Blanchard, and in Seattle, a Blanchard could get away with anything—even adultery, and maybe even murder.

Chapter Seventeen

Catherine did not know that her youngest child had been kidnapped until three hours after the time Natalie usually arrived home from school. That day, she was out at the Bluff, and by the time she returned to the Highlands, the ransom note had already been delivered, left at the gate of the compound by a man dressed as a messenger from Frederick & Nelson's Department Store. There was no reason why the gate guard should think anything was amiss; the delivery truck bore the distinctive green and white emblem of the store, and the box in which the kidnappers had left their instructions was a familiar-looking parcel. Dozens of such packages, from the finest stores in Seattle, were regularly delivered—there was nothing unusual about it.

The delivery van was found later, abandoned on a side street near the waterfront after it had been reported stolen from the store's garage. The uniform worn by the kidnapper was also found, along with Natalie's schoolbooks and tasseled blue stocking cap. These items were located at the precise moment that Catherine Blake learned that the only way she could meet the demands outlined in the ransom note was to sell the Bluff.

"What do you mean, you can't give me the money?" she demanded.

Her brother Matthew refused to meet her eyes, but Lucas stared at her balefully. "I told you, your ALKCO shares are not available. You signed them over to us to pay off your husband's debts, and we cannot in all good conscience lend money against mortgaged collateral," he said.

She was dumbfounded. "This is my daughter's life we're talking about!" she cried. "This is your niece!"

"That's true," said Lucas, "but we have a responsibility to our other shareholders. As you know, the Depression has hit everyone very hard. Even ALKCO. The value of your holdings is nowhere near what it was even six months ago. If we liquidated everything that is not otherwise encumbered, we might be able to come up with enough money to pay the ransom. But that would take weeks, the way things are."

"Then take the radio stations," she pleaded.

"Don't be silly, Catherine, what would we do with two radio stations?" Matthew said. "They're practically worthless. No, I'm afraid there's nothing to it except to sell the rest of the Alki property. That's entirely free of encumbrances—we could certainly borrow against that. But only if we had clear title to it."

"It's worth a great deal more than the money they've demanded," she argued. "What if I sold you a portion of it?"

"That wouldn't do," said Lucas. "In order to facilitate proper development of the site, we'd need it all. I hardly think you're in a position to haggle—after all, as you yourself just said, it's Natalie's life you're talking about."

Added Matthew, "Perhaps you should discuss this with Leighton, my dear. After all, Natalie is his child, too."

Catherine shook her head. Leighton's solution to the problem posed by the ransom demand was the same as her brothers'. "Now we'll see what really matters to you, your daughter or your goddamned Bluff!" he had said, taking a perverse pleasure in his wife's dilemma.

"She's your daughter too!" she said.

"Is she?" he asked cruelly. At that moment, she knew her marriage was over, and that her innocent friendship with Colin might very possibly cost her her youngest child's life.

She left Leighton at the Firs then—he was already drunker than she had ever seen him, and she knew he could not—would not—help her.

Nor could her mother, whose inheritance from Abel was all in ALKCO shares, as was her own. Broadview was Maddy's, and she offered it to Catherine, but huge mansions were a glut on the depressed real estate market, and in any case Maddy had borrowed against it some months before to help her sons keep ALKCO from going under.

"All right then," Catherine told her brothers. "You can have it. How long will it take to get the money?"

"I think we can get it for you by tomorrow morning, when the banks open," said Matthew. "We'll have the papers drawn up as soon as possible. Once you sign them, I'm certain we can make the funds available immediately."

"In unmarked bills, with no sequence," she reminded them, "all three hundred thousand of it."

"We understand," said Lucas, and Matthew added, "If there were any other way, of course we'd be glad to do it. We know how much the Bluff means to you. But at this time, in this market, there is no other way. Our hands are tied."

Catherine left the ALKCO office, a welter of emotions swirling through her. She feared for Natalie's safety. The kidnappers had promised that they would not harm her as long as their demands were met, and she believed them; she had to, or she would not have been able to function. There was no doubt in her mind that Natalie, alive and unhurt, meant more to her than the Bluff— more than anything. More than her sons, who had more Blake in them than Blanchard, she often thought—they had always been closer to Leighton than to her. More than Arabella, who was a silly, empty-headed ninny—a sweet child, but with none of Natalie's intelligence, spirit, or self-confidence.

Catherine sighed. It was probably Natalie's willfulness that had gotten her into this mess; even at her young age, her stubbornness defeated any attempt to control her. She had demanded to be allowed to attend public school, and Catherine, remembering her own forced attendance at Forest Ridge and her unhappiness at not being permitted to go to South High with the rest of her childhood friends, had acquiesced. And Natalie had refused to allow anyone to drive her to or from school—not Inga, not Mason, not even Catherine herself.

I should have insisted, Catherine thought as she came out of the Alkco Building. If I hadn't let her talk me into it, she wouldn't be in this trouble. If I had kept closer watch on her, taken better care of her, they wouldn't have taken her. And at the thought of what might happen to Natalie, her composure cracked and tears filled her eyes, so that she didn't see the big shambling man who had been waiting for her.

"Catherine, dear heart, what can I do to help?" Colin McKay's arms went around her, right there in the middle of Third Avenue, at high noon, with half of Seattle watching, but Catherine was so glad to see him that she didn't care.

"How did you know?" she asked. She had not seen him since that day in Caleb's house on the Bluff three years before. She could not face him, embarrassed as she was by what had happened there—by the scene Leighton had made, the fight that had ensued between the two men, the threats that had been leveled, and her realization that it was her own failure to hold her husband's affections that had led to it all. If she had been a better wife to Leighton, she thought, it never would have happened— she would never have met Colin McKay, or invited him to the Bluff, or allowed their friendship to flower. She would not have needed what he gave her: the knowledge that she was still beautiful, still desirable, still valued by a man. And by the time she realized that it was not she who had been at fault—that Leighton's own nature rather than her failings were responsible for the demise of their marriage—Colin's telephone calls and letters had stopped and his efforts to see her had ceased.

She and Leighton hardly spoke these days. When he was at home, he closed himself in his study and drank until he passed out and Mason undressed him and put him to bed. His womanizing had reached such proportions that it barely raised an eyebrow among their friends, who nevertheless did not wonder why Catherine didn't leave him. In families like the Blanchards, one did not divorce, no matter the provocation. And Catherine had filled her days with her music, her children, her radio stations, and, of course, the Bluff.

Colin took her arm and led her to his car. "I have some friends in the Department," he said cryptically in answer to her question. The kidnappers' instructions had been quite clear—no police, no publicity. But she had ignored the first of them—the Blanchard influence was strong enough to keep information about the incident from leaking to the press—and she agreed with Maddy and Leighton that the authorities had to be called in. They were proceeding discreetly. In the forty-eight hours since Natalie's abduction, they had traced the delivery truck and gotten a description of the Buick driven by the kidnappers, although they had not been able, yet, to trace it farther than a few miles outside the city, where the trail of the criminals ended.

"What are you going to do?" Colin asked.

"Comply with their instructions, as soon as I put my hands on the money," she said.

"You can raise it, then?" Colin McKay was not unaware of Leighton's financial problems, or of ALKCO's, either; he made it his business to know his adversaries' weak points.

"I'll sell the Bluff," she said simply. He knew how much that decision cost her. She was a proud woman and he knew what Caleb's Bluff meant to her—she had once told him that from its unspoiled wilderness, she drew the faith and strength that most people found in church. "We are all made better, more divine, by proximity to nature," she had said, "as if by putting a small and insignificant creature such as man next to His most magnificent creation, God set us an example and gave us reason to believe that He exists."

Remembering that, Colin did not hesitate. "You don't have to sell it," he said. "I can get you the money."

She looked at him in surprise. "You?" she said. She knew of the poverty in which he'd been raised, and the shabby old pre-war Ford he drove and the threadbare suit he wore confirmed that he could not possibly have access to the fortune the kidnappers had demanded for Natalie's release. But perhaps he did not know how much money was at stake, she told him gently, not wishing to wound his pride.

"Three hundred thousand dollars," he said, and once again he surprised her. His influence must be much greater than she had imagined—only the chief of police knew exactly what the ransom note said. "I'll have it for you tomorrow at noon."

"But what—how—" she began.

He put a finger to her lips. "Things are not always as they seem," he said. "I have ways."

"Colin, I can't allow you to do this!" she protested. "You can't possibly raise that kind of money that quickly. And I couldn't pay you back, not for a long time, anyway . . . not until things improve, and I can sell the stations or my ALKCO shares."

"Don't worry about paying it back. Once Natalie's safe, I'm sure the police will be able to nail the bastards who did this and recover the ransom. Now, I won't hear another word about it, Catherine. You mustn't sell the Bluff—not if you don't absolutely have to."

"What if I sold it to you?" Anything was preferable to turning the land over to Matthew and Lucas. If somehow, by some means she couldn't possibly imagine, Colin McKay had three hundred thousand dollars available to him, she would deed the Bluff over at once.

"That won't be necessary," he said, but she insisted.

"I'd rather do this—call it collateral for a loan," she said. "At least until this nightmare is over, and I can pay it back."

"If you prefer," he replied. "But there's no reason to put it in writing; your word is enough for me. This Depression can't last forever. One of these days we'll turn the corner, like Mr. Roosevelt says. Once he's inaugurated, he'll get the economy going again, and then you can pay me back."

"All right," she agreed, but when she met him at Blanc's the next day at noon, and he gave her the money—in used out-of-sequence bills, in a paper-wrapped bundle tied with thick brown twine—she gave him a handwritten promissory note establishing his right to take possession of her property at Alki if she defaulted on the loan. It was as legal and aboveboard as she could make it without asking the advice of her banker or lawyer, something Colin had told her she must not do.

"You have as much to lose as I do if word of this gets out," he said, and while she understood what the gossips would make of the unorthodox arrangement between them, she did not comprehend what he had risked to bring her the money. Before she accepted the parcel, she asked him again how he had managed to accumulate such a huge sum. "Wise investments and some good luck," he told her, "but it wouldn't do to let the fellows I represent know about it—if they thought I was rich, they'd never trust me." He took Catherine's delicate, pale hand in his own big, freckled one. "None of that matters, Catherine. What matters is that you get Natalie back, safe and sound, and then we can decide what to do about the rest of it."

"The rest of it?"

"Well, yes," he said softly. "You and me."

"Colin, if this money is contingent on our . . . friendship, then I can't accept it," she said.

His face reddened in embarrassment. "Of course it's not!" he replied indignantly. "Look, if you think for one minute that I —that we—that I'd do anything as low as that, take advantage of this terrible thing that's happened to you—well, then, you must think I'm no better than your brothers. Or your husband, for that matter!"

Her eyes softened. "Of course I don't think that, Colin," she said. "It's just that Leighton and I—I know you won't understand this, but my . . . position means a great deal to me. And my marriage vows."

"Even if he's already broken them?"

"Even if," she said. "That's why I've never—why we haven't—" She blushed, and David felt a surge of compassion for her. She was trapped by the conventions of her world, and took seriously its insincere piety.

"There are no strings attached to that money," he said. "You must do whatever you think is right, now and always. I would never pressure you, in any way. But if you decide—when you decide—to leave him, I'm here."

He didn't believe that she would not divorce Leighton, that she would remain in a loveless marriage when there was no reason to do so. And as he tore the document she had prepared for him into tiny pieces, as if to demonstrate his trust in her, neither of them had any idea how wrong they both were.

Natalie was released, unharmed, the evening of the day the kidnappers picked up the ransom. She had been intercepted on her way home from school, chloroformed and thrown into the trunk of a Buick automobile. Her abductors hid her the first day in a deep pit covered with tin, lined with boards and braces, with posts to which her hands were cuffed. The pit was located in logged-off country that belonged to ALKCO—it was nearly impenetrable, with no roads or trails leading into it, just infrequently planked paths through clear-cut woods to abandoned logging camps, with only stumps and splintered wood to mark where majestic Douglas firs and blue-tipped Sitka spruces had once stood.

After her release, on a dusty county road two miles from the nearest town, she marched into the first public building she came to and asked to make a telephone call. As soon as Catherine heard her voice, she shrieked with relief, then hurried to her. As she held and kissed her daughter, she thanked God silently for Colin McKay. Certainly she would have given up the Bluff to secure Natalie's release. But because of Colin, she hadn't had to.

"Where's Father?" Natalie wanted to know, wriggling free of Catherine's embrace.

"Waiting for you at home, darling girl," she said.

"Waiting for both of us, isn't that right?"

"Yes," she said sadly. "Waiting for both of us."

Chapter Eighteen

Catherine waited while the porter collected Ruth's suitcases and placed them in the back seat of her automobile.

"So you've done it finally," Ruth said, as they drove off, but Catherine shook her head.

"Not the way you think," she replied. "I haven't divorced him —I've just left him."

"And moved back to Broadview?"

"For now, anyway," said Catherine.

"I'm surprised. I would have thought you'd go to the Bluff."

"I considered it, but the girls can't bear it, and it really is quite isolated," she replied. "Since the kidnapping, I don't feel entirely secure there—I'm busy with the stations and often not home until late, and Inga wouldn't hear of it. I couldn't possibly manage without her, especially now."

"How are you and Maddy getting along?" Ruth wanted to know.

"Swimmingly," said Catherine. "Of course, she's as bad as you are about my getting a divorce—she thinks I should marry again."

"Does she have anyone in mind?"

Catherine laughed. "I believe she'd be thrilled if I favored Jonathan."

"Jonathan Cape?" Ruth chuckled. "I take it she doesn't understand about men like him."

"Exactly," said Catherine. "She's surprisingly modern in a number of ways, but that isn't one of them."

"What about Colin?"

Catherine sighed. "You're as bad as Mother," she said. "Neither of you understands—I don't *want* to marry again. I have a very full life: my girls, my stations, my friends, and my music. Leighton goes his way and I go mine. I'm taking Arabella to Boston—she's starting at Wellesley this year—and then Natalie and I are going abroad. I was hoping to convince you to join us."

"As a matter of fact, I'm going myself, in two weeks. I'm afraid I'll have to cut short my visit here," said Ruth. "I'm going to Spain. There may be something useful I can do for the Loyalist cause."

Catherine was horrified. "But there's a war going on, Ruth!" she said.

"Exactly," her friend replied. "And soon it will spread. You know, I don't really think you should make the trip."

"And miss Bayreuth and La Scala? Don't be silly, Ruth, it's perfectly safe."

"Now, perhaps, but who knows for how much longer? I think you should reconsider."

"Well, I don't," said Catherine firmly, as she pulled up in front of Broadview. "Here we are—oh, look, there's Mother—she's been dying to see you. I haven't seen her this excited in months."

"How is she?" Ruth asked. Maddy waved from her bedroom window, and she waved back.

"Not very well, I'm afraid. She had a bad winter. She was sick with pneumonia, and we thought we were going to lose her, but she rallied, thank heavens. She doesn't go out as much as she used to; she's turned the *Journal* almost completely over to Jonathan, although she has a new project, a library at the university. Between that and her books, she seems content. And Natalie, of course—the two of them are as thick as thieves."

"And how is my favorite goddaughter?"

"As stubborn as ever. She'll be the death of me yet. But you'll see for yourself—I believe she's agreed to grace us with her presence this evening."

"It sounds like you two are at odds again," said Ruth.

Catherine smiled. "Aren't we always?" She turned to Ruth, her smile broadening. "Oh, my dear, I'm so glad you're here. My life always seems satisfying and complete, but when you come every summer, I realize that it's missing something . . . someone. Mother used to say that there were only two people in the world who really understood her, and she didn't know it until Aunt Sonnet died. That's how I feel. The only one I can really count on is you."

"Who was the other person?" asked Ruth curiously.

Catherine shrugged. "My father, I suppose," she said. "Who else could it have been?"

* * *

Maddy thought her daughter looked unwell. Catherine's grooming was impeccable as usual, but there were circles under her eyes and her smart new Poiret suit hung on her slender frame.

She knew Catherine was not sleeping well—she heard her moving around in the big house at night, long after the servants were abed.

"Are you having problems with the stations these days?" she asked.

"No, Mother, as a matter of fact we should make a nice profit this year," she replied.

She had purchased the first one against all advice, but insisted that the land the station stood on, at least, would be valuable some day. And she had bought another station during the Depression, when the property was available at fire-sale rates.

She'd been right about the site of that first low-killowatt transmitter; five years after she took it over, she had sold the Queen Anne property for twenty times what she had paid for it, and with the proceeds she expanded the reach of the B&B Broadcasting Company as far east as Pend Oreille and as far south as Portland.

Catherine's "little hobby," as Matthew and Lucas called it, was doing quite nicely, thank you, she told her mother. What had begun as a way to keep her from brooding about how things were between her and Leighton—and incidentally provide a source of income for her friends when the symphony couldn't afford to pay them a living wage—had proven so successful that even the wag who had remarked that sow bellies and Sibelius seemed an unlikely combination was forced to admit that Catherine Blake's blend of agricultural bulletins, weather reports, news, and classical music seemed to be paying off.

That comment did not amuse Catherine. "Sibelius?" she said. "Obviously the man has never listened to one of my programs." For music that had not stood the test of time—which meant anything composed after the nineteenth century—was not permitted on her airwaves. She chose the programs herself, bent over the Empire desk in her sitting room with sheets and scores from her own enormous collection. Then she dispatched her selections to her managers, who never deviated from her play lists.

"Well, something must be troubling you," Maddy said. "It doesn't have anything to do with Colin McKay, does it? According to the *Times,* he seems to be in a bit of a fix."

Catherine's teacup rattled in her hands. "What on earth makes you say that?" she asked nervously.

Maddy shrugged noncommittally. "I had the impression that you were rather good friends."

Catherine removed a cigarette from a slim gold case and lit it. "He has been very devoted to the symphony and the Ladies Musical Association, if that's what you mean. He's raised quite a bit of money for us."

"They say he stole three hundred thousand dollars from that union of his."

"Oh?" Catherine struggled to remain calm. "Come to think of it, I did hear something about his attempting to organize the Boeing mechanics—I believe Kurt mentioned it. Apparently Dave Beck is trying to do that as well, and his Teamsters have trumped up these charges to discredit Mr. McKay."

"I see," said Maddy agreeably. "That isn't why you've been so skittery lately, is it?"

"Of course not, Mother, where did you get that idea?" said Catherine with annoyance. "Actually, it's Natalie I'm worried about."

"It seems to me that if you did a little less worrying, she'd be fine," Maddy said tartly. "Let her go off to that photography school in New York the way she wants to."

"I don't think Manhattan is the right place for a young girl, especially in wartime," Catherine replied stiffly.

"It didn't hurt you any, and you were younger than she is."

"That was a different time—and Natalie is a different girl."

"You can't keep her here forever," said Maddy. "Catherine, the kidnapping was years ago—put it to rest, why don't you? Natalie has dreams of her own. And I don't believe they include marriage to that Wright fellow you're so keen on."

"Don't you think he'd make a good husband for her?"

"It doesn't matter what I think, or you either—what's important is what Natalie thinks."

Catherine stubbed out her cigarette, ignoring Maddy's look of disapproval. "What could she possibly know, at her age?"

"As much as you did when you were twenty and married Leighton," said Maddy, but when she saw the look on her daughter's face, she regretted her words. She hadn't meant to hurt her, but it was too late now.

Catherine stood up, indicating that the conversation was over. "Good night, Mother," she said. "I've an engagement this evening; I may be back quite late. Don't wait up for me. You need your sleep."

"I can sleep when I'm dead," said Maddy. "Catherine . . . ease up on the girl, why don't you? She's got a good head on her shoulders. . . . She'll do fine in New York."

"Perhaps after she finishes at the university—then we'll see," Catherine answered. She bent over and kissed Maddy's papery cheek, then drew her mink stole around her shoulders and picked up her bag. "I'll send Beverly in with your medicine now. Good night."

"Good night, my dear," said Maddy. "Have a pleasant evening." And by the time Catherine had descended the stairs and let herself out of the house, Maddy was asleep, drifting in a dream, or perhaps a memory, of a little girl who shrieked with delight as she galloped along a beach on a chestnut mare, her small, compact body nestled safely in the arms of a tall, red-haired man whose eyes, like hers, were the color of the sea at daybreak.

*   *   *

Catherine drove away from Broadview, wondering what sixth sense had enabled Maddy to put her finger on the source of her concern. When she had moved·out of Leighton's house and into Maddy's mansion, Colin had come to call a time or two, but the intimacy he desired had never materialized, much to his disappointment. And true to his word, he had not pressed his suit. She did not want to cause him pain, but neither had she wished to upset her well-ordered existence.

She cared for Colin, but she never felt for him the passion Leighton had once aroused in her—perhaps, as she had once told Ruth, that came only once to a woman. Instead she poured that passion into her stations and her children. She had earned the power she now possessed, and she followed her father's dictum: of those to whom much is given, much is expected. The police had recovered most of the ransom, and she had returned what they recovered to Colin; the rest she repaid over the next three years. And now the interest on her debt was due. Only she could explain why he'd taken the union's money, refute the allegations that he had embezzled it for his own gain, prove that he had replaced it all. She had the proof: her own copy of the promissory note she'd given him that afternoon at Blanc's, the note he'd destroyed. She shuddered, thinking what a field day the newspapers would have if they got a look at it, what the gossips would say. But this evening, at the place it had all begun, she would pay back the last installment on her debt to the man who loved her.

·Natalie: 1940-1962·

Chapter Nineteen

Natalie trudged slowly up First Hill, deep in thought. As she turned onto Minor Avenue she saw her mother's automobile driving away in the other direction and sighed with relief—at least she would not have to deal with Catherine this evening.

Natalie and her mother had never been especially close. Her grandmother said it was because they were so much alike, but she didn't think that was true. Catherine only cared about appearances—the right clothes, the right address, the right people, the right behavior. None of that mattered a fig to Natalie. She had permitted her parents to present her to society and smiled dutifully as two hundred guests passed through the receiving line at the Sunset Club at her debut, but she refused to participate in the other festivities marking her eighteenth birthday. "For heaven's sake, Mother, this isn't New York society, it's only Seattle," she protested, "and besides, I don't need to be presented to those old bores—I've known them since I was born!" People were interesting because of who they were, not who their ancestors were, she declared.

Catherine never did anything that wasn't proper and appropriate—except, perhaps, when she made a smashing success of her radio stations. That surprised a lot of people, but not Natalie, who knew that her mother had a will of iron and a determination of equal strength.

"I'm doing this for you," Catherine told Natalie. "These stations will be yours some day." But Natalie didn't care about them—she had her own ideas about her future, which did not include being stuck for the rest of her life in provincial Seattle, where being a Blanchard was a burden one could never be rid of.

Her future here was all planned out for her, principally the expectation that she would marry one of the suitable scions of a proper pioneer dynasty—a Denny, perhaps, or a Terry or a Boren or even a fat-faced Wright, like the fellow who persisted in calling on her, despite her attempts to discourage him. He was not her idea of a husband. A husband, in fact, was the furthest thing from her mind.

What was on her mind as she approached the part-timbered brick and stucco mansion that dominated the entire block was the light—with her new lens, she might be able to capture that pale strip of silver between the mountain peaks just purpling into darkness and the jagged line of clouds that hovered above them, like an echo manifested in the heavens. She reached into the camera bag slung over her shoulder. If she worked quickly, she might get it.

She didn't understand why people complained that Seattle was so often dark and gloomy. She knew better, knew the way the light could polish the sky to a pearly luster just before the rain began to fall, or how the clouds slipped past ahead of a storm, revealing on the grayest afternoon an undercoat of glistening blue. What she saw through the camera's eye she tried to compose in ground glass—"Dangerous art," her teacher at the university told her, but she didn't understand him at first. Her pictures were pretty but sentimentalized, devoid of the more subtle emotions she felt when she saw a beautiful sunset or watched light ripple through water.

She had her first camera when she was twelve, a simple box affair that gave way to an Ica Reflex and then to a Graflex. Her brother Nick, who was very skillful with equipment, helped her master the intricacies of developing and printing her own film and had built her a darkroom in a corner of the potting shed.

She wanted to go to New York to the Institute of Photography, but Catherine wouldn't hear of it, so she made the best of the instruction that was available in Seattle, chafing under the protective custody that made anonymity difficult—when she moved from landscapes to human subjects, even the strangers she would like to have photographed knew who she was and were self-conscious about posing for her. She was seventeen before Catherine allowed her to go about unaccompanied, and even that permission was yielded with reluctance.

It was the kidnapping that made her that way. Natalie had thought it was something of a lark—terrible things didn't happen to little girls like her. What was worse was what came afterward: her mother's constant, nervous vigilance that suffocated her like a shroud.

She shot several rolls of film before replacing the camera in her bag and turning into the driveway of Broadview. The gas lamps set on ornate wrought-iron gateposts had just been lit; they flickered in the early darkness, casting an orange glow on the manicured gravel drive that led to the mansion. The top floor of Broadview was dark except for the library on the southwest corner of the house, and only the palest amber light shone through the stained-glass oriel window set into the ornately carved mahogany front door. But on the floor between, every room that faced the street was lit up.

The top floor was her grandmother's; Catherine lived in the apartments below, as Natalie had done until she entered the university. Her small, cramped dormitory room was a hovel compared to her spacious bedroom at Broadview, but she loved it; it was the only place she did not feel under constant surveillance. She was a halfhearted student—she stayed in college only because it was her single opportunity to get away from Catherine's overprotectiveness. Her real life did not happen in class, it took place behind her camera and in the pictures in her mind; the way it did for her grandmother and her books, she thought, as she ascended the stairs to Maddy's rooms. Surely Maddy would understand why she had to get away.

Beverly Westwind opened the library door just as Natalie was about to enter.

"How is she?" Natalie asked.

"Better now that you've come, I'm sure," Beverly said. "She told me today the Lord must have His hands full if He's not ready for her yet. Go in—she'll be delighted to see you. I think she gets lonely up here, so many of her old friends have passed on."

Beverly was Johnny's grandniece; her almond-shaped green

204· JANE ADAMS

eyes testified to the blood link between the Blanchards and the Westwinds. None of the Westwinds were mentioned in the Blanchard family tree meticulously traced in the family Bible. But they were like mountains hidden by the fog—just because you couldn't see them didn't mean they weren't real.

"Hasn't she had any visitors today?" asked Natalie.

"Just that man from the Pioneers Association, wanting to make sure he gets his hands on this house after she's gone. She pretended she couldn't remember who he was, and then she closed her eyes and made out like she was sleeping."

That was Maddy's characteristic way of dealing with people she thought boring—pretending to be dotty or ignoring them in favor of a book. Catherine had said it more than once, "Words are more real to her than people or events, and they always have been."

Natalie didn't believe that. Maddy's books were what her cameras were to her, a way to see, to make what was real understandable. Some of the happiest hours of her childhood had been spent in Maddy's library, where she had dreamed away a thousand afternoons, curled up in the window seat watching the light change in the sky while cedar logs spit crackles of red-hot sparks against the fan-shaped brass fireplace screen. Often the only other sound in the room was the scratching of Maddy's quill pen as she wrote in her journals, those enormous ledgers, one for every year, that lined the topmost shelves. "Take it out of your head and put it down on paper," she often said. "Then it won't clutter up your mind and you'll have room to learn something new."

It was a habit Natalie had never acquired—she had her cameras to make a moment or a feeling last, a way to put her experience in order and learn from it.

Before she went into the library, she tidied her hair, straightened the seams of her stockings, and composed herself—Maddy cared a great deal about a neat appearance. Maddy had been confined to her room after suffering a broken hip some years before, but her eyesight was still sharp and very little escaped her attention.

When Maddy saw who her visitor was, she clapped her hands in delight. "My word, it's Natalie. . . . Here, dear, let me get a good look at you!"

Maddy's eyes were button bright in her wrinkled face, and her white hair was plaited in thin braids that framed her long, narrow countenance. The years had not shrunk her as they often did with the aged; she was still nearly Natalie's height, although her body was frail, and she moved with difficulty.

Beverly brought them supper on trays, and they chatted about everything and nothing for a time, until Natalie brought up what was uppermost in her mind.

"Gram, I have to get out of here," she said, and Maddy, sensing the desperation in her voice, sat up straighter in her chair.

"Yes, you do," she said. Natalie, who had feared upsetting her, breathed easier. "Oh, I know why Catherine's kept you wrapped in cotton wool all these years," Maddy said, "but you're practically grown, and it's time you had your chance. I suppose it's still that art school in New York you want to go to, hmm?"

"Not exactly," Natalie answered carefully. "I believe I've had enough formal education for a while."

"Oh, you do, do you?" Maddy's eyes gleamed. "Perhaps you're right. Those pictures you're always taking—if you ask me, they're as good as the ones in this magazine." She picked up the issue of *Life* that rested in her lap and held it out to her granddaughter. The war in Europe was prominently featured, and it gave Natalie the opening she needed.

"I'm going there," she said firmly. "I don't have it all figured out yet, but I'm going."

"You have any idea what you're getting yourself into?" Maddy asked. "There are people being killed over there—not just soldiers, either. Bullets don't care whether you're just taking pictures, you know."

"I know that," said Natalie, who hadn't really thought about the danger involved, only about how desperate she was to leave Seattle and that her camera would be her passport out.

"I suppose Europe isn't any farther away from Seattle than Fall River was," Maddy said. "And you're not much older than I was when I ran away from home."

"Really? You ran away? But I always thought—"

"You always thought exactly what I wanted you to think, and so did everyone else, but that was a long time ago, and if you can't tell the truth when you're ninety-one years old, then I guess you never can," said Maddy. "Have you thought any about how you'll get over there? I don't imagine you can just buy a ticket, seeing as how it's smack in the middle of a war."

"No, I haven't." Natalie didn't really have a plan, just an idea and a need.

"I hear those bombers they're building out at Boeing are flying over practically empty," Maddy said. "Now if you happened to know someone who could get you on one, I imagine they might be willing to give you a lift."

"I don't know anyone who—" she began, but then a thought came to her, and her eyes lit up. "As a matter of fact, Johnny Gasden is working out at Boeing now," she said. "He was rejected by the Army—flat feet, they said—but Boeing took him on as a test pilot."

"That the fellow who used to hang around with Nick? Always banging around in that garage where they built flying boats?"

"That's the one," Natalie replied. "Oh, Gram, you've given me a wonderful idea!"

"Far as your mother knows, I didn't give you anything," said Maddy, and winked conspiratorially at Natalie. Then a look of sadness came over her weathered old face. "I know you have to go," she said. "A long time ago, I felt that way too. But I'm an old lady, and it pains me to think I might never see you again."

"Oh, Gram, you're indestructible," Natalie said. "You'll outlive us all."

"Maybe, but what for? So I can sit around and listen to a bunch of old coots tell stories to anyone who'll listen about things nobody cares about any more?" Maddy replied. "When there's no one left to call you by your first name, you're past your time."

Natalie took her grandmother's hand and clasped it wordlessly to her own soft young cheek. A few moments later she left, and Maddy laid her magazine aside and sat back in her reading chair. It'll be over soon, she thought—we'll all be dead, and no one left alive to remember our rememberings. Something in her heart turned over, like a message from within—or from far away, she considered. Soon, she told him silently. . . . I'm coming soon.

Chapter Twenty

"I'm going to go, you know. Whether you help me or not, I'm going to go." Natalie stuck out her chin defiantly.

Paul Hawkins, editor and publisher of the Seattle *Clarion*, leaned back in his chair and studied her. Natalie's eyes flashed bright with determination, and a flush of high color stained the pale oval of her face. She turned to leave the messy, crowded little cubicle that was his office, but he held up his hand.

"Not so fast," he cautioned her. "Sit down and we'll talk about it." He reached for his pipe and tobacco pouch and swung his legs up on his desk.

She waited but she didn't sit. She stood there, hands on her hips, daring him to doubt that she meant what she said. She was tall for a woman—nearly six feet tall in those ridiculous high heels she was wearing. Come to think of it, he thought, the kid didn't look at all like her usual self today.

He was used to the limp, tan raincoat she wore in winter and summer, the careless combinations of garments that looked salvaged from one of the Skid Road mission donation boxes, the stockings that bagged over unpolished shoes and the watch cap that kept her frizzy hair plastered to her head instead of springing out in all directions as it did whenever the weather turned damp.

His wife Sally had said that Natalie always looked as though she walked through old Maddy Blanchard's attic and wore whatever stuck to her. But that overgrown, dowdy, gawky girl who was always pestering him for assignments—Nat the Nuisance, Sally had dubbed her—bore little resemblance to the carefully groomed, fashionably dressed young woman who faced him now, except for the same stubborn determination that had led him to hire her in the first place.

"I don't expect you to give me a job because I'm a Blanchard," she'd said earnestly a year before.

"Far as I know, you're a Blake," he'd answered noncommittally. "And if I hired you it would be in spite of that, not because of it. The *Clarion* isn't exactly your folks' kind of newspaper, you know."

Paul Hawkins's newspaper didn't attack people like Natalie's family lightly, though he never missed an opportunity for a sly jab at them here and there. And it was partly because her earnestness amused him, and because she wore him down by turning up at his office regularly until he gave in, that he hired her. The other reason, which he did not admit to anyone, was that he got a kick out of the idea of having Abel Blanchard's granddaughter as an employee.

She had walked out of the university's journalism department one day and into his office, begging for a job. At first he was amused by her; soon he came to respect her. She worked hard, and she was good—her pictures were distinctive, unusual, and memorable. Some were more than just photographs, they were stories without words, like the spread she'd done on the hobo jungle down on the flats. The Depression was over, and now the tarpaper shacks and tin lean-tos of Hooverville housed war workers, who crowded into a city that had grown too rapidly to shelter them all. That was the first set of her pictures he syndicated. He did not think it would be the last.

He could not pay her much—the *Clarion* didn't have the deep pockets of the *Times* or the *Post-Intelligencer.* But as he told Sally, Natalie was the kind who wanted to work so much that she didn't care.

"That's no problem when you're a Blake and a Blanchard both," Sally said enviously. Paul's wife came from poor farm people in Carnation. She hadn't grown up in the Highlands, and she focused all her resentment of those who had on Natalie. It didn't help that she had had to take a swing shift job working for Natalie's brothers after the Hawkins's landlord—taking unpatriotic advantage of the wartime boom—doubled their rent. Kurt and Nick Blake were still making the seaplanes they'd been building since they started in a little factory on Lake Union, toys for rich men who needed a way to get to their fancy fishing and hunting camps up in the Islands. But some of the electronics they'd developed in the process had military uses, and their business had expanded rapidly. Actually, Paul didn't think Sally minded working at Blake's all that much, but when she needed an object for her bitterness, the kid was convenient.

Still, the kid—who was not a kid at all but a determined, capable young woman with the clout of Seattle's most powerful family behind her—was not particularly convenient right now. Despite her talent, there was no way Paul Hawkins was going to send her to the front. He lit his pipe and considered how to break that news to her without alienating her entirely.

It would have been easier if she didn't look quite so . . . well, elegant, he thought. She wore a green crepe dress with padded shoulders and a pleated skirt, and her silk stockings were a paler shade of the same color. On her arm she carried a short jacket with a Persian lamb collar, and her ears were studded with creamy pearls that matched the double strand around her neck.

"What are you all gussied up for today?" he asked.

"A War Relief luncheon at the Sunset Club," she replied with a grimace.

"A command performance by Catherine the Great, hmm?" he said.

Her eyes flashed an angry green. She was very sensitive about her parents—especially her mother. Catherine Blanchard Blake was not a subject Natalie often cared to entertain, but he had no choice. His voice was gruffer than he felt. He liked the girl, and he knew things around the office would be a lot less interesting without her.

"What do you suppose your mother would do to me if I let you get killed by the Huns?" he asked. "Come to think of it, what would the rest of your family do to me—to the *Clarion*? They'd have my balls for breakfast and close down my paper for good measure, that's what they'd do!"

She refused to accept that, so he tried to put it in terms someone like Natalie could understand.

"I send you overseas, and I'm risking my own investment—
all the training I've given you," he said. "I'm about to make us
both a lot of money; I've had an offer to syndicate that series you
did on the internment camps. I don't need pictures of guys
getting their heads blown off, I need more stuff like that. And
you're just the girl to give it to me."

She had put her guts into that assignment, covering the forced
departure of Seattle's Japanese Americans for the camps in
Idaho. The family she'd photographed, the Tsutakawas, were
well known to her—Nori, the eldest daughter, had been her
closest childhood friend. Their sorrow and disbelief, and Natalie's anguish, were clear in every picture.

Behind the lens of a camera, Natalie could escape who she
was. With it as a shield, she kept people at a distance, kept them
from knowing her while she probed their hearts and minds and
reflected what she saw there in her pictures. After she finished
the Tsutakawa shots, she hadn't turned in anything that good
for a while, just the usual: cats stuck in treetops and sunsets over
the bay. But then she seemed to snap out of it; he knew she was
learning the rest of the job, being a professional, and he was
proud of her.

But pro or not, she wasn't going overseas, and he told her so.
"I can't afford it," he said flatly. "You want to be a fancy war
correspondent, talk to someone with the money to send you over
there. Go talk to the Blethens."

He knew she couldn't and wouldn't. Blethen would no more
put Natalie's life in danger than he would. Less, even—the
Blethens were close friends of the Blanchards. Paul Hawkins's
Clarion was an insignificant little rag compared to the *Times,* and
nobody important paid it much mind. But it was his paper, and
his livelihood, and while it was nice to poke the powerful once
in a while, he knew the people who controlled Seattle could
crush him in a moment. His newspaper existed because they
allowed it to. And no matter how good a photographer the kid
was—and she was pretty good, he'd admit it—he wasn't about
to jeopardize his future to help her avoid the one they had all
laid out for her.

"I can pay my own way," she said stubbornly. "You don't

have to keep me on salary. What if I get over there on my own? If I sent you pictures, would you run them?"

"It depends," he replied carefully. "If they're any good—maybe."

"You know they'll be good, dammit."

He didn't want to close the door. Someday she would be a very important person in this town. If he could find a way to help her and himself without bringing the wrath of the Blanchards down on him, he would.

"Officially I can't do anything," he said. "Oh, I might be able to wangle you some credentials, but if you get over there—and I don't want to know how you're going to manage that—you'll have to get Ike or somebody to validate them. If you send me something I can use, I might print it. But that's as far as I can go."

A spark of hope flared in her eyes, and she threw her arms around his neck. "That's all I need, Paul—that will do it. You won't be sorry, I promise!"

I probably will, Hawkins thought. Like Sally always said, when you shake hands with a Blanchard, be sure you count the fingers you get back.

*   *   *

The strong wind blowing in from Elliott Bay threatened to blow Natalie's hat off her head, but the gusty, moisture-laden gray weather did nothing to dampen her spirits as she hurried along. The downtown streets were crowded with men in uniform. They stopped to stare at the tall young woman, slender as a birch tree, with the long, lean torso, narrow hips, and beautifully shaped legs. A group of white-hats spilled out of a Second Avenue tavern, and one of them whistled at her appreciatively.

She was no longer gawky, though she often felt that way. And her looks were arresting—splendid cheekbones and pale, creamy skin stretched taut over an aquiline, patrician nose and a small, square chin. Her lower lip was full and sensuous, and her coppery hair lit with amber glints like those that sparkled in her clear green eyes.

As a child, she had always felt clumsy and unlovely—her

mother was the true beauty in the family; everyone said so. Until she got used to her height, she tripped over everything. And Catherine was forever telling her to stop slumping, which she did to hide her high, full breasts, which in adolescence embarrassed her greatly.

No one had whistled at her then, and she grinned at the sailor as she made her way through the traffic. At the Savoy Hotel a one-armed man in a doorman's uniform was arguing with a khaki-clad young soldier who clasped the hand of an equally young, hugely pregnant girl. "I told ye, laddie, we're full up," the doorman was saying as Natalie passed them. "Now why don't you and the missus just go down to the ladies at the Aid Society. Maybe they'll be able to find you a room."

On the steps of the Post Office at Union Street a newsboy hawked the afternoon edition of the *Times*. "Extra, extra!" he called. "Allies launch new offensive, Luftwaffe bombs London!"

A thrill ran through Natalie. Beyond the gray-green mist that rolled in from the Pacific and hovered, trapped between two mighty mountain ranges, things were happening. In Seattle, they had happened long ago, before her time, she thought. And she hurried off to keep her appointment with a world at war.

Chapter Twenty-one

Natalie was no stranger to the capitals of Europe—
she had often accompanied Catherine on shopping trips to the
Continent. But in the spring of 1942, London was greatly
changed from the genteel, civilized, elegant city she knew.

Even the newsreels had not prepared her for the devastation
all around her. In the first two years after Great Britain declared
war on the Axis powers, the city had been bombed and burned;
centuries of history, architecture, and a way of life destroyed by
German UXBs, parachute flares, incendiary bombs, and "bread-
baskets," demolition clusters that exploded in midair and rained
death and destruction on both civilian and military targets.
Lodgings were hard to come by—London had become the nerve
center of the Allied effort, and hotel rooms were scarce and
frightfully expensive. Still, there were ways and means, especially for someone whose mother, before the war, had been a
regular and valued customer at a fine hotel like the Connaught.
Catherine's name was useful, and so was Natalie's cache of
American dollars, though when she had unpacked and spent an
afternoon retracing her steps through familiar streets and to
remembered haunts, her affluence made her feel so guilty that
she immediately set about finding less ostentatious lodgings.

It took several days before she located a flat on Duchess Street
—it was let to her by a fatherly gentleman who had sent his own
family away to the relative safety of Switzerland and thought
the young American girl was daft to put herself in harm's way.
And that first night in the flat when the air raid sirens sounded

and she stumbled down into the shelter of the tube, heard bombs exploding and buildings toppling, she thought he was probably right. But the people around her were stoic, and that British unflappability, even in the midst of such havoc and danger, calmed her own fears. " 'Tain't the ones you can hear that'll harm you, lass," said the white-haired, robe- and pajama-clad elderly man who sat next to her on the hard bench, his gas mask hung incongruously around his neck and his furled umbrella under his arm. "It's the ones you can't hear that do the real damage. Old Jerry's just going through the motions tonight, simply rattling our cage—we've got 'im on the run, you know."

She spent the first week in a frustrating round of calls: at Scotland Yard, for a police pass that would enable her to move freely around London, at the Ministry of Home Security for the clearances necessary to validate her *Clarion* credentials, at every office in Fleet Street where she could show her portfolio and clips and apply for a job.

She called round at Grosvenor House and listened patiently while an aide to Ambassador Kennedy explained that, in case she didn't know it, there was a war going on, and he had better things to do than help a foolish American girl who had some romantic notions about her career. Thus she was surprised when that same aide appeared at Duchess Street two days later with a letter from her father, which had come that morning in the diplomatic pouch marked PRIORITY—HAND DELIVER.

"I'm afraid I didn't know who you were," the aide apologized, and handed over the communiqué from Leighton. "Of course, I'll be glad to do anything I can to expedite things for you."

Her father's letter included a draft for a thousand pounds, a list of people in London who might be useful, and a handwritten note.

Look after yourself, don't take too many foolish chances, and remember that, while being who you are may seem in Seattle a limitation on your personal freedom and professional aspirations, in other places it can and will open doors to you that might otherwise be closed.

Support from such an unexpected quarter was a welcome surprise, even though Natalie had few illusions about what had prompted it. In spite of the civility that marked relations between her mother and father, she knew that—though it was said to have been a great romance in the beginning—there was little love between them now. She still remembered the day she had come home from grammar school to find Catherine packing up their belongings and supervising the movers. She had run upstairs. Her room, freshly repainted and redecorated only a month before, was completely empty—even her fourposter bed, with the blossom-sprigged sheer silk curtains that framed it like a sultan's tent, had been dismantled and removed.

When she went back downstairs, her father had just arrived. Catherine's high heels beat out a staccato tattoo on the marble floors as she moved back and forth between the movers and the boxes. But when she confronted her husband in the rotunda, there was no hint of nervousness in her demeanor and no tremor in her voice.

"You're leaving," he said. His words were a statement, not a question, and Catherine did not disagree.

"You're going to Broadview?" Leighton asked, and when Catherine nodded Natalie felt the knot of tension in her stomach loosen slightly. Broadview—that might not be so terrible. It was better than the Bluff; she had feared, at first, that Catherine was exiling them there. Great-uncle Caleb's house was old and damp; when the wind howled through it, she thought the building would blow right out to sea, and the sound of the surf pounding against the cliffs was so loud she couldn't sleep. There was no one to play with for miles around except for Indians, whom she had been afraid of ever since her brothers told her that the bluff was the site of their burial grounds—that their spirits walked the land at night, and that sometimes they snatched little girls right out of their beds, took their scalps, and threw their headless bodies into the sound. And Arabella, who was four years older and given to teasing just as Kurt and Nicholas were, told her about Sara Blanchard, their grandfather's first wife, and how she had died mysteriously on that same bluff—her ghost, said Arabella, still haunted it.

No, she couldn't bear living at the Bluff. But Broadview wouldn't be so awful. She could tell her friends they were moving because her grandmother was old and infirm. Then no one

would say, as they did about her friend Amy Burke, that her
parents were getting a divorce so they could marry other people.
When she asked her mother if that was why they were leaving,
Catherine said, Don't be a foolish goose, neither of us is marrying anyone else, where did you get such a stupid idea? And then
she said, with that uncanny knack she had of anticipating Natalie's thoughts before they were clear in her own mind, that even
though Maddy pretended that she was as strong as a horse, she
was really quite frail and old and needed them to care for her.

When Natalie had repeated that to her grandmother, Maddy
pursed her lips. "If it suits her to say that, so be it. I just hope
she doesn't believe it." And then she changed the subject, and
no more was said.

Natalie's bed and her other belongings were sent to First Hill,
and on her first morning there, she woke up and looked out at
the snow-draped mountains staggered against the western sky
like a line of high-stepping dancers flinging their petticoats over
their heads. Snuggled under the feather quilts, she thought
about her father, lonely and abandoned in the big house at the
Highlands. She thought about Mrs. Dickinson, the housekeeper,
and Inga, the nanny, and Mary, the cook, and Ahito, the gar-
dener, and Mason, the butler. She thought about Jezebel, her
golden retriever, who could not come to Broadview because
dogs made Maddy sneeze, and about the enormous old madrona
tree that brushed up against the nursery window, its peeled
reddish skin like cool silk beneath the scratchy bark. She
thought about the parties her parents used to give, the way the
music and laughter rang through the house and floated upstairs
on nights after the boat races, which her father, with his beloved
yacht *Hera*, usually won. And then she thought about the nights
when he didn't come home, the silence that filled the rooms like
dust—and when he finally did, the angry words like rifle shots,
exchanged between him and her mother. And then the First
Hill streetcar clanged, and there was a knock at her door, and
Mrs. Erickson came in with a tray laden with hot oatmeal,
strawberries and cream, and freshly made muffins, and she
thought that Broadview, after all, might not be too dreadful—
might, in fact, be quite nice. There was a Japanese girl her own
age who lived a few doors away. And when on Sunday evenings

Natalie and her sister returned from weekends with Leighton at the Firs, she was not sorry to be back at Maddy's.

Divorce was not mentioned in Natalie's presence. Her parents were correct and even polite to each other when family or other public occasions required their joint presence. On Sundays they worshiped together in the Methodist Church, and Leighton came to dinner afterward at Broadview. They all went to Nick and Kurt's graduation from Stanford, and at Christmas the whole family, Leighton included, embarked for Honolulu, although Catherine and Leighton had separate suites at the Royal Poinciana Hotel.

Natalie and her father had not been especially close before the separation. But as she grew into young womanhood, he paid more attention to her: he showed her and Arabella off to his friends at lunches at his club, picked them up in his sporty roadster and whisked them off to play doubles at the Tennis Club, or took them away on weekends to ski at Snoqualmie Pass or sail up to the Islands on the *Hera*.

Though he was affectionate and appreciative, kind, and even courtly, Natalie never felt completely comfortable with her father's attentions—she suspected him of using her in the undeclared but still real war between him and Catherine. When her photographs first appeared in the *Clarion* he praised them extravagantly, and he was quick to encourage her. He was also generous with his support of her work—he bought her the most advanced cameras, the newest film, insisted that she continue with her studies and perfect her skill. He was her ally in the futile battle with Catherine about going to New York, though it did no good—Catherine was adamant.

You have an exceptional talent, and these are the times in which you can most fully exploit it, he wrote to her in London, and when she called round to see the people he had suggested, she discovered that he had already written them letters of introduction. At the suggestion of a man Leighton had sailed with in the years between the wars, she went to the Black Star Agency in Fleet Street. But it was two weeks before she could even get in to see the editor, two weeks of waiting on hard wooden benches in cigarette-littered hallways, and when she finally secured an appointment, the fellow looked over her credentials, said, "What the hell is the Seattle *Clarion*?" and showed her the door without even looking at her photos.

She was leaving the photo agency's offices, her portfolio suddenly a heavy weight under her arm, when a cheerful voice interrupted her musings. "Why, it's Natalie Blake! What on earth are you doing here, child?"

She looked up to see the friendly face of Mary Marvin Breckenridge. Natalie had met her at one of Catherine's Sunday evenings two years before, when the acclaimed photojournalist had shown her documentary film about the Frontier Nursing Service in Seattle. She had come to Broadview with one of Catherine's artist friends, and Natalie liked her immediately. She was a tall brunette with a long horsy face and a ready smile—"Call me Marvin, everyone does," she said. After seeing some of Natalie's photographs she had told her to look her up when she got to New York—now, she told Natalie, she was living in Europe, married to a diplomat and therefore had to give up her work for Black Star. That didn't stop her from taking Natalie by the hand and marching her back into the editor's office. "This young woman has enormous talent—you'd be a fool not to take her on," she declared. Finally, Natalie was promised a tryout, and they left the offices for lunch at the Savoy Grill, where Marvin insisted on paying. In that hushed, gracious room, the war seemed a million years away. But it was not, and from the veteran correspondent, Natalie learned how to cut through red tape, what channels to use, where to buy groceries, where to get a gas mask, and who could be helpful at OMI and SHAEF. "Your brothers are quite important to the war effort—use whatever leverage that can give you," she said. "And isn't your mother an old friend of Clementine Churchill's?"

Natalie nodded. On her last visit to England, they had taken tea with Mrs. Churchill, an otherwise boring afternoon enlivened only by the vivid presence, for a few moments, of the First Lord of the Admiralty. Back at home, Catherine had organized the Seattle chapter of Bundles for Britain—and for her efforts she had had several notes of appreciation from Mrs. Churchill.

"Well, don't hesitate to mention that either," Marvin told her briskly. "You'll need all the help you can get if you're determined to be here. I can't imagine what your mother was thinking of, though—" Marvin's eyes narrowed as she assessed the guilty face across the table. "She does know you're here, doesn't she?"

Natalie nodded. She had left a note for Catherine the night she left Seattle and had written her once she arrived in London, apologizing for her secretive departure and asking Catherine to try to understand why she had felt compelled to leave. She did not think her explanation would suffice, or that her mother would easily forgive her. But she would deal with that at a later time; as her grandmother was fond of saying, as soon as her head caught up with the rest of her. And when she parted with Marvin Breckenridge an hour later and went out into the April sunshine and looked around her, Seattle, and Catherine, seemed to belong to another world.

While the war was still being fought on the home front, the main action had shifted that spring to the Continent, where British commando raids had begun. With the money from Leighton, Natalie purchased a Sunbeam Talbot, and though gasoline was strictly rationed, her press credentials enabled her to find enough petrol to drive out of the city. She photographed other war victims—the slum children evacuated out of London, the wives waiting for word of their fighting men, the hospitals full of the wounded. She sold her first pictures to *Life* three months after she arrived; when segregated units of American GIs arrived in England and violent incidents followed, she caught them on film, the first photographer to do so.

London itself was a city still besieged. Air raid precaution signs were everywhere, rubble from the bombings was covered by more rubble before it could be carted away, and most of the vital industries as well as the shops and stores were kept going by the young, the infirm, the militarily unfit, and their mothers, wives, and daughters. The graceful parks were torn up with trenches, and the nightly BBC broadcasts dutifully reported the latest casualty counts. Yet in spite of all this there was a kind of reckless gaiety, a brave laughter in the face of death, that made friendships quick and easy, liaisons urgent and desperately romantic. There were late nights of feverish drinking and dancing and many handsome men in uniform were eager to court the pretty Yank photographer; she was friendly with most of them, infatuated for a short time with one, but so intent on her work that hardly any man made more than a temporary impression. Johnny Gasden managed to get to England every couple of months and kept her supplied with news from home as well as with food parcels and other items that were scarce in London. Her Aunt Ruth rang up as soon as she found out that Natalie was in London—her mother's oldest friend had been doing relief work in Russia and was now in England organizing more aid for that beleaguered country. She was the first to tell Natalie that the rumors she had heard about concentration camps in Germany were more than just rumors. Ruth had met two young Jews who had managed to get away, and their report of the atrocities being committed horrified Natalie. "Americans are not fully informed on just how awful things are, and even the ones who know are keeping quiet," Ruth said. "Later they'll say they didn't know, it wasn't their fault—when the Nazis have worked the remaining few to death in the armaments factories, there won't be a Jew left in all of Germany, and America won't even mind—they've wanted us dead since the beginning of history anyway." She fixed Natalie with her penetrating stare. "The tide is turning. The Allies will win the war, though not until thousands more have died. And when they do—when it's over—someone has to go and make a record, so the world will never forget what has been done to my people."

Ruth worried about Natalie. "You must promise me not to try to leave England—there are enough news correspondents and photographers out there already getting killed every week," she said. Natalie evaded such a commitment. She had already applied for permission to fly with a bombing mission and photograph in action the planes that had been built in her own back yard—she knew she would find a good market for those pictures in Seattle. It took months to arrange. She fumed while male correspondents flew off with the heavy bomber groups, and she was only allowed to shoot as they departed or returned from their missions. True, she had no actual combat experience, as many veteran photographers did; on the other hand, she had hundreds of hours of actual flight time and a pilot's license as well. Her brothers and Johnny Gadsden had been her instructors, and she was as used to the cockpit of an airplane as she was to the driver's seat of an automobile.

She was determined to wangle the necessary permission any way she could; meanwhile, she worked on accumulating and testing the equipment she would need: the Speed Graphic a Signal Corps lieutenant "liberated" for her, a rigid metal K-20 "borrowed" from an army colonel, electric mittens so her hands, at the high altitudes flown by the B-17's, would not freeze on the lever of the camera.

Finally, the coveted permission came through and she hurried to the field, so excited that it was not until the briefing officer and meteorologist gave the ready signal that she realized the fluttering feeling in her stomach was more than exhilaration. It was fear, a sudden awareness of her own mortality, a realization that people could die on this mission, and not just those on the ground.

Once airborne, she busied herself photographing the interior of the Flying Fortress from every angle: the crew at their posts, the bombardier's exit into the bay once the plane left friendly territory and crossed into enemy skies, the frighteningly young airman who put away his Bible as they approached the target. As they roared toward their goal, the pilot began a series of evasive maneuvers not unlike those she had experienced before, flying with Kurt and Nick in one plane as they pretended to shoot Johnny out of the skies in his. But this was not a friendly rivalry, she reminded herself—this was war, and the stakes were much higher than the drinks or dollars they had waged on those youthful challenges.

Her photographs from that mission made *Life*'s centerfold— the plumes of white, black, and red smoke and fire marking the on-target landing of the bombs dropped from the B-17's bays, the threads of return fire from enemy antiaircraft installations, the terror and triumph on the faces of the crew as they flew through hell. It wasn't until after the plane turned away from the target and the pilot announced, two hours later, that they were in sight of their home base, that she began to shake; it took all her self-control to keep from crying with relief. At the post-flight debriefing, she learned that six of the planes that had gone on the mission had not returned: two had exploded in midair, one she had watched take a direct hit and plummet to earth like a shot bird before the pilot could eject, and the others were not yet accounted for.

Natalie was not ordinarily a drinker, but when she left the operations shack, she went in search of the pub she had noticed just outside the airfield's perimeter. A half hour later, the pub was full of the bombardier group crews, all shoving each other in a desperate need to get to the bar, down their first glass, and loudly demand the next. Then they settled down to serious drinking, and an enthusiastic rehash of the mission—all but one man, who stood slightly apart until he noticed her and came over to where she was sitting. Without waiting for an invitation, he joined her, and she did not object. She was lonely. She felt apart from the others, not just because she was a woman, but because she had been an observer, and not a participant, in their mission of death.

The man who came to sit with her was the gunner with the Bible; after they landed, she had watched him climb out of the bomber, take off his helmet, and vomit into it. Then he had looked up and seen her aim her camera at him; he had touched his forehead in a mock salute before disappearing into the operations shack. She followed him there and watched his anxious face as he listened for word of the missing planes, and when he entered the pub, he saw her immediately and had again saluted her. She felt his eyes on her as he drank the first traditional glass of whiskey with his comrades. Then he left them and came to sit with her. Without speaking, they watched the others, who in a short time became very drunk; their language grew coarse and their behavior raucous. But the gunner seemed to sink deeper into a heavy silence.

Finally he spoke to her. "They're trying to erase it from their minds so they can go back up there tomorrow night," he said.

"Then why aren't you with them?"

"There's not enough whiskey in the world for that," he replied.

He did not speak again, but when he rose to leave, she said, "Are you going back to the base?"

He replied that he was, and she gathered her cameras. "I'll go with you," she said. "Perhaps by now they've had some word about the others."

He said nothing, and she followed him out of the pub. It was a cool, starry night, moonless and damp; it reminded her of home, the musty autumn smell of the earth making ready for winter.

"Did you—do you know any of the men on the planes that aren't back yet?" she asked.

"The bombardier on the *Ginnie Mae* is my brother," he said, and because she did not know what else to say, she took his hand in hers and silently went with him back to the base.

There was no word yet of the missing planes; they drank bitter coffee and smoked endless cigarettes as the night paled into dawn. Each time the door of the shack opened, he looked up—and between times he told her a little about himself. He was from a small town in South Carolina and had been a farmer before the war. He looked quite young in his bulky flying suit, like a boy masquerading in grown-up clothes; underneath his ruddy tan there was a pallor to his face, and his fingernails, on work-roughened, reddened hands, were bitten to the quick.

Finally, they heard the sound of a plane, its engines sputtering like a hacking cough, and ran outside to watch it land, a medic team pushing past them with stretchers and bags of straw-colored plasma, a fire crew spraying the runway with foam and warning them to stay back.

Less than a thousand feet above the field, the rear section of the plane suddenly burst into flame, and the half that remained veered wildly to the left. Then it plunged straight down, hitting the tarmac with an earsplitting, ground-shaking *thwack* that sprayed pieces of metal and other unrecognizable objects within inches of where they stood.

"That was the *Ginnie Mae*—that was Dick's plane!" the young airman said, his face contorting in a mask of pain. He ran forward, but the heat drove him back from the burning mass that was all that remained of the bomber.

He turned away then, walking with a grim, determined stride to the farthest corner of the airfield. She followed him, stopping when she heard his footsteps stop, and in the light reflected from the still-burning wreckage of the *Ginnie Mae*, she saw the tears stream down his cheeks.

She did not know what made her leave her camera where it was and approach him, her arms held out to embrace him. Or why, when he led her to a barracks room that was silent and empty, she allowed him to take off her clothes, and unzip his flying suit, and make love to her with an urgency so fierce that his climax, when it came, resounded with the pain she felt when he entered her, and his tears, afterward, were indistinguishable from her own.

They lay there together for a while, and then the sirens clanged, signaling the pilots to man their aircraft. He dressed hurriedly, his mind not on her now but on what was ahead, and when he was fully clothed, he bent to kiss her cheek and murmur a quiet "Thank you." And then he was gone, and in minutes, so was she.

Chapter Twenty-two

Maddy Blanchard's funeral cortege lumbered along the fogbound avenue like a pod of whales swimming through sea mist. Except for the hearse, the cortege included most of the limousines that had delivered the same dignitaries, a week before, to the dedication of the Abel Blanchard Memorial Library at the University of Washington.

Although the library was Maddy's legacy to Seattle, it was Abel's name that was chiseled in granite letters above the portico. "Your father always said you can't have a great city without a great university," she told her children, "and a university without an excellent library can never be great."

If he'd been consulted, Abel would have preferred an office building like Joshua Green's, or a skyscraper like L. C. Smith's. The typewriter millionaire's tower at the bottom of the Skid Road was the tallest building west of the Mississippi. But Maddy had never shown any interest in monuments to commerce. She had kept the *Journal* going even during the Depression, thanks to Jonathan Cape's canny management and her small but steady subsidy. Some of the *Journal*'s promising young writers had even managed to pierce the green curtain that blocked the view of influential New York critics, and when their work was published and praised beyond Seattle, Maddy was especially gratified. But it was the library to which she had devoted most of her energy in the last years of her life, and that she had lived to see her dream become reality, intoned the minister, was proof that her mission had enjoyed God's favor.

She died peacefully in the big wing chair in her library on the second day of 1944. The funeral was delayed while Catherine tried to find Natalie. She was with the Russian army, following their advance toward Sevastopol and the recapture of the Crimea, and the Black Star editor cabled that he would attempt to locate her. But after four days, Catherine allowed funeral plans to proceed, hoping until the last that Natalie would get her message and return home in time to bury Maddy.

When the hearse pulled off the main street and wound slowly through Lakeview Cemetery, Catherine still did not know if Natalie had received her messages—or, if she had, whether she had tried to respond. Catherine and Maddy had never been close, in spite of living together for so long; today, Catherine regretted that, and it made her long for Natalie's presence. She wished she could apologize for all the things she had not done, and for some of those she had—to her daughter as well as to her mother. She was sorry, now, that she had not tried to heal the breach Natalie's departure had opened between them. If she ever got the opportunity to make it up to Natalie—for Maddy was beyond her reach now—she vowed, she would.

Natalie had always been the most difficult, least tractable of Catherine's children. Almost from infancy, she was stubborn, willful, and fiercely independent. As a young woman, she had scorned Catherine's attempts to guide her toward the life that was best for her. Catherine believed that, no matter how self-sufficient or dedicated to the pursuit of a career, a woman's only true happiness lay in marriage—in a home, children, and a loving husband. She herself had failed at the last; perhaps that was why Natalie had run away. If she had stayed with Leighton, might Natalie have stayed in Seattle? It was not the first time she had asked herself that question.

She wished she had replied to Natalie's first and only letter from London. Her calculated silence was an effort to indicate her displeasure and her feelings of betrayal; when it did not work, when Natalie did not come home, she recognized her mistake. She could not bring herself to make the first gesture of reconciliation—still, she had not abandoned her daughter. She tried with her considerable influence to ensure Natalie's safety, even her success. She wondered if her daughter knew why she enjoyed the access she did—at the Office of Military Information, at SHAEF, at the American Embassy, even at Number 10 Downing Street. Her family connections permitted Natalie to pursue her work unfettered by the restrictions that hampered other journalists. Because of Catherine's behind-the-scenes maneuvering, Natalie was allowed to earn the acclaim that her talent and perseverance merited. Because of her, Catherine thought ruefully, Natalie was in the thick of the fighting—in greater danger than anyone, even her mother, could possibly protect her from. Natalie had no idea of what she owed her, and Catherine wondered, as they approached the cemetery, if she would ever have the chance to call in that debt.

She stepped out of the limousine, a heavily veiled and elegant figure in a simple Mainbocher dress of black wool crepe, over which she wore a full-length mink coat. She was flanked by her sons and by Leighton and Arabella. Her brothers and their families completed the circle around the grave's yawning rectangle.

As she had at the church, Catherine acknowledged the condolences of the wealthy and powerful who had gathered to pay homage, again, to Maddy Blanchard. She pointedly ignored William Boeing's outstretched hand—she would not forgive him for aiding Natalie's escape, however indirectly. Nor Johnny Gasden either, toward whom she directed an icy glare. He had become practically a member of the family, since the time Nick first brought him home, and she had hoped that Natalie might return his obvious affection. His antecedents weren't especially grand, but he was clever and well-spoken, ambitious and hardworking—very much as Leighton had been, she thought, watching him from beneath her veil, but without that opportunistic streak or that need to dominate and possess every female he met that had been her husband's downfall.

She had had great hopes for Johnny Gasden, but he had proved himself unworthy of them. Catherine was a woman who held few grudges, but those few ran strong and deep; neither Nick, who was Gasden's closest friend, nor Kurt, who knew how important Bill Boeing's goodwill was to their own business, dared to attempt to persuade her that her bitterness toward either man was unjustified.

The minister began to read the funeral service, as a white federal marshal's car stopped at the far edge of the cemetery and a man got out, accompanied by two burly officers. They walked alongside him, their eyes searching the crowd. The trio made their way through the stone gardens, past the mausoleums of Maynards and Dennys and Borens, pioneers who, like the woman they had come to bury, had journeyed far from the homes of their birth and, like her, had found their eternal rest on this gentle green slope overlooking the bay.

When Catherine saw who it was that had interrupted Maddy's final rites, her face paled beneath her veil and she would have fallen if Kurt and Nick had not held her. As Colin McKay came toward her slowly, the crowd parted to make way for him. When he reached her, he held out his hand; ignoring the shock of surprise that rippled through the mourners, she took it, and they remained that way, still and silent as the marble statuary that surrounded them, until the minister cleared his throat and once more began the funeral service.

Later, in the privacy of their own homes, the guests would gossip about the appearance of Colin McKay at Maddy Blanchard's funeral—about what kind of strings had been pulled to permit him to leave the federal prison at McNeil Island and attend the burial of a woman none of them had any idea he had even known. They would speculate about the relationship between Colin McKay and Catherine Blake and discuss in detail how Leighton Blake had reddened with anger, turned on his heel, and left the cemetery. And how, after Catherine tossed the first handful of dirt on the coffin, just before it was lowered into the ground, another car had pulled up to the graveside—a taxicab this time—and from it alighted a tall young woman with hair the color of a new penny, dressed in gray slacks and a military jacket on whose collar shone the gold insignia of a war correspondent. In her hand was a single white rose, which she dropped on the coffin before turning to her mother, who, despite the arms that held her, slumped into the first faint of her life.

*　*　*

Catherine's sitting room was a fine frame for the beautifully composed portrait she made, seated on a silk damask Louis XV sofa, surrounded by the lovely objects she had collected over the years: Battersea snuff boxes jumbled artfully on a graceful, gilded étagère, a pair of K'ang Hsi porcelain birds on the marble mantel of the fireplace, a Renoir painting of a bather that glowed with the same soft hues as the Aubusson carpet.

She was a slender, fine-boned woman with coloring that startled like a tropical bird, even softened as it was by the years. Her hair was still the color of fire when it first breathes air, and her eyes were still that vivid tourmaline green, though her skin, dusted lightly with a faint spattering of freckles, had lost the fine translucence of long ago.

She had changed into a russet robe of Dynasty silk, and her face was surprisingly youthful for a woman of fifty-four, though tiny lines at the corners of her eyes hinted at her age. On her lap was the score of Beethoven's last sonata, the C minor, and as the expressive tones of Leopold Godowsky's recording died away, she let it slip to the floor and leaned her head back on the sofa, lost in thought.

Maddy's death had not been a shock to her. She had stunned Catherine only twice: once when she told her not to marry Leighton if she didn't love him, no matter if she was carrying his child, and the other time when, shortly after Natalie's kidnapping, she suggested that she formalize her separation from him "and perhaps make a new life for yourself." Maddy had seemed to know about Catherine's friendship with Colin McKay and, without in any way condoning it, treated her with unusual tact and delicacy after he was convicted and jailed.

She wondered this evening, with her mother only hours in her grave, if she had known the truth about her relationship with Colin. After his highly publicized trial, she had spoken rather cryptically about duty and honesty; perhaps in some way she knew that Catherine owed him a debt of honor. What she did not know—what no one knew—was that Catherine had pleaded with Colin to let her testify in his defense at the trial, to reveal the reason he had taken the union's money and prove his contention that every dollar of it had been replaced and repaid. But Colin had refused. "You would not sacrifice your position to marry me, I cannot allow you to do it to save me," he said, and when she gave him the copy of the promissory note that she had kept, he did as he had done with the original several years before—tore it into small bits and pieces and then tossed it in the fire that was burning, that evening, in the house at Caleb's Bluff.

He had gone to prison shortly thereafter, and how he had wangled permission to attend the funeral was beyond her comprehension. They had had only a few moments, after the service was concluded, before his guards indicated that it was time to go back. He had looked strong and well; in their brief conversation, he told her that prison life was actually quite healthy and even enjoyable. "I have time to read, exercise, and even play music," he said. "I've organized an orchestra among the inmates."

She had laughed. "When you get to heaven, you'll organize the seraphim and cherubim," she told him.

"Not for a while yet," he responded. His eyes searched her face. "The years have been kind to you—and you've returned the compliment."

"I see you've found time for Byron, too," she said.

"Among others." He took her hand in his. "Will you be all right?"

"Yes," she responded. "Will you?"

"I've eighteen more months, and then the rest of my life ahead of me. Or the rest of ours. Haven't we wasted enough of it?"

"Now you've blown our secret, you mean?" she parried, but he could tell she was pleased that he had come and not unduly concerned, any more, with the rumors that would surely follow his departure. Still, she would not give him the commitment he hoped for. "Perhaps," she replied. "When you're free . . . perhaps."

She could not refuse him then—not when he had to return to that dreadful place. But now, hours later, her head once more ruled her heart, and she knew that she had given him false hope. She had tried to keep him from going to prison, but he had refused. Having destroyed his own reputation to secure hers, he had made an alliance between them even more unthinkable.

In the emotion of the moment, with her mother's body being lowered into the grave, it had seemed possible. After all, what else did she have to look forward to in her old age? Her sons had their own lives, her brothers and their families bored her, and even her stations held little interest or challenge any more. Now that Maddy was gone, Broadview would be turned over to the Pioneers Association, historically preserved for future generations as Abel had willed it. She would have to make a new home for herself, and she had decided to return to the Bluff, which remained, as it had always been, her one true home. She would welcome Colin there, as a guest and as a friend, but she would not marry him or divorce Leighton. For now she had a reason to live up to her name and her heritage, to prosper and endure. Natalie had returned, and although Maddy was dead and Colin back in prison, in Catherine's heart a spark of happiness flickered and fanned into a flame as bright and alive as the one that burned in the hearth before her.

* * *

Natalie knocked at the door of the sitting room, and at Catherine's "come in" she smoothed her hair and entered. After the funeral, they had returned to Broadview, each in her own way mourning the death that had brought them together again. Her estrangement from Catherine had troubled Natalie in those first months in London, but then, caught up in a new life, she had ceased to worry about it. Catherine never had responded to her letter, but that first Christmas after her departure, Natalie sent her a photograph that said everything she could not put into words: a picture of an elderly woman at Waterloo station, clutching the empty sleeve of a beribboned sergeant, as she waved goodby to a raw-faced youth in a private's uniform. There were tears in the woman's eyes, but her head was held high and there was a proud smile on her face as she saw her remaining son off to war. That picture, Natalie saw, hung over her mother's writing desk, and it gave her the courage she needed to walk toward the sofa, drop to her knees, and lay her head in Catherine's lap.

"I'm sorry," she said softly, and she felt her mother's hand stroke her hair.

"She had a long and useful life," Catherine replied, as if Natalie was talking about the funeral. "Now stand up and let me look at you."

She complied with her mother's wishes and stood as Catherine inspected her.

"You've become handsome," she said, "and you've filled out some, though you look quite exhausted. Are you sure you're not ill?"

Natalie still wore her uniform trousers, though she had changed her blouse and jacket for a long, loose smock of cashmere wool in a heathery green that matched her eyes. The angular figure of her girlhood was gone—she looked womanly, Catherine thought, changed in some imperceptible way. Was it the fullness of her figure or her eyes? she wondered. They were older than her years, full of the death and destruction she had witnessed, and beneath them were deep circles.

"It was a long flight," Natalie said. "I'm tired, that's all. I'd been working for three weeks, and when I got back to London and checked in at the office, they gave me your cable. I came as soon as I could."

A friend at SHAEF had arranged priority seating for her on a flight to the States, and she had managed to get to Seattle in twenty-four hours. She had arrived at the cemetery as Leighton was leaving it. He had waited and driven her back to Broadview afterward.

"Aren't you coming in?" she asked when he drew up before the gate. She would always think of this house as her grandmother's.

"No, I think it's better that I leave you two together," her father said. "If I know Catherine, she's already making plans for you, and I wouldn't dream of interfering with them." He reached over and kissed her cheek. "I imagine you have your own plans as well, my dear; you always have. When you've struck your bargain with her, come and see me, won't you? I've missed you too, you know—and I'm proud of what you've accomplished, just as she is."

As she watched her mother rise from the sofa to turn off the phonograph, she remembered her father's words. Knowing that she would need all her wits about her, she refused the drink Catherine offered.

"Well, I'll have one anyway," said Catherine, and lifted her glass in Natalie's direction. "To the prodigal daughter," she pronounced, "and her safe return from the wars."

She led Natalie to the sofa and gestured for her to sit down. "Don't be sad for your grandmother," she said. "She had a useful life and lucky death. She left her journals to you, you know—she said at the library dedication that if you didn't want them, she'd like them burned."

"I thought she'd want them to go to the university," said Natalie, surprised.

"So did I," said Catherine, "but she was quite adamant about it. She said she'd rather see them destroyed than fall into the hands of outsiders."

"I don't know what I shall do with them, though of course I want them," said Natalie. "Someday I'll have a place to keep them . . . until then, would you look after them for me?"

"Certainly," said Catherine, "though you should start looking for a house now. When the war is over, housing will be difficult to find. There's the Bluff, of course—I'll be moving out there shortly, and while there's ample room for you there, I imagine you'll want to be closer to town."

Natalie sighed. Clearly her mother thought she intended to take up once more the life she had gone so far to avoid and had no idea how impossible, at this particular moment, that was. For a moment she deliberated—what if she told Catherine the truth? But then she looked at her mother, surrounded by her possessions, the embodiment of moral rectitude, and knew how foolish that was. "I don't think you understand, Mother. I can't stay."

Her mother's face suddenly sagged—she looked smaller, older, than she had just a moment before. "Must we go through this again?" she said. "I understand that you had to try your hand at a career, but you've done that now—and quite well, too. But there are the stations—I hoped you'd want to take them over. And there's the *Journal*, too—Maddy often said she was saving it for you. That should be more than enough to keep you busy, at least until you—"

"Until I find a suitable husband and settle down to a suitable life," Natalie finished. She did not miss the anger that flared in Catherine's green eyes.

"Is that so dreadful?" she demanded. "To want you here,

taking your proper place in society, with a husband and children?"

"Mother, there's something I have to tell you," Natalie began, but Catherine interrupted her.

"If it's about a man, you needn't," she said sharply. "I'm not so old-fashioned as to believe that in your travels you might not have—well, succumbed to a wartime passion. Is he someone suitable?"

Natalie grimaced. "I don't believe you'd have thought so," she said. "In any case, it doesn't matter now."

"It's over, then?"

"In a manner of speaking."

"Then what is the problem?"

"The problem is that I don't belong here any more, Mother. I can't stay. I have . . . responsibilities."

"You have responsibilities here, young lady, and I suggest that you remember them!" Catherine said angrily. Natalie felt the old resentment—that, and the certain knowledge that she should not have come. Extricating herself from her mother's grasp was not going to be easy. She felt all her confidence, all her self-assurance, melt away in the face of Catherine's determination.

"I don't think this is a good time for us to talk," she said. "We're both tired, and we'll probably say things we'll regret later." She stood up and went to the door, but Catherine's voice stopped her.

"I want to settle this now," she said. "There are things to be done, arrangements to be made."

"Not tonight," Natalie said with a finality even Catherine was forced to acknowledge. "Tomorrow," she said. "We'll talk tomorrow."

After she left, Catherine walked to her writing desk and touched the photograph Natalie had sent her so long ago. You're home now, she said silently and fiercely. And this time, I shall not let you go!

Chapter Twenty-three

Catherine's mind wandered as Kurt droned on, enumerating with deadening logic the reasons why he proposed to sell off the assets of Blake Aviation, for which he needed her vote in the upcoming board meeting. Catherine's investment in the company was now worth a great deal of money—a third of a million dollars, exactly the amount needed to purchase the television station she was thinking about buying.

"Look, Mother, it's very simple. Since the war ended, we've shrunk our payroll by three quarters," Kurt said. "We've got labor troubles, thanks to Dave Beck and his Teamsters, and barely enough capital to make it to the end of the year, if the mechanics don't go out on strike and we can finish the contracts we have. Boeing will pay us a good royalty on our engineering patents, and ALKCO can develop our property in Bellevue. All those GIs who fought the war for a house in the suburbs will grab it in a minute. You'll get enough money to buy your television station, and Bill Allen has made Nick a very generous offer: a vice-presidency, Boeing stock, and a free hand in R and D."

Kurt sat back in his chair, a satisfied smile on his face. Around him his uncles, Matthew and Lucas, old but still closely involved in the family business, nodded in agreement. Nick, twirling his water goblet around in his fingers, shook his head.

"Bill Allen's a nice guy, but I don't want to work for him."

"No, you want to beat him at his own game." Kurt cracked his knuckles in a gesture of annoyance. "You can't, brother—he's too far ahead for you to catch up. He's got the resources to ride things out until the next war, but we don't."

"We're farther ahead with radar technology than he is, and he can't fly his passenger jets without it."

"It'll be ten years before he's sold one of those things, and meanwhile, he's got fourteen million dollars' worth of contracts for those Stratocruisers of his—"

Catherine studied her sons, wondering as she often did at how different they were, and yet how alike. Kurt reminded her of her father. He looked like Abel—big, clumsy in his movements, with an open, innocent face and watery blue eyes under brows as pale as his thinning blond hair. And, like Abel, he was earnest, thoroughgoing, dependable, and conservative—the exact opposite of his twin brother, who was mercurial, quick, and clever and as brilliant as lightning zigzagging across the sky. They were like two sides of a coin, one onyx, the other gold, she thought as she watched them, their heads bent over the sheaf of papers Kurt had brought to the meeting. Kurt had inherited her reddish-gold coloring, and Nick had Leighton's ruddy skin, spirited black eyes, and luxuriant, thick dark hair. Since infancy they had shared each other's passions, despite the differences in their personalities. They sailed, skied, and climbed together, making their first ascent of Mt. Rainier when they were only thirteen; on skis or in climbing boots, they had conquered every peak in the Northwest and most in California and Alaska. During prep school and college they often double-dated, and Catherine frequently thought they were wrongly paired with the young women they courted. The serious, thoughtful girls always seemed to prefer Nick, while the silly, frivolous ones, vain and empty-headed, were always attracted to Kurt. Or perhaps it was the boys who did the choosing, or thought they did. Men, thought Catherine, were not always very bright, which is why it was really too bad that they had all the power.

In business—until now—the twins complemented each other so neatly, it was hard to say whether their company would ever have amounted to anything if they had not managed to combine their strengths and abilities as smoothly as they did. Nick had had the idea for their first flying boat, the sleek little wooden seaplane that could skim you over to one of the islands dotting Puget Sound or the Gulf of Canada, or even to the isolated green dots in the southeastern seas off Alaska. And Kurt had found the money to build it and the land east of the lake to put up a proper factory. The military bought their product, and then they had hired skilled workers away from Bill Boeing, thus beginning a friendly rivalry that continued even after Bill retired and his successor turned the airplane factory into the huge entity it was now—four times the size of Blake Aviation and, as Kurt pointed out, in a much better financial position to ride out the postwar recession.

Kurt had made Blake Aviation successful because he resisted the impulse to take imprudent risks. He admired people like Bill Allen, who was running Boeing these days and chancing everything on the passenger aircraft market, but he had no desire to emulate them. Nick wanted to gamble—to keep building planes, even if the military was no longer buying them, and make them technologically superior to Boeing's. Catherine was worried that their differences on this crucial matter would tear the family apart. This was the first time they had ever been at odds, and she wanted to put a stop to it. For, in the end, family was what counted. Friends, business, even romantic love came and went; the bonds of blood were stronger and more important than any of those.

Or should be, she thought as they continued to wrangle. It was hard to concentrate on what they were saying, to keep her mind right here and not thousands of miles away. The boys would settle their differences—or she would, if they ever stopped talking long enough to let her tell them what she had in mind—and they would close ranks against outsiders again. But there would still be an empty seat at this boardroom table, an empty place in her heart, that could only be filled by the one person who did not care at all about the family business—and even less, Catherine suspected sadly, about the family itself.

According to the morning *Times*, Natalie was in Tel Aviv, or had been, as recently as the dateline on the photographs in the newspaper. When the British Mandate in Palestine expired, the Jewish state of Israel was declared—and, as expected, was attacked by the combined air forces of Egypt, Syria, and Jordan. Her daughter was there; wherever there was a war, Natalie Blake and her cameras were sure to be in the thick of it. This small brushfire between her brothers probably wouldn't qualify, Catherine thought wearily—the Blanchards and Blakes never inflicted mortal wounds on each other.

Or did they, she wondered? Catherine had not seen or heard from Natalie since the night of Maddy's funeral. The next morning, she was gone . . . no note of explanation, none of apology or regret.

Catherine was devastated. Had she, once more, driven her daughter away? In trying to help her, to guide her toward the life she was meant to live, had she succeeded only in shredding the already tattered remnants of the bond between them? For weeks, she tortured herself with guilt and recriminations; then, in an exercise of great self-control and mental discipline, she had put Natalie out of her mind. But not out of her heart. Every time she picked up a magazine or newspaper and saw her daughter's photographs, she ached anew for her.

Natalie's career had grown far beyond even the realm of Catherine Blake's influence. In early 1944, she had entered Rome with the Allies—and those pictures won her her first Pulitzer nomination. Then she seemed to drop out of sight; Catherine made no official inquiries, but from Ruth Straus she learned that Natalie had resigned from Black Star and was said by her editor to be on an extended leave of absence, though he believed she was still somewhere in England.

When the robot bombs, the revenge weapons called *Vergeltungswaffen* by the Germans, rained their death and destruction on London that summer after D-Day, Catherine made another attempt to contact Natalie. She learned that her daughter's house in Duchess Street was one casualty of the bombing, reduced to rubble by a V-2. Fortunately, Natalie was elsewhere that afternoon—five miles away, photographing the Guards Chapel in Whitehall, where two hundred people who had taken cover from the air raid were dead or dying.

"When I heard that Duchess Street was burning, I went round immediately," Ruth said. "Natalie lost everything."

"But not her life."

Catherine felt a tremendous relief, but although Ruth agreed that it was a miraculous stroke of luck, there was something in her voice that belied her words. Or perhaps it was the bad connection; Catherine had managed to get a direct link-up with London, but there was a lot of static on the line.

"Where is she now?" Ruth was the only person who knew how out of touch she was with Natalie, the only one for whom she did not need to construct the tissue of half-truths and omissions that concealed from others the true state of her relations with her daughter. Ruth had been Catherine's only real friend, her sole confidante; despite the distance that separated them, they remained close, maintaining their friendship with letters and cables and telephone calls. When Natalie was younger, it was Ruth who mediated the friction between mother and daughter; now it was Ruth who linked them, however tenuously, and was a friend to both.

"I'm not sure, exactly." Ruth was vague. "She didn't tell me her plans—just that she was taking a leave for a time, and would be in touch."

"When she is—" Catherine began, and Ruth broke in.

"When she is, I'll let you know," she said, and Catherine had to be satisfied with that.

It was months before she heard anything of her daughter again, though by late autumn Natalie was in Greece—one of her photographs of the Allied occupation of Athens made the cover of *Life,* and in April of the following year, so did her picture of the funeral train that carried Franklin Roosevelt home to Hyde Park from Warm Springs.

Catherine hoped then that Natalie might come home; by V-E day, she was sure of it. But then Natalie entered the concentration camps with the Allied troops. She went to make a record of the atrocities visited on the Jews, and it was that record that earned her her second nomination and her first Pulitzer Prize.

In the years since then, Catherine had not heard one direct word from Natalie. She followed her peregrinations around the world in the press but refused Leighton's suggestion that she make the first move in attempting a reconciliation. "She'll be at the Pulitzer awards ceremony in New York," he told her. "Why don't we both go?"

But by that time Catherine's pride had hardened into a carapace of bitterness. "She knows where I am. If she cares, let her come to me."

"Suit yourself. If you change your mind, let me know; we're all going in the Blake plane, and there's plenty of room."

Immediately after the ceremony, Natalie left the country again, going first to India, then to Palestine. She should be here today, Catherine thought as she pretended to take an interest in what Kurt and Nick were saying. It's her future we're talking about.

The purchase of the television station was her bait to lure Natalie home again. Radio stations didn't appeal to her, but the new technology that made the transmission of moving images possible—that might tempt her. It would be some time before the primitive facility Catherine was planning to buy was operational, but that fit in with her plans. For surely Natalie would not stay away from Seattle forever. Soon she would come home —she had told Ruth she was considering it. She was tired of war, she said, tired of death. She was going to the Far East next, she wanted to photograph Hiroshima, complete her record of man's inhumanity to man. After that . . . well, she told Ruth, after that she would see. Perhaps it was time to make peace with her family; perhaps she was ready, or soon would be.

When she was, Catherine would have something to offer her, an outlet for her energy, a new challenge that could not fail to excite her. And as she looked down the long expanse of the mahogany table at her sons and brothers, she made her decision.

"Kurt, I think you're right," she said. "The land is too valuable to keep. If we act now, we can probably realize a considerable profit."

"I thought you were the one for whom land meant so much," Nick said bitterly.

"Not your land," she said. "That's perfect for the kind of development ALKCO has in mind now. No, I will agree to Kurt's plan—on one condition."

"Which is?" Kurt asked.

Catherine addressed her other son. "Nick, would you agree to leave building airplanes to Boeing and concentrate on developing your instrument landing system? If you do, I'll give you the landfill on the southeast edge of Caleb's property, but only for a laboratory and research facility, not a plane factory or a housing development. Could you build on that property without disturbing the wetlands? Without polluting the breeding grounds for the waterfowl?"

Leighton, who had thus far been silent, looked up. "Where I wanted to put the shipyard?" he asked. "That land?"

"Ten acres," said Catherine. "But only for research—offices and laboratories. No smokestacks, no furnaces, no chemical wastes, and no ugly little houses."

"Catherine, do you realize what you're doing?" Lucas was apoplectic. "That property could make us millions with some other kind of development—Lockheed and Bethlehem have been after it for years!"

"For steel mills and shipyards . . . yes, I know. Well, Nick, what do you say?"

Her son leaped up from his chair and hugged her. "I say terrific!" he cried. "With my share of Blake Aviation and your land, I'm in business!"

"And how will you buy your television station?" Lucas asked.

"I'll expect a goodly share of stock in Nick's company for that land, which I'll borrow against. I believe certain bankers in Seattle share my confidence in Nick. There is some additional acreage that's already been logged off that I'll sell Kurt, substantially below market value but not dirt cheap. I hope he'll bring it to ALKCO in return for a substantial position with the company. I think he can develop it carefully, so it isn't an eyesore and doesn't ruin what's left. Remember, I've shares in ALKCO too —and I think Kurt's particular talents will be an advantage there."

"And your inheritance?" said Leighton bitterly. "Your precious birthright from Caleb, that you wouldn't part with when I needed it?"

"You never had any business in shipbuilding to begin with," Catherine said, "as subsequent events proved."

"If it hadn't been for that bastard McKay, I could have kept the yard going—" Leighton began, but Catherine stopped him with an icy stare. Despite his bitterness, Leighton had been fortunate to get out of the shipping business as cheaply as he had. The Depression had practically ruined him. By the time war broke out, his maritime empire was in shambles, reduced to a few tugs and barges that not even the merchant marine wanted. He had a seat on the board of his sons' company, where his military contacts paid off, and he was a director of ALKCO as well, thanks to her. His personal wealth was not great—she was many times richer than he—but very few people outside the family knew it. Only a few small passenger ferries that plied the inland waters of the sound flew the Blake Lines' distinctive flag, and now that the state was taking over the trans-sound lines and building big new boats that would carry up to five hundred cars, even their days were numbered.

"I don't think this is the time or place for raking up old history," she said. "Besides, a shipyard would have destroyed the landscape, whereas a small laboratory will hardly change it. And Nick . . . I shall want to be consulted on the design, by the way."

"I won't get in the way of a single one of your old mud hens, Mother," he told her. "And . . . thank you."

"You're welcome," she said. "Leighton, will you dine with me this evening? There are some things we need to talk about—privately."

"Do I have any choice?" he asked. "Did I ever?"

"Why, certainly," she replied. "You always did . . . from the very beginning."

* * *

"I want to give you half of what I realize from the sale of the property to Kurt," Catherine told her husband over dinner that evening. "Perhaps I should have given you the land when you wanted it, but I was hurt and angry, and I didn't like what you wanted to do with it. Because I held on to it, it's become much more valuable, even if I charge Kurt only a fraction of what it's worth. I believe you deserve half of what he gives me for it."

"Why are you giving me this money now?" he asked. He couldn't believe there wasn't some motive other than sheer generosity behind her move—Catherine had become a very calculating woman.

"I want you to buy a place out in the country, or on one of the islands, for your girlfriends," she said. "I don't like your having them at the Firs; I still own half of that, as you know. I would like it someday to go to Kurt and not be spoiled for him

. . . you know what gossips all our neighbors are, and even if you don't care about the talk, it wounds Kurt deeply."

He was silent.

"You'll have enough money to do whatever you like, as long as you're discreet about it," she reminded him.

"Very generous of you," he said dryly. "I don't understand why we don't simply divorce, Catherine. Then you would be as free as I to live your own life, to marry McKay."

"I have no intention of marrying Colin—or anyone else, for that matter," she replied.

Leighton obviously believed her, for he stared at her appraisingly for a long time. "I've a better idea. Why don't we let bygones be bygones and start all over again?"

She was still a great beauty, and he had not forgotten the fires that burned in her once, and surely still did. She was stronger than he, more powerful, considerably wealthier. No trace of the pliant, innocent girl she had been remained in the elegant, self-assured woman who faced him now across the table in the dining room at the Bluff. In fact, he admitted, she was more exciting now than she had been since the very beginning—she was a challenge, and he could never resist a challenge.

She must have been thinking the same thoughts, remembering the passion they once shared, for her cheeks flamed red as her hair, and she struggled to regain her composure.

"I don't think we . . . I'm not certain I could—" she began, but Leighton, seizing the moment, cut off her words in the way he knew best. Rising from his chair, he lifted her out of hers and gathered her in his arms.

"Of course we could," he said easily, stroking the blue vein that led to the pulse at the base of her throat, that quivered under his touch. He bent to kiss her, and she breathed in the remembered smell of him, felt his body harden against hers, and her own soften and moisten. His tongue searched her mouth, his hands cupped her buttocks under her thin silk dress, and then her breasts, and her nipples hardened when his lips brushed them.

And then she backed away, remembering how he had always silenced her this way, always used her body's need for his to gain an advantage, settle a dispute, forgive the unforgivable. Forcing her breathing to quiet, she gathered her dignity about her like a cloak and steadied her voice.

"I don't think so, Leighton. There's been too much I can't forget—nor can you. I bear you no grudges, and I hope you bear me none—for the sake of the children, if nothing else."

"For the precious Blanchard name," he said cynically, and she colored.

"That too," she admitted. "I took vows once, and I have kept them, despite what you believe. I have never had any man except you."

"You're a beautiful woman and a passionate one, Catherine," he said. "It's a shame to waste that on a lonely old age."

"Oh, I won't be lonely," she said. "I have the stations, and my music, and the children—"

"Except Natalie," he interrupted. A look of pain crossed her patrician features, threatened to fill her eyes with tears, and he cursed himself for a fool; despite the other women, she had been the best in almost every way and he had no real desire to hurt her; he only wanted to remind her that her power was not unlimited.

"Except Natalie," she agreed.

"You still have the Bluff," he said, not unkindly. "And someday Natalie will come home. As soon as her head catches up with the rest of her, as Maddy used to say."

And then he touched her hair gently, and took his coat from her, and when, before stepping out into the rain-freshened night, he saw forgiveness in her eyes, he truly hoped that she saw it in his as well.

Chapter Twenty-four

Catherine sprinkled sugar and cinnamon on the latticed crusts of the pie and then popped it in the oven. By the time the sweet smell of the last of the fall Macintoshes baking in a buttery shell perfumed the air, the kitchen was spotless—the butcher-block counters lightly polished with mineral oil, the dirty dishes stacked in the dishwasher, the copper pots and ladles and wooden spoons rehung from hooks on a wrought-iron baker's rack.

She looked around the room, satisfied. When she'd moved out of Broadview and back into the house on the Bluff, her first task had been to modernize the kitchen. It was designed by the same firm that built the kitchen for the morning cooking show on her television station—new appliances finished in harvest gold, from the two-door refrigerator with its separate freezer to the magic machine that washed and rinsed and dried glasses, dishes, and even cooking pots. The counters weren't that dreadful-looking Formica; except for the marble square she knew was responsible for her skill as a pastry maker, they were oak, and so was the floor. That much of the original kitchen she had kept, plus the wood stove on which she had cooked as a bride, though she added a modern oven set into one wall.

She had changed this house—in which she spent those happy first months after she and Leighton were married, while she was carrying the twins—in other ways, too; it bore few traces of that earlier time. She had knocked out walls, enclosed the entire western face of the living room in wood-framed sheets of glass, and added a second story, a suite consisting of a bedroom whose western wall was also glass, a small office, and a dressing room and bath.

The old bedroom on the first floor had been remodeled too; she had extended its walls and nearly doubled its size, modernizing the bath and refurbishing both rooms. She had always lived in houses with comfortable quarters for visitors, and the spare room, as she called it, was often occupied—by Arabella, when she was between marriages, by one or another of her grandchildren, especially Jessie, Kurt's youngest and her favorite, or by an old friend from out of town, like Ruth Straus, who was there now, taking a nap before dinner.

Tonight's special dinner party was for Ruth—Ruth, who had come back to Seattle after the war, accepted a position in the sociology department at the university, and been fired from her job and driven out of the city by the Canwell Committee. This committee, like the House Un-American Activities Committee in Washington whose tactics and strategies it reflected, had investigated the faculty of the university and found it, in the words of one of members, "riddled with Reds." Albert Canwell, a state senator from Spokane, was the direct inheritor of a tradition begun in the twenties by Attorney General Palmer and continued in the present by a Wisconsin senator who had blackened larger reputations than Ruth Straus's. Neither he nor anyone else ever proved that Ruth was a Communist, but everything else about her was grist for the Canwell mill: her solidarity with Socialists in the early days, her trip to Russia with Anna Louise Strong in the twenties, her relief work after the war in the Soviet Union, and her close associations with people who were known to have been members of the Party. She was a Jew, and she was from New York—with the other counts against her, that was more than enough. She had left Seattle and had not returned since, though she and Catherine had seen each other often in New York. Catherine traveled frequently these days, since her radio stations were part of a national network headquartered in New York, and legislation relating to the regulation of her broadcasting properties often required her testimony in Washington.

"You are almost as famous as your daughter," Ruth commented, when a national magazine profiled Catherine. Under the headline THE QUEEN OF THE EMERALD CITY, the piece fairly gushed over her wealth, power, and substantial contributions to the cultural and civic life of Seattle. It quoted her as saying, "I am not a political person," but told the apocryphal story of how she personally escorted a black doctor from the newly formed Group Health Cooperative, denounced by the medical establishment as socialist, into ALKCO's offices, demanding that the man be allowed to buy a home in an all-white development, else she would give her stock in the family company to the NAACP. The truth was not as colorful, and reflected the more genteel manner by which she usually got her way—in this instance, by convincing her brothers that selective integration of some of ALKCO's suburban subdivisions across the lake would relieve the pressure from the growing black middle class on ALKCO's more exclusive and expensive residential compounds in the city itself.

"She is as elegant as most New York or San Francisco socialites, who, while they might be as beautifully and fashionably dressed as Catherine Blanchard Blake, do not have her considerable business acumen," said the article. "She aptly deserves the sobriquet of 'Catherine the Great,' a title bestowed upon her by captains of industry and civic leaders who have been challenged to match her vision of what a city blessed with Seattle's natural resources can become."

What the story did not mention was that her younger daughter, the eminent photojournalist, was a stranger to her, or that her elder one was an embarrassment, a vain, flighty, pathetic woman who blundered into disastrous romantic liaisons, the last with a fortune-hunting Italian with a bogus title. Nor did it comment that her marriage to Leighton Blake, who was described as "one of the great figures in Seattle's maritime history," was a marriage in name only, or even mention her rumored romance with the notorious Colin McKay.

Colin was not her lover, but he was one of her two best friends, and tonight both friends would help her celebrate her sixty-fifth birthday, one night before the lavish celebration Nick insisted on throwing to mark that occasion.

As Catherine lit the candles surrounding the bowl of pink and white camellias on the French country table in her plank-floored

dining room, she thought how glad she was that Colin had
finally accepted her terms for their relationship. Prison had
mellowed him—he had learned to accept what could not be
changed, he told her, and he no longer pressed her to marry him.
There was no physical intimacy between them, except that of
old friends who were easy with each other—in all the evenings
he had been her guest at the Bluff, he had never attempted more
than a warm embrace or a chaste kiss on her cheek.

He had put his own life back in order, with some quiet help
from her. Without his knowing it, she had arranged for him to
be offered a position with the symphony, of which she was an
influential patron; he was an accomplished flute player, and his
years in prison had given him the opportunity to devote his time
and energies to the music that had brought them together in the
first place. There were still many of his former union colleagues
who remained loyal to him, despite the boss rule Dave Beck
imposed on Seattle's skilled labor force. Two years after Beck
forced Boeing to settle with the aerospace mechanics, the local
got out from under his grasp, and though Colin was barred from
holding any union office, he counseled the men he had once led,
helping them with behind-the-scenes negotiations in advance of
regular bargaining sessions, so that to the outside world Seattle
seemed like a city undisturbed by union bellicosity. He understood, as he always had, what the working man wanted—a secure job, a home, a car or boat, however modest, a decent life in
a decent unspoiled community. And in the postwar building
boom that choked the city's streets and highways, polluted the
lake and the sound, and overtaxed Seattle's ability to absorb its
growing population, his was a voice for a careful, controlled
expansion that would not destroy for either the old-timers or the
newcomers the city they remembered or envisioned.

Her time with Colin was private and was spent mostly at the
Bluff, where she kept up her tradition of entertaining on Sunday
evenings. Tonight, in addition to Colin and Ruth, she had invited Jonathan Cape and the protégé he had chosen to take over
the *Journal,* as well as a University professor and his wife,
friends of Ruth's from the old days. There would be wonderful
food, good talk, and, of course, music.

She gave the gracious, welcoming room a final appraisal and went upstairs to change for dinner. She could hardly wait.

*   *   *

"We'll be docking in fifteen minutes, Miss Blake." The steward left, taking Natalie's cases with him, and after a final check to ensure that none of her belongings were left in the cabin, she closed the door behind her and followed him down the first class passageway and out onto the promenade deck.

One lone fireboat and a small tug shared the waters of Elliott Bay with the S.S. *Lurline* this gusty March afternoon. Natalie could remember when the arrival of the *Lurline* crowded the harbor with dozens of gaily decorated boats, sail and power, all tooting their horns and shrieking their whistles to announce that the finest passenger liner on the trans-Pacific route had returned from the Hawaiian Islands and was back in its home port of Seattle. In years long gone she had made this crossing often; her parents spent the Christmas holidays at the Royal Poinciana, and aboard this very ship she had first worn her hair up and first been kissed by a young man.

During the war, the steamship had been converted to a troop carrier, but now it was completely refurbished, restored to its original graceful beauty. No expense had been spared in its restoration, but it was clear from the diminished number of travelers aboard, this week before Easter, that the *Lurline*'s days as the reigning queen of the Pacific were numbered.

A silvery glint in the slate-colored sky caught Natalie's eye, and in the contrails of the jet plane overhead she read a confirmation that soon there would not be enough passenger traffic to justify the leisurely five-day ocean voyage between Hawaii and Seattle, even on a ship as fine as the *Lurline*. Seattle's busy port might not notice the loss—from what she could see of the derricks, cranes, and other heavy machinery at the south end of the harbor, the city's maritime eminence was still assured. But she herself would mourn the end of the way of life symbolized by the *Lurline*'s elegance.

Natalie had loved those Christmas voyages, from the day after Thanksgiving, when the huge steamer trunks were carried down from the attic, to the hour of arrival in the great harbor

of Oahu, where golden-skinned youths swam out to greet them
with sweet-smelling leis of orchids and ginger blossoms. Nostalgia for those days had made her change her plans at the last
minute, cancel her flight from Honolulu, and book passage on
the ship instead. She wasn't sorry, for she saw now that it might
be her last opportunity; the new jets would soon make ocean
travel obsolete. As if to underscore her thoughts, the sleek, silvery plane that had passed overhead a few minutes before returned. It made a pass above the ship and then sped away for a
short distance before turning around and heading, it seemed,
directly for the *Lurline*'s smokestack. It was a small plane, but
it looked huge in the sky—dangerously low, she thought, watching as it dipped its wings even lower, in a kind of salute to the
ship. In seconds the plane was gone again, only a thin line of
smoke to mark where it had been.

"That must be Johnny Gasden, playing games with Boeing's
new toy," said Thom Hayden, the *Lurline*'s executive officer,
who had materialized at her elbow. "I hear he's testing some
new radar system that lets those jets land in any kind of fog or
bad weather. That's Nick Blake's brainchild—begging your par-
don, ma'am," he added, with that automatic deference everyone
in Seattle showed her family. "The man's plumb crazy," Hayden went on, as the plane circled the ship and dipped its wings
again. "I'd better go raise him on the radio and tell him to cut
it out before he scares our passengers to death!" Executing a
small half bow, he turned on his heel and left Natalie leaning
over the polished brass rail, thinking about Johnny.

How had he known she was coming home today? she wondered, for she knew the message in the dipped wings was meant
for her. Only Nick knew she was returning, and she had sworn
him to secrecy, for up until an hour before she boarded the ship
in Honolulu she had not been sure, herself, if she would go
through with it.

The note from Nick announcing his party in honor of Catherine's birthday had made her think, for the first time in many
years, of home. She had picked it up at the Tokyo office of the
international photo syndicate for which she had worked since
the war; she had just finished shooting in Korea, a pictorial essay

on the thousands of half-American war orphans left behind when U.S. troops pulled out of the country.

She thought about it again after hitching a ride on a MATS flight from Seoul to Tokyo, planning after a brief visit with the Tsutakawas to head back to New York, where she kept an apartment as a base between assignments. She was tired of her life; she longed for a change but didn't know what else to do besides the work that had earned her her fame, her fortune, and her independence.

She tried to talk to Nori about the feeling she had of being rudderless, without direction or ambition, but her girlhood friend could not empathize with her frustration. "I wish I had your choices," she told Natalie, in the cramped apartment in the middle of the city where she lived with three generations of her family. Her parents had chosen after their release from the internment camps to return to the country of their birth, and her own two children now played quietly at her feet. The fish market the elder Tsutakawas had owned for years had been confiscated when they went to the camps, and their home and other belongings sold out from under them. They would never feel safe in the United States again, they said. Nori had not wanted to go to Japan, but she was unmarried and thus had to follow her mother and father and, in time, marry the young man they selected for her. That afternoon she wore the traditional kimono and obi and spoke to her husband and children in soft, compliant tones, but her dissatisfaction and resentment were evident, at least to Natalie. "If I were free, like you, I would travel and do important things," she said sadly, and Natalie pitied her friend, who had had her own dreams of independence and adventure.

"Maybe someday you'll come back," she ventured.

"When the old ones pass on, perhaps," Nori replied. "My husband promises, but many things can happen." Then she changed the subject, and they talked of old friends and shared memories until Nori's father came home, accompanied by a small, wizened old man whom he introduced as Sensei Hiroto, a Zen teacher—"a *roshi*," he explained for Natalie's edification. She watched him closely as she shared the family's evening meal of soup and fish and rice, and he listened intently when she tried to describe to the Tsutakawas why she was thinking of leaving the syndicate.

"I've seen too much of war and dying," she said. "I'm full of it, so full I feel empty, if that makes any sense."

Sensei Hiroto nodded. "That is the beginning of fullness," he said. "They are the same, though they may seem different." And then he talked in his musical voice for what seemed like a long time, although it was actually just a few words spoken over the course of an hour. She didn't remember, later, what he had said, but his words had seemed full of meaning. And when he invited her to accompany him to his retreat on the lower slopes of Mt. Fuji, she accepted eagerly. He did not promise her anything; he said only, "Time goes from present to past, and if you come to find enlightenment, you will be driven by karma, and waste your time on the black cushion."

Enlightenment was not what she sought, only peace, some surcease from the images that flooded her brain and the cries that rang in her ears. The cries of a Jew at Bergen Belsen, blue numbers tattooed on a wrist so thin it was translucent, as American soldiers lifted him as gently as they could onto a stretcher. The screams of an old woman buried under the rubble of the King David Hotel in Jerusalem after the explosion. The sobs of a fifteen-year-old girl when she saw in the reflection of a rippling pond in a park in Nagasaki the ugly radiation burns that destroyed her face. The screams of a young boy abandoned on a muddy road near Seoul. And especially the thin wail of an infant trapped in a burning building in the bomb-struck West End of London, a cry she hadn't heard but imagined nightly, in her dreams.

After a month at the retreat, she no longer heard the cries and felt ready to move on. Nick's note weighed heavily on her mind —there was unfinished business waiting for her in Seattle, and it was past time to complete it. That thought put her on a plane for Honolulu, and almost onto one bound for Seattle, but at the last minute she hesitated. Perhaps she was not ready to return to the city she had left over a decade before. And when she saw the notice of the *Lurline*'s sailing, she thought the extra five days might strengthen her resolve, calm her nervousness, help her face whatever was in store for her in Seattle: angry words, studied indifference, or worse. She had no idea how Catherine would react to her arrival, but she was glad that Johnny Gasden, at least, was pleased that she was home.

He must have wangled her arrival date out of Nick—he had always managed to track her down, wherever she was. He had turned up in London several times, his smile like a letter from home, his warmth genuine, his casual friendliness a welcome antidote to the confusion of those early days. He had appeared in the syndicate offices in Tel Aviv the night independence was declared, and they had danced in the streets. In Korea he had found her too and urged her, as he always did, to come home.

"I'm not ready," she told him.

"You can't run away from who you are forever," he replied.

"Yes I can," she said, almost believing it. In Seattle, she was who her family was. But to the rest of the world, her own reputation gleamed as brightly as the Blakes' and Blanchards', and any respect or admiration she received was for the woman she had invented to replace the one whose life was so predictable, and so rooted in the past.

Now she was not just Abel's grandchild or Catherine and Leighton's daughter. She was Natalie Blake, whose photographs were famous, whose work had earned the highest accolades of her peers and the admiration of her public. So why, she wondered, standing at the rail of the *Lurline* as the boat nudged its way into the sheltered moorage of Elliott Bay, did she feel so much like a child again? She had changed greatly in her years away—she was different now, she reminded herself, and she held on to that comforting thought as the city, which had also changed, came into view.

An errant ray of late sunshine lit the six hills that curved around the harbor. The downtown skyline was crowded with new buildings, and silvery lines of highways snaked around it like arteries encircling a heart. The waterfront, however, was still the same bustling, lively place it had always been, even, as now, cut off from the rest of the city by an ugly elevated viaduct.

The traffic clattering across the viaduct was so noisy it almost drowned out Thom Hayden's voice as he came on deck again. "I see they've sent a car for you," he said, pointing to the long dark limousine that waited at the pier, its engines raising small puffs of smoke in the chilly air. "And look—even the mountain has come out to welcome you home!" In the southeast sky the strong spring wind had blown the lowering clouds to one side, the sun had suddenly turned the sky from gray to brilliant blue, and, against it, Rainier's snowy crescent summit stood out clear and sharp.

The last time she had seen the mountain it had been a dark outline in a moonless sky, glimpsed from the blacked-out port-hole of a Flying Fortress carrying her back to London. She was sick the entire time, sick from guilt for sneaking off again like a thief in the night, sick with worry at the uncertain future that awaited her. Since then, she had traveled thousands of miles, so why did she suddenly feel as though her journey had just begun?

Chapter Twenty-five

Natalie had stayed in many hotels over the years: hot dusty ones with peeling wallpaper and softly humming fans circling lazily overhead, cheap new ones flung up overnight with paper-thin walls and blond imitation-wood furniture, and gracious, timeless ones, where the manager apologized for not being able to offer the small luxuries that had been available before the war—any war. But she had never spent a night in Seattle anywhere except in her own room, in her own home, and she felt more of a stranger in the tasteful elegance of the Olympic Hotel than she had ever felt in any foreign country.

When she refused Nick's invitation to stay with him, he had offered the use of the suite his company maintained in the hotel erected on the original land of the University of Washington. Dismissing the car and chauffeur he had put at her disposal, she unpacked her things, changed into comfortable trousers and walking shoes, tucked in her purse the small new camera pressed on her by a colleague in Japan, and left the hotel.

She walked slowly up First Hill in the gathering dusk, feeling excited, mysterious, and vaguely guilty. When she passed people who looked familiar, she averted her eyes; she did not want anyone to recognize her, at least not until she faced Catherine.

Her mother did not care for surprises, but Natalie needed whatever advantage her unexpected arrival would offer. Her mother was a formidable adversary—that was how she thought of her, how she had, in her mind, always perceived Catherine's powerful, controlling love.

As she walked, enjoying the chance to stretch her legs after the confines of the ship, she noted that many buildings she remembered had disappeared and others had taken their place. The Sorrento Hotel, set on the brow of First Hill, looked much the same—its Italian Renaissance design and European garden courtyard reminding her of a palazzo overlooking the Bay of Naples—but right next to it a gleaming new hospital building took up most of the block. The graceful trees lining Madison Street were gone, and so was the row of pullman houses built for people of small means before the crash of '93. There was one pullman left, incongruously set between a gas station and a nurses' residence. The house was meticulously maintained, the turned porch posts and wood friezes below the dormer gables freshly painted, the rosebushes tidily pruned behind the picket fence that enclosed the small yard and set the building apart from its neighbors, like a proud woman holding her skirt away from the mud.

She turned off Madison Street and passed a Greek Revival mansion where Queen Marie of Rumania had once been entertained and, farther on, a red-brick Georgian house where she had danced at Betty Bloedel's wedding reception. Now it was a rooming house, and next to it there was a squat two-story office building.

A series of doglegs brought her to Broadview, which was dark and shuttered. A discreet sign gave the mansion's name and, below it, in raised gold-leaf lettering, a brief provenance. Reading it induced a disturbing melancholy—she felt as if her birthright had been given into the hands of strangers. She turned away, noting that the view, at least, had not changed; stretched before her, shrouded by the dark gray-blue twilight of early spring, were the landmarks she remembered: the hills, the mountains, the bay. Lights twinkled on the water. A ferryboat pulled out of its slip, a tug hauled its cargo north to Alaska, and the flags outlining the illuminated superstructure of the *Lurline* at the pier flapped briskly in the wind.

Moving on, she passed the Tsutakawas' old house, painted a different color now, its once-groomed lawn overgrown and in its driveway a new, torpedo-nosed Studebaker. She went to the end of the street and turned west again, down Pike Street, past

Frederick & Nelson and the Bon Marché, past the ornate, gilded
movie theaters, until finally she came to the ramshackle collection of wooden buildings and canvas-draped stalls that was the
public market. It was eerily silent now that the truck farmers
who came each morning to sell their produce and the hundreds
of shoppers who arrived all day to buy it had gone home for the
night.

First Avenue was an unrelievedly ugly expanse of taverns,
burlesque theaters, pawnshops, and stores selling war-salvage
surplus. There were knots of people on every block: impassive
Indians and brawny, beery loggers; heavily made-up women
whose breasts spilled out of their blouses; unshaven men with
blankets clutched around them who begged her for coins as she
passed. She ventured farther down the avenue, into what—
before the fire—had been the center of the city: Free Speech
Corner. Socialists and radicals and anarchists and Wobblies had
once held forth here on soapboxes, and Joe Hill's rebel girl
Elizabeth Gurley Flynn had climbed a lamppost and chained
herself to it, screaming down at the vigilantes who pursued her.
And here was where the prophets of the House of David had
preached, those bearded patriarchs in odd clothes who ranted to
anyone who'd listen before they went off to barnstorm the
Northwest, playing baseball against local teams who could
never defeat them.

Finally she came to the small French restaurant where she
had agreed to meet her brother, right at the foot of the old Skid
Road. A short, dapper man with a tidy mustache took her coat
and showed her into a small private room at the rear of the
brasserie; Nick was already there, sipping a cocktail. He stood
up when she appeared and kissed her cheek warmly. She apologized for being late—she'd been walking around, lost track of
time.

"After all your travels, Seattle must seem very small and
provincial," he said, but she shook her head.

"It seems larger than I remembered, and smaller—the same,
and yet different."

"And so are you," he replied.

"Well, thanks!" She grinned. "Have I gone to fat, then? You
always said I would."

"Not at all—you look wonderful. But what you've done, where you've been: to people here you're bigger than *Life*—no pun intended," he said.

She liked both of her brothers, valuing different qualities in each. She had seen them occasionally after the war, in Europe or Asia, on their trips abroad, or in New York. Catherine, too, traveled widely these days, back to Europe for clothes and culture, and to New York as well. But she had made no further attempts to contact Natalie, who suspected that, between her sons and Ruth Straus, Catherine was kept apprised of her whereabouts. Kurt had tried repeatedly to convince Natalie to make the first move in reconciliation, but Nick, who was more intuitive than his brother, had let her alone about it, and she was particularly grateful to him for that.

They talked of places she had been and things she had done, and he told her about people they both knew and something of the changes that had taken place in the city while she was away. She showed him the clever little minicamera she had been given in Tokyo. "The Japanese have taken up where the Germans left off," she said, "and their determination to rebuild their economy is stunning."

He examined the camera carefully. "If you think this is something, you ought to see what they're doing with radio, optics, computers—anything that uses transistors in place of vacuum tubes. 'The land of the rising sun' is apt; they'll eclipse us someday." He smiled. "But we've got a few gizmos in the works that ought to keep us a step or two ahead of them for a while—good old American know-how, yours truly included." Then dinner was served: fresh salmon, tastier than anything she'd eaten in Scotland or Scandinavia; the first asparagus of the season; and a salad of spring greens and slivers of apples and almonds, tossed lightly with sweetened vinegar.

"When are you going to announce your presence to Catherine the Great?" he asked her. "You're not going to just appear at the party and maybe give her a heart attack in the middle of the cherries jubilee, are you?"

She laughed. "No, I wouldn't mess up your elaborate preparations like that. I'll see her tomorrow, don't worry—in plenty of time for her to recover for the party. How is she?"

"She's quite hale—she still rides every day, and she can ski any of us into a tree. She's busy with the symphony, and of course the stations, though she's stretched to the limit financially. She had some trouble about renewing the license on the radio stations—there are people east of the mountains who don't care for the political views of the stations, and they're making things tough for her. Her advertising revenues have fallen off, for the same reason. And she's heavily invested in the TV station—I think there are some problems there, too. She can handle all that; you know Mother. But there's trouble with the Bluff again."

"What kind of trouble?"

"Johnny Westwind died recently, and his grandson Pete is suing to overturn the disposition of the property to Mother. Says he's Caleb's only direct descendant and the Bluff's his. Especially the Mound. That's always been the jewel of that property, you know."

Natalie was shocked. "Does he have a case?"

"Not one a good lawyer would touch, but he's found some shyster. They're all litigious as hell, those Indians, since Congress gave them their civil rights; a lot of tribes are making these native land claims; next they'll probably be saying the salmon in the rivers is theirs too. The Bluff's not trust land, so that's not an issue here, but get a bleeding-heart liberal judge and he might see things Pete's way, especially since there's clear evidence to support his contention that the Mound, at least, is sacred land and rightfully belongs to his people."

"Mother must be dreadfully worried," said Natalie.

"That's putting it mildly," her brother replied. "It's going to cost a lot of money to defend against the suit, and meanwhile, taxes on the property are sky-high—it's practically the last stretch of undeveloped land in the city, and the waterfront alone is worth a fortune. The Cousins, who are running ALKCO with Kurt these days, want to buy Pete off and sell the whole parcel."

"That's nothing new, they always have," she said.

"True, but this time it may come down to the stations or the Bluff—she merged them with ALKCO a few years ago, because it made good tax sense, but now they've got her in a corner. Even Kurt is against her on this."

"And you?"

Nick was thoughtful. "I owe Mother a great deal; my loyalties are with her, as well as a substantial chunk of my own stock. But frankly, I could use some more of the land—we're growing so fast, we don't have room to expand. My people are working in cramped quarters, and we really need to enlarge the lab and the office complex. It would mean clearing several more acres, which would put some ducks and birds and a couple of beaver dams out of business. But we're stretched to the limit—we've got a lot of new government contracts. Our manufacturing facility is ten miles away in the Kent Valley; it's a nuisance."

"But you're not going to do it?"

"Not now," Nick replied. "Look, Nat. Mother's not a young woman. She's healthy as a horse, but she's still sixty-five. I can hang on a few more years the way things are—Caleb's Bluff means a lot to her. Later . . . well, we'll deal with that when the time comes."

"Mother can stand them off," Natalie said. "She always has."

"If she wants to."

"What do you mean?"

"She told me years ago that she felt Johnny should have had the property—after all, he was Caleb's son. And he would have cared for it the way she has. I told her fine. But it's not Johnny we're dealing with here. Pete's a loaded gun, he's angry, militant, a real troublemaker. He claims it's his ancestors' burial site he wants to protect, but I'm not so sure. The Cousins think he just wants money, but I suspect he wants to embarrass the Blanchards."

"Digging up the past would do that, wouldn't it?" she said.

"More likely bring in a harvest of Great-uncle Caleb's other wild oats—apparently he was quite a fellow with the ladies—and mortify Mother. You know how stuffy and proper she can be."

"I certainly do," Natalie agreed.

Her brother paid the check and they left the restaurant. "Johnny Gasden sends you his love," he said, and Natalie brightened.

"I got his message at the hotel—and the one in the sky."

"He's in love with you, you know . . . he always has been."

"And I love him too—but not that way."

"Well, that's good. Mother has had it in for him ever since he helped you get away."

She sighed. "She still thinks she can run my life, doesn't she?"

Nick shrugged. "The real question is, is she still doing it?"

She cocked her head to one side, considering. Was it true? Was she still acting—reacting—to Catherine's desires for her, or were the choices she had made her own?

"I don't know," she told her brother. "To tell you the truth, I really don't know."

* * *

She got out of the car at the entrance to the winding road that led to the Bluff; within minutes, as she walked past the wall of coniferous trees that bordered the eastern edge of her mother's land, all signs of the city outside it vanished. No buildings were visible, no sounds could be heard. She was in a forest that had been old when she was born.

The Douglas firs, with their furrowed bark, and the western red cedars with their reddish-brown coats that grew in narrow strips, were on this land when the Indians lived there; the western hemlock, its bark like chocolate, was a relative newcomer, only a century and a half old. The forest was dense with shrubs and wildflowers: trillium was already blooming, in advance of the salmonberry and bleeding heart that would blossom in April, and the miner's lettuce and elderberry that flourished in May.

The silence was broken by the *ratatat* of pileated woodpeckers, a flock of them, red-crested and lively. They needed the old growth forest to survive, and in the largest tree trunks she saw the oval cavities that signified their presence.

A glistening brown Douglas squirrel scampered up a tree, chasing another, which chattered its birdlike alarm to alert the other creatures of the woodland to the presence of a stranger in their midst. The morning clouds had burned off, and sunlight sparkled in the treetops, which formed a cathedral ceiling overhead. After several minutes the road widened, and at the end of it was Catherine's house.

Natalie took a deep breath and ascended the stairs of the

redwood deck that had replaced the sagging old porch she
remembered. She rang the cowbell hung on the double door,
whose top half was open; she could see into the enormous, open
living room, separated from the kitchen by the huge stone
hearth that dominated the interior.

"Who's there?" It was not Catherine who came to the door but
Ruth Straus, and Natalie hugged her delightedly.

"Aunt Ruth, what are you doing here? I thought you were in
New York!" She was overjoyed—if anyone could make her re-
union with Catherine easier to bear, it was Ruth Straus. Of
course, she was pleased to see her for other reasons; she pro-
foundly loved this worldly, feisty, sharp-tongued woman who
had been her friend as well as her mother's, custodian of their
feelings about each other and their secrets too.

"I expect I'm here for the same reason you are," said Ruth,
hugging Natalie back. "Nick told me he'd written you, but I
didn't really expect you to come."

"I thought it was time," Natalie said simply, and the older
woman nodded.

"Long past," she said. "Your mother's upstairs. Shall I tell her
you're here?"

"No, don't bother, I'll go on up. . . . My, she's really done a
bang-up job on the old homestead, hasn't she?" Natalie said, as
she followed Ruth inside.

"Ruth, I thought I heard the bell ring—" It was Catherine's
voice, from the top of the stairs.

Natalie looked up, and they stared at each other for an endless
moment, in which neither of them spoke. Even Ruth seemed to
be holding her breath.

Then: "Hello, Natalie," her mother said evenly, descending
the staircase and coming toward her.

"Hello, Mother," Natalie began, but then her voice broke, and
somehow they were in each other's arms, while Natalie tried to
hold back her tears.

Catherine held Natalie close until her own sobs broke the
silence between them, and then she pushed her away gently,
dabbing at her eyes. "If I'd known I had to turn sixty-five to get
you again, I'd have done it a long time ago," she said, but
there was no rebuke in her voice. "This is the best present I
could have . . . the only one I really wanted."

"If you'd told Nicholas that, you'd have saved him a lot of trouble," Ruth said, and the three of them stood in the middle of Caleb Blanchard's first and last home in Seattle and grinned at each other.

"There's coffee and some pastries," said Catherine. "If I'd known you were coming—"

"I didn't know it myself until a few days ago," Natalie said easily, "but coffee sounds wonderful." She followed her mother into the kitchen, looking around her curiously as Catherine fussed with a tray and carried it out through sliding glass doors to the courtyard.

They sat down at a small wrought-iron table beneath a gaily striped umbrella and looked at each other. Catherine seemed unchanged by the years—older, of course, but her eyes were the same, green and direct, and her hands steady as they held the fragile china cup. She was still slim and elegant, dressed in a soft rose Chanel suit trimmed with braid, her blouse a soft froth of paisley silk beneath the collarless jacket. At her throat was a double strand of pearls, and she wore the emerald earrings Leighton had given her long ago. She looked poised and perfect, exactly as Natalie remembered her.

"I'm due at the station shortly for a meeting with my managers," she said. "I could cancel it, of course, but . . ." She hesitated for a moment, and then continued. "If you'd like to drive in with me, we could talk on the way. And then I'll show you around. We've just built a new facility, and it's quite something—by Seattle standards anyway. Of course, if you'd rather stay here and visit with Ruth until I'm finished, that would be fine."

"I'd be delighted to come with you," Natalie said, with a heartiness she didn't quite feel. "I've only been in a TV station once or twice, and then just briefly. Perhaps Aunt Ruth could join us later . . . we could have lunch at the Georgian Room, the way we used to."

"That's an excellent idea," said Ruth. "I've nothing to do until the shindig tonight . . . Catherine?"

"I'll have my secretary reserve us a table," she said. "I'll call her now and tell her we'll be in shortly. There are some other meetings she'll have to reschedule."

"Not on my account, Mother . . . please," said Natalie. "I want to run out to the Firs, too, and see Father before this evening."

"He's not well," said Catherine, "but you'll be a tonic. He's very proud of you, you know."

And are you, Mother? she wanted to know, but she did not ask. Instead she said, "Is it serious?"

Ruth Straus snorted in derision. "All that gallivanting around finally caught up with him," she commented, but Catherine, to her daughter's surprise, defended Leighton.

"The doctors think it is," she said. "But you know your father —he still thinks he's a young man, refuses to give up his whiskey and cigars."

"So does Mr. Churchill," Natalie said.

"Oh? Have you seen him recently? And Clementine . . . how is she, the dear old thing?"

"I haven't been in London for years, Mother," Natalie said carefully, trying not to look at Ruth. "Except passing through."

"That's right. You used to have a flat there, didn't you."

"Yes, but that was a long time ago." She felt Ruth's cool hand slip into hers and squeezed it tightly. When her mother left the room, she said, "She doesn't know, does she?"

"No," Ruth replied. "I don't see that she has to, either, unless you want her to."

"Someday maybe I'll tell her, but now now," Natalie said.

"Tell me what?" Catherine was back, a Burberry raincoat tossed casually over one arm, an alligator handbag on the other. "Natalie . . . you're not going away again, are you? I mean . . . not immediately?"

"Not immediately." Her daughter smiled. "Maybe not for a long time." She was rewarded by the look of contentment on her mother's lovely face—that, and something more. Acceptance, perhaps. Or was it just the old Catherine, scheming, planning, trying to recapture her in that skillfully woven web of power, obligation, and love?

You're here to start again, not open old wounds, she told herself sternly as she followed her mother out of the house and into her luxurious Lincoln sedan. Give her a chance—she may not have meant to, but she gave you one, a long time ago.

Chapter Twenty-six

Watching the news director put together the evening telecast on KBBB-TV, Natalie couldn't help but reflect that the man didn't have much of a feel for what was news. Instead of sending the station's only remote van to the scene of a major fire, he had ordered it to City Hall to televise the mayor's proclamation of Brotherhood Week. So when Catherine asked her as they were leaving the station what she thought of the operation, she hedged a little.

"You have some very creative people working for you. That huge telescopic lens they rigged up is quite something."

"Yes, it is, isn't it?" Catherine said proudly. "Al and Earl came up with the idea, and we tried it out at the hydroplane races last summer. They managed the most amazing long shots—our coverage was splendid. It's quite simple. They took an astronomical telescope and added a side-mounted lens and mirrors that couple the picture into the camera's pickup tube."

Natalie was impressed with her mother's command of the technical aspect of television; she herself knew almost nothing about it.

"How was your meeting?" she asked. After giving Natalie a brief tour of the station and introducing her with barely suppressed pride to everyone from the receptionist to the station manager, Catherine had turned her over to an intern from the university's school of communications and disappeared into the conference room.

"Frustrating," Catherine replied. "It costs a great deal to run a television station, it's much more complicated and costly than radio. Without a network affiliation, it's difficult to sell enough advertising to keep our heads above water, much less turn a profit. And then there's the decision to be made about colorcasting—that's the coming thing, you know, and the first station to have it will get a network, certainly. But the investment is enormous, and I don't know how we'll manage it. We really need a shot in the arm. So many of our advertisers canceled their contracts at the end of the year, it's quite demoralizing. But you don't want to hear my depressing tales. . . . Oh, good, here's Ruth."

"Hello, darlings, have you had a pleasant time together?" Ruth beamed. "Did you get your famous daughter in front of the cameras instead of behind them for a change?"

"Heavens, no!" Natalie protested. "I've no desire at all along those lines."

"Well, what lines are you thinking along?" Catherine asked. Her mother always got right to the point, Natalie thought uncomfortably.

"It's too soon, the girl just got home," Ruth said, giving Catherine a warning look. "Leave her be, Catherine."

"At least until her head's had a chance to catch up with the rest of her." Mother and daughter repeated the familiar phrase at the same time, and Ruth Straus laughed heartily with them. Then luncheon was served, during which they were interrupted frequently by people who stopped to chat with Catherine Blake and, incidentally, be introduced to her celebrated daughter.

It was a happy, relaxed homecoming—not at all what she had expected, Natalie thought, as she drove out to the Highlands. How long would it last? How long before she had to think about the real world? About the lease on her apartment, which expired in June, and about the new book she had halfway promised an editor. Right now all that seemed very far away—Seattle was truly at the very edge of nowhere, as she had often described it to friends, about as far as you could go without falling off the end of the continent. Still, the sight of the mountains, hard-edged against a tarnished silver sky, made her feel peaceful and content, and she was glad she had come.

Traffic thinned out beyond the city limit sign; she smiled as she passed the roadhouse where she had drunk her first illicit whiskey with a hard-faced boy named Lars. She'd been giddy with recklessness that night, for the Jolly Roger was a notorious speakeasy during Prohibition, a glamorous fortress with an octagonal lookout tower offering a good view of the highway so that "guests" could be warned of an impending police raid.

Of course, her mother had found out; few of her youthful transgressions escaped Catherine's notice. That one had resulted in her removal from the local high school and her forced enrollment at Forest Ridge, a school Natalie had hated then but now, enveloped in a general feeling of goodwill, remembered with fond nostalgia.

She hummed along with the music from the radio as she drove through landscape that had once been mostly rural, covered with brushy verges and clovered hills. East and west, on either side of the highway, she glimpsed rows of cheerlessly similar houses, each with its own patch of newly sodded lawn and a single scrawny tree that looked to her eyes like an elderly tenant stubbornly refusing to move after the others had been evicted. Soon she turned off onto the unposted road that wound down through more densely wooded hills to the gatehouse.

The guard waved her through, and a few yards farther on she slowed to make way for a foursome of hardy golfers who were playing through on the course that bisected the compound.

Mason, her father's long-time servant, was an old man now, and so was her father, she thought, as Mason showed her into the sitting room. Leighton was seated in a leather chair in front of the French doors that led to the terrace, and he rose with an effort to greet her. Even in his seventy-third year, one could still see the handsome, debonair man Leighton Blake had been. The coal-black hair was silvered at his temples, but shards of light still danced like fireflies in the inky depths of his eyes. His body was still trim; she remembered when he clapped his hands imperiously for Mason to bring them drinks that he had once moved with a sinuous grace. His complexion was ruddy, marked with a thin tracery of red lines, like a road map, from wind and sun and whiskey. He was immaculately barbered and groomed, and about him was a faint aroma of the patchouli and orange bark he had always favored. He wore fawn trousers pressed to a knife edge and a beige cashmere jacket over a tattersall checked shirt, into which he had tucked a navy-blue ascot; his shoes gleamed with the richness of cordovan leather, and his nails were buffed to a pink glow as he raised a glass to her.

"To the conquering hero—or shall I say heroine?—who has returned to the land of her birth, and not a moment too soon!" he said, draining his glass and holding it out for a refill. She poured it for him from the crystal decanter, and she saw his hands tremble as he lifted it to his lips.

"It comes and goes," he said, noticing her look of concern. "The doctors say it's nothing: an effect of the gout, probably. All those years of good living and then suddenly being presented with a bill—well, that's to be expected, but it doesn't seem fair, does it?" His eyes twinkled, regarding her fondly. Sipping her cocktail, she looked around. A Queen Anne secretaire and a pair of lacquered Regency tables flanked the French fireplace, where a cheery fire blazed. The green and blue tones of an antique painted chest were repeated in the Dhurrie rug and in the tints of the botanical prints from Brookshaw's *Pomono Brittanica*. On a clear day the view from the drapery-swagged windows reached all the way to Whidbey Island, but today Useless Bay was shrouded in rain-filled clouds moving slowly but inexorably south along the near shore of the sound.

Her brother's wife had not made many changes in this room; it still bore Catherine's distinctive taste. Kurt and his family had moved into the Firs—"Ostensibly to keep an eye on the old man but actually to make sure he doesn't sell it out from under them," Nick had told her.

Her sister-in-law entered the room. "Natalie, how wonderful to see you," she said in her high, musical voice. "What exotic corner of the globe have you come from?"

"Asia," she replied. "Korea, and then Japan. By the way," she added, addressing her father, "I saw the Tsutakawas there. They asked to be remembered to you."

"Is the old man still alive?" Leighton asked, and when she nodded, he sighed. "He tied the best flies around—Josh Green used to wonder where I got them, but I never told him." He chuckled, remembering, and then he seemed to doze off, and

when Elizabeth put her finger to her lips, Natalie followed her
out of the room.

"He needs to nap, to conserve his strength for tonight," she
said. "Kurt promised to be home early, but he probably won't
get here until it's time to leave for the party. He'll be sorry he
missed you."

"We'll all be together this evening," Natalie promised, and
her sister-in-law, whom she had always liked, brightened. "Yes,
we will. . . . The children will be so excited, meeting the world-
famous Natalie Blake! Jessie simply dotes on you—she has an
entire scrapbook of your photographs and is quite the little
shutterbug herself. And Mark and Dory—they were just infants
the last time you saw them, but they're quite grown-up now."
She chattered away as she walked Natalie to her car. "Have you
seen Arabella yet?" she asked.

"No, but I will, tonight." Natalie saw her older sister from
time to time, usually in New York, where she was always surrounded by hangers-on, often very young men with perpetual
suntans and no visible means of support. Whenever Natalie
came back from a shoot, she found a sheaf of messages: *At the
Pierre, do call,* or *Drinks with the most divine Brit tonight, hope you'll
join us,* and once, *Why aren't you ever here when I need you?*—a plea
she found rather odd, considering that they had never been
close. Arabella had had two husbands and a brief fling at an
acting career; her son was at Le Rosey in Switzerland and her
daughter a boarding student at Foxcroft. She kept an apartment
in the Gainsborough, one of Seattle's fine old residential hotels,
but was rarely there, according to Catherine. "However, I expect she'll show up this evening, just to keep an eye on her
inheritance," her mother remarked frankly. It was clear that she
had a rather jaundiced view of Arabella. "She has never learned
to make herself useful," she said, "and I'm afraid she never will."

Natalie said good-bye to Elizabeth and drove back to town. It
had been a long emotional day, and there was a long night ahead.
It would be a Blanchard Occasion—bread, bores, and circus—
of the kind she had always dreaded. But she was somehow looking forward to this one. Odd, she thought, how Seattle was
beginning to grow on her.

*   *   *

The crystal sconces cast a rosy glow over the diners seated on either side of the eighteen-foot expanse of ivory damask, Georgian silver, and Limoges china. Venetian glass goblets reflected the candlelight from the chandelier that hung above the table like the teardrop of a Valkyrie and refracted it into multicolored slivers, prisms of indigo and gold.

Catherine, at the head of the table, let her glance linger on her family, assembled this evening, all of them, for the first time in over a decade. There were her handsome, successful sons and their wives and children—Nick had justified her confidence in him, and so had Kurt. And Arabella—Catherine frowned, unaware that she always did when she beheld her elder daughter. She was such a foolish creature, a pushover for men and always weak ones. Not forty yet, but she looked older; she had inherited Catherine's delicate frame, but she had put on a great deal more flesh, so that she looked like a stuffed sweet. She wore her straw-colored hair in silly ringlets that accentuated the puffiness at her jaw, the extra folds of flesh at her throat; and her enormous breasts, those pale mounds of milky flesh, threatened to spill out of the fitted bodice of her royal-purple Hardy Amies gown.

Catherine had small tolerance for weakness, and she considered an inability to control one's appetites, for food or other sensual pleasures, just such a debility. She watched Arabella pop another buttery little biscuit into her mouth—that was five. Catherine could not keep herself from counting what Arabella ate.

But Natalie—ah, that was quite a different story, and a happier one. She still couldn't get over Natalie; her joy at her return overshadowed the brief pang of sadness she felt, wishing Colin could be here too.

Her younger daughter had grown into quite a stunning woman, with an air of quiet confidence she had lacked as a girl. She was as elegantly groomed and fashionably dressed as—well, as she herself was, she thought, chuckling at her own vanity. Catherine's gown was a Charles James creation, black velvet with a puffed, gathered, and dropped hipline and trumpet-flared skirt. With it she wore the emeralds Leighton had given her when the twins were born. Natalie's two-piece brocaded silk suit shimmered blue and green like an imperial peacock; it had a high collar and closely fitted sheath skirt slit above her knee like a cheongsam. In her hair she wore jeweled chopsticks, a touch of fancy that set off her almond-shaped eyes so that she looked faintly Eurasian. Catherine was pleased to find her so attractive. Talent and intelligence were useful, but beauty would always serve a woman best, especially if she was unmarried and no longer a girl.

Tonight's dinner was for family and very close friends only; afterward, Broadview's great doors would be thrown open and several score more people would join them for dancing, dessert, and champagne. Nick had arranged with the Pioneers Association to hold Catherine's gala in her childhood home. Later, perhaps, there might be an appropriate chap or two that Natalie would like, a suggestion she had broached gently to her daughter during cocktails. "Maybe, but not any of those twits you used to push at me," Natalie said, equally gently. She giggled. "For all your theories about how blood tells, Mother, some of Seattle's bluest is down to a thin, watery gruel. Too much inbreeding, I'd say—didn't all of them marry their cousins?" In spite of herself, Catherine had laughed too. Well, she might have a surprise or two for Natalie. Seattle was full of a lot of interesting people these days, many of them newcomers from the East Coast, as cosmopolitan as she was. They had migrated west determined not to re-create the urban blight they left behind, so they were often in conflict with the locals, who thought growth might not be so terrible and felt that a stronger economy, one not tied to the Boeing Company's fortunes, would offset any ill effects of new industry. The recent emigrants were smart, well-educated, well-to-do professionals—lawyers, architects, planners, and the like—who camped and hiked and skied enthusiastically and got up petitions every time the natives did something they feared would despoil the natural beauty of their adopted home. Catherine liked them, for the most part, though they were sometimes a little too pushy, a little too convinced of their own right-headedness and too quick to argue. Quiet persuasion was her way, which was always easier if one had the power and position to enforce it. She would need all of that to convince Natalie, this time, to stay—well, not the power, perhaps, since she already knew that wouldn't work with her stubbornly independent daughter.

But position: that was something else again. Being a citizen of the globe was all well and good, but this was where Natalie belonged. And as she exchanged a smile with her husband, seated at the other end of the table and watching their youngest child with equal fascination, Catherine thought she had just the position to tempt her.

Chapter Twenty-seven

Natalie read the entry from Maddy's journal twice before she was sure it meant what she thought it did.

She had been thinking of doing a book about the city in its early days, photographs of its historic buildings before they yielded to the wrecker's ball, and she had taken to reading the journals, year by year, for a while each evening before she fell asleep. Her years away had given her a new appreciation of Seattle. It was complacent and provincial, removed from the rest of the country and even the world, at least the one she was used to, where things happened quickly and events had a way of eclipsing the moments that enriched her here—a lingering multicolored sunset; a taste of air like wine, crisp and clean and heavy with fruit and wood; a quiet walk through shady streets at night, secure that danger did not lurk around the next dark corner. Maddy's journals told of a past she could imagine easily —Seattle was changed now from those days, but in many ways it was still the same.

She had sat up in bed when she read it the first time.

June 7, 1889. Yesterday momentous, to say the least. The fire destroyed thirty blocks—A. estimates millions of dollars lost, though no lives, thank God. It is still burning in places—A. so distraught I cannot burden him further. Seeing the blaze from the ferry on returning from the Bluff, I thought it an hallucination, the hell to which·He, on account of my sin with C., has surely consigned me. I will pray God for guidance and mercy—perhaps in time I shall be able to ask A.'s.

Yes, it meant what she thought it did, though no further entries for the next several weeks referred to her "sin with C." And then she came to this:

Sept. 7, 1889. Despite the Peruvian bark, which succeeded only in making me quite ill, and the patent medicine which is supposed to bring down courses, I am with child. No quickening yet, but abortion at any time now out of the question—Doctor would not permit it, my life in no danger in spite of my advanced years. He expects no problem except curbing A.'s high spirits when he learns of it— if he only knew!

The next entry was dated a week later.

Sept. 14, 1889. Sonnet suggests a sea tent—she says the Indians used laminaria to dilate early in pregnancy, and some of her girls have also. What to do? I would be breaking God's law—but I have already done it, and this is the punishment. C. must never know.

And then:

Sept. 22, 1889. Told A. this evening—he was delighted, of course. If he knew the truth, he would be devastated.

She did some mental arithmetic: her mother had been born nine months after the Great Fire. Was she Caleb's daughter? It certainly seemed that way.

Should she tell her? Were it not for Pete Westwind's lawsuit, Natalie decided, she would not; Maddy had a right to her secret, and nothing would be served by raking up this one. Would it destroy Catherine to know her true paternity—or would it help her establish, once and for all, her claim to the Bluff?

There was only one way to find out, she decided, picking up the two journals she had brought with her this morning.

She buzzed her mother. "Can I come up for a few minutes? I have some things I need to talk over with you."

"Five minutes, dear. I'll be done with this dreadful paperwork then," Catherine replied.

Natalie got up from her desk and looked through the glass walls of her office at the staff, busily preparing for the midday newscast.

The B3-TV team she had assembled was hard at work, enclosed in the cocoon of the newsroom. In the two years since she had joined the station, it had never occurred to her until this moment that television news was created in a room with no windows.

She was hooked that very first day; she knew it as well as Catherine, and she didn't even mind the triumphant look on her mother's face when she said yes, she wanted to work at the station. She didn't know much about television, but that didn't matter; she knew cameras and she understood news, and her own reputation made up for her inexperience in the medium. Not that she needed it—being Catherine's daughter was enough. But it gave KBBB the edge it needed: advertisers reconsidered their budgets, the national networks were suddenly more interested in affiliating, and even the vendors of the new color equipment were glad to provide what the station needed, knowing that having the famous Natalie Blake behind their cameras would be a public relations bonanza.

Of course, strictly speaking, she was not behind them; usually she was at her desk, sifting through the day's stories, deciding which national events ought to lead the first few minutes of the newscast, which local ones should follow, where the remotes should come from, how to deploy her crews and equipment, and, most challenging of all, attempting to make the B3 newscasts profitable instead of loss leaders for the station.

Right now she had an important decision to make: whether to send Kevin Scanlon, a correspondent she had known in Korea and lured to Seattle, to Washington to narrate live coverage of Dave Beck's investigation by the Senate Rackets Committee. A cross-country TV feed would be an innovation, but it wouldn't be cheap. Still, Beck was big news in Seattle. He had dominated the labor scene of the city for over three decades, and local interest in the investigation was intense.

She had wanted to discuss it with Catherine, but she was preoccupied with the lawsuit, really afraid this time that she might truly lose the Bluff. Natalie did not know if what she had to show her mother would help or hurt her in her case against Pete Westwind. All she knew was that she couldn't put it off any longer, so she walked out of her office, through the newsroom, and climbed the back stairs to her mother's private office.

* * *

"Does this mean what it seems to mean?"

Natalie couldn't read her mother's expression. Before her on the leather-topped desk lay Maddy Blanchard's journal, the familiar handwriting sharp and slanted on the neat ledger pages.

Her mother was quicker than she had been—after reading the entry the day after the fire, she flipped ahead to September right away. Then she looked up at her daughter. "So that's why she wanted her journals burned instead of seen by strangers," she said mildly.

Natalie was surprised. She had expected almost anything from her mother except this calm acceptance. Her own conception was of doubtful origin, to say the least—she, who was so blood proud. But then, Caleb had been a Blanchard too.

"I always wondered, you know," she said. "People always said I looked more like him than like Father—the eyes, I suppose, the coloring. For a time I thought that was why he left me the Bluff, not just because I loved it as he did. But now, I wonder. Do you suppose Abel ever knew?"

"There's no evidence of that in the rest of the journals," Natalie said. "But Mother, if it's true, wouldn't that help with the lawsuit? I mean, if you are, in fact, Caleb's direct descendant —his daughter, not merely his niece—that would give you an even stronger claim to the Bluff."

"And how would you suggest I publish this news, on the evening broadcast?"

Natalie knew Catherine's aversion to the merest whiff of scandal was strong, but surely her land was more important than that. Or was it?

"I know you are trying to help, my dear, and I'm certain you've been troubled by this discovery, as I am. But I think I'll fight Pete Westwind on the merits of his own case, which is questionable, if what the lawyers tell me is true. In fact, I had planned to offer a settlement of sorts—one that should spike his guns and still keep most of the Bluff safe. This only confirms my sense that that is the right thing to do, and it may blunt his attempts to embarrass us with a lengthy and public trial," said Catherine.

"What kind of settlement?"

"Now that will be my secret, won't it?" she teased. "Oh, don't worry, dear, I'll tell you at Thanksgiving dinner. When the Cousins hear of it, they'll think I've gone daft and seek to have me committed. I shall need your support."

"You have it," Natalie replied wholeheartedly. She had slipped more easily than she could have imagined into the life she had made in Seattle. As she told Johnny Gasden a few days after Catherine's birthday party, "I feel less like an anthropologist in the jungle wondering why the natives are stoking up the fire under the pot, and more like I really belong here."

He grinned. "I told you Catherine would get you if you didn't watch out—and even if you did."

"Well, maybe she did, but what of it? I needed a change." The pull of the familiar was stronger than she had dreamed it would be; almost against her will, she felt herself drawn back to her roots. Within weeks she had bought a house near Volunteer Park with a fine view of the bay and plenty of space for a darkroom, though she was too busy at the station to do much of her own work, and when she did, it was mostly studies of light and landscape. She had made new friends, including one who was more than that—and since Catherine had weathered the news about her mother's hidden past with such equanimity, she decided that perhaps it was time to bring up another topic, which was potentially almost as explosive.

"I may bring a guest to Thanksgiving dinner," she said to Catherine, "if that's all right with you, of course."

"Why, certainly," said Catherine. "Someone I know?"

"Rafe Lenhart."

Once again, her mother's reaction surprised her. "What an excellent idea!" she said. "Did you know he and your Aunt Ruth were chums in the old days? They went through some bad times together."

"I'm glad you feel that way. I thought, with his record and all, you might have a different attitude," said Natalie.

"Why? Because he went to jail for his beliefs?" Catherine snorted. "Some of the best people I know have gone to jail for worse reasons." Or better, she might have added. Colin McKay, dead of a heart attack, must be chuckling in his grave—her daughter and the radical newspaperman who had been convicted of violating the Smith Act! "What is Rafe up to these days?" she asked.

"Living in a tugboat on the lake—interestingly enough, the *Kodiak Sue,* one of Father's old boats. He gave me the Blake Lines flag. He calls me Landlady."

"That's better than Catherine the Great," her mother shot back, and they both laughed. "And what else?"

"He's writing, mostly, a book about his experiences, and his politics—with Rafe, they're indistinguishable. He's still a reformer; he still thinks the little guys can beat the big ones if they stick together," she said. He had come out of prison unrepentant, he told her, the shaggy, bearded, pipe-smoking man she had met at a citizens' meeting to protest the destruction of the lake's residential neighborhood by the proposed new freeway.

They had gone out for coffee after that first meeting, and as they spent other evenings together, she liked him more and more. He had a dry, generous wit and a worldview wider than most people she knew in Seattle. He had been a Democrat, a Republican, and a Communist, he told her—but never at the same time.

"Is this a serious friendship?" Catherine asked.

"I think so," Natalie replied.

"The Cousins will have a tizzy, an old leftie like Rafe Lenhart at Thanksgiving," Catherine said, obviously relishing the prospect of making her brothers' stuffy sons uncomfortable. "And when they hear what I propose, they'll surely know the world has gone to hell in a basket. It should be a very interesting evening."

* * *

If the Cousins were perturbed by Natalie's escort and his unsavory past, they pretended not to be. Thanksgiving was held at the Firs; Leighton was so crippled now it was difficult for him to leave the house. Seated across from Rafe, Natalie watched him lovingly—she wondered what he would have to say, later, about her family.

What they had to say about him didn't matter, except Catherine, who by now had all but given up hope that Natalie would marry. "I must say, being your own woman doesn't seem like such a bad thing to me any more," she had commented recently, ignoring the fact that in all but name she had been exactly that for several decades. "Still, it's a shame you've not had children."

Natalie held her tongue. There was no reason to upset her mother. The only person besides Ruth who knew her secret was Rafe.

She had told him after the first time they made love. They were lying facing each other in her bed, his cool fingers learning her face like a blind man.

"I had a child once," she said.

"Tell me." His voice was soft and low.

"In London, during the war. She was killed by a bomb when she was three months old." She closed her eyes, remembering how she had come home to Duchess Street, seen the fire trucks at the end of the mews, and begun to run, screaming. Her baby was in there—her baby, born of the young airman whose name she never knew, and Hannah, a young refugee woman Ruth had found to mind the infant when Natalie went back to work a month after the delivery in a private clinic on Harley Street. She had kept her pregnancy and the birth a secret from everyone except Ruth; she supposed she would tell people, later, that she had adopted the child. It was plausible enough; there were plenty of refugees of all ages in England in those days. But her baby was gone, perished with the others in the house on Duchess Street.

Rafe listened to it all and then he made love to her again, more tenderly this time, sucking her nipples so sweetly that for a brief moment it was like an infant at her breast. When he was inside of her he kneaded her belly, pushing it as she strained against him, harder and harder, and in a way it was like giving birth again. The next morning he asked her to marry him.

"I don't know how that would fit into my life now," she temporized.

"Let me know when you figure it out," he said, so laconically that she tugged at his beard and pulled him over onto her with a giggle, and they spent the rest of the day in bed, telling each other all the small secrets of their lives, all their histories, the first people they had loved and the last, until now. Natalie had decided; as she watched him now, deep in conversation with her mother, she couldn't wait to tell him.

* * *

The Firs was especially lovely tonight. In the pale yellow dining room, Catherine's taste still prevailed. The walls were marbleized, finished with a grapevine frieze. A vert antique niche housed an Empire terracotta stove with an Egyptian motif, and a pair of Empire mahogany jardinières held masses of golden chrysanthemums. Twenty chairs were drawn up to the table as the turkey was presented with a flourish—Kurt carved, plates were passed, and even Rafe's presence did not change the comfortably predictable conversation. They discussed what people in Seattle always discussed at table: whether the skiing would be good this winter and if they should add another room to the cabin at Paradise; the prospects for a big winter steelhead run and the dismal record of the Husky football team; whether the amazing O'Brien brothers could pilot the Seattle University Chieftains to a championship again; and whether Boeing would be hiring to meet the orders for the new passenger jets. No arguments disturbed the quiet tenor of the meal. All views were heard respectfully, and no voices were raised in dissent.

Finally, after coffee was served and Arabella helped herself to the last slice of mince pie, Catherine rapped gently on her wineglass.

"I have an announcement to make," she said. "I have settled the lawsuit against the Bluff."

A hubub of voices arose before she continued.

"I've turned over the Mound—the old burial grounds and an acre surrounding it—to the All Indian Tribes Council, which will administer it as a park, jointly with the city and Pete Westwind, who will be its director. The city has given him a salaried position, and I have given him a small grant for a memorial of some kind—perhaps a building, a nature and crafts center where the old ways can be preserved and celebrated."

Then, enjoying the look of complete stupefaction on the Cousins' faces, she rose grandly from the table. "We'll play some music now. . . . Jessie, have you been practicing the Brahms?"

Chapter Twenty-eight

Natalie came awake the morning of her wedding day with a start. She had had the nightmare again. Except that this time it wasn't the baby trapped inside the burning building, it was Rafe, not on Duchess Street but at Broadview, which was all ablaze. He stood in the flaming doorway, his hand outstretched to her, and this time she got there before the fiery timbers collapsed on him, but this time she kept running, past him, past the house, hearing his screams trailing into a thin keening cry behind her.

She hadn't had that nightmare, or any like it, for a long time; without thinking, she did what she used to do to shake it off, pulling on her old sweat pants and sneakers, slipping out of her house on Prospect Street in the early morning stillness, and running down the tree-shaded street to the entrance of the park. She ran around the reservoir twice, and then up the gentle rise to the art deco building that housed the art museum, past the marble camels and elephants that flanked it, down the hill behind it, and through the huge old trees that studded the grounds of the park. The sky was the color of ashes, leaking rain a few drops at a time, like mercury from a barometer; by the time she arrived back at her house, the dream had all but disappeared, and she scrubbed the last traces of it from her memory as she sank into a cross-legged position on the floor, closed her eyes, and began counting her breaths silently, until at last there was nothing in her head except the sound of her exhalations and the comforting spaces between them.

Later, in the shower, she thought of the ceremony that in a few hours would change her name and also her life. She had never thought she would marry—at first, there was too much living to do, and later, too much that had happened while she was doing it. She had never lacked for the company of men, not only because she was lovely to look at but also, as Graham Carleton had once told her, because she held something back. It was not an intentional aloofness but a protective veneer that had been part of her almost since childhood—since the kidnapping, she supposed, though she thought it had really begun after the baby's death.

There had been no man she really trusted until Rafe, though she had been in love once before, and infatuated a few times. Graham Carleton had been a diplomat at the British Embassy in Washington when she met him a few years after the war. She had commuted between the nation's capital, her apartment in New York, and whatever foreign location her work took her to, for nearly a year, and when he was transferred to Egypt and asked her to marry him, she nearly did. But he had very different ideas about how a wife should behave—he expected her to give up her career and devote her efforts to advancing his. And as an American married to a Brit, especially one in the Foreign Service, she realized, she would be letting herself in for a lifetime of Yank bashing. She wasn't all that patriotic; she considered herself a citizen of the world. Still, it was infuriating to listen while America was constantly run down and derided by those who were so deeply in its debt, and Graham was as bad as his friends and colleagues.

All that might have been tolerable, loving him as she did, if it hadn't been for his reaction when she told him about the child she had borne. He was stunned and seemed to feel that she had betrayed him.

"Not that I expected you to be—well, entirely pure," he said. "After all, you're a grown woman. I knew there might have been another man in your life before me. But to have slept with a stranger and then to have his child . . . well, you must admit it's a bit hard for a chap to swallow."

Later, he had tried to make amends, but she had been so cruelly hurt by his first response that she drew even further back, into herself, and when he left for Cairo she knew she would not see him again. She did not see any man more than casually for some time after that. She had a brief fling with a colleague, a burly Scots photographer with a thick brogue, merry eyes, and a wife and child in Edinburgh. That ended badly, and she put marriage out of her mind. She had her career, she was financially independent, and, as Nori Tsutakawa had said, she was free to do whatever she wanted, wherever she chose.

Since coming back to Seattle, she had met a number of men, but until Rafe, none of them interested her more than slightly. Like Graham, they all had definite, extremely old-fashioned ideas about a woman's proper role. So did most of the women she met, women who she had hoped would be her friends. If they were married, they rarely had careers or even jobs, and even those who were forced by economic pressures to work considered her unnatural because she wanted to be more than just some man's wife—any man, she often thought, considering how dull and unappealing the husbands of many of them were.

Her mother was the only woman she knew who understood the particular pleasures of making decisions, wielding power, having responsibility—all the components of making a differ- ence, giving something back to the city that had given her family so much. But even Catherine would have preferred that Natalie marry.

"It's not too late to have children, you know," she said, shortly before Natalie met Rafe Lenhart. They were sitting on the redwood deck at the Bluff, watching the setting sun streak the sky pink and scarlet. The wind blew the fragrance of ripening fruit in from the orchards, mixing its sweetness with the dank brine smell of the outgoing tide. "I would like a grandchild to leave this to," Catherine added, "someone who would love it as I do."

"You have several grandchildren already," Natalie replied, but her mother shook her head.

"None who wouldn't sell it for a few pieces of silver," she said. "Not Arabella's children, or Nick or Kurt's either."

"What about Jessie?"

Catherine brightened for a moment at the thought of her

favorite grandchild, but then she frowned. "No . . . Kurt would sell it out from under her before she could say no, and she can't wait to shake the dust of Seattle off her heels and follow in your footsteps anyway."

Natalie smiled. Jessie was her favorite too—about the age her own child would have been, she thought wistfully. Then she told her mother about the baby she had had, and lost; she hadn't planned to do it, and was hesitant at first, and nervous. But Catherine's face softened with love and sympathy, and at the end of Natalie's recitation she held her arms out to her youngest child and rocked her in her still-strong arms, as the sun slid behind the flame-tipped mountains.

*   *   *

Catherine was a constant surprise, Natalie thought now as she unpinned the muslin drape that protected her wedding gown and slipped it over her head. There had been no judgment in her eyes or her voice when Natalie told her, just as there had been none in Rafe's when she told him. Both her mother and her lover had cried for her loss and rejoiced that she had found the strength to surmount it.

Later, when Natalie introduced Rafe to Catherine, her mother had been similarly supportive and enthusiastic, despite Rafe's checkered past and modest origins.

Natalie thought it was because her mother had all but given up hope that she would marry, but once again she underestimated Catherine's values. Money and family and position and appearances all still counted with her, but in her long lifetime she had learned that other things were important too. "Rafe is a fine man," she said, "and he's managed not to be bitter and resentful at what his political beliefs cost him. Oh, I don't think being a Communist is a good thing, mind you, but quite frankly, I'm rather relieved that he's not tiresome about his disenchantment with the Party the way so many of those old radicals are. And Rafe is a decent, intelligent person, and he obviously loves you a great deal. Tell me . . . how does he feel about your working?"

"He says he's grateful that I have something to do that enriches me," Natalie replied, "though he's concerned that I've all but given up my photography. He keeps nagging me to get back to the book on old Seattle."

It had been a long time since she'd picked up a camera—the book was progressing much more slowly than the city itself, which was engaged in a new round of tearing down, building up, and booming, due to Boeing's ascendancy in the aerospace industry and the World's Fair that was due to open in two years: Century 21, it was called, Seattle's bid for greatness.

"I think you should, too," Catherine said. "It would be a shame to let all our history disappear, and I hope you'll finish that book someday. But I have conflicting feelings about that, because I would like to make you president of the station, and that will leave precious little time for anything else, especially now that you're getting married. You've done a superb job, you know. We're in excellent shape, financially and otherwise, and the credit for that goes to you."

KBBB's success was due not only to Natalie's canny sense of television's potential but also to her ability to lure talented professionals to the city. It was not an easy task—"In New York they call Seattle the foreign desk," said one veteran reporter—but enough others came to make up for him. They were drawn to the Northwest by the promise of pleasant surroundings and good working conditions. Some of them were dissatisfied with the slower pace of life, what that same correspondent called "the everlasting amiability of it all," but others stayed, enjoying the gentle ebb and flow of the professional backwater, content to let national acclaim or larger salaries pass them by.

Natalie did not hesitate. She had big plans for the station— not just KBBB but the other one, the one in Portland that she hoped to convince Catherine to buy. "I'm glad you think so," she said, "and I accept—happily, and with thanks. You won't be sorry."

"I don't expect to be," her mother said. "Speaking of Rafe, I would like to give him the *Journal* as a wedding present—if you think he'll accept it, that is. He's an excellent journalist; I liked his ideas for making the *Journal* more responsive to the needs of the city, and I hear the Bullitts are going to offer him a chance to run that new magazine they're starting up, so I thought I'd beat them to the punch."

Natalie grinned. "You want Rafe to give Stim Bullitt a run for his money, right? Or do you just want to give his wife a run for hers?"

Catherine snorted, but Natalie knew she had struck home. Dorothy Stimson Bullitt had her own group of television and radio stations, and her husband, a liberal lawyer, had been talking for some time about founding an alternative to the largely conservative, unremittingly boring newspapers in the region.

"Let's just say I think that Rafe is more than up to the job," Catherine said. "It's no great bargain, you know; since Jonathan died, the *Journal* has been losing money. We've been through three editors in the last six years, each one worse than his predecessor. I'll give Rafe two years to show a profit—or at least to get the *Journal* out of the red. Would he take it, do you think?"

"I think he might see it as a challenge," said Natalie. "His book is done; it will be published in the fall. He's thinking of starting another one, but he's not quite ready now. Anyway, you can ask him yourself—he should be here soon. And Mother . . . thank you for my promotion. I'll try to do you proud."

"You already have, dearest girl," she said. "A long time ago."

*　　*　　*

"Do you, Natalie Blanchard Blake, take this man to be your lawfully wedded husband?"

Rafe squeezed her hand reassuringly and Natalie took a deep breath. "I do," she said, and behind her, in the sudden hush that followed the minister's question and her response, she heard her mother's soft sigh.

That makes two of us, she told Catherine silently, as Rafe slipped the simple gold band on her ring finger. I never thought it would happen either.

She had not wanted an elaborate wedding—"Mother, I'm not a girl any more," she'd said—but Catherine insisted. Finally they had compromised: only about a hundred family members and friends had gathered at the Firs this afternoon to watch the couple exchange their vows. But Blakes and Blanchards made up nearly half that number; Rafe's family consisted only of his widowed mother and Alex, his twelve-year-old son, who lived with Rafe's former wife in Bellevue but spent weekends with

Rafe on the *Kodiak Sue*. Now he would be spending that time with both of them, in her house near the park. Rafe was moving in with her; he had relocated the offices of the *Journal* onto his tugboat, in a cost-cutting move that pleased Catherine and lent the newly revitalized magazine a certain cachet among the educated, affluent readers, many of them newcomers to the city, whom he hoped to attract. Alex was a sweet, shy boy, and Natalie liked the prospect of being a mother to him, even part-time—she hoped it was not too late to become pregnant herself, but if that didn't happen, at least she would have a stepson. She had grown fond of the boy, and he seemed to return her affection; "You're a natural at this stuff," Rafe told her when she convinced Alex to put on skis for the first time. He was small for his age and not comfortable at team sports, but after a few spills he got the hang of it and in one brief season advanced so quickly that soon he was almost as good as she was.

When Reverend Bain pronounced them man and wife, Rafe lifted the short veil that covered her face, took her in his arms, and kissed her tenderly. "I love you, beautiful lady," he said, and as she whispered back, "I love you too," the last vestiges of her doubts, and her dreams, disappeared.

Then they turned together and moved down the aisle between the rows of chairs set up in the music room for the occasion, as the chamber orchestra struck up the joyous music of the recessional. She saw her mother wipe a tear from her eye and then give her handkerchief to Leighton, seated next to Catherine in his wheelchair. Her niece Jessie blew her a kiss, and so did Aunt Ruth, and Nick raised his arms over his head like a fighter claiming victory. On Johnny Gasden's pleasant face there was a flicker of something that might have been regret, had she looked closely. But she did not—her own eyes were so teary with happiness she could hardly see anything, but she felt her husband's firm grip on her arm and walked with him out of the flower-banked room and into her brand new life.

* * *

The flurry of publicity that accompanied Catherine's dedication of the Longhouse on the Mound a year after Rafe and Natalie's wedding did the Blakes and Blanchards great credit, although by then Leighton had been dead for four months, and Catherine privately expressed to Natalie her relief that he had not lived to see her gift realized. "The Bluff was always between us," her mother said, "though perhaps it needn't have been. But I made my choices, and by and large I'm not sorry." They stood a few feet from what was left of the Westwind family; Pete, the man who had started all the fuss, did not appear to share Catherine's enthusiasm for the ceremony. Probably he had hoped to wrest more than recognition or even his new position from Catherine, but her maneuver had generated such a positive response from his own Indian community and the rest of the public that he had been disarmed.

When Catherine presented him with the deed to the Mound, he accepted impassively; later she said to Natalie, "Ironic, isn't it, that Caleb's love of the land should be upheld not by his red descendants but by his white one?" The Mound's disposition seemed to make what remained of Caleb's legacy even more meaningful to her, more precious. She was in semiretirement by then and spent most of her days at the Bluff. Natalie visited her there frequently; Catherine's business instincts were sound and her counsel useful, and on matters that pertained to the financial management of the stations, and especially KBBB's position in the city, Natalie continued to seek her advice.

Natalie was happier than she had ever been. Her life was complete in every way. And then Catherine had a stroke, a very serious one, and as she lingered on, all that unseasonably clear and sunny spring in 1962, Natalie wondered how she would ever get along without her.

Chapter Twenty-nine

It was a family legend that the bed in which Catherine lay dying as spring stretched into summer and summer into autumn had come around the Horn in 1866. It was said that Maddy Douglas brought it with her from Fall River on the *Continental,* and that in it Maddy had been born and Catherine conceived, and in it Catherine, like her mother before her, would surely breathe her last.

What was true, thought Natalie as she gently wiped her mother's lips with a cloth dipped in gardenia-scented water, was that legends were created when reality threatened what really mattered—money, land, and sometimes love. And what was also true was that the blurry gray-green mist that hid the Olympics from view this rainy afternoon had always clouded the distinctions among them.

"The vu-vu-vultures are ga-ga-ga—" Catherine said thickly. It was difficult to understand her since the stroke. Sometimes only Natalie could interpret her mother's sounds.

"Gathering," Natalie finished for her. Her mother was right, unfortunately. The Cousins had been to visit again; in anticipation of Catherine's demise and the long-awaited opportunity to develop the last twenty-five acres of her land, they gathered often at her bedside. Kurt and Arabella were almost as greedy; as for Nick, he had told Natalie long ago that he would not stand in the way of the others' plans. She supposed, when it came to a decision, she would be outvoted by her siblings; in fact, considering the contention the land had stirred up in the family for over a century, pitting brother against brother, father against daughter, and husband against wife, it was probably just as well.

"Ff-ff-for ch-ch-chilrun," her mother managed, and Natalie nodded. Preserving the land for future generations was all well and good, but how? Taxes were prohibitive, and who cared, anyway? Not her brothers or sister, and perhaps not she, either. It was her heritage, and part of the history she shared with them, and so would always hold a special place in her heart, but it was also a burden she wanted, finally, to put down.

She wiped a tear from the corner of her mother's eye—she could have wept herself for Catherine's agony, trapped practically speechless in a withered and decaying body, but she did not. Catherine was counting on her to be strong, to hold everyone at bay—even death, she sometimes thought.

She had engaged nurses around the clock. It would have been more convenient to move Catherine to a hospital, or even her own house, but her mother refused to leave the Bluff, and Natalie acceded to her wishes, even though it was inconvenient to drive all the way out here twice or even once a day. A few weeks before, when Catherine's condition had worsened alarmingly, Natalie had turned most of her responsibilities at the station over to her general manager and moved into the farmhouse; Rafe came every night and stayed with her in the guest suite. She spelled the nurses, bathing and changing and feeding her mother, and the rest of the time she roamed the property, picking the apples and plums, salvaging the late vegetables from the garden, and occasionally taking the old cedar canoe from the boathouse and paddling around the sound. To keep Catherine's spirit from flagging, she told her what was happening on the land—how the bittersweet was turning orange with the ripening of autumn, how the squirrels were secreting their nuts and berries for the winter to come. She gathered oysters and clams from the beach, mushrooms from the woods, and the last of the dahlias and chrysanthemums from the cutting garden. And she took photographs, which she showed Catherine when she spoke, so that her mother could see the Bluff through Natalie's eyes, imagine it as she had seen it so many times, in so many seasons past.

Catherine held on until just before Thanksgiving, when Natalie told her what the doctor had just confirmed, that she would have a baby early in the summer. "Blu-blu-bluff . . . for your ch-child," she said. "Don't let . . . don't let g-g-g-go," she managed, and Natalie—giving in, finally, to the tears she had held back for so many weeks—squeezed her mother's hand tightly and did not let go of it until Catherine had taken her last, agonizingly labored breath. Then she drew the sheet up around the body, gently closed her mother's vacant eyes, and went out to tell the others.

*　　*　　*

The terms of Catherine's will were simple: the stations went to Natalie and everything else—half of her shares in ALKCO and all her stock in Nick's company, as well as the rest of her extensive holdings—were divided among Kurt, Nick, and Arabella. Or, rather, Arabella's two children; Catherine had established a trust that would support her elder daughter comfortably, but on her death her share of Catherine's estate would pass to her offspring. That came as no surprise to anyone; Catherine had often told Natalie and her brothers of her plans for Arabella's inheritance. "She'll give it away, or let some man take it from her; at least this way I know my grandchildren will not starve."

It was the clause pertaining to the Bluff that surprised them all. "The property known as Caleb's Bluff," it began—and there followed a legal description of the remainder of Caleb Blanchard's donation claim—"shall be preserved in its present boundaries and entirety until and unless surviving children of the testator—Kurt, Nicholas, Arabella, and Natalie, as tenants in entirety—shall unanimously and in concert agree on its disposition, with all named beneficiaries thereto to share equally in any monies realized therefrom." The will also disclosed the establishment of a trust, funded with the other half of Catherine's ALKCO stock, that would pay taxes and maintenance on the property.

There were two codicils to the will, both of which had been added just before Natalie's wedding: the first gave Rafe Lenhart full ownership of the *Journal,* and the second pertained, once again, to Caleb's Bluff. "If on the death of the last surviving child of Catherine Blake the property remains in his or her possession, it shall pass to the issue of Natalie Blake, if any; and, if none, it shall be given as a donation to the City of Seattle, with the stipulation that no incursions be made on its natural state, except as they further the creation of a park, to be open without charge to the residents of the City and to be known as Blanchard Park."

"She's done it now," Natalie whispered to Rafe after the will was read. "She's going to have her way, even from the grave. That damn property—will it divide us forever?"

"You're not going to sell it then?" He kept his voice low. Kurt and Nick and Arabella were all talking excitedly with the Cousins, across the living room of the farmhouse; they had gathered to hear Catherine's final words and to scatter her ashes, as she had wished, on her beloved Bluff. Natalie had sprinkled them in the orchard earlier that day. The rest of them would have preferred that their mother be interred with the other Blanchards, and Leighton too, at Lakeview Cemetery. "She'll never know, and it would be much more appropriate," Kurt said, but Natalie ignored him and followed Catherine's instructions.

Her brother did not protest. If their mother wanted her precious fruit trees fertilized with her remains, why not? By the spring the trees would be gone anyway—the trees, the gardens, the brushy slopes, and the fern-filled woodlands.

Natalie knew what Kurt and the rest of them were thinking, and she thought how easy it would be to go along with them— to rid them all of the curse of Caleb's Bluff. But was it a curse or a blessing? Could it be something that brought them together, instead of dividing them? Could it be a balm instead of a bane, a source of strength and renewal instead of a well of bitterness? Inside her, the baby moved—a flutter at first, like a butterfly's wings beating against the air, and then, as if to underscore her thoughts, a quickening that was definitely a kick.

"Not now," she told Rafe. "Maybe not ever." It would not be easy; her brothers were strong, her sister was selfish, and her cousins were greedy. But it had not been easy for Catherine, either, or for Caleb before her. They had been Blanchards—they had been up to it. Would she?

She didn't know. But as soon as her head had a chance to catch up to the rest of her, she would think of a way.